W9-BVG-633

IN A WORD...
SUSAN HILL'S SIMON SERRAILLER MYSTERIES ARE—

"Superb."
—P. D. JAMES

"Stunning."
—RUTH RENDELL

"Elegant."
—NEW YORK TIMES

"Atmospheric."
—NEW YORK JOURNAL OF BOOKS

"Somber."
—WALL STREET JOURNAL

"Timeless."
—WASHINGTON POST

"Chilling."
—NEW YORK TIMES BOOK REVIEW

"Gripping."
—STRAND MAGAZINE

"Compelling."
—KIRKUS REVIEWS

"Electrifying."
—SAN FRANCISCO REVIEW OF BOOKS

"Gritty."
—BOOKLIST

"Ominous."
—ENTERTAINMENT WEEKLY

"Outstanding."
—LIBRARY JOURNAL (STARRED REVIEW)

"Taut."
—PUBLISHERS WEEKLY

"Intelligent."
—TIME OUT

"Brooding."
—WASHINGTON TIMES

For
Katherine Fry,
Who has meticulously copy-edited every Serrailler novel
from the beginning, saved me from myself innumerable
times, and knows far more about both the books
and Simon than I ever will.

This edition first published in hardcover in the United States in 2022
by The Overlook Press, an imprint of ABRAMS.

Originally published in 2021 by Chatto & Windus, an imprint of Vintage,
Penguin Random House UK.

Abrams books are available at special discounts when purchased in quantity
for premiums and promotions as well as fundraising or educational use.
Special editions can also be created to specification.
For details, contact specialsales@abramsbooks.com or the address above.

Library of Congress Control Number: 2021947022

Printed and bound in the United States

1 3 5 7 9 10 8 6 4 2

ISBN: 978-1-4197-5964-2
eISBN: 978-1-64700-581-8

ABRAMS The Art of Books
195 Broadway, New York, NY 10007
abramsbooks.com

A Change of Circumstance

of

Circumstance

A SIMON SERRAILLER CASE

SUSAN HILL

The Overlook Press, New York

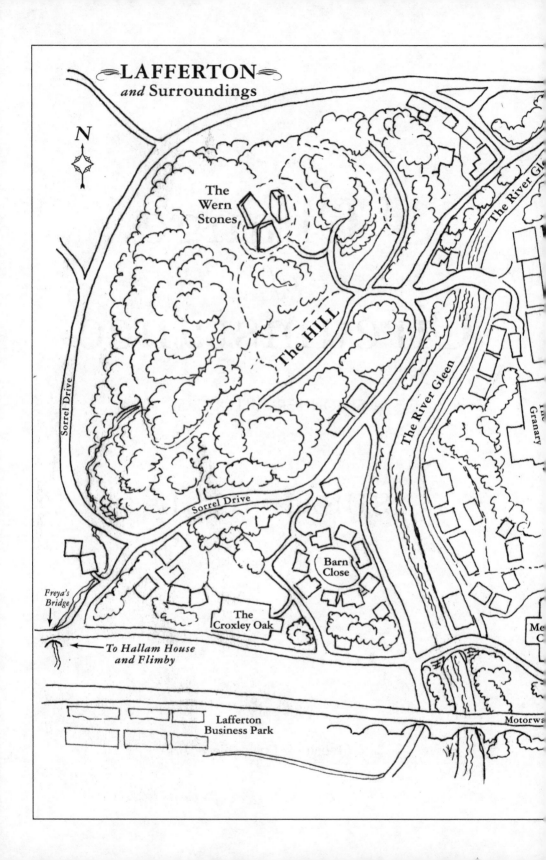

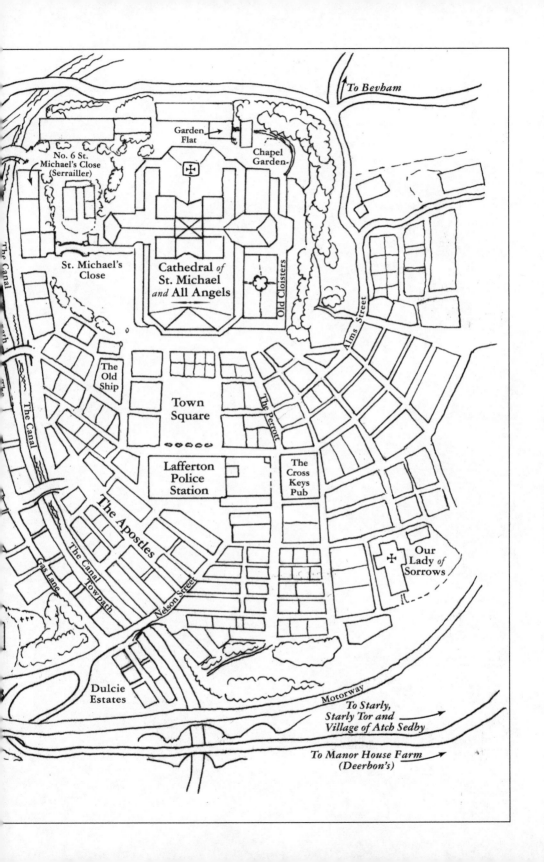

One

January, and Christmas vanished without trace. The pavements of Starly village were greasy under a day of drizzle and there was an unhealthy mildness in the air.

A police patrol car, a dark grey saloon with 'Doctor' on the windscreen and Detective Chief Superintendent Simon Serrailler's silver Audi were all parked on double yellow lines outside the Chinese pharmacy. Crime scene tape was stretched across a side entrance that led to the flat above the shop with a uniform constable standing by the gate to keep back the prying public of two teenagers straddling their bikes and smoking ostentatiously.

The pathologist in the upstairs room with Serrailler was one he did not know, a completely bald man with white eyebrows and lashes. He was also a man of few words.

'Overdose?' Simon said.

A nod.

'Can you say when, roughly?'

A shrug.

'And you'll know more when you get him on the table, yes, OK. What's happened to forensics?'

The doctor ripped off his gloves with the particular tearing sound that always set Simon's teeth on edge, and swung his rucksack onto his back. The older ones still carried bags.

'Heroin.' His tone said everything.

1

The body was hunched forwards, syringe still hanging from his arm. His age had been put somewhere between seventeen and twenty.

'It's everywhere.'

The pathologist glanced up at a New Age poster half peeling off the wall.

'Love. Light. Peace,' he read aloud before he left.

Serrailler's phone beeped.

Bypass closed. Rerouting – eta 25 minutes.

But he was used to being alone with dead bodies.

The room was filthy, damp, with bare boards, the corpse the purple-brown bruise colours of a Francis Bacon painting, but at least there was not yet the rotten-sweet smell of death. The boy had a shaven head, dirty feet, was wearing a soiled vest and shorts. His skin had erupted in sores and boils among the thicket of tattoos, his eyes were half closed, his mouth hung open, and he was emaciated, but his skull was well shaped, his fingers long and, in spite of their filth, delicate.

Serrailler felt anger, at the waste of life, anger, despair and disgust, but the feelings were impersonal, and about the squalor of the scene not about the young man whose body was now such a revolting mess. It had not always been like that and, whoever he was, he had been, in the phrase, 'somebody's son'.

On a first quick search there had seemed to be nothing in the room to identify him, or to confirm that he had lived here – indeed, that anyone had, none of the usual signs of habitation even of the most basic kind, no sofa, table, crockery or kettle, no bedding. No bed.

The pharmacy had been closed when he had arrived a few minutes after the patrol car, on a job he would never normally be involved in at this early stage, but he was one of the few members of CID left standing, in the flu epidemic that had swept through the station, in spite of the fact that they were all supposed to have been vaccinated back in October.

Footsteps sounded on the stairs, as the forensics team arrived, apologising, cursing the traffic.

'Thanks, guys. The doc's left and the van should be on its way. Sorry to leave you with him.'

'He won't bite,' one said, unpacking his equipment. The other sniggered.

Simon looked at her, then down at the body with sudden sadness, and a strange urge to defend him, whoever he was, protect him. Someone else should be here, he thought, someone close to him, not a copper and a load of clue-seekers. Someone to pray for him. What was it the priest would say? 'Go forth upon your journey, Christian soul.' But had he even been a Christian?

'Do we know who he is, guv?'

Serrailler shook his head.

'I'm heading back.'

Back to the station, not back home where he should be, enjoying two days off.

He stopped by the PC on duty beside the gate. He looked cold. 'Once the body's gone and forensics are done you can go too – just leave the tape and make sure you check that the flat door is fully secured.'

'Guv. Oi, you two!' But the boys had already spun their bikes and were off, doing wheelies round the corner and away.

Two

'I don't want to go in there, Doc.'

Cat Deerbon sat with 95-year-old Lionel Brown, waiting for an ambulance. She had called it nearly an hour ago, hearing him say over and over again that he wouldn't be taken into hospital, that once you went in you never came home again, that he would walk out and get back home. 'I'll do it somehow.'

He had been found on his living-room floor, having fallen during the night. He had pneumonia and he was seriously dehydrated as well as hypothermic. Cat had her hand on his as she looked out of the window. Each almshouse had a long strip of garden, some better tended than others, but now there was only frozen grass to see and a few shrivelled flowers, plus, in Lionel Brown's, a bird table and a lilac bush close to it, both holding an array of bird feeders, fat balls, seed cakes, on which a robin and several blue tits were feeding now.

'Yes and that's another thing and another reason why I can't go. Who else is going to look after my birds? There's a party of long-tailed tits comes down morning and afternoon, easily a dozen of them, they flock down like a gang of kids. Well, I'll tell you who'll look out for them, nobody, that's who, and my birds have grown used to it, they rely on me, I feed them every day. They won't know what to do if it's left empty.'

'But I can see some peanut feeders in the garden next door, I'm sure your neighbour'll look after them for you.'

'What, her? She's got a broomstick parked inside her back door, I've seen it.'

Cat laughed. His skin was pale ivory and translucent as an honesty pod, his finger bones felt like winter twigs under her hand.

'Are you getting warmer? I can find you another blanket.'

'No, I'm all right now, you've made it lovely and cosy in here, Doc, which isn't what you went to college all those years for.'

'I'll make sure you're wrapped up well when you leave, it will be colder in the ambulance. When it comes.'

'I am not going in an ambulance, I'm not going anywhere, I've already told you.'

Cat thought he had probably had a mild stroke, fallen and been unable to get up, or else simply tripped over, though he had no broken bones and his contusions were only superficial. When the almshouse warden had found him on her morning check, she had found Lionel alive, though as she had said, 'Only just.'

The twelve almshouses, built and endowed in the sixteenth century by a local landowner, had dark red-brick walls, tall, barley-twist Elizabethan chimneys and rather small rooms, but all of them had been modernised within the last ten years and the warden installed in an adjacent, newly built bungalow. The founding benefaction had been augmented over the centuries by several large bequests and the money shrewdly invested by the trustees. The last doctors' surgery in Starly had closed several years ago, following the major changes in the NHS, with GP home visits a rarity. Nobody in the almshouses had a car and the warden had spent too much time driving residents in and out of Lafferton for medical appointments. The problem had been solved by another benefactor, anonymous – though Cat had a shrewd idea of his identity – who had set up a fund to pay for registration of every almshouse resident with GP care from Concierge Medical.

She still wondered occasionally how Chris, her first husband, would have dealt with it, given his steadfast opposition to private medicine, thought about how much he would have objected when she had, as he might have put it, 'gone over to the dark side'.

'I know I'm going to die, Doc, I should have died last night, shouldn't I?'

'Not "should have" – but you easily might have done, that's why –'

'And I'm all right with that, I'm old – I'm too old. But I'm not dying in that hospital. My wife, Lois, did that and it was terrible, and I'm not having it happen to me. Why won't you just take some notice of what I keep saying? Why doesn't anyone take notice of you when you're old? I'm ninety-five but I'm still all there, I'm the same person I always was and I know what I want and why, but nobody takes any notice. I thought you'd be different, but you're not.'

His eyes were full of tears, not of sadness but of frustration, of apprehension and deep loneliness, and Cat felt ashamed of her own obtuseness. She had been thinking medically, which was right, but over her years as a GP she had prided herself that she always thought of her patients first and foremost as people, individuals, who needed and deserved more than fast diagnosis and treatment. It was those other things that took the time, but which were as vital as the medicine and which had always given her deep job satisfaction.

She stood up. 'You're absolutely right, Mr Brown, and you do right to remind me. I'm sorry. Listen, I'll help you as best I can but I am not going to promise that I won't ask you to go into hospital. I can't do that, it would be irresponsible of me, and I would rightly be held to account if I gave you anything but the proper treatment. But I am going to make absolutely sure it is the best thing, I promise you that.' She took his hand again. 'Deal?'

His temperature had started to go up because she had covered him in blankets and a duvet, he had a hot-water bottle and the heating was now on. He had drunk two large mugs of sweet tea and one of water but he still needed intravenous hydration, his blood pressure was much too low and his breathing rattled. But his sight and hearing were fine, he had no numbness or paralysis, and although his speech had been slightly slurred when she had first arrived, it had improved. Nevertheless, even if his stroke had been minor and transient, at his age he was at high risk of suffering another, and it would be negligent not to send him into Bevham General for rehydration, and a full assessment – the stroke unit there was outstanding.

She was still holding Lionel's hand, mulling it over, when the ambulance arrived and the paramedics were knocking on the door, accompanied by the warden, Sadie Logan.

'I'll go with you to the hospital, Lionel, it's not a problem.'

Cat was relieved but still asked her if that was part of her job.

'I make it my job. What chance would he have in that A&E scrum trying to make his voice heard? Shall I let you know what happens?'

'Yes, please do – the hospital will report back to me but not for ages.'

She took the old man's hand again. 'You do know you have to go, don't you? You have to be scanned and fully assessed and I can't do that, but you won't get to stay in unless they are sure you need to, they haven't enough beds to keep fit and well people in them.'

'You'll get a thorough going-over,' Sadie said.

'Makes me sound like a carpet.' But he winked at Cat, and the wink gave her the reassurance she wanted. If Lionel Brown was making a joke of going to hospital, then he was reconciled to it.

Three

'Hey, you!' Cat slowed at the corner of Starly Square, lowering the window to call her brother. A few minutes later, they were sitting at a corner table in the Dreamcatcher Cafe. Cat looked at the menu.

'I once had dandelion coffee here, but it's gone. Espresso. Cappuccino. Flat white . . . heavens, quite normal.'

'Nothing in Starly is normal. Go out there, it's like walking through a pack of tarot cards. Do you remember Dava? And that guy who called himself a psychic surgeon?'

Cat shuddered. 'And Freya,' she said.

Freya Graffham, the detective sergeant, victim of a psychopath, who had engaged in a killing spree in Lafferton, some ten years ago. She had also been the first woman in Simon's life Cat had thought he might actually have married. Now, he met her eye briefly as their coffees came.

'This isn't real milk.'

'Of course it isn't real milk, this is a vegan cafe, it's a dairy-free zone. It'll be soya or oat or almond.'

'Or breast, even.' Simon raised his hand-thrown pottery mug, decorated with the symbol for the star sign Aquarius.

'Don't be mean.' Cat lifted her own cappuccino with the design for Pisces.

'Anyway, what's brought you up here?'

They traded news and cases, catching up for the first time since Christmas.

'What a way to die,' Cat said, 'on the floorboards of a freezing cold flat above a quack herbalist, with a syringe in your arm.'

'You don't know the half of it – you in your private patient world.'

'You'd be surprised. Anyway, that's not like you – the disapproval.'

'Sorry, sis. I don't really . . . I'm just feeling a bit below par.'

'Hope you're not getting flu.'

'Had my jab. Which is more than you can say for half the station, apparently. They get it provided, nurse in the station, and they still don't go for it.'

'Don't start me on anti-vaxxers – odd for policemen, though.'

'Oh, they're not anti-vaxxers, they just can't be bothered.'

'It's just January with you, then.'

'Right, and I'm ready for a proper winter now . . . frost and ice and deep, deep snow.'

'And limb fractures everywhere.'

'Only I could do with a proper break . . . oops, didn't mean that one.'

'Really? What about Morocco? Sun there.'

'The Alps . . . I haven't been skiing for –' He stopped and glanced down at his prosthetic right arm. 'Maybe not. You know, skiing hasn't even been on my list of things I'll never be able to do again – and it's a pretty short list.'

'So it should be.'

'Somewhere, anyway.' Simon finished his coffee and gestured for another. 'You?'

'Yes, let's go for it. There's time.'

'Until something kicks off.'

Four

The only actual cooking their dad did was a fry-up, which they had every morning, and that was it for the day. Otherwise, there were the tins and frozen packets they opened themselves. School dinners were free though there was never enough in them. But it wasn't food the Ropers lacked. The Ropers – Tommy. Connor. Brookie. Alf.

That Wednesday morning, Brookie nearly missed the bus.

'Where's my trainers? Where's my trainers?' Nobody took any notice. Someone had always lost something, in the jumble sale that was their home. Brookie raced back upstairs.

His bed was head to tail with two others, and all of them spurting out mattress entrails, with assorted coverings, blankets, old curtains, thrown about anyhow. Tommy had a duvet, a new one, that had been still in its packaging when found in a skip but there had never been another and even that had no cover.

'Brookie!'

The door slammed shut, frying pan and crockery slid off the draining board into the sink. Brookie ran after the others, trainers undone, as the bus was pulling up to their stop, Connor on first as usual, and straight into a seat. He stuck his leg out. By now Brookie should have been ready for it but he never was and crashed over sideways into some girl's lap, to mass cheers.

When a day went wrong at the start, that day went on going wrong, and Brooklyn's days were mostly like that now. He missed the primary school at Starly that they had all just walked

10

to, so they got an extra half-hour in bed, and there were other things about secondary school he wasn't keen on. He staggered into the last window seat and started drawing stick men on the steamed-up glass.

At the end of the day he was still trying to catch up with himself, shoving his things into the plastic carrier that served him for a schoolbag, when a boy who seemed to have taken against him, for no reason Brookie could fathom, shoved him hard from behind, knocking him over and sending the carrier flying. He didn't bother to retaliate but by the time he had gathered up his scattered belongings, including his pencil case that had rolled under a bench into the mud, it was twenty to four and the bus had left. He knew better than to expect his brothers to ask the driver to wait a minute for him, even if the driver would. He looked along the line of waiting parents' cars in case he saw anyone who might be going to, or even near, Starly, but it was dark and hard to make anyone out as he walked up and down, trying to stop the split carrier bag from spewing out its contents again.

Brookie never wasted time feeling sorry for himself because it was just the way things generally were, and he was used to it. 'Shit happens,' his dad said, half a dozen times a day.

'You lost or what?'

The man's voice, close by him yet apparently coming out of nowhere, made him lose his hold on the carrier bag completely.

'Here, let me. What are you like, Sam?'

'I'm not Sam,' he said, wiping water off his pencil case.

'Sorry, could have sworn you were. Is this yours?'

'Yeah! Great, thanks.'

'So who are you?'

'Brookie Roper.'

'Course you are, should have known, only it's dark, right?'

'OK.'

'Looking for your mum?'

'I . . . no. I just missed the bus.'

'Your fault or the bus's? Still, whatever – you missed it.'

'Yes.'

'Where'd you live?'

'Starly.'

'Then lucky you, Brookie Roper, it's where I'm heading. I was just dropping off my girl's homework books . . . she's off sick.

'What's her name?'

'Her name? Amy.'

'What year is she?'

'You'd make a good cop – what this, who that.'

'Sorry.'

'You're all right. So, do you want a lift to Starly or what?'

In the man's van and clutching his carrier bag, Brookie said, 'I'll be home first, the school bus stops everywhere, it's really boring.'

'Whereabouts?'

'Mercer Close but you can drop me anywhere.'

The bloke didn't seem old. He had one those stupid man-buns of which there were a lot in Starly.

'What's your name?' Brookie asked.

'Fats.'

'That's not a name.'

'Well, it's mine. What does Brookie stand for?'

'Brooklyn.'

'There you go then.'

It didn't take long without all the stops, and the man dropped him on the corner, and drove straight off. When the others got in they foraged about in the kitchen for their tea. The TV went on and there was the usual fight over the remote. Brookie made some toast, spread with the last of the peanut butter. Nobody said anything about him not being on the bus. They probably hadn't even noticed.

Five

Still January, but the damp mild air had given way to a north-east wind that cut down the lanes and sent Saturday shoppers looking for warmth so that even at ten minutes past ten, Cat could not see a seat in the brasserie, until Rosie waved to her from a table in the window.

They had not met since well before Christmas. Sam had come home but Rosie went to her own family in Manchester, partly to get down to work – her med school final exams were this year. Cat made her way through the packed tables, thinking how neat her son's girlfriend always was, tidy, well presented and stylish, even on little money. She was wearing a navy-blue jacket with large, tangerine-coloured buttons, which she would have found and sewn on herself, in place of whatever uninteresting ones had been there.

Rosie started speaking before Cat had settled herself, a girl who was always focused, never wasted the moment.

'Can I ask you about a big specialty recruitment drive that's going on?'

'There's always one. What is it this time? In my day they wanted everyone to go into infectious diseases.'

So far Rosie had not been able to settle on a career direction once she had qualified, though she was very sure of what she did not want to do – any form of surgery, anything that would keep her in a research lab, or general practice. The last time she had talked to Cat about it, she had been veering in the direction of neonatal.

'I went to a great session – this consultant was really inspirational, encouraging us to widen our horizons, look beyond the obvious.'

'I'm not sure anything in medicine is obvious, not even A&E.'

Rosie smiled. 'We haven't had a catch-up for so long you wouldn't know, but I've been thinking seriously about A&E.

'It's a killer.'

'I know, but this is a different bit of A&E and there aren't enough going into it.'

'Which is what every spokesperson for every specialty will tell you.'

'When people have spent six years being involved with bodies they tend to look at – well, bodies. I was too, but after this talk – not so much.'

'Ah, you're talking about psychiatry – I'm slow on the uptake this morning.'

Rosie gave one of her rather infrequent, sudden smiles. She was not a miserable or gloomy girl but her default facial expression was thoughtful and rather serious.

'Yes! It was a light bulb moment, Cat, it really was. She was so interesting, she really made her case –'

'Of course she did – she was recruiting.'

'Oh. Yes, I guess.'

'And why not? Listen, it's easy to be swept away by a pitch from someone passionate about their specialty, but have you thought about it and gone over every aspect of it since her talk? What exactly is it about psychiatry that suddenly appeals to you more than all the other options? It's a long way from neonatal.'

Rosie's expression changed again but Cat could not read it.

'I always said I thought you'd be good at that – you have a calmness and a gentleness but you're quite decisive . . . well, usually.'

'And I have very small hands! I know.'

'That and Sam doing midwifery. What a team!'

There was a long silence. They sipped their coffees. The brasserie hummed. Rosie looked up. 'What do you think?'

'What I think isn't relevant, it's your career. Psych isn't something I could have done, though it has a lot of relevance to general practice of course – a GP often has to be a therapist, or should be, though there's precious little time for it in the NHS now. Was your recruiting sergeant talking generally, across the whole psych spectrum? It's pretty wide of course.'

'She went quite deeply into adolescent psychiatry and eating disorders because that's her field, and then to the other end of the spectrum but that's definitely not for me.'

'Geriatrics? Dementia?'

'Yes. I mean, what can you do about ageing? It just happens.'

Cat thought about Lionel Brown. But how young Rosie was and so how differently she saw things. Had she been the same when she was newly qualified? She suddenly remembered saying to a nurse, after a difficult time with an elderly patient in A&E, 'When I hit sixty, take me outside and shoot me.'

'I tell you what, Rosie, – forensic psychiatry is absolutely fascinating – the sharp end, pretty tough – but you're very clever and if you're interested in the place where the law meets medicine meets a human being, I think you'd find it worth looking into.'

'Hm. Actually the eating disorders stuff got my attention. I had a room-mate in my third year who was anorexic and it took me a while to spot it, but in the end I got quite involved. Bit too involved really.'

'How?'

'Honestly – I think I was impatient with her. I just couldn't understand why she was doing it, I kept asking her why she didn't just . . .'

'Eat?'

Rosie nodded. 'I still think that, so I'd be no good, would I?'

Cat didn't want to influence her one way or another though her first thought was that she would be well suited to the right branch of psychiatry. She had to take her time and look into it in depth and detail. It was easy to be swept away by one charismatic lecturer. She remembered having been passionate about dermatology as a student, merely because she had fallen for one consultant as had a good many of her friends.

15

'They're desperately short of psychs of course, but that isn't a good reason for going into it – has to be the right fit for you.'

'I went to another talk that was pretty engaging too – I'd have gone a long way to hear her.' Rosie named a prizewinning cardiologist.

'My God yes – she's often referred to as the humble genius.'

'I know why. There she was, this great doctor, and she said two things that really hit me. One was "We really know so little about the human body, even today". The other was "Doctors don't heal and we don't cure. The body itself does that and we give it a bit of technical assistance." Do you think that's true of the mind as well?'

'Pretty much. The other way of putting it is "Most things get better of their own accord". Maybe that's true of the mind, but it's definitely "most things", not "all". Interesting questions, Rosie. I know it's full on at the moment, and he's in London, but have you seen Sam lately?'

The girl picked her empty coffee cup, did not meet Cat's eye.

'You know how it is.'

'This was always going to be tough – a bit of a test. Chris and I had to run our early relationship from two different continents when he was to Africa for a year. It can be done if you set your mind to it. You make it work.'

Rosie picked up her bag from the floor and the bill from the table but Cat whisked it away.

'You can pay when you've qualified.'

'Thank you very much. I have to get back to my studies but I'm so pleased we met.' She often spoke rather formally.

'Where are you at?'

'Neurology. Epilepsy. Brain electricity.'

'Good luck with that.'

'I really don't understand half of it.'

'Nor me but don't say anything. I'm not sure when Sam's next up but why don't you come to Sunday lunch whether he's home or not?

If Rosie replied, her voice was drowned in the hubbub they walked through as they left.

I like her, Cat thought, but I can't always read her, and especially now. She had been good for Sam, settling and focusing him, helping him to grow up a bit, but where they were, let alone where they might be heading, it was impossible to tell. And they were very young. Too young.

Her phone beeped with a voice message.

'This is Sister Daly on Osler Ward, Bevham General, for Dr Deerbon. It's about your patient, Mr Lionel Brown. He keeps asking to see you. He doesn't seem to have any family and he's quite distressed, so if there's any chance you could pop over, I think it would help.'

It was Cat's long weekend off. She had an afternoon of batch cooking and baking ahead after doing the jobs in town, with a choir practice that evening, and she needed to finish her book group choice before they met on Monday. Kieron was collecting Felix from Saturday-morning school. It was the sort of domestic day she loved. But now, there was Lionel Brown. Concierge Medical did not usually visit patients in hospital – no GP did, partly because the hospitals did not like it and preferred to get on with their side of the job, so the fact that Lionel's repeated request to see her had prompted the ward sister to ring was significant.

A section of the bypass was bring resurfaced and under temporary traffic-light control, and a sudden hailstorm had already slowed everything down, so that the quick trip to Bevham General took Cat forty-five minutes. The supermarket run would have to wait.

He was in a four-bed ward off a larger one, where the level of noise should not have been tolerated. Visitors milled about, talking and laughing loudly, two small children raced about unrestrained, trolleys screeched. There was the usual smell of stew and antiseptic. Since when had any hospital ward been allowed to turn into bedlam?

One of the beds in Lionel's bay had the curtains drawn round; in the next, a tiny, ancient, waxen figure was deeply asleep and snoring. The third bed was vacant. He was beside the window but the view was of the adjacent building's concrete wall.

He had shrunk down into himself and was thinner, his skin was grey and he had the inward-looking expression Cat had often seen on the faces of very old people who had lost all interest in the life around them. His eyes were half closed and he was lolling forward, the pillows slipping down the bed frame on which he was propped. She put her hand on his.

'Hello, Mr Brown . . . Lionel?'

No response.

'It's Dr Deerbon. Would you like me to sort out your pillows? You'd be a lot more comfortable.' He grunted. Cat moved him gently forward until he was leaning on her arm while she quickly rearranged and plumped his pillows. He smelled, a stale, old-body smell. Then, he opened his eyes suddenly.

'I knew you'd come, Dr Cat, I knew it, I told them but they weren't having any of it.' The words came through a bubble of phlegm in his throat.

'There you are! Hello. Can I get you some fresh water . . . or anything else? You still don't look very comfortable.'

'Ha, you don't expect comfort in here, Doc. I'm all right, I'm fine, and I want you to tell them that please and then to take me home, and if they don't like it, bugger them, because I'm not going to die in here.'

'Have they worked out why you collapsed yet?'

'Oh, they don't tell me anything. Haven't they told you?'

'I'm afraid not. We eventually get a letter but not until you're discharged. Has anybody been to see you?'

A scream from the opposite bed made Cat start but the old man only shrugged. 'The entire time,' he said, 'night and day – a screech, then he goes back to sleep. Nobody pays any heed.'

The screech came again but the figure still lay flat, apparently unaware of the sound he was making. A nurse appeared, glanced round, then left again.

'You are going to take me home, aren't you? There's plenty of pushchairs standing about, you just grab one, get me into it and we'll go, they won't even notice.'

'I can't do that and you know it.'

He gave a short laugh. 'Meaning you won't.'

'Can you even imagine what trouble I'd be in?'

She looked at his chart, saw the meds he was written up for were to thin his blood and prevent him having another stroke. There was no note of any therapy. He had been on a rehydration drip. But he needed more frequent monitoring than he appeared to be getting and she wondered why he was not in the stroke unit. She went to find someone to talk to, conscious of the need to be tactful, as well as of the usual staffing and bed shortages. The same melee in the ward continued and there was no one at the nurses' station, let alone any sign of a doctor.

As she left, another screech from Lionel's ward echoed down the corridor after her.

Six

Simon glanced at his watch. 'All right, five more minutes.'

DC Denzil Aberra, recently graduated to CID, looked around the conference room. Four of them, not including Serrailler.

'They can't all still be sick.'

'Two are, guv – it's a bugger this flu, it drags on and on. I should know.' DC Fern Monroe coughed.

'I feel for you, Constable,' Simon said, avoiding her eye, as he tried to avoid her altogether these days, since he had made what had turned out to be an error of judgement in taking her out to dinner. 'You're all up to speed with the young man found dead of an OD in Starly?'

'Moron.'

Serrailler gave DC Sandhu one of his quick, hard glares.

'For anyone who, for some mysterious reason, has not yet looked at this . . .'

The photograph came up on the screen and Serrailler enlarged it. They had all seen their share of dead bodies in various states, and plenty of them those of addicts, but there was still a faint intake of breath. At the skin blotched with dark, livid patches where needles had probed and twisted repeatedly, searching for a usable vein. The bruised face and the skeletal torso, bone showing through ragged skin. Scabs, sores. Hypodermic hanging off the arm. Little of the room was visible but it was the body, and in particular the face, that Simon wanted them to focus on.

'Path report is pretty straightforward. Heroin OD, and the toxicology says it was contaminated. We've got a growing number of junkies – there's been a huge spike in the past six months – and the dealers can't keep up with the demand they've created for themselves, so they're mixing it with God knows what to make it go further, creating a much more dangerous substance. It doesn't work for long of course, because word gets round, but it buys the dealers time till better supplies come in. This guy here, we've no idea who he is or how long he's been living such a shitty life. I'm not here to give you an elementary lesson in substance abuse, but because there's an explosion of it on our patch, and those nearby, we need to keep up to speed – sorry.'

'Stay sharp,' Bilaval muttered.

'OK, look hard at the photo again. This is what addiction does to a young man's body, not to mention his mind, and his spirit, his willpower, his emotional balance, his judgement.'

'Do we know how old he was?'

'Pathologist says around twenty. He was somebody's son, somebody's mate, boyfriend, maybe even some kid's dad. Whose? We have no idea. Common blood group, no surgical scars, teeth were rotten and many were missing. The impressions are still doing the rounds but I don't hold out much hope. We have fingerprints, there's no criminal record, he doesn't fit the description of any local misper. We've widened the search and my hunch is that we'll get an ID from within fifty miles or so. OK, continue to look hard at him, and go on looking, until his image is burned onto your mind. Then try and see him before he started to resemble a butcher's carcass. Do a sort of mental identikit. Have you ever encountered him, whatever the context? Could he have done the MOT on your car, sold you a pair of boxers from a market stall, served you a pint or a coffee? If you get a shadow of a nudge to your memory, stop. Go back over it. Anywhere, any time. His family are out there, maybe just across town. He probably won't have been living with them for a while but there'll be someone he belongs to and they will be anxious. Even if they know he'd turned into a junkie, they will want to know where he is.'

'Seasonal worker?'

'Unlikely, wrong season, people don't come here to get casual jobs in winter. No, he's local. Maybe he's even from where he was found.'

'Sustainable Starly.'

'Whatever. The biggest problem we have with a body in this sort of state is that we can't go round showing his photograph to all and sundry to try and get an ID.'

'GP surgeries?'

'Maybe. Bevham General records haven't come up with anything but they don't have photographs of patients, only staff. This isn't easy, I know. Still, follow the slightest lead, eyes and ears open. You know the drill. All right, let's get out there and find out who he was. Thanks.'

He was away and down the corridor fast. Fern Monroe had been sitting near the door hoping to catch his eye but he'd shot past her, closing the door behind him, and vanished.

'Fern . . .' Donna Merriman's voice was low.

As Fern moved, Denzil Aberra jumped forward to open the door. He was the sort of man who did that and somehow never caused offence, he was so delightful and friendly, warm. Fun.

'Hey, how are things? You settling in?'

He had only been in Lafferton a month, over from the Met and to their station's gain, as Fern intended to tell Serrailler, if she ever got the chance to tell him anything. As well as being an all-round nice guy, Denzil was sharp and ambitious, but never banged on about his old force, as ex-Met bods were prone to do. He had stirred up the Lafferon CID, which was under-manned, even before the flu epidemic, they felt stale, they were sick of winter, and they were getting on one another's nerves.

'Cup of tea?'

'Sure. How's Pearl?'

'Still really sick. I'm a bit bothered to be honest and the midwife said if it went on much longer she'd have to go into hospital, but what can they do there that they can't do at home? She's safer at home.'

'Not necessarily. They'll put her on a drip to keep her hydrated and give her some nourishment that way too – she needs it and the baby needs it, Denzil. Hospital's the best place for her.'

'I hate those places. You go in with one thing and catch something else while you're there. Happened to my grandad, only he never came out at all.'

'Well, that's not going to happen to Pearl, she'd only be in a couple of days, get her right. This doughnut is disgusting. What do they make them out of?'

Denzil reached over and took it.

'You still like it here?'

'I love it.'

'We love you too.'

'Thanks. It's a quieter life as well.'

'You don't miss the London buzz?'

'Nope. And I reckon I can go further here – too many climbing on top of each other to get promotion in the Met.'

He wiped sugar off his fingers and finished his tea.

'This OD case . . .'

'We never used to get them here. Bevham did but Bevham's different. Now we're seeing them on our patch all the time.'

'They'll never get an ID on him. His mother wouldn't recognise him.'

'You're wrong there. This isn't the Smoke. If he's local, someone will fetch up here to tell us and he'll be recognisable to his family, even in that state.'

'I haven't been up to that village where he was found – Starly. I might go and have a sniff around.'

'Off you go, and if you think you smell weed as well as joss sticks, you do.'

'Just weed?'

'Yeah – it's all gentle hippydom and free spirits fifty years on, Denzil. Our boy won't have got his fixes in Starly, even though he was found there. But you'll see the place for yourself. Actually, I've got a soft spot for it . . . I like a bit of chilling out every now and again.'

The sun shone as Denzil walked slowly down the street that led into the square, where racks of Nepalese and Indian scarves fluttered, next to multicoloured, mirrored cotton bags, and skeins of brass bells, wind chimes and bamboo pan pipes jingled softly. The smell of patchouli and incense drifted through open shop doors. It was the warmest day since last autumn. Denzil looked at the notices on boards and in windows, adverts for yoga classes, meditation groups, tarot readers, vegan caterers, holistic therapists, dreamcatcher workshops, t'ai chi, past-life researchers, Buddhist retreats. The cafe had set two tables out on the pavement, so he got a mint tea and watched the few people out shopping, the sun on his face. A gentle place, he thought, calm and quiet but probably not prosperous. He wondered how the shopkeepers made much of a living, except in summer, when there were a couple of big music festivals. There was a post office-cum-general store and a greengrocer, but no butcher, bank, bookies, supermarket. Presumably, everything had to be bought in Lafferton or at the hypermarkets in the new retail park west of Bevham. Who lived in Starly? The young and single, the elderly, whose village had grown with the New Age arrivals, some thirty years ago. After them had come the alternatives and the eco-warriors. Somehow, people survived here in bubbles of hope. Starly – gentle, peaceful, amiable Starly, with the discoloured, half-naked body of a young man alone in an empty, dirty room above a shop. Did anything else that spoke of squalor and self-harm, violence and other dark things lurk behind the tolerant, peace-loving face of this village?

He walked along to the Chinese pharmacy and looked up. The flat above was curtainless and clearly still empty and the sun shining on the windows showed up a film of dirt – who bothered to clean windows in places like that? But the chemist's shop windows below were sparkling, the displays well ordered. It was open.

Denzil went in as a woman and young child left and he waited until the door closed behind them before showing his warrant card. No shopkeeper wanted a police visit advertised to the world, and as soon as he had glanced at it, the man went over, locked the door and turned the sign to Closed.

'Please come into the back.'

There was a cubbyhole office and a small stockroom, with shelves of jars, bottles and boxes labelled in Chinese script. The man was younger than Denzil had expected, small, slightly plump, with rimless glasses. He looked apprehensive.

'If this is again about the terrible incident in the room above, I know nothing. I was away, I was in Manchester at my uncle's funeral, I have already made a statement about it.'

'And your statement has been checked, there's nothing at all for you to worry about. I am not here to ask you about the day the body was found, I want to know about the time before . . . weeks before.'

They were standing face-to-face in the tiny space but now Wang Lin got a high stool from the stockroom. He wiped it with a sheet of paper from a kitchen roll before inviting Denzil to sit.

'You own the flat above the shop?'

'No. I don't own the shop either. I rent, but I am a tenant on a lease of thirty years. Six have passed.'

'So you sublet the flat, you don't live there yourself?'

'No, I live in Bevham, but the flat is nothing to do with me. I just know that it's been empty for a while.'

'So you didn't let the place to the young man who –'

'No, never. I have already said all of this.'

'Have you seen his photograph?'

Mr Wang held up his hands. 'Please, not again. So horrible and so sad, it was very hard to look, but I don't know him, I never saw him in my life, so far as it was possible to tell. Yes, it is a very shocking photograph.'

'How do you think he got into the flat? Did he break the door down, or a window?'

'I have already told this . . . there was no sign of breaking in. Maybe someone gave him a key?'

'Do you have a key?'

'No, no. I am sorry.'

'That's all right, don't worry, Mr Wang, no one is blaming you for anything. Now, I presume you're only here in the day, during shop hours, but do you ever hear anything, maybe footsteps, people moving about, sounds that might make you think someone could be dossing up there?'

'Nothing.'

'Any car parked outside the entrance to the flat?'

'Oh, anyone could do that, parking is allowed. Different cars come and go there all the time, sometimes shoppers, sometimes people who work in Starly.'

'Do you remember the people who rented it in the past? Did you see the tenants much?'

Wang did not reply for a moment. Denzil watched his face but read nothing.

'Would you recognise them if they came into the shop?'

Wang took off his glasses and wiped them on another sheet of the paper towel. He looked troubled.

'I don't know. But why? I don't want anyone brought in here, do you understand? I want nothing that could make trouble for me. I have a good business, people come from a long way sometimes, I am a trained herbalist, I am well respected.'

'There won't be any trouble, the most that would happen at this stage is some photographs would be shown to you, see if you recognise anyone. We might get lucky.'

Someone rattled at the shop door and Wang leapt up. 'I have to open up, I have been closed for too long, customers will be very annoyed.'

'No problem, I'm leaving now. Thank you, you've been very helpful but if you do remember or anyone comes in, here's my card, direct line, station number as well . . .'

Wang was already at the door with his hand on the latch. Denzil had kept his last question until the herbalist was about to open the door.

'Do you sell illegal drugs, Mr Huang? Do you have any opiates on the premises?'

'No, I do not. I would never do this. I am qualified and I am licensed. I would risk losing everything, my business, my reputation. Never.'

'Good. Thanks for your time. Better let this impatient customer in.'

Wang saw Denzil walk away as the woman started to explain to him about her father's ulcerated leg. He fetched a small jar of ointment, labelled it and printed off an instruction sheet. 'If there is no healing in five days please come back, and then I will give him powders as well. But if he has any temperature or sign of infection then you must see the doctor or go to the hospital. Please keep a careful watch.'

The woman had questions, he had to go over everything again before she left. The shop had been empty for ten seconds when two men pushed their way in, dropped the lock and turned the sign to Closed. Wang held up his hands.

'No! No, I have nothing to tell you, I have been away at my uncle's funeral, I have –'

'Shut it, Wang.'

He did not know their names. In the beginning, they had phoned to warn him, now they just came in like this. It had been going on for more than a year.

'Anyone out the back?'

'No.'

'OK, usual routine, stay here, no opening up if someone rattles on the handle.'

'Listen to me, I do not want this any more. Please.'

'What was the cop after?'

'What cop?'

The taller one cleared his throat, then spat out a gobbet of phlegm onto the floor.

'That one. Now turn round, Wangker.'

They were in and out of the stockroom in little more than a minute.

'No treasure hunting, all right? And if the cop comes back, we were after some of the lotus flower johnnies.'

Seven

Two people had come forward to say that they knew the dead drug addict. The first had decided quickly, on seeing the photograph of the dead body enlarged and also receiving a detailed description, that he had been mistaken. The second was sent packing by the duty sergeant without getting as far as CID.

'Nutter, guv.'

'You sure?'

'Put it this way – every time we put out a request for more information or an ID, he turns up. Every. Single. Time.'

Serrailler was not having a good day. He had come up against a brick wall on a reinvestigation into a cold case, the murder of an elderly man whose family had never accepted 'By person or persons unknown. File remains open. June 1987.'

At 11.10 he downloaded a report on firearms containing a large number of graphics, which had crashed his computer. IT had told him they might get round to it by the end of the afternoon but no promises. Simon groaned, picked up his jacket, pushed his blond hair back from his forehead, and walked out of the station. The coffee in the canteen was undrinkable, but at the end of the road in the Cypriot cafe, it was the best outside London. He was thinking about his first double espresso as he started to cross, saw a car bearing down on him, calculated that he would outrun it and sprinted, but he had misjudged its speed and had to leap for the pavement. The silver BMW convertible stopped dead with a squeal of brakes and a slight skid, the

28

driver leaning on the horn. He went over to apologise, summoning up all his best, rueful charm.

'Bloody hell, what were you thinking? That was nearly one dead Chief Superintendent,' Rachel Wyatt said.

Deep violet eyes in a heart-shaped face, creamy skin, hair pulled back in a comb. In the seconds it took him to lean in through the passenger window, Simon had a flashback to the first time they had met, placed next to one another at the Lord Lieutenant's Banquet, gold and silver plates, crystal glasses and chandeliers catching the light from hundreds of candles, and the diamonds round her neck and at her ears, beautiful jewels but somehow not at all ostentatious.

He blinked, the banqueting hall vanished and Rachel was in the driver's seat of her car, still looking cross.

'Hey, were you heading to the station?'

'No, I was heading home.'

'Going in the wrong direction.'

'I've moved. And you had better move too or you'll lose another of your lives. How many would it be now?' A van had slowed behind them and waited as Simon still leaned on the door, talking to her, looking at her.

'Pull in over there.'

The van driver blasted his horn, Rachel shrugged and did as he suggested, but once parked, she did not switch off the engine.

'I was just going down to the Cypriot to get a decent coffee. Come with me, I need to talk to you.'

'Need?'

'Yes – and want and would love to.'

She hesitated.

'Park in the forecourt – you can use the space next to me.'

'Where it says "Strictly police officers and station staff only"?'

'Right.'

Rachel smiled.

'Too long,' Simon said, when they had sat down. 'Where have you been?'

'New Zealand. New York.'

'By yourself?'

Her look silenced him.

'I was told that New Zealand was a boring provincial country, and provincial it certainly is, but boring – not entirely, and so beautiful. I can't remember if you've been?'

'Once. I flew over from Oz for a week when my sister and brother-in-law spent a year there. Lovely scenery, quite boring. New York now . . .'

'Love it or hate it.'

'Love, but it must be about eight years since I was last there.'

'It's changed a lot – but then again, it hasn't changed at all. New York doesn't change, it just reinvents itself every decade.'

'We should go. I've got some leave to use up . . . let's do it, Rachel.'

She turned her head away, to look out of the cafe window at nothing in particular. Drank her coffee.

'I'm sorry,' Simon said.

She took a moment before looking at him again and he could not read her expression. Not annoyance. Not surprise. What?

'You're a bit like New York,' she said. 'You've changed, and then again – you haven't.'

He could not process that and she did not explain, so he set it aside, to think about later.

'How's the bookshop?'

'Fine.'

'Profitable?'

'More or less.'

'Still a labour of love.'

'Why not?'

Her cup was empty and he started to get up.

'No, Simon . . .'

But he had already caught the attention of the barista.

'I have changed,' he said. 'I used to be incautious but losing the arm made a difference.'

'As in crossing the road without looking both ways.'

'Whereas you . . .' He touched her hand. 'You haven't changed in the slightest bit.'

She would not meet his eye.

'Still beautiful. Still the same woman.'

Then she did look directly at him, so that he caught his breath.

'How can you possibly know that, Simon?' she said.

'I know that I want to.'

In the silence between them then, he had a moment of absolute clarity in which he did know, he knew everything – Rachel and what she had meant to him, what they had had and, more than anything, what he had been. A complete bloody fool, he thought.

More people had come in and he sensed that one of them was looking at them from across the cafe.

Their coffees arrived but Rachel poured some water into hers, drank it quickly, got up.

'Rachel . . .'

'No.'

'I'll walk back with you.'

'And if someone has put a notice on my windscreen, you are going to deal with it, right?'

'Of course.'

He held open the door and put his hand on her back as they left.

Fern Monroe watched until they were out of sight before taking a sip of her coffee.

'So,' Donna said, 'who was that?'

Eight

'Hello!'

The man stepped out of nowhere so suddenly that Brookie dropped his carrier bag into a puddle of muddy rainwater.

'Man, what are you like?'

Brookie stared down at the textbooks, pens and mess of assorted rubbish, but his expression was not of dismay just of numb acceptance. Stuff happened. To him.

'Come here, let me . . . Look at the state of you. Can't you even find a new placky bag or what?'

Brookie started to scrabble about in the puddle. 'No.'

'Hang on, hang on, let's do this properly. '

'I'll miss the bus again.'

'Never mind that, I'll give you a lift, and I've probably got an old bag in the van. Now hold these – no, not like that, they're dripping wet.'

Fats went round to the back of the van and rummaged about, while Brookie tried to stop the rainwater dripping all over himself and the seats, even though the seats were already filthy and split here and there.

'Here, better than that other rubbish.'

He held out something in a shiny new plastic cover.

'What's this?'

'Present.'

'Who from?'

'Me. Now open it, shove your things in and let's get going, I've got stuff to do.'

The rucksack that came out of the packaging had strong maroon waterproof fabric with black piping, and black straps, and smelled of its newness, inside and out.

'What are you giving me this for?'

'Must be mad. Anyway, it'll do you, won't it?'

Brookie stared at it, then stroked it, then very carefully stowed his things inside.

'You sure?'

'Yeah, now shut up before I change my mind.'

Brookie was silent for the first bit of the journey, just holding the rucksack close to him, but as they turned onto the country road, he said, 'Why were you at my school again?'

'Seeing a man about a dog.'

'You got a dog?' Brookie dreamed hopefully and regularly of having his own dog.

'Nah, it's a thing people say, see a man about a dog.'

They swung round a corner too hard, almost tipping into the ditch. Brookie was glad when they stopped at the corner.

'You'd better say you found it on a skip.'

'Why? I want to tell my dad you –'

'No, you don't, you keep this between us. A skip, I said.'

'Oh. Only –'

'Only nothing. Get it?'

'OK. Hey, thanks though, it's really cool.'

'You're all right. Slam the door.'

The van rattled off. It had only one working back light. Brookie watched it go, holding the rucksack tightly, but worrying about it. Because you found a lot of stuff in skips but not shiny new bags in their wrappers from the shop. Not usually.

He raced upstairs with the bag when he got in, was putting it between his mattress and the wall when Tommy came in.

'Where'd you get that?'

'What?'

'That bag.'

'It's old.'

'Doesn't look old. Where'd you get it?'

'Found it.'

'Liar.'

'In a skip.'

'What skip? Where?'

'Mind yours.'

'You nicked it.'

'Off a skip isn't nicking.'

'I want something next time then.'

'OK.'

Tommy dug his younger brother in the ribs, then dodged away. Brookie pulled the rucksack nearer, partly because he couldn't believe he'd got it and didn't have to put up with any more plastic bags. But mainly because he didn't trust his brother.

Nine

'Guv?'

Serrailler paused on his way up the stairs.

'Young woman brought this in ten minutes ago – just dropped it on the desk and ran. I didn't get a proper look at her, I was dealing with a couple of scroats. Might be something and nothing.'

To the Police, Lafferton.

Regarding the photo in the Bevham Gazette, I think this may be a picture of my brother. None of my family have seen him since autumn when he called at our mum and stepdad's house, I was there and saw him. He was in a bad way. His name is Liam, if it is him. It's not easy to tell for sure. Please let me know what I should do next.

Yours sincerely

Lynn Vines (Mrs)

There was a mobile number beneath her name.

'Will you ring this number, Hawkins, and ask Mrs Vines if she can come back to the station?'

DC Hawkins took the letter. Like Denzil, he was new, ambitious and annoyingly youthful.

'Might be a good idea if you could bring her in yourself. Don't let her ask about her brother – talk about something else. How about the weather?'

'If she asks me any questions, guv?'
'Still the weather.'

Lynn Vines was in her early thirties, carefully made up, wearing
a good Puffa jacket and orange hat with a fur bobble. She looked
so nervous that he asked his secretary to bring tea, in a pot, on
a tray, with biscuits. He knew the psychological value of the
gesture, which was more than the sum of its parts and gave out
a signal that this was an informal visit, for a conversation not a
questioning. The tea plus his soothing chat about the recent
floods after the thaw and the cheering sight of the first crocuses
on the Hill, took fifteen friendly minutes, by which time the
young woman had visibly relaxed.

Simon set down his cup. 'Mrs Vines, can we talk about your
brother, Liam? Are you happy to?'

She nodded.

'But first I do want to thank you and stress how good it was
of you to write the note and to come in here. It's never easy, I
do understand, police stations can be intimidating places, except
for those of us who work in them.'

'I saw it in the local paper, I think I said, but even after I'd
read it, and then looked at that photo, I didn't really connect it
with Liam, not straight away.'

'I'm sorry we had to make that public but we had no other
way to find out about the young man. It is a distressing photo,
I know. We made sure that the paper printed it on the inside
pages and that parts of it were blurred. So, you didn't think
straight away that it was your brother?'

'No, because the face . . . well, it wasn't very clear or how he
really was – of course it wasn't, but it's not like you expect
anyone to look, is it?'

'No.'

'But I kept returning to it, and anyway, Liam's always in the
back of my mind. I phoned Becky, my sister, she'd seen it on
her phone, only she didn't want to even go there, she scrolled
down from it. But then she was like me, she went back and she
just knew. When I rang her she said that. "It's Liam."'

'Tell me about him. Was the time you went to your mother's house when he was there the last time you saw him?'

'Yes.'

'Do you know if they'd been expecting him?'

'Oh no, I didn't have to ask, they wouldn't have been, they'd given up on him. He just turned up sometimes. That's how it's been with him for over a year. He'd show up and then disappear again, none of us'd set eyes on him or heard anything for weeks.'

'May I have his full name, please?'

'Liam Joseph Payne.'

'His age?'

'Twenty-two. He was twenty-two on Christmas Day.' Her face clouded.

'Did he have a job?'

'Ha, yes, well – he actually trained as a mechanic at Kinnocks, got a paid-for apprenticeship, he was very lucky and he did all right, they were pleased with him, they get people onto proper career paths there if they work hard, it's a good firm, and Liam did work, he was really keen, talked about it non-stop at the beginning.'

'How long was he there?'

'Getting on for three years. And then he just upped and left. ' She snapped her fingers. 'Mum was furious with him, only he said he was bored, he wanted to be more his own boss, wanted to branch out, he had this mate with his own garage, bloke who restored old cars and steam engines, if you believe it, he did them up, got them working and sold them for a fortune. They were going into partnership. So he said.'

'And did he?'

'God knows. No, I'm sure he didn't. He was living at home then, with Mum and Derek, only he was never there. Mum said he'd turn up, empty the fridge, have a shower, which she said he definitely needed, then sleep round the clock. He never said much but he had some nice new gear, designer stuff, trainers, and I know those, you don't get change out of three hundred quid. Anyway, then he said he was moving into a flat with some mates in Bevham, he'd be back for Bonfire Night. We all generally go to that big bonfire and fireworks up at Starly Tor so I was really pleased, he'd been to that every year since he was a little kid, we all have, I thought, well, it means something to him. Only he never turned up. It was then . . .'

She was biting the inside of her cheek and her face took on a distant look.

'Something was wrong?' Simon asked gently.

She nodded but was still silent, and he waited. He never tried to take the words out of anyone's mouth, or jump ahead of them.

Eventually, she said, 'He turned up a few weeks later. He looked awful. Terrible. He looked like death. He's a handsome lad, Liam, and, look, I know, he's my brother, I love him, but he has a lovely open sort of face, beautiful eyes, and he's always been a warm person, friends with everyone. He's a bit of a softy – you know?'

Serrailler nodded.

'If anyone was to forget your birthday, it'd never be Liam. And something else, he's always been fit, he worked out, went running, on his bike, he was never ill – when we all had coughs and colds and stuff Liam never did. So when he came home that day, I didn't recognise him, if I'd seen him the street I'd have walked past him. I'd never seen anyone look like that. He was thin as a stick, with these dark, hollow shadows under his eyes, and he was an awful colour – his skin was sort of doughy, but with all these sore-looking spots, like teenage ones only way, way worse, they were like boils, I mean, who has boils nowadays? His fingernails were all bitten down and raw, and black and – and this is awful . . . he smelled.' Abruptly, she burst into tears.

Simon knew that pressing her to continue at this point would not only be unproductive but also insensitive and unkind. She spent several minutes with her head down, a pad of tissues pressed to her mouth. He went out and got her some chilled water from the machine, partly to give her a few moments by herself.

He had kept an open mind while she had been talking, as to whether this was a likely ID for the dead junkie or a false alarm, but at this moment, he had a gut feeling that they had the right man – not that they had been inundated with likely prospects.

She blew her nose, and took the cup of water Simon held out. 'What happens now?'

'We have a number of photos of the person you think is your brother, Liam.'

'It is him.'

'And I don't want you to have to see more than absolutely necessary because I know this is extremely distressing, but a dead body can look different from different angles, so I'm asking if you would be able to view just a couple more, so that you're absolutely confident. If you find you're not quite as sure after all, then it won't be in any way your fault. OK, do you think you can do it?'

She nodded. Her tears had gone and he knew they would not come back. Not now. Not yet.

'Thank you. Right, these were all taken by a forensic photographer and –'

'It's OK, I get it, they weren't done to make him look pretty.'

'Sorry. I'm going to show them to you on my laptop so that they are as clear as possible, but before I do, can you confirm one thing? That so far as you know, nobody reported to us that your brother was missing, at any time since you last saw him alive?'

'I'm certain nobody did and I'd have known, unless it was one of his mates, only they'd never have thought of doing it, and definitely not before they'd checked with home first. Like I said, he'd been coming and going, he'd disappear for weeks and then just turn up so nobody exactly thought of him as – well, missing.'

'Fine. Here we go then. You just have to look at these, as carefully as you can bear to.' Simon clicked quickly through the first photos, of the flat exterior, then the room.

'Is that – my God, was he living there?'

'We're not sure yet. Possibly. Now, take your time . . . deep breath.'

'I'm OK.'

He showed pictures of the man's head. Chest. Left arm.

'Oh God.'

'Take a moment . . . look away if you need to.'

'It's him. That's Liam. That's Liam dead, only he looks like he did that last time . . . except he wasn't that colour, he was, like, ashy white . . . doughy, I said. That's his tattoo.'

'I don't think you need to look at any more.' Serrailler closed the file.

'Is that it?'

'No. There is something else, I'm afraid, but it doesn't have to be you, it can be another family member.'

She looked at him in dread. 'I know what you mean. I know and I'm . . . I don't know how I'd be.'

'That's understandable and pretty usual, so who else do you think might be able and willing to identify your brother?'

'Won't the photograph do? By itself – because that's Liam, I'd swear.'

'I'm afraid not.'

'Not Mum or Derek, I don't want them to have to go through that. Would I – anyone – have to touch him?'

'No. You would have to look at his face only and just for long enough to be able to say for certain that it either is or is not your brother. Someone will go with you and be there, you can ask for a female officer.'

'Couldn't you, Mr Serrailler?'

'Of course I could, Lynn. So, will you do it?'

'I have to. It's my brother.'

Seeing her off, Simon prayed that it was, and then wondered if the prayer was entirely appropriate.

Ten

*Hey. So good to see you. Can we talk? I would like us to. Coffee break
doesn't count. Have leave, Thursday to Monday, week after next. Nice
quiet hotel, somewhere beautiful? Let me know soonest. Love S*

As he was pressing 'Send', Denzil Aberra put his head round
the door. 'Got a minute, guv?'

Simon waved him in, glad of the interruption, which would
distract him from listening for the ping of a reply to his text. He
had an hour before he had to be at the mortuary.

'Starly.'

'Right. You've had second thoughts about our Chinese herbalist?'

'Yes and no. I haven't got anything new, he hasn't been in
touch, only I've just got a niggle.'

'Respect it. What?'

'I believed him when he said he didn't know anything about
the flat above. He isn't the landlord, the entrance is separate
from his shop. Whoever came and went, he most likely wouldn't
have seen them – none of his business. But I still got a sense of
something . . .'

'That he wasn't telling you the whole story?'

'Maybe. I wasn't there long, but it's still clear in my mind . . .
the more I go over it, the more I think he was bothered about
something . . . he was nervous all the time I was there.'

'A lot of people are anxious if they have a cop coming through
the door to ask questions, or had you not noticed? It doesn't

matter if they're guilty of anything or nothing. The worst of the lot can be as cool as you like, the most innocent party can be shaking with fear, so you can't rely on the initial reaction. Having said that, it's always worth noting. Go on.'

'He didn't like me being in the shop because he didn't want customers seeing me, he'd turned the notice on the door round to Closed the minute I'd shown him my warrant card, and I get that, but he was twitchy . . . he gabbled a bit. I don't know.' Denzil shook his head. 'Sounds like a load of nothing, doesn't it?'

'Not necessarily. Did everything look as you'd expect?'

The DC shrugged. 'No idea, guv, never been in a Chinese pharmacy before, but yeah, it was all neat, well arranged and very clean. I went into the back, tiny little office area and a stockroom, all orderly. No rubbish lying about, very hygienic.'

'What's your plan?'

'The thing is, I've no reason to go back, have I?'

'There's always a reason, you make one, you're checking on something he said, or on a date or a time, you ask if he's heard anyone in the flat since you were there, seen anyone hanging about outside.'

'Could do.'

'Listen, you haven't been here long and I don't know you very well but you don't strike me as being unconfident, so have faith in your own judgement. What's the worst that can happen?'

'I get nowhere. Again.'

'What else are you working on?'

'Filing a report on two break-ins. Nothing interesting.'

'It's all interesting, DC Aberra.'

'Guv.'

'Finish your report – I have a feeling two break-ins at the Old Ribbon Factory apartments might turn out to be a few more.'

'I'm with you there. More than half those places are unoccupied during the day, that's well known, easy enough for anyone to clock, wait till mid-morning when they're all safely behind their desks. Burglar's paradise.'

'Right, I want you staying on that for now. Go back over your notes, see if there's any pattern, any link, which I'm pretty sure there will be, then go over there, sit in your car, walk about, move, rinse and repeat, you know the drill. Keep in touch, take photographs of anyone hanging about. It's a slow game but this is just the time we might catch someone in the act . . . and if there's nothing today, go back tomorrow.'

Denzil left, looking downtrodden. Serrailler didn't blame him. He had given the new DC a perfect example of the dead-end jobs which, once in a blue moon, came good. For the time being he wanted the DC kept busy and away from Starly. When a member of CID had been identified in a particular place, he was better deployed elsewhere, if possible, until people lost interest.

By five to three he was parked at the hospital and checking his phone. Seven work emails. Nothing from Rachel. So, she was away, seeing friends, in the bookshop, at the hairdresser, some-where else which had no phone signal. Where?

A small blue Hyundai came slowly into the reserved area, and Simon put away his phone.

'Mrs Vines . . . you can park here, next to me.'

Lynn Vines was wearing a black coat, dark grey trousers, black boots. Mourning of a sort.

'Thank you so much, Mr Serrailler, I'm so grateful to you for being here. I didn't know if you would.'

She spoke warmly, but her expression was oddly blank, as if she had determined not to show anything of what she felt, any trepidation, reluctance or distress. She might have been about to walk into an office or a shop, rather than a hospital mortuary.

She paused briefly at the door of the viewing room and closed her eyes, so that for a moment Simon wondered if she was going to back out or start to cry. But she did neither; she took a deep breath, straightened her back, and went in.

'Thank you,' Simon said when they were back by their cars. 'I do know how hard that was. Will you be all right to drive your-self home?'

'I'm fine, I'm better than I thought I would be which maybe seems strange.'

'No. It can be a great relief.'

'I feel that. I was dreading it and I was praying it wouldn't be Liam, but now I know, I can face what happened to him. It's a rubbish sort of life, Mr Serrailler. How can anyone see that photo of my brother, in that dump of a place, and think there's any glamour or any cleverness in it? Do you know what I hate most? Those smart people who think they can shoot up or snort coke at parties and it's just a bit of fun, a high, all friends together, they can afford it, no harm done. Jesus. If they knew, if they saw . . . he wasn't a bad boy, you know – he was a bit weak, but he was only twenty-two, for God's sake. He really didn't have any bad in him.'

'I'm sure of it . . . not many of the ones who end up as he did are bad. Stupid sometimes, easily led, weak, as you said, but not bad. It's the dealers who are bad, not the victims – because that is what they are. That's what Liam was.' He touched her shoulder. 'Thank you again. Are you going to see your family now?'

She nodded. 'I have to tell Mum and Derek, and my sister . . . they're waiting to hear. What will happen next?'

'There will be an inquest. Identity is established now, and the cause of death, so it should be quite straightforward.'

'Will anybody be – will you find out who led him into this?'

'Almost certainly not, I'm afraid. Liam was the only one who could have told us that.'

'So he just went up there into that crappy room and killed himself.'

'He won't have meant to kill himself. Either he had a contaminated batch of heroin, and whatever was in it caused his death, or he may not have used for a while, so his system had been without a heroin fix for long enough to react massively when he did inject again. I'm pretty sure this was unintentional, Lynn.'

'We won't know, will we? We won't ever know.'

'I'm sorry. Listen, there are people you can talk to about this . . . you should think about getting some kind of help. It can be just a phone call or two. Don't let it overwhelm you . . . you're

44

going to grieve, of course you are, but things can fester if you let them. If you want me to put you in touch with someone, give me a call, email me. I have to go but don't forget. And thank you again for doing this. You're very courageous.'

She was still standing beside her own car, staring at nothing, when he drove away.

Eleven

There had been a frost the previous night, and a thaw during the day, so that Starly's pavements were slick and black, and as he turned to lock his car, Serrailler slipped and went down on his back, stunned for a moment, feeling a pain in his lower vertebrae which did not bode well. His height meant that he had suffered intermittently from back pain since his late teens and it had worsened in the last year. He could still walk long distances but his climbing days were numbered. He could still do most things but he suffered for it afterwards.

He was so used to his prosthetic arm now that he forgot it most of the time. It did not greatly hamper him and though he had played his last cricket match he was happy to umpire. But as he tried to get to his feet now, he put his weight on his left arm and slipped again.

'Have you hurt yourself? Bloody potholes in these paths.'

The man looked no younger than seventy.

'Thank you, that's kind, but I'm fine.'

'You don't look it. Here, hold on to me and let me take your weight, use your other arm to steady yourself.'

He did so and was upright in three seconds. His coat was muddy and his trousers wet but otherwise he had got off lightly. He simply felt a bloody fool to have needed help from an old man with a stick, who was now walking away without fuss.

He sauntered across the road, and along the row of shops. He bought a copy of the *Bevham Gazette* and a bottle of water

46

from the all-purpose shop, and as he came out again, glanced along to the corner and the Chinese herbalist's premises. He walked purposefully towards and straight past it, looking sideways as he reached the door and noting that the shop had one customer.

His car was parked at an angle in the short row of spaces on the other side of the square, from which he would have a good view of people going in and out, and he had barely settled in his seat when the customer left the pharmacy and turned the first corner out of sight. For forty minutes, no one else went in. Simon drank his water, read his paper while glancing up every so often, missing nothing. Shop and street lights were on now. The sky was heavy with rain as the evening closed in, though it was not yet five, but he would wait until closing time.

At five to five a car stopped on the corner. One person stayed at the wheel, one person got out and went quickly into the herbalist's, head down, jacket collar turned up. Serrailler was across the street in seconds, just out of sight of both the occupant of the car and the shop, phone in hand, switched to camera. With luck, there might be just enough light, but he was ready to memorise the man's features too. Might be nothing, might be something. His strong instinct was that it was something. He edged forward, close to the wall, to try and glimpse inside the shop, but from this angle it seemed to be empty. He was debating whether to move any further, and then the man came out, head down again, dived into the car and they were gone but not before Simon had taken a dozen quick shots. They might have noticed the phone light if they had not been focused entirely on getting away. It had looked like a robbery but it was all too quick.

He had his hand on the door handle as the chemist locked it from the other side and turned the notice to Closed. Serrailler rapped on the glass but the man waved his arms, shouting that he was shut, pointing to the sign. The next minute he had switched off the lights.

He could do one of two things. Wait until the man left, on the way to his car, or come back tomorrow in daylight. The building was empty, dark and silent. No one appeared but a car door slammed and an engine started in the side road leading past the entrance to the flat. Simon swore at himself for making such a rookie mistake. The images he had on his phone were poor but one might be recognisable and he forwarded them over with a request to have them checked against records. Not that he was hopeful of a result.

He had two emails from work, of no particular interest, one from his father, asking why he had not been to visit him 'for several weeks', which was intended to make him feel guilty but did not, and in any case, it was barely one week since he had taken Richard out for a pub lunch, a stroll and a half-hour of his complaints and disapproval.

There was nothing from Rachel. No text, no email. He sat looking at the screen, changing his mind about whether to send another message or wait longer, starting to key one in, deleting it, putting the phone away, picking it up again.

Hi again. Did you get my last message? Would love it if we could get away. x S

He checked his spam folder. Nothing.

Twelve

Brookie threw his bag onto the pile in the hall and as he turned round Connor tripped him up neatly from behind.

'Leave off . . . what you done that for? I'll get you back.'

'Try.' He bent over and picked up the bag. 'This int yours.'

'Yes it is. Give it back.'

Connor held it above his head. 'Not . . . you never had that before.'

'Give it back.' Brookie made a dive, which was useless because his brother spun out of his reach, the bag still above his head.

'OK, don't then.' He made to go into the kitchen but now Connor blocked his path.

'You tell me where you got it, you'll get it back.'

'Or what?'

'I'll throw it.'

'Don't be stupid. I want to get my tea, come on, I'm starving.'

'Nope. You nicked it, didn't you?'

'Found it.'

'Yeah.'

'It was on a skip and you know I only had a placky bag and that broke and then I saw this and getting stuff off a skip int nicking. Now give it here.'

He lunged at Connor, butted him forward, Connor kicked him in the shin and they fell in a heap, blocking the doorway. The rucksack went skidding across the floor and hit the skirting board. Books and pens went all over, Connor throwing himself on them while Brookie went to the table and bagged the last of the bread. The other two had switched on the television and were together on the brown leather sofa, the best find of anything they'd ever got from a skip. The only slightly worn parts were the armrests and that wasn't right through.

'Where the fuck did you get this, Brookie?' Connor whistled.

Brookie was putting margarine and peanut butter on his bread and didn't look round.

Next thing he knew, Connor was shoving something under his nose.

'Amazing what you get off a skip. Not. Where'd it come from?'

It was still under his nose. A small slab of black metal.

'That's not mine. That was never in my bag.'

'Where else did it come from then? Fall off the ceiling?'

The mobile phone gleamed as it lay in Connor's hand.

'Come on, where'd I get that from? Let's see it.'

Connor lifted his arm in the air. 'Finders keepers.'

'Not yours, give it here. It was in my bag.'

'You going to tell me the truth?'

Brookie just stood. Connor lowered his arm and looked at the phone carefully, turned it on, looked at the screen, turned it off. 'Works,' he said.

'Come on, Connor, hand it over.'

'Owner might ring it . . . then you answer it and they'll have you for nickin stuff.'

'How'd they know who it was answering?'

Connor's silence acknowledged the truth of that.

Brookie grabbed his bread and four biscuits and went to sit on the sofa to watch *Jamie Johnson* with the other two but he didn't take the programme in properly. Connor was at the table, eating the broken bits at the bottom of the biscuit pack and playing with the mobile. He was sure his brother had nicked it, and he didn't know what he thought about that.

Thirteen

Hi G. Wanted you to see this as I don't suppose you have. Thought you'd want to know. I've scanned it from the paper. Don't let it bother you, you've moved on. Stupid idiot, and he's how old, 55? Hope you and Liv are OK. Noelline xxx

Below was the announcement.

TONKS. To Madison (née Bulmer) and Jeffrey, magnificent twin sons, Isaac Jeffrey and Noah Patrick, first grandchildren for Kay and Patrick Bulmer. Life is wonderful!

This was why Greta didn't open her messages before she started work but always waited for lunchtime, or at least until her coffee break. 'You've moved on.' What did Noelline know? But if you had asked Greta Tonks the previous day if that was true, she would have said a firm yes, that she had her life back, a good life and one she was perfectly happy in, and that she and Olivia didn't need Jeff, didn't miss him, managed very well without him, thank you. Of course, when it had happened she had not felt any of that, she had been devastated, torn apart and certain she could not survive, let alone make a go of being an abandoned and then divorced woman with a daughter and modest earnings.

It was only fourteen-year-old Olivia who had held her mother back from a nervous breakdown. Greta thought her daughter had heard and seen far too much, yet they had struggled through, damaged and bereft but more or less intact. Jeff had faced the full onslaught of her shock, rage and distress and of his daughter's pale, cold withdrawal, for no longer than a couple of weeks, before he had bolted to 23-year-old Madison. Noelline, who lived nearby, reported back on his marriage, then their new house and the way the two of them were always about and lovey-dovey, but had never mentioned a pregnancy. So why now? Did she think telling Greta about the twin babies was necessary and might, in some way, be good for her state of mind, or was it just gloating, disguised as friendly concern, and if that were so, what was friendly about it?

She went to make her coffee two hours earlier than usual, because she needed to do something and the news had shot the morning's work to pieces before it was started. She would hardly be able to concentrate on checking solicitors' bills for possible errors and inaccurate charging, a job she had done for the past ten years, as a freelance for various legal firms, from home.

She opened the back door onto the side of the garden which caught the late-morning sun and stood looking out but not seeing, hands round her coffee mug. It was very still and freezing cold.

She had thought all of her bitterness and anger at what Jeff had done to them had begun to fade. It was almost two years ago. The misery, regret, self-blame had left her quite soon because she was intelligent, reasonable, clear-sighted, and was sure that she had not been in any way at fault. They had had a happy marriage, at ease with one another, devoted to their only child, for whom they had waited seven years, and because they were so relieved and grateful for Liv, they had never been sad that she was an only one.

'Why?' she had asked Jeff over and over again in the first few dark days. 'What is wrong with me? Why aren't you happy in our marriage? I thought you were. I'm sure I always have been. What's happened?'

He had said nothing, there was nothing, he too had been happy, and he still loved her, there was nothing wrong. The only thing that had happened was Madison, with whom, at the age of fifty-three, he had fallen suddenly and insanely in love. Yes,

Greta said, yes, it is insane, you are mad, you are out of your mind, and I know this happens, it's an illness, it's a fever. Read Shakespeare. You had drops poured into your eyes. No, I am sane and wide awake and nobody drugged me, I was where I was, and suddenly, everything turned upside down and I am where I am, he had said.

You can't argue with it, friends had told her, you can't cure it, you have to hope he'll wake up and know himself for an idiot. Don't try and stop him, let him go and you keep your pride. I give it six months, less even. It can't last. He'll be back. She's twenty-one, for goodness' sake! He won't marry her.

He had married her.

Greta stood quietly, sipping her coffee, expecting to feel something . . . a wave of grief, jealousy, pain. But it was laughter, gloating laughter, without a trace of rancour or envy in it, laughter that he was fifty-five and married to a girl thirty years younger, with newborn twins boys. Olivia had not been a difficult baby, but still Jeff had not found life with an infant at all easy, he had moved into the spare room because he couldn't deal with the loss of sleep, he had found ways of escaping from the house when Liv had cried and been irritable and demanding. And now, here he was again times two, and the future held rowdy, energetic, space-filling toddlers and small boys and then lumping great older boys, on and on as far as the eye could see. Greta smiled and went on smiling, as she put her empty mug in the sink and went through to the office to start work. It was gone ten. Olivia had her dance class this afternoon, after which she went into town for a pizza or a shake with one or two of the other girls, then they would wander in and out of the shops, happily browsing and trying on things they would never buy. Nice girls. Mia. Naeve. Amelie. Sometimes they were picked up in town by someone's parent, but mostly they got the bus. None of them lived far out. Yes, nice girls. Olivia was the talented one, the best dancer. She only lacked a bit of confidence but that would come. She was middle of the road academically, and thought she wanted to do nursing, but that could change. Greta tried never to push her, but privately she thought her dancing would take Liv into the future, one way or another.

Her hands froze on the keyboard. Olivia. She had not wanted anything to do with her father for over a year but then there had been Christmas and he had wanted to take her for a special dinner, have an early celebration and her presents, and Madison had sent a bracelet and a flowery little card, saying how she really really wanted them to be friends.

And Greta had minded, not because of Jeff himself, let alone the young woman, but for fear that Olivia would be bribed and made up to. Changed.

So what would she think about the twins, her two half-brothers? New babies were a draw, Olivia liked children, she was fourteen, almost of an age to babysit or help out, to love them, because they would be lovable and they would make up for the siblings she had not had.

Greta rearranged her back cushion. Logged on. She always worked on Saturdays, and took Tuesdays off, to shop and meet friends when the town was quieter, but now, because of Noelline's message, she was behind before she had started, and all she could do was think about the babies. Isaac and Noah – trendy little names, and there had been no reference to Jeff's mother, Moira, and his late dad, only to the other grandparents. The new in-laws.

Oh for God's sake, woman, stop it, leave it be.

She wished Noelline had never butted in, all concern, to tell her about it, 'thought you would want to know' while probably smirking behind her hand.

Fourteen

'Shakes or ice cream?'

Mia rolled her eyes, Amelie shook her head. 'Can't, I've got to buy some shampoo and then I'm broke.'

'Doesn't your mum buy that?'

'Used to but now it's got to come out of my allowance.'

'What else did you spend it on?'

But Olivia interrupted. 'I'm paying for the desserts, you just have to buy your own pizzas. I think I want a vanilla shake with cream and chocolate sprinkles.'

'You sure, Liv?'

'Would I offer?'

'OK, can I have a double salted caramel with cream and caramel drizzle?'

'Amelie?'

'Banana pancake please, with banana ice cream.'

'Pancake after pizza?'

'It doesn't cost any more.'

'Thinking of your waistline.'

But they were all slender, all energetic dancers and sports players.

'That's over fifteen pounds, Liv.'

'It's OK, Mum gave me twenty.'

'Love your mum! Are we going into Venables after? I need to look at boots.'

'Need to?'

'Birthday in three weeks.'

'Yeah, I'll come with you, they'll have had new stock, we can try on.'

'I can't, I've got to meet my dad, sorry.'

'Didn't think you saw your dad outside Christmas.'

Olivia was ordering and didn't answer, but when she turned round, Mia said it again.

'Yeah, I see him now. Sometimes.'

'Is it . . . OK?'

A shrug.

'Must be weird though. His wife's only a year older than Bethany. Can't imagine my sister being married to a bloke as old as your dad.'

'Are you going in for "Strictly Bevham"?'

'No. Listen, sorry, I didn't mean to poke my nose in.'

'It's OK. I think it'll be rubbish, not worth the trouble. Mrs Palmer isn't interested, she said anyone wanting to enter does it off her own bat.'

'Well, she would, she isn't the Queen Bee so it's of no interest. She is actually a good dance teacher or I wouldn't still be going but she's such a snob.'

'I've never actually *had* a pupil who lived in Bevham.'

The desserts came.

'Oh. My. God, will you look at that! Thanks so much, Liv . . .'

'Thank your mum.'

Olivia watched the other two go off arm in arm towards Venables, Lafferton's only and quite small department store, before turning down the snicket beside the cab rank. She didn't know why she had said she was meeting her dad, she hadn't even thought of him for a bit, let alone seen him. He sent her funny cards, emails and expensive presents, but he never suggested they meet, apart from last Christmas, and that was fine with her, she had spent two years steeling herself against any feelings for him. And it was all right. Mostly. Her mother had said from the beginning that she would never get between the two of them, Liv must do as she liked and see him whenever she wanted to, he was her father, and there would be no resentment from her, but Olivia

56

knew that actually Greta wanted anything but that, she wanted the two of them to be a tight, self-sufficient unit.

She came out into the bottom end of town, where the scuzzy betting shop and tattoo parlour were, the boarded-up nightclub and the back of the multi-storey. She glanced round. But he would be there before her, he always was.

The Black Cat Cafe had Formica tables, and a flashing, banging, screaming slot machine. An old man was shoving coins into it and leaning on the glass front, staring at the whirring orange and neon-blue things going round, looming out and back, crashing down. The place smelled of stale chip fat and tea leaves.

'Thought you wasn't coming.'

He was right at the back in the dark corner, furthest away from the counter. He had a cup of tea in front of him, a can of Coke opposite.

'Thought you'd gone cold on me.'

Olivia opened the drink can, though she was not going to drink and did not look at him. He was weaselly, with three rings in one ear, but he had a face you didn't remember. She never could. It was weird, a sort of blank, you thought about him and you got the earrings and the ginger hair and that was it.

Her heart had begun to thump hard.

'Just the one this week. It's too bloody quiet.'

'I can't.'

He sucked the tea through his front teeth, and stared at her. His eyes were too pale, as if someone had washed the colour out.

'I think I need to go to the doctor, get my ears checked, because I didn't quite hear that.'

'I said I can't. I can't this week. And not . . . not any more.'

'Ah.' He wiped his mouth with the back of his hand, picked a sugar lump out of the bowl. 'And why would that be, Miss Posh? I think you're joking, winding me up, aren't you? Least, I hope you are.'

Liv felt sick and cold but now it was out, she had said it and she meant it. She had been thinking about it for a week, but this morning, she'd changed her mind, because she was frightened of him. But when she'd seen him, a skinny, weaselly little ginge with earrings, it was as if she'd been slapped in the face – slapped awake.

'No. I can't. I think someone knows about it.'

'I bloody well hope you didn't tell them.'

'No. I just . . . think. And my mum.'

'You swore to me your mum never noticed anything,'

'She doesn't. Mostly.'

'Lying little cunt.'

Olivia flinched. She had never been sworn at in her life but since the Weasel it happened all the time, and if nothing else about this made her feel bad and dirty, the swearing did. Her mother never swore, her father did occasionally but only ever at the car when it wouldn't start or at bad drivers who couldn't hear him.

'Right, now we've got that out the way, like I said, there's just the one, and it's a big one, mind, mess this up and you'll be in more trouble than you are now and you won't get your pocket money either.'

'I don't want it. I said.' She drank from the can. 'I'm not in trouble. I haven't done anything.'

He sniggered. 'You sure about that, with the stuff I could tell about you?'

Olivia pushed her chair back.

'Sit down.'

Something in his voice made her hesitate, but if she didn't go now . . .

'You heard.'

Then it was something in his face, his eyes, hard, mean little eyes.

She sat down.

He looked at her and went on looking. Finished his tea. Looked.

'Right. Get to the bog.'

She gave in.

She went to the dark box of a lavatory to the left of the counter, with the bulb that only just gave out light, and the smell of blue cleaner that made her retch. She had to count to a hundred.

When she came back to the table, he told her to sit down again.

'Now listen up. Everything like normal, on your phone in half an hour.'

'I don't –'

'What?'

'Nothing.' She picked up the can, but it was empty. He'd drunk it then. She shuddered, thinking about it on his mouth before she'd put it to hers.

He leaned across the table, his eyes on her, his breath smelling.

'Just so's you know, miss. No way are you packing it in. No way. But if you're ever so bloody stupid . . .'

'What could you do?' The tears were in her throat and at the back of her eyes, she didn't know where the nerve was coming from to let her ask.

'Do you want to know? You sure about that? It won't be nice easy jobs like carrying an envelope and dropping it in a letter box, you'll be through with all that. You'll be entertaining some of my mates, keeping them sweet, know what I mean? Two, three, maybe more of them. That's what you'll do.'

Bile rose into her mouth, bile and fear.

'Know what I mean, darling?'

She stared down, forcing the tears and the bile not to come.

'Yes? No?'

Eventually, she nodded.

'Right.' He stood up, nearly shoving the chair over. 'Stop here as usual, five minutes on the clock.'

The door opened and closed. Three other men were in the cafe, and sat together. Olivia glanced over. They weren't taking any notice of her but she picked up her jacket and bag, and though it had been barely a minute since he'd left, she risked it, and went, took the quick way back into town, to the bus stop, to people, shops, safety.

The envelope was in her inside pocket. She didn't touch it.

She was still carrying it when she rounded the corner beside the jeweller's and crashed straight into Amelie.

'Hey, thought you were meeting your dad.'

Olivia took a step back.

'Don't look at me like that, Livi. What's happened?'

'I ought to get back, Am, I've got stuff I have to do.'

'Do it later. Come on. Listen, I've got this big problem, Liv, it's really bugging me, I need to talk to someone about it.'

'Oh. OK then, you should have said. Let's head to the park – I hate the town when it gets like this.'

It was busy in the park but they found a corner out of the way, sheltered from the wind by laurel bushes, and huddled into their coats. They had got hot chocolates at the stall and sat warming their hands on the paper beakers, Liv feeling better after the time in the cafe with Fats, simply because her friend needing her took her mind away from her own problem.

'You know I'll always help you if I can, Am, so what's wrong?'

'That's what I'm asking you.'

'I don't get it.'

'I'm fine, Livi, only you're not – obviously you're not, and you haven't been for ages. I worry when you look like this.'

'Like what? I look perfectly normal.' Olivia stood up. 'I thought this was you wanting me to help with something.'

'Sit down. It is. I want you to tell me what's happening . . . You're miles away a lot of the time, you look worried and you don't have a laugh with us. Is it your dad? Because honestly, that's a shit situation and I don't blame you but you can't let him get to you. He's made his bed and I bet it's bloody uncomfortable – honestly, why do men keep their brains in their trousers?'

Liv laughed in spite of herself.

'Fat lot you know about men.'

'Yes, well –'

'I'm fine, really. I don't care now.'

'Liv . . .'

'No, I don't. I worry about my mum but she's a lot better as well. Come on, I'm freezing.'

'Only, if it isn't that, if there's something else, you can tell me. I won't tell anyone else, not the others, nobody, I swear.'

'I'm OK. There's nothing. Well, I've had awful toothache for a month, it wakes me in the night, but I'm terrified of going to the dentist.'

'Is that all?'

'Sure.'

'You doughnut, I'll come with you, it'll be fine. I'll even hold your hand.'

Liv shoved her, she shoved back, chocolate splatted onto the path, and they went off arm in arm. The package was still in her inside pocket, the meeting with Fats was a block of cold stone in her stomach, but for now, she had convinced herself that nothing was wrong except an imaginary toothache.

Amelie knew that it was imaginary, knew Olivia too well to be fooled, knew that something was seriously wrong. Knew that there was no chance of her revealing what it was, not to her, not to anyone. She had known Liv since they were in reception, and even then, though she had never understood why, Liv had kept some things locked inside herself.

Fifteen

Cat drove up to the front door, but after switching off, did not move for several minutes – did not reach over to the back seat for her bag, which she had thrown there after her last call, did not open the car door, but just sat, eyes closed. The night air came in through the half-open window, smelling of frost. It was very still.

Since five that morning she had barely found time to eat, one call after another coming in. Luke was in London for the day, and she had not felt that she could pass on any of her calls to the new young doctor Concierge had taken on. Clemmy Rice was very good and would prove a great asset, but for now she lacked the experience to handle one unusual emergency after another in a long day.

She opened her eyes on a half-moon in a starry sky, and when she finally got out, saw that the lawn was already frosted white and the driveway shingle glinted. She stretched, feeling as she had at the end of a shift as a junior doctor in A&E. Everything ached. She let her mind linger on the prospect of a large gin and tonic, and a hot bath. Kieron was home, so there might even be something prepared for supper.

She put her hand to the doorknob, and as she did so, shivered slightly, with a vivid sense of the cat Mephisto emerging out of the darkness to weave round her ankles, miaowing softly in welcome, waiting to be let in. But Mephisto was in his grave, which was still faithfully visited and kept up by Felix.

Felix? Another moment of panic before she remembered that he was safely staying with his friend Marcus, sharing the construction of a Lego Hogwarts Castle.

'Hey, I'm home!'

There was a groan from the kitchen.

Kieron was sitting at the table, left leg up on another chair and what appeared to be a wet tea towel draped across his knee.

'What have you done?' Cat dropped her bag and coat on the sofa and went to her husband.

'It was so stupid. I was just coming down the stairs . . . my phone rang and I slipped.'

'When you say coming down the stairs, you mean running?'

'I'm not five, Cat, but it wasn't my fault, and it bloody hurts.'

'I'm trying to establish the facts – and will you stop shielding your knee with both hands, that's what kids do.'

'Why are you being so mean to me?'

She got up and went to the fridge. 'Here, drink this.'

'Is it vodka?'

'Water with ice. You'll be dehydrated.'

'I pity your patients if you're like this all the time.'

'I'm not. All right, let me do what I sometimes do with children – if I put my hands behind my back and keep them there, will you show me your injury? Honestly, Kieron.'

He made a face but lifted his hands away. His left knee was very swollen and livid, though the skin was unbroken. She put her hand out and he winced back.

'It's really painful, Cat.'

'It looks it but I have to touch to find out exactly where it hurts most. I'm not going to put any pressure on.'

'No, don't. I think I've broken my kneecap.'

'I doubt it, that's actually quite hard to do. Does it hurt here? Here?'

Kieron pulled his leg back at her touch and yelped but she went on gently prodding and testing.

'OK, I'm going to put another ice pack round it, you're going to hobble into the sitting room and put it up on the sofa, on a pile of cushions, and then I'll get you some painkillers.'

'I need something a lot stronger than that. Can I have a large whisky?'

'No.'

'I have fractured my kneecap, haven't I?'

'I don't think so, you've probably ripped a tendon. I'll be able to tell more in the morning.'

'I don't think I'll last till the morning.'

Cat laughed, putting her arms round him. 'Come on, into the sitting room and then I'll make us something to eat.'

'I bet you're going to have a drink.'

'Too right I am.'

She managed to help him there, limping and hopping and groaning, and settled him on the sofa with his leg up.

'Now, stay there . . . here's the paper, you can do the crossword.'

'I don't think I'll manage that, my brain feels peculiar.'

'How's your head?'

'I didn't do anything to my head.'

'No but you might have a headache. Do you?'

'I think I do actually.'

'Does your back tingle? Have you got a peculiar taste in your mouth?'

His eyes widened. 'What would that mean?'

'Oh sweetheart, if I can wind you up, you're fine.'

'I thought doctors were supposed to be sympathetic.'

'So we are, except when their patients have more than enough sympathy for themselves and some to spare.'

She went into the kitchen, poured herself a large gin and tonic, and then got Kieron's painkillers. His knee was going to be far more painful tomorrow and for quite a few days after that and he needed proper relief, and though she was as sure as she could be at this stage that he had not broken anything, she still might need to take him in for an X-ray. She was off duty now, and a trip to Bevham General was the last thing she wanted, especially at the weekend when 'Please be aware, the waiting time is currently four hours' would be chalked up on the board.

'Right, sit up a bit more on those cushions and take these. How's it feeling?'

'Awful. I don't think you appreciate how much pain I'm in.'

'I do actually, I've done it myself and worse. Try breaking a leg in three places and a collarbone, on the ski slopes.' She leaned over and kissed his cheek. 'Darling K, I really am sorry and I do know how much it hurts and I promise when these kick in it will feel so much better. I'll get us something to eat and then you should go to bed.'

'Bed? I don't think I could get up the stairs.'

'Yes you could, once you've got pain relief.'

'No, I think I'd better sleep here.'

'Crumpled up in an uncomfortable position and likely to roll off onto the floor? I don't think so. I'm going to make us scrambled eggs because there isn't much else in until I go shopping tomorrow, and you need something light but nourishing.'

'I could try a whisky.'

'We've already vetoed that. I could make it an omelette with mushrooms and top it with grated cheese . . .' Her voice tailed off as she saw car headlights sweep up and drive. 'Who the hell's that at this time of night?'

'I'm not up to seeing anyone, Cat, if it's the station . . .'

The front door opened and they heard Wookie the Yorkshire terrier hurl himself off the kitchen sofa and skitter into the hall, barking little yelping barks of excitement. Friendly, welcoming barks.

'It's the station only not the station. You up to seeing him?'

'Hey . . . ?' Simon loomed into the doorway, ducking his head as he came in. 'Everything all right?'

Kieron groaned.

'Oh. Have you taken a tumble? What did you do?'

'Hold on, before you settle down to a debrief . . . Si, are you here to eat? Drink? Just passing by?'

'What's on offer?'

'Drink you know what, eat is a fairly meagre omelette and, if I can find any at the bottom of the freezer, possibly some rather elderly frozen chips.'

'Do me, thanks, sis. I could murder a Scotch. Been in Starly most of the afternoon. Kieron?'

'No!'

Simon followed his sister into the kitchen.

'Is it as bad as it looks?'

'Probably a torn tendon – painful and can take ages to heal. I haven't quite said that yet.'

'I did it to a ligament.'

'God yes, also skiing, I remember. Dad made you carry on regardless for the rest of the day and you were clearly in agony.'

'How old were we?'

'Twelve? Thirteen?'

'Can he really not have a Scotch?'

'Not with the painkillers. I'll have a Coke with him, I've had one gin and I don't want to rub salt in the wound. What were you doing in Starly anyway, or don't I ask?'

'Actually, yes, you do, it's why I'm here. I need to pick your medical brain.'

'Honey, I haven't got one left to pick tonight. Can it wait?'

'Well . . .'

'All right, you go and talk to K, I'll get supper, after which we'll help him up to bed and then I'll try but it's probably a question of how long I can keep awake. You can stay over.'

'I ought not. I'm off duty but there's . . . stuff.'

'And is that stuff you also want to talk to me about?'

'Sort of.'

'Well, take this in to him and try and get his mind off his bloody knee.'

'Harsh.'

'Get out . . .'

Kieron had his eyes closed.

'I tried on the whisky, but she wasn't having it, sorry.'

Simon pulled a small table closer and set down the Coke. 'How is it?'

'Very painful. I can't believe I was just walking down the bloody stairs . . .'

'I know what you mean. Injury like that, the least you want is something to boast about – shinning over a fence with barbed wire on top after an armed robber, that type of thing.'

'Piss off.'

Simon sat back with his Scotch, trying not to look as if he were relishing it.

'Can I run something past you?'

'You can try but my head's a bit fuzzy.'

'What's the doctor put you on?'

'Not sure. Probably those powerful prescription-only jobs.'

'Yeah, they make you see double and then wallpaper starts to bleed.'

Kieron shot him a look.

'County lines,' Simon said.

'Christ.'

'OK, if you only want a run-through of last month's speeding figures . . .'

'I could have you demoted.'

'For?'

'Pissing off the Chief Constable. But yes, county lines. It's been on my mind as well . . . we need a day conf.'

'Soon.'

'If I hadn't done this knee . . .'

'Your knee won't stop you being in the ground-floor meeting room. How soon can we get bods over from Bevham? It's bad there as well. Could we arrange it for Wednesday? Thursday latest?'

'Funny – you used to be the one who said –'

'Said we wasted far too much time fretting about drugs, drugs ops, uniform manning the underpasses, going into the school talking to the kids . . . So we did, but that was then, this is now, and it's going to get out of hand fast. Ours are pretty likely to be coming from the Smoke.'

'Or Brum?'

'Possibly. Doesn't really matter where they come from, they're hitting us, they're targeting our kids, and it's making me angrier than I've ever been – well, probably. I don't care what the idiots who take drugs do to themselves, frankly – I'd rather they didn't ruin their lives, but if they're adults, they have a choice, and you and I both know that the choice comes at the start. Don't do it. But if you're idiot enough, be prepared for the conse-quences. But getting young kids involved, bribing them to do the dirty work? It's the pits, and I'm furious with myself for not seeing the way it was going. This has blown up over the last, what, year, eighteen months max. And it's only going to get worse.'

'Thank you for that information.'

'We have to throw everything at it now – a blitz.'

'What have you got in your sights, Simon?'

'I've got Starly in them.'

'The junkie in the flat?'

'It started with that but I think that was maybe the tip of iceberg, or even unrelated. Liam Payne wasn't a kid, he'd been a junkie for a while. Having said which, yes, I do want to focus on Starly for the next week.'

'How many bods?'

'Just me. Start flooding the place even with plain clothes and word'll be straight out – it could be already.'

He filled Kieron in on the Chinese herbalist, and the men who had been caught on camera. Kieron's painkillers were obviously working because he was focused on the conversation, half sitting up now, his knee ignored.

'I'll leave you alone there then, just use any other bods as and when. You'll be needed in the conference though, and by then you might have got something more.'

'It's spotting the kids they're grooming and making use of, as much as spotting the dealers. Get to them and it's a lot easier.'

'Don't be so sure. They'll have filled them with the terrors of hell about saying a single word. These men know how to keep kids on side. Step carefully.'

Cat called from the kitchen, and Simon helped Kieron hobble through.

'Nothing like a nice chat about crime to put the colour back in your cheeks. You look better.'

'It's an optical illusion. I feel worse.'

'So you're not up to eating? Maybe if I hold the spoon?'

Kieron sat down, drawing in his breath sharply, but said nothing.

Sixteen

'Olivia?'

'In the hall.'

'You know it's my turn to do the after-church coffees with Marianne? I don't suppose you could come and help?' Greta came down the stairs. 'What are you doing?'

'Going for a run. So I can't, Mum, sorry.'

'You never can. It wouldn't hurt you, you can run later.'

'I'll help you next time. I'm going now or I'll get cold before I start.'

She was wearing just her tracksuit and trainers.

'Are you meeting anyone?'

'Mia might come. I'm going round by her house anyway. You'd better go, hadn't you?'

'Just be careful and try to run where there are other people around, don't go off into Starly Woods alone. Got your key and your phone?'

Olivia rolled her eyes.

Ten minutes later, she had run through Starly, and headed out towards the fields, where the spring onions and young carrots were grown by the thousand and rows of caravans housed the foreign pickers, in season. Now, they were not yet ploughed and the ground was dark with pools of water. She ran more slowly, then dropped down to a walk, as the road was so muddy, before turning up a track that led across a field to some barns. Beside

them was a row of half a dozen old cottages, in various stages
of decay. But the last one had unbroken windows, old cars and
bits of motorbikes littered around, and smoke coming out of the
chimney. A dog barked crazily as she approached but it was
safely held back on a short chain tied to a post, and could only
leap and lunge at her helplessly. No one came out but a voice
shouted something from inside the end house. Olivia had the
packet ready in her hand and she dashed towards the door and
shoved it into the letter box, barely pausing, before starting back
along the track.

'Oi!'

She did not look round or stop, she had done what she was
forced and paid to do, and she didn't want to see or talk to the
man with the belly hanging over his trousers and wearing a
filthy vest and jerkin, the man who leered at her and made
sucking noises between his teeth. She ran, never mind if she
slipped and fell over, she always felt like this after she'd been
there, the fear and the panic came then, not as she went across
the field towards the place. She would tell him she wasn't going
again. Not anywhere again. Not doing it again. Not doing it.
Never. Never doing it. She ran in time to her own voice.

Not again not again not again not again . . .

A stitch in her side drew her up, and as she bent over to ease
it, an image of her father flashed across her mind, her father by
himself, looking stern, as if he were telling her off, but was
finding it hard to be entirely serious, and she reached for her
phone, suddenly needing to see him or speak to him at least,
needing him around her but at home and as it used to be. He
would have been able to do something, help her, she would
have told him about the Weasel and he would have somehow
sorted it all out, she was quite sure. But why wouldn't he do
that anyway, even though everything was different and he was
not at home with them? He still existed, she could still see him,
and then he could, he would, because he was her dad. Nothing
changed that.

There was no signal so she ran on closer to the village, found
a wall to sit on and then the ringing tone came at once.

'The person you are calling is not available . . .'

70

Olivia snapped it off and jogged about on the spot for a few minutes. He was on the phone but he would answer now, or soon, she would just keep on ringing.

'Yes?'

He sounded cross and distracted and out of breath and that was never what he said when he answered his phone, he said his name, 'Jeff Tonks here.'

'Dad?'

In the background she could hear a baby crying.

'Dad? Where are you?'

'Olivia? What's the matter?'

'I said where are you?'

'At home.'

'What's all that noise?'

'Oh God, one of them, I don't know which one, I can't tell.'

'One of what? Dad, what are you talking about? I want to come and see you.'

'Christ no, Livi, not now, we couldn't cope.'

'What do you mean? Who's there with you?'

There was a silence so that for a moment she thought the signal had gone. Then a sigh. She waited, very cold now and needing to move.

'We've got twin boys, Madison and I, they're a couple of weeks old.' Another silence and then, as if he were pleading with her, trying to get her on side. 'Livi, you have two baby brothers. Aren't you pleased?'

Olivia dropped the phone and bent over to vomit on the verge.

Seventeen

'What was that beep?'

'What?'

'You heard me.'

'Yeah. Didn't hear no beep though.'

'You hear it, Tommy?'

'Shut up, I keep missing the target.'

'You're supposed to be doing geography stuff not playing that.'

'Who says?'

'You'll get in trouble again.'

'There, I heard it then, Brookie.'

'Dunno what you're on about.'

The phone had beeped at him last night after they'd gone to bed and he'd had to scrabble about to find it and then finger it all over to press the off button in the dark. It hadn't mattered because the others had slept through it. He hadn't been sure what to do, never having had a phone of his own, none of them had except their dad. There was never enough money. So Brookie's phone was fair game.

'Give it me to look at or I'll tell him you got it and he'll think you nicked it. You did anyway, didn't you?'

'No.'

'All right, if you say where you got it we might believe you.'

He wished he hadn't got it, like the bag, they'd gone on about that as well, but a rucksack out of a skip was all right, they'd believed him, just about, because it was what happened with stuff. Just not with new phones.

There'd been a message. And then another one. Asking if he was there, telling him to reply.

He could say he was sorry, say he hadn't known how to work it, say he'd lost it for a day, say his brothers had found out and then his dad and he'd said Brookie wasn't to use it, he had to give it back, so he wanted to do that, when could he and where?

Only he hadn't said all of that. He'd said nothing.

The phone worried him – no, it actually scared him. He'd slipped it into his bag on the hall floor with the pile of other things, bags and jackets and boots and some stuff Connor really had got off a skip, a golf club, an old garden badminton net, and a couple of cans of paint, half full. They were doing up some houses at the back of the primary school and there was always a full skip, usually of stuff they couldn't do much with, old kitchen worktops and cracked washbasins, wall tiles, wood with nails sticking out. But then on another day there'd be treasure.

'Tommy, you got any money?'

'Nope.'

'Alfie . . .'

'What for?'

'Get some chips.'

'I'll have chips!'

'And me . . .'

The truth was there hadn't been that much for tea, Dad had been to the food bank late and all the best stuff was gone. He only went once a week, he said he could manage the rest, but that meant tonight was tinned spaghetti hoops on one slice of toast each. Alfie looked at his brothers. He'd had a good school dinner and his mate had shared two KitKats and a bag of Hula Hoops with him. He had £2.43 in his jeans pocket in tens and coppers, picked up over a couple of weeks from the street. Alfie walked with his eyes down everywhere. He was patient and it worked, he found money all over the place.

'OK, Brookie, go and get chips with that, and don't start eating them yourself.'

He grabbed his anorak and the phone, went out. It was very cold and quiet but the fish and chip shop was a beacon and he plunged into the sizzling warmth and the golden smell, fourth in line, looking at the battered fish, sausages, breaded roes, and his stomach groaned and ached in response. Two people came in behind him, a bucket of chips splashed into the hot fat, his mouth could feel them, his tongue was already licking them round, just a bit too hot, greasy and beautifully satisfying. He turned Alfie's money over in his pocket.

'Well, well, well.'

Fats was one of the two behind him, the other was a man who looked seven foot tall and wore sunglasses, which made no sense.

'Our Brookie. You getting for yourself?'

'Not just me.'

'Your dad in?'

'Why?'

Fats laughed. The queue moved up nearer the high metal counter where the fish lay still sizzling under the lights.

'Thought you'd have been in touch, you know, when I messaged.'

In his head, he said that he couldn't, he'd told his dad, he had to give the phone back, here, have it now, but instead he just stared at the fish, the rows of drink cans piled on top of the counter, the tray of little wooden forks.

The woman in front went out of the shop.

'Next?'

Brookie opened his mouth but he didn't get a chance to speak because Fats had elbowed past him.

'Large fish, large chips, peas, sausages, for . . . how many, kid?'

Brookie stared.

'Jeez, and I thought you was a sharp lad . . . Four, is it? Five?'

'Five.' There were four but the word had slipped out.

'For five. Do his, then us after.'

The woman gave him an odd look.

There were two plastic carrier bags full of hot-fat-smelling parcels, they were in his hands, and he was out and running again, no thanks, no anything, and it was only when he slowed at the crossroads that he panicked suddenly, because he had to have a story to tell the others and he couldn't think of one. He'd found a tenner. The shop lady had given him them free. Yeah, right.

'Fuck, Brookie, what you got there? How'd you pay for this lot? Fuck!'

'There's a man I know, he was in there, he got them for us.'

'What man? There's twenty quid's worth in here! Who is he?'

'Don't know his name.'

'Fuck off.'

'Frank.' The name slipped out of his mouth too.

'Frank what?'

'Dunno. Come on, they'll get cold, shall I get plates?'

'Plates?'

He couldn't sleep and the springs digging into his back were hot pokers. Then the phone screen lit up. Brookie grabbed it in case it beeped and woke the others. It didn't but the message still showed.

Enjoy your dinner?

He wouldn't answer, though he knew he ought to. Fats had spent all that money.

Great thanks.

Good. Story?

What did that mean?

You still there?

Yes. But I have to go to sleep now.

Right. 4.10, Spinners Lane.

I can't.

You'd better.

What's it for?

Tell you then. 4.10.

I can't.

You will.

The screen went dark.

He would. Fats scared him now, though he didn't exactly know why, but he'd given him the bag, which wasn't any big deal, and the phone, which was, and then forked out on the fish and chips for all four of them.

He had to.

Brookie switched the phone off, pushed it inside the split in his mattress and closed his eyes. Behind them, hundreds of golden fish swirled about, dancing in a sea of bubbling fat.

Eighteen

Cat was already curled on the sofa, shoes off. Simon set his beer down.

'OK, so what's this –'

But her phone rang.

'Leave it, you're not on call.'

She shook her head and mouthed 'Sam'.

'Hi, sweetheart . . . How are you? Sam? You've got a bad signal, I can hardly hear you . . . OK, that's a bit better . . . Yes, I'm fine, sitting here having a drink with Simon . . . What's up? Sammy?'

She looked at the screen for a few seconds.

'Bloody signals,' Simon said.

'I'll call him back, see if that's any better. Sorry . . . Damn, now it's gone to voicemail.'

'Does he get to see Hannah much?'

'Sometimes. He went to her show and took her out for supper, and she's been over to his nursing digs, but they're both busy. I do worry about them, though, being in London.'

'Course you do. Let's hope he rings back or you'll be wide awake all night.'

'I'm wide awake now, so you might as well hit me with your questions . . . Hang on, Wookie's snuffling at the door.'

Simon jumped up. 'Come in, little rat.'

'Don't call him that.'

Wookie trotted over to the sofa and jumped up, settling close to Cat, and then nudging her. She rolled him gently over and started to scratch his tummy.

'Chinese herbal medicine – what do you know about it? What do you think about it?'

'Ha, how long have you got?'

'All night.'

Wookie made a chain of contented snuffling noises and burrowed down.

'I can only talk about it generally, I don't know any individual practitioners and I haven't much idea how they run their practices, though I have had the occasional patient who's consulted them. The first thing to say is that they're perfectly legit – they're not quacks. We don't subscribe to the philosophy behind their medicine but they do have one, and they train for a long time. The main problem is that some of the stuff their pharmacies sell is unlicensed here and potentially quite harmful – you just don't know what's in that little bag of herbal mixture you're buying for your sore throat and they don't often have Western training alongside their own, to learn about potential interactions between our meds and theirs, which is pretty complicated.'

'Can you find out about their qualifications?'

'Possibly. I've never tried. Are you thinking of the one in Starly?'

'Yes.'

'That junkie who died in the flat . . .'

'The flat is unconnected with the pharmacy – same landlord but two separate rentals, so far as we can ascertain, though we're having a certain amount of difficulty tracking down the landlord but that's not unusual. My gut feeling is that the death had nothing to do with Mr Wang, though it's made him twitchy.'

'Do you wonder?'

'Do they need any sort of licence to retail or is it like half the other whacky quacks in Starly, you just set up and call yourself what you like?'

'Well, they don't need a medical licence. It's a grey area because when given by qualified practitioners some of their treatment is good – it works. Acupuncture does but that's pretty mainstream now, and lots of the herbs they use are very effective, and also often pretty powerful, but that's no different from the stuff naturopaths give – not so different at least in origin from some of the drugs we use, come to that.'

'Digitalis from foxgloves.'

'Yes. A lot of Western medicine originated in plants because that's all they had – read up on the medieval monks and their infirmarians – though drugs have come a long way from their sources and are now chemically engineered. I wouldn't myself send a patient to a Chinese herbalist but I don't disapprove of them in general, they just ought to be more strictly regulated so that only fully trained people can set up – trained in Chinese medicine, but also about where their treatments intersect with ours.'

Cat finished her drink and looked at the empty glass, as Simon got up to take it.

'Thanks – half a glass this time please. I suppose I'd better check on the invalid.'

'I don't sense any desperate anxiety on the part of the invalid's physician.'

'He'll live.' But she looked round as she went out of the door. 'Actually, it's quite nasty. He'll be in a lot of pain tomorrow – but I won't tell him that.'

Kieron was fast asleep, breathing quietly, head on a pillow which he had scrunched up as usual into a small, strange shape. Cat sometimes lay listening as he twisted and turned and pummelled it until it was exactly as he liked it, a job that could take several full minutes, but after he was settled he slept quite peacefully in the same position all night.

The effect of the painkillers she had given him would wear off during the early hours but for now Kieron was comfortable. As she straightened the bedcover, and looked down at him, she had a flashback to Chris, lying curled towards her, his face marked by weeks of pain, his skin the colour and texture of parchment, Chris, dying of a brain tumour beside her in a situation over which she had no medical control except of the palliative sort, and by those last days, even that was too little. Chris.

She saw him at that moment in place of this husband, now, with only a hurt knee, painful, yes, but a dot on the pain scale, to the ten of Chris's tumour. She leaned over and kissed Kieron's cheek. He stirred slightly but didn't wake.

Going downstairs, she remembered that Sam had not rung back, Sam who had come into the bedroom just as Chris had died lying beside her. He had climbed onto the bed and lain between his mother and father, and been held close, in the great peace that falls like a shawl, wrapping the dead one and the watchers around.

'Thanks for the drink . . . I said a small one.'

'I know you did.'

She yawned.

'You should go to bed, sis.'

'No, I've got a second wind now.'

'Are you hungry? I could make a bacon sarnie.'

'No, first, there's no bacon, and second, sit down again. She looked at her brother steadily, with the look he could never dodge.

'It wasn't only Chinese medicine, was it? Or even at all.'

'Of course it was.'

'You could have googled what I told you.'

'Yes but I needed a doctor's take on it.'

'Oh, really.'

Simon shifted around in the chair, finished his beer slowly. Cat knew better than to say anything else, confident, as a result of long experience in this situation, that he would eventually either talk or think better of it and get up, saying curtly that he was off to bed. She stroked Wookie's ears and he made a soft grunt of contentment in his sleep.

'Do you think he misses Mephisto?'

Cat shrugged. 'Hard to tell. He was very quiet for the first couple of weeks, he didn't stay out in the garden for long and kept sniffing round everywhere. I think he's forgotten now.'

'Another cat?'

'Not unless Felix gets a longing for a kitten but I don't think he's very interested and Wookie wouldn't be entirely welcoming.'

Silence. Simon looked at his left hand. Turned it over. Back. But Cat did not ask about the prosthesis now, he managed it well, it gave little trouble, and if he needed to consult anyone, it would be the experts, not her.

She looked at his face, turned away from the lamp, his white-blond hair catching the light – angel hair, she had thought when they were growing up. He had been taller than either her or their brother Ivo before they entered their teens. She and Ivo had had more in common, playing strange made-up games and being wannabe doctors from the start. But it was Simon she had adored.

Still? She looked at him again. No, not adore, she had become aware of his flaws, and he often infuriated her, mainly in his relationships with women, evading, backing away, making bad choices, hasty judgements and half-deliberate mistakes. Causing pain. She had been so lucky, in her first, happiest of marriages to Chris, difficult though he had been in some ways, and now, straightforwardly and contentedly, with Kieron. She had not looked for a second chance and it had never been the wholly absorbing love affair that had been her marriage to Chris, nor had she wanted that again, even if she had believed it possible. 'The arrow only strikes once,' her stepmother, Judith, had said in an unguarded moment, but Cat had accepted the truth of that and agreed. It did not invalidate her very different love for Kieron, or her life with him, and she recognised and gave thanks for her own good fortune. Ivo, in Australia, had a wife and now a daughter, and might as well live on another planet. Photographs came, short phone videos of Lauren, first in her pram then her buggy, laughing, splashing in the sea, waving to the camera on cue, Ivo sometimes in the background, his fair hair now perman-ently in a buzz cut, face like Simon's and yet less handsome, the features just out of true, the nose larger, ears more prominent. It was five years since they had met up and she knew that if they ever did again, they would have to travel across the world because Ivo would never return to Britain, even for a couple of weeks, at least while Richard, their father, was still alive.

Cat felt herself slipping into a half-doze, the second wind having been brief, but she surfaced when Simon's phone buzzed a message, and he picked it up in a split second, his face open with hope, before he read and tossed it aside.

'Work? Thought you were off.'

'I am but if there's any data they send it anyway. Nothing important.'

'So not Rachel.'

It was a dart flung wildly but she saw it hit home before her brother's face closed up in the old familiar expression. 'Don't. Just do not go there.'

She was awake again and knew better than to take any notice. 'Tell me.'

There might follow anything, from a storming out to total silence or a quiet 'Goodnight' and a move to the door, to a snarl of displeasure – she was used to them all, took each one as it came and simply pressed on.

Very rarely indeed had she seen Simon's face change so quickly, from being blank of expression to being visibly distressed, so that she recognised at once that he was asking her for help, asking her what he should do, asking her to sort everything out, as he had when they were children and Cat had momentarily been the one who knew best and who could make things right and not the mildly annoying sister.

She wanted to get up and put her arms round him, and then to provide a ready solution, but instead, she remained sitting with her legs tucked up under her. 'I never want to pry into your life, Simon, you know that well enough, though it's worth repeating from time to time, but you also know that I will help if I can, though I usually can't.'

She expected him to get up and fetch another drink, offer to make coffee, anything to distract her from himself, but he simply sat, head back, eyes closed.

Wookie stirred, and struggled up, before leaping from the sofa and trotting out towards the front door to be let out. Cat followed him. It was bitterly cold again, an east wind whipping round her legs. The little dog came racing back from the bushes within a few seconds and shot into the kitchen to await his late-night biscuit. She took her time over it, leaving Simon to work out how he wanted to play things – pretend nothing had been said, go up, wait for her to return. She was dropping with tiredness but if he wanted to talk to her, she would listen.

Wookie crunched the last of the small treat and then made for his bed, scratching about to rearrange the fleece as he liked it, turning round and round, before finally settling, back to the room, head buried, where he would be, apparently not having moved a millimetre, until the next morning.

'Funny little Wookers,' she said, scratching his ears. 'Goodnight.'

Simon was sitting staring into space.

'I can last about another few minutes before I fold, but if you're not ready to talk tell me so I can go to bed now.'

'I just get no reply,' he said quietly.

'From Rachel?'

'She could say "Sod off", or "I'll talk to you later", but what's silence supposed to mean?'

'What do you think it means? What exactly did you say in your messages?'

'Oh, you know . . . are you free? Can we have dinner? I'd like to have a few days away somewhere, will you come with me? That sort of thing.'

Cat raised an eyebrow.

'And when were you last in touch?'

He told her about the near-miss outside the station.

'We went for a coffee. She needed it.'

'Idiot. But that was a chance meeting – what about before that? It's ages, isn't it?'

'A while but why would that matter?'

'Oh, Si, think about it! Women like Rachel aren't just sitting about waiting for you, or any man, for that matter. She's attractive – no, she's beautiful – she's single, she's rich, she has a house and a business and –'

'You're telling me she's a good catch.'

'Not in so many words, no, and it's a hateful phrase. She's a whole lot more. Why do you want to see her? Why invite her away for a weekend? You need to ask yourself and then answer yourself – not me. Tell yourself the truth.'

'Not sure I know it.'

'You never do.'

'Don't I?'

Cat saw that he was closer than he had been for a long time to admitting real feelings, to himself and then perhaps to her, and after that, just possibly, to Rachel. She had known him be mad about this woman or that, be delirious with optimistic happiness, only then to be overwhelmed by doubt, immediately after which he was ruthless in extricating himself. She had only once seen him truly vulnerable through love and that had been with his CID colleague Freya Graffham, murdered by the serial killer she had been close to unmasking. Simon had clammed up and had never talked about her since, but for a while after he had met Rachel, Cat thought his feelings had been as strong all over again, and possibly they had, but he had backed off as usual, taken fright, and Rachel had simply removed herself from his orbit. Simon might not have been badly hurt but she certainly was.

'I'll tell you one thing, bro, if you don't mean this seriously, if it's about taking up with her again because you fancy a nice cosy weekend occasionally, no strings, then don't message her again. Leave it. It's unkind to her and you'll make a fool of yourself – only, knowing you and your affairs as well and as long as I have, I don't actually care too much about that. But Rachel is a very special person and I do care about her, and if you mess her around again, I'll kill you.'

'No you won't.'

'Don't push your luck. But I'm serious, Simon.'

He was silent for a few moments, looking down at his feet.

'You think I'm not?' he said in the end.

She was saved from having to answer by Kieron calling her from upstairs.

Simon got up at the same time and headed for the spare room with only a quick 'Goodnight'.

Nineteen

'Cat?'

It was nearly midnight and she had just nodded of. Beside her, dosed up with more

painkillers, Kieron slept deeply.

'I'm so sorry, I know you're not on call –' Luke, sounding genuinely apologetic.

'No, I'm bloody not. What's wrong?'

'I've had a vicious migraine all evening, thought it would clear and I'm maxed out on meds. I'd call Clemmy but she's going to a wedding tomorrow.'

'Has anything come in?'

'No, it's very quiet and if this clears up sooner I can take over.'

'Of course. Switch the phone over to me and let's pray no one rings.'

'I'm really sorry, Cat, but I wouldn't be fit to drive, I can hardly see and I'm dosed up.'

'Don't worry about it. I'll call to see how you are tomorrow.'

'I owe you.'

'Forget it.'

She fell asleep still holding the phone and when it buzzed her half awake again she thought for a moment that she was still on the call to Luke.

'Oh, Dr Cat? This is Sadie Logan, at the almshouses. I know it's an awful time, I am so sorry, but it's Mr Brown.'

*

The warden was standing at the open door of Lionel Brown's almshouse, in her dressing gown.

'I looked in on him about ten last night and he was settled in bed, not asleep but he said he was fine, though I've been a bit worried about him this week, he's complained several times of a sore leg, but he wouldn't let me look at it or send for you or anyone, so I thought he'd just banged it on a chair leg or something.'

They were standing in the hall, and Mrs Logan was whispering.

'But not long ago, he rang the bell and went on ringing it so I didn't even use the intercom to speak to him, I just came straight round. He was shivering, he said he hadn't been to sleep for the pain in his leg, it had got worse. I think I did right to call you, Dr Cat, and I'm sorry it's so late.'

'Don't worry.' Feeling as she did, Cat might have suggested an earlier call would have been better but she said nothing, knowing that it was a fine line between calling unnecessarily, and waiting too long.

There was a faint smell in Lionel Brown's bedroom, one Cat recognised instantly. He was lying in bed on his side, and his left leg was half out of the covers. She could feel the heat coming from him as she went near.

'You poor thing, you're feeling rough, aren't you? I can see.'

He sighed and half looked at her, but his eyes were dull and his face seemed to have sunken in under the cheekbones. The smell was stronger, the heat from his body greater.

'What happened to your leg, Lionel? Did you fall, or bang it on something?'

He seemed to be gathering his strength in order to focus and then reply.

'It's not been right since I came out of the hospital. It wasn't much though, just like a little sore place. Nothing.'

'May I have a look? I'll try not to cause you any pain but I do need to see.'

She lifted the bedcovers.

What had indeed probably been a small spot that he had scratched, was now a long mass of suppurating ulcer, the stench coming from it making her gag. The bedclothes were wet with pus and she did not need to take his temperature, the fever must be over forty. His skin was damp, his face red, but underneath the surface flush, it was like candle wax.

'All right, this is very serious, Lionel. You've got a rip-roaring infection here and I am ringing for the ambulance. You should have rung us, or got Mrs Logan to ring, days ago. I know you haven't wanted to cause bother, but I also know how much pain you will have been in and it's dangerous to leave these things.'

Lionel Brown was struggling to sit up. 'No,' he said, shaking his head over and over, 'I'm not going back in that hospital, ever, I said that to you, and I won't go in any ambulance. I'm staying here.'

Cat put her hand over his. 'Listen,' she said quietly, 'I'm not going to lie to you. If you don't go to hospital to have this treated, you will die here. I can't look after this, I don't have the drugs or the facilities, and it's not right for you to be here – this is an infection you could pass on. So, I'm sorry but I'm over-ruling you, because you need the sort of treatment and care only the hospital can give you.'

She turned away, calling the emergency number.

Lionel was rolling his head from side to side on the pillow, mumbling 'no, no'. The warden stood at a distance from the bed, hand over her nose and mouth, eyes full of alarm.

'How did he let things get like this, Dr Cat? Why didn't he say anything? No, you don't need to answer that, I already know. He's dreaded ever going back to that place.'

'Bevham General is a very good hospital but he wasn't looked after well on the ward, I agree, and I'm going to put in a complaint. He got this infection in there and even a small sore should have been spotted and dealt with.'

As the paramedics, with infinite care and gentleness, were getting Lionel Brown into the ambulance, the warden touched Cat's arm. 'He isn't really going to die, is he? I mean, they'll sort it out once he's there?'

'The important thing is that he doesn't get sepsis. If he had stayed here without treatment that's probably what would have happened and he could well have died in a few hours' time.

His age is against him and this infection has got a grip, but he's going to the right place, they'll do everything possible. Have they got your phone number?'

'Yes, they put me as his next of kin last time he went in.'

'Good, then they'll ring and report on how he is as soon as they can, and you can call yourself in the morning.'

'It is morning. Can I get you a cup of tea or anything, Dr Cat?'

'Thanks, I'm fine, I'll scoot home now and get back to bed, but I will phone the hospital myself tomorrow, and you and I will be in touch.'

'I did the right thing in ringing you, didn't I?'

'Indeed you did. Now you get to bed too, you've done everything possible. They're all very lucky to have you here.'

Sadie Logan flushed and shook her head, but Cat had meant it. By no means every sheltered housing warden she had had dealings with was as caring and concerned.

She took a few deep breaths before she started the car, and kept the window half open but she was good at keeping herself awake and attentive on night calls. It was when she got home that tiredness would fell her.

'And please God, no more tonight.'

She had not known such exhaustion since she had been a junior hospital doctor on duty six nights out of seven. She dumped her bag on the hall table and locked the front door, but when she went into the kitchen to get a glass of water she felt a chill draught round her ankles. The side door was closed and bolted but the cat flap, which they had not got round to sealing up since Mephisto had died the previous year, was slightly open, probably blown in by the wind.

Only there was no wind, the night air was freezing and quite still. No human could enter through a cat flap but a stray animal might, in which case Wookie would have gone crazy.

Wookie was not in his basket, or in the sitting room into which he occasionally sneaked if the door had not been properly closed, to sleep in illicit bliss on the sofa. Cat's study door was shut but she checked in case, as her desk chair had a handy cushion to which the little terrier was also partial.

She was not only tired now, she was annoyed, and with annoyance went worry, neither of which would be conducive to sleep, however tired she was.

After a ten-minute search of the house, including attic and cellar, she had not found Wookie.

'Si . . . Simon, sorry, SIMON.'

He woke and sat upright in one movement, fully awake immediately.

'Have you see Wookie?'

'What? Of course I haven't, I've been asleep. I thought you were.'

'I've been out on a call.'

'Jeez, sorry. What do you want me to do?'

'I've been everywhere, you know what he's like, I thought he might have got into Felix's room but all the doors are shut.'

'Sofa.' Simon lay back and was about to close his eyes. 'Or somewhere, hiding. That bloody dog could vanish up a vacuum cleaner pipe.'

'The cat flap was ajar.'

'Oh bloody hell.' He was upright again.

'He's been known to sneak out through that, which is why I keep it locked, but the lock can slip and it obviously has. He must have heard a fox or a badger moving about outside.'

'Have you tried just opening the front door and calling him?'

'No, but I'm going to. I just thought you might say you'd seen him or . . . God, this is all I need. I'm absolutely wiped out.'

'OK, I get it. You go to bed.'

And he was up and into his trainers and sweater.

'Put your jacket on, Si, it's absolutely freezing, that's partly why I'm so worried – if he's out in this without his coat on . . .'

'Fifty p says he'll be waiting on the step.'

'But he would have barked.'

'Yes, imperiously. Now *go to bed*.'

Twenty

'You're late.'

Brookie took a step back. Fats sounded different, more like he had sounded in the phone messages, and his expression was different, not friendly, not as if he found him a bit daft, a bit of a joker . . .' Honestly, boy, what are you like?' This Fats, waiting for him in a half-dark street, was rougher, and annoyed, as if he might raise his fist because it wasn't ten past it was nearly half four.

'I couldn't –'

'Shut it. Just don't keep me waiting again, all right? Here.'

He held out a small brown Jiffy bag sealed with clear tape. Brookie hesitated.

'Take it.'

'What's in it?'

'None of your business, sunshine. Put it inside your anorak, stuff it in the pocket.'

'Pocket's got a hole.'

'Jeez, then under your sweatshirt, anywhere it can't be seen and you can't bloody lose it, which is what a stupid kid like you would do, I don't know why I've bothered, there's plenty of others.'

'That's OK, I don't mind.'

'What?'

'Give it to one of them. I shouldn't be here.'

'No, but you are, so that's that, no going back now.'

'I don't want to.'

'I don't care what you want or don't want, doesn't interest me. You don't interest me. Maybe if you do this right you will but at the moment I'm having other thoughts.'

It was cold standing in the street, his jeans might have been made of tissue paper, the wind cut through them to his skin, and his anorak had no lining. He wished he hadn't come at all. He wished everything and he knew it was all useless, because whatever he had to do for Fats, he had to. Whatever.

'You know Mars Lane?'

'Sort of.'

'Do you or don't you?'

'Yes. I know where it is.'

'Go there, walk all the way to the end, there's a track, go up the track, not far, you'll see a couple of mobile homes.'

'That'll take me ages, I've got to be back for five.'

'You listen. You go to the second one, you shout "TAKEAWAY". Then you drop your packet on the caravan step and scarper. Don't wait for anyone, don't hang about at all, just leave it.'

'You could drive there in your van.'

'I could, but I ent. You're going, on foot, or a bike. Yeah, a bike'd be OK.'

'I haven't got a bike.'

'Then bloody nick one. Plenty of bikes in passageways.'

'I can't do that –'

'Then you walk, don't you? Tell you what though, if you get this one right, I might give you another job, and if you get that right, and the next –'

'Is this a job? A job you, like, pay me for doing?'

Fats laughed, but it wasn't a laugh with any fun inside it, it was a laugh that shot out like spit, then stopped.

'You're a funny one, you. Now get off. When you've done it, like I said, exactly like I said, you text me.'

'On what?'

'The phone that belongs to me that you're looking after.'

Brooklyn wondered if he could turn and run, and whether Fats would grab him if he did, grab him and take him some-where and kill him.

'You have still got it?'

'No. Not on me. I could lose it.'

The gobbet of a laugh spat out again.

'This is wasting time, my time, your time doesn't matter. You leave that packet and you get home, running all the way, and you find the phone and you text me, right?'

'What do I text?'

'Assuming it's all gone smoothly, you press two little keys,' Fats said. 'O and K, and then you send it. Now, can you manage that?'

There was no chance for him to agree, or not, because somehow, Fats had disappeared, slipped into the shadows of the street and gone. Brooklyn touched the packet, wondering what was inside it, then zipped his anorak right to the top. If all he had to do was deliver one thing, it might not be so bad.

Twenty-One

BEVHAM GAZETTE

4 February
*An investigation is under way into post-mortem examinations
conducted by pathologist Dr Kirk Shenfield, who took early retirement last week after fourteen years in his post at Bevham General
Hospital. A spokesman for the Area Health Trust declined to
release details of the cases but said that 'certain discrepancies and
anomalies' had been noted in a recent check, after queries had
been raised by families of deceased relatives whose post-mortem
examinations had been performed by Dr Shenfield. 'It is therefore
our intention to conduct a re-examination of certain cases by an
independent pathologist from an outside Health Trust. Families
and the relevant authorities are being kept informed.'*

'Where's Simon?'
'Out looking for Wookie again. I'll join him when I've helped
you up. I can't bear to think of the poor little thing lost some-
where in this freezing wind.'
'Wookie will turn up. Dogs do this sort of thing.'
'Wookie has *never* done this sort of thing, and what do you
know about dogs?'
'I had a dog.'
'When?'

'When I was eight. It got run over.'

'Well, there you are then. Right, I'll get breakfast . . . hang on, that's Simon back.'

Cat shouted to him from the landing but from the tone of his voice in reply, she knew he did not have Wookie.

'It's below freezing, I've been about three square miles calling and whistling, I've looked in ditches and a few outbuildings, I've had a word with the people at Crown Cottage and they'll keep a lookout. I also went up to the main road and along that for a bit so I'm sure he hasn't been run over. I don't what else we can do except maybe get some posters up around the area, pin them to trees and poles. If you've got a decent photo of the Wookster I'll sort it out and we can print them off straight away. Right, I need some hot coffee.'

Cat stood in the kitchen doorway, thinking about the past twenty-four hours, about Sam's call, about Lionel Brown, about Rachel, about Kieron's knee, but, for the moment, mainly about Wookie, small, silky silver-tan, hair over his eyes, noisy, bouncy, needy, good-natured little Wookie, resilient after the death of his friend the old cat Mephisto, fiercely protective of the house in the face of strong gales rattling the windows, foxes squealing at the end of the garden, mice scratching, the postman making the letter box clatter. Wookie, out all one freezing night and still out, on his own, possibly hurt, barking furiously without being heard. But no, if he had been barking someone would have certainly found him.

'There were a lot of reports of dog snatchers around the patch last autumn,' Simon said, pouring boiling water into the cafetière.

'Thank you for that.'

'Nothing lately though and they wouldn't be hanging around in this weather – well, I suppose in a vehicle they might but it's a long shot, they tend to come on these pedigree dogs by chance and grab them then.'

'Will you please shut the fuck up about dog snatchers? And K wants to talk to you, he's getting dressed. Take him a coffee.'

'How's his knee?'

'Not terminal.'

As he went out, Simon touched her shoulder. 'Sorry, sis. We'll find the little bugger, don't worry.'

'OK.' Simon handed back the phone to the Chief, after reading the newspaper clip. 'So, Dr Shenfield resigned before he was pushed. Were all these cases ours? I've worked with him quite a lot.'

'We'll find out. But he did the PM on the junkie from the Starly flat.'

'That didn't show anything unexpected . . . heroin overdose, self-administered.'

'Has the body been released?'

'God yes, they've had the funeral – last week I think. I accompanied the sister to ID him and it was all going forward from there. Are you worried it wasn't kosher'

'Not necessarily but go over to BG, there'll be an on-call pathologist. Try and dig out some answers.'

'All right, though technically . . .'

'What?'

'I'm off duty. It could wait till tomorrow morning.'

'I don't want this hanging around, Simon.'

'Understood, but weekend's not the best time day to request info.'

'All right. I take it you have important plans?'

'Finding Wookie. Cat isn't going to rest until we have closure one way or another. I could put someone onto the Shenfield thing, but if we leave it till tomorrow I'll find out a lot more myself. If there's anything going on the medics will close ranks as usual, but I know a fair few to talk to. Drink that and then I'll help you get downstairs, before I go out dog hunting again. Leave no stone unturned.'

'How much luck do you think you're going to have this time?'

Simon shook his head as he heard Cat coming upstairs.

Twenty-Two

'Adam Iliffe.'

'Morning, Adam. Simon Serrailler.'

'Now let me guess . . . you need a big favour, there's a body you want us to fast-track up the queue – right?'

'Wrong. Can we meet up?'

'Talking of that queue. Full day.'

'This evening?'

Adam sighed. 'All right, seven? Can't be too long, there's a new infant at home.'

'That's great. I don't want to keep you from – him? her?'

'Him. Jacob. It's OK, I know you – it'll be urgent.'

'Bit confidential too.'

'As ever. Right then, my village pub. Won't be busy on a Monday at that time. The Wheatsheaf at Castlesett.'

'Know it. Thanks, Adam. and it's my shout.'

'I should bloody hope so.'

He had been right, they were the only ones in the bar other than a man with an iPad who did not look up. Outside, the temperature had already dropped below freezing and the landlord was topping up the fire with fresh logs.

'How are things?' Serrailler raised his glass. They sat at a table away from the blaze.

'Overstretched. Too many "causes unknown", too many elderly dying alone having been apparently fit when seen the previous day. Always natural causes but . . .'

'Hypothermia?'

Adam nodded. 'Too much of that as well. '

He was a medic Simon had known for ten or so years, a six-foot-four hefty prop forward with a broken nose – the sort of doctor Cat always marked down as an orthopaedic surgeon. 'Brawn and saws.' But Adam was a tender-hearted soul, always emphasising that he did not deal with bodies but with people – who just happened to be dead. He taught his students respect first, anatomy later, he had invented a technique which cut the time it took to do a couple of procedures and was both highly regarded and well liked.

'I gather there's a vacancy for the top job.'

Adam gave him a look. 'Thought it might be about Shenfield.'

'He'll be replaced presumably?'

'He'd better be – not so much in terms of seniority as just numbers. We need at least three more pathologists and we'll be lucky to get one.'

'Think you'll move into his shoes?'

Adam shrugged. 'I ought to but my guess is they won't replace at top level.' He finished his beer and held out the empty glass.

'So what's the story,' Simon asked, setting down the second round of drinks, his own being a tomato juice, but Adam lived a couple of hundred yards from the pub so he took up his fresh pint enthusiastically.

'It's a bit odd – muddy waters and nobody's sure exactly . . . off the record by the way?'

'Yes, except if there's anything I need to act on I will, with your name kept out of it. You know the score.'

'Only none of this is confirmed, nothing was actually discovered – or, correction, it hasn't been yet but they are investigating. They couldn't pin anything on Shenfield – who I respected, by the way, I learned a hell of a lot from him, he was a good man and a good, careful pathologist – didn't set the world alight but which one of us does? It's just a steady game, most of the time.

Anyway, over the last few months, a couple of people noticed that he wasn't altogether on the ball. A junior doctor and one of the mortuary technicians came to me about him – and this was separately, neither knowing about the other, which is what made me sit up. Shenfield would forget the odd thing, make the odd slip – nothing major, just pretty unusual mistakes for a man of his status and experience . . . you know, picking up the wrong instrument, starting to do something he had already done. On one occasion, he seemed unaware of it and had to have it pointed out to him, and then apparently he just looked confused. It wasn't hard to see what might be happening.'

'Dementia?'

'Of some sort, yes, probably. Although it wasn't quite as urgent to have him stopped as it would be if he were a surgeon oper-ating on the living, it still couldn't be ignored. And then a couple of discrepancies in his case notes were spotted, another technician mentioned something he himself hadn't been happy about . . . some omission.'

'Do you know which cases are under review?'

'Not the details. Shenfield's full path reports will have to be taken line by line.'

'Are any of them police matters?'

'You'd have to be the judge of that. I can let you know more when I know more myself, and there may be nothing, it's only suspicions, queries, not a done deal.'

'Understood.'

'The prof was always the most meticulous path, and incred-ibly hard-working – his team used to complain that he'd always fit in another, if there was a backlog, – and he was a devil for ferreting out the truth too – if something didn't seem quite right, he was on it and he'd find it. He was inspirational.'

'Until recently.'

'Last couple of months. None of what's been happening lately was in character. No, it's early signs of dementia, no question. Right, another half and then I'd better get home. You?'

'I'm fine, thanks.'

'Limit to how much spicy tomato juice you can take.'

Adam went to the bar. A few more people had come in but this was not going to be a busy night.

'So,' he said, sitting down again with, Simon noted, not a half but a pint, 'what's your worry?'

Serrailler filled him in on Liam Payne.

'What do you think doesn't add up?'

'It's pretty nebulous and if this business over Shenfield had never arisen, I doubt if I'd have given it another thought. There was the glimmer of a shadow, not from the scene itself but because of where it was and some probable dodgy dealings in the Chinese herbalist below, and even that we can't be certain about because there's no evidence – yet.'

'The path verdict was death from an OD?'

'It was. How difficult would it be to discover that it wasn't?'

'You mean if it was suicide or administered by someone else instead?'

'Yes.'

'The suicide or OD are more difficult, strangely. There was a lot of work done on this quite a few years back – 2009 I think, but I'd have to look it up to confirm that. It was really about the difficulty of judging the amounts of a substance in live bodies, dead bodies and then dead bodies that have been in the deep-freeze for a bit because everything changes and then changes again. It's quite complicated but I can get some stuff over to you.'

'I'd appreciate that. But are you saying the amount of heroin that had been injected and would have proved fatal can't be accurately determined in a PM?'

'With all caveats, yes. It's not quite as straightforward as that makes it sound.'

'Nothing is. What about the administered?'

'That's easier. Examination of the injection site, position of syringe if it was still inserted when the first photos were taken, position of the body, any other injuries and, if there were, were they recent, ante- or post-mortem –'

'And if they were sustained on the spot or elsewhere?'

'That's more your job – I mean, if you drag a body across any surface, you leave traces. Did the forensics find anything like of that sort?'

'No, and the PM report doesn't record anything found either – traces on the skin, particles.'

'But you're not happy?'

'I'm hovering.'

'Want me to take a look?'

'At the report? If you think you might find something, yes please, Adam, that would be above and beyond.'

'Well, no promises on the result, but if I did find any cause for concern you'd have grounds to apply for a second PM.'

'Difficult. The coroner released the body and they've had the funeral.'

'Not cremation though because then you are buggered.'

'No.'

Adam looked at Simon over his glass.

'Then I know what your next move is.'

'Indeed.'

They both stood up, but before they left the bar, Adam reached into his pocket.

'Indulge me,' he said, and scrolled down his phone screen briefly, before handing it over. 'He was a few weeks premature, so he was in the special care baby unit – bonding is really important, with both parents. Skin to skin. Jacob's fine now, by the way.'

The photograph was of Adam, with his shirt front unbuttoned, showing a broad, muscular and thickly haired chest, against which a tiny baby was curled up, half inside the shirt, wearing a tiny blue cotton hat and some leads and wires. Adam's large hand was supporting him, making the little boy's body look even smaller by contrast, and his head was bent down to look at his son with an expression of such deep tenderness and concern, an attitude of such protectiveness, that tears stung Simon's eyes.

'You should get home to him,' he said.

Twenty-Three

'Hello, Livi.'

'No.'

'No what?'

'I'm not Livi.'

'I think you are. Don't switch the phone off, Livi.'

'I don't want to talk to you. Stop ringing me.'

'Did you deliver? Livi? Yes or no.'

'I don't want to talk to you. Just leave me alone? I don't want anything to do with you any more.'

'Too late for that.'

'I told my dad.'

'Of course you didn't. Did you deliver, I said?'

'Yes, and I'm never doing it again.'

'You are, you've got a phone, and if you're a sensible young lady you'll get the new iPhone and money in your pocket. Nothing more for today, nothing tomorrow, but I'll text you on Wednesday.'

'I can't, I've got an exam.'

'In school time maybe but this is after school, isn't it?'

'I can't.'

'Don't forget your phone to get the text.'

'No. I'm not doing any more, and you can't make me, you can't do anything.'

There was a brief sound, a snort or a snigger, and the phone went dead.

All right, she just wouldn't do it, like she'd told him. Keep the phone switched off, don't pick up any messages. Or even ditch the phone, chuck it away, there'd be somewhere she could lose it, then she'd tell Dad. Yes, that.

She wanted to see her dad. She had money for a bus fare or maybe she'd get a taxi, and when she got there, he'd phone her mother to say she was with him, stop her worrying. And see her brothers – half-brothers – if she wanted to see them. She wasn't sure. It had always been just her, though she used to long for a sibling and had no idea why one hadn't come. She had stopped asking about it ages ago because it never went down well.

She was cold but she could borrow something to wrap up in from Madison, when she got there. Probably. If they were the same size. She'd never actually seen Madison.

Dad. Madison. Babies.

She ran until she was in a proper street not on a track, and then called the cab number her mother had made her save to her own phone, in case she was ever in trouble. She'd laughed at that. Not now.

There was a flash new Mini Cooper in the drive.

'Hold on, I'll get my dad.' The taxi driver nodded but watched her go up the path, knock and then immediately ring the door-bell, having trusted her about the fare – but not altogether.

It was a long time. She rang and knocked again and eventually, as she danced from one foot to another, he came, socks but no shoes, open shirt, looking harassed.

'Oli—'

'Dad, I'm sorry but can you pay the taxi? I said you would, he's waited.'

He glanced over his shoulder into the house, looked annoyed, looked worried.

'Who is it? ' Her voice, inside somewhere. 'Jeff?'

He came back up the path. 'You're taking a bit of a liberty, taxi here, taxi there, money doesn't grow on trees, Olivia, and what are you doing dressed like that?' He stopped himself, then, stood and put his hands on her shoulders. 'It's freezing, you should have a coat and boots, what's wrong?'

She was shivering. She wanted to hold on to him, to hug him, but didn't.

'You'd better come in anyway. That taxi cost fourteen pounds.'

The house smelled oddly, of new carpet, wet clothing, and something like soup or gravy.

'Jeff, what's going on, I need you to – Oh.'

They stared at one another.

She was tiny, like a malevolent bird, Olivia thought, with long blonde hair tied back in a scrunchie, extremely small hands and feet and ears, legs like flower stalks in skinny black leggings. She was wearing earrings that changed from blue to green when she turned her head.

'What are you doing here? Jeff, I need you to get the new box of nappies from the garage, I can't carry it, only don't bang the door and wake them, for Christ's sake.' But then she turned a smile on him like a sudden flash of sunlight, and Olivia saw very white teeth and a pink tongue that licked her lips briefly, like a cat. Her father looked at her, then at Madison, a strange, empty look, as if for a split second he had no idea who either of them was. Grey, Olivia thought, he looks grey, and weary. He had stains on his shirt and pouches under his eyes.

'Do you want something, Oli, a cup of tea or . . . what have we got, Mads? I don't know.'

His wife went to him, put her hands on his arms and raised herself up on tiptoe. Then she kissed him on the cheek, on the mouth, and smiled. 'Jeff,' she whispered, and it was a whisper like a hiss, 'nappies.'

'Sorry, yes.' He turned away. 'Sorry.'

'So, what have you come here for? If you want to see your father, which of course you have every right to do, it's really best to meet him in town, for tea or something, you know? Or at least you could make an appointment, not just turn up. We've only five minutes ago got the twins off, they've been yelling for hours. I don't know. Have they got tummy ache or something? Anyway, what are you dressed like that for, where's your coat?' She headed out of the room, not waiting for Olivia to reply. 'If you want a drink or anything, look in the fridge.'

The kitchen was like Madison, shiny, gleaming, new – and a tip, strewn with bottle steriliser, bottles, baskets of baby clothes and towels, milk, three or four dirty mugs, half a loaf on a plate, some bananas. How could her dad live in this, when he was the fussiest man on the planet, always wiping down surfaces and putting things away, in a cupboard, in a drawer, in the bin? There was a mop and bucket in the middle of the floor.

'Have you come to ask Jeff for money? I bet you have, and it's nothing to do with me, only we're not that good at the moment, reorganisation at work so he's had a bit of a demotion, the twins cost a bloody fortune, and God knows what it will be like later, shoes and all that, so don't expect much, he gives your mother money already, that ought to do you.'

Her father came through with a large box of nappies, half carrying, half pushing it. 'Jeez, Madison, how many nappies do they get through?'

'Hundreds, shitty little things.' She laughed and her earrings glittered.

'Oli, are you having anything? I'll make some tea actually. You want tea, sweetheart?'

Madison sat down at the kitchen table and pulled a packet of chocolate digestives towards her. 'Thanks.'

When he had the kettle on, Jeff looked at a baby monitor, like a mini television screen, with a microphone and a control panel. It showed a white-grey picture of a room with two cribs pushed close together. Two bodies, one twisting over and back, the other still.

Olivia watched her father watch the babies, peering at them with such close attention, such concern. Love. Yes.

'Can I see them?'

'Christ no, you go up there and that'll be that, two hours of screaming.'

'Why do they do that? Scream, I mean?'

'God knows. The health visitor woman said colic or wind, I don't know. I think they're just playing up.'

'Of course they don't, they're far too young to know how to do that, they just haven't settled yet,' Jeff said, without looking away from the monitor.

Olivia went to stand beside him. It was like seeing an old black-and-white film on a TV with bad reception. She couldn't make out what the babies looked like, even how big they were, they were just blobby outlines on the screen. A mobile was fixed over each crib, with plastic jungle animals on stalks but they weren't moving.

'That's Isaac.' Her father pointed to the restless little body on the left. 'That's Noah. He was a bit smaller when he was born and he's much more placid. He never moves when he sleeps, but look at Isaac, tossing and turning. Funny, how different they are, how they've got their own personalities already.'

The kettle shrieked but he did not seem to hear it, he was absorbed in looking at his sons.

'Jeff . . .'

'What? Oh, yes, sorry, sorry.'

Madison rolled her eyes.

You could have done that, Olivia thought, you could have made the tea.

Madison was chomping on another biscuit.

'I wish I could . . .'

'Well, you can't. They're not very interesting anyway, babies don't do much. Be better when they can play with you and you can take them for a walk, give me a break.'

Olivia could not make her out. 'You don't seem to like them,' she said.

'I bloody adore them, I'm crazy about them, what do you say that for? And Jeff does, can't you tell?'

'Yes.'

'Well then. You're a weird one, but I suppose it's your age, I was like it.'

'Like what?'

'Weird, hormones starting to play up and all that. Anyway, you didn't say why you weren't properly dressed.'

'No,' Olivia said, pulling the packet of biscuits over, 'I didn't.'

'Uh-oh, Isaac's awake.' The wail came at full volume through the monitor. Madison groaned. 'Leave him, he might go off again.'

'You know he never does, sweetheart. I'll go, I'll go. Coming up to see them, Oli?'

But as he asked, her phone rang. Olivia hesitated.

'Better get it.'

'No, it's OK.'

'Your mum?'

'It won't be anything. I want to see the twins.'

The babies had fallen silent again but Jeff still went stealthily into the room that adjoined the main bedroom, into which Olivia carefully did not look. The curtains were drawn and there was only a dull grey light from the overcast afternoon but it was enough for her to see at least Isaac clearly. He had gone back to sleep curled in a tight ball but his face was turned towards her. As she bent a little to look her phone rang.

'Sorry, sorry . . . Oh God.'

The baby had hurtled awake and into a loud wail, and as she fled the room, the second twin woke too.

'Bloody hell, now look what you've done.' Madison came thumping up the stairs. 'Stupid girl.'

'I didn't –'

'Oh get out of the way. Jeff?'

Olivia huddled at the kitchen table, staring at the half-empty biscuit packet and the remains of her tea and the screaming of the babies came to her from two directions, upstairs and on the monitor, and she heard her father and Madison, voices alternately angry with each other and then soothing as each held a twin and tried to hush them.

When the phone rang again, it was his number on the screen. She ignored it, and then switched the whole thing off. She was never answering that phone again, was going to throw it away the minute she left here. She wanted to leave now but through the window she could see sleet coming from a darkening sky. She had no coat, no boots, no money.

It was twenty minutes before first Madison then her father came down.

'I'm driving you home,' he said. 'Now.'

'I need the loo.'

'OK, second on the left.'

'And then you're gone,' Madison said, 'and I'd prefer it if you didn't come back here, actually, see your dad somewhere outside when you have to, I think anything else is going to upset us all.'

'I don't –'

'Sorry, but this is our new life together, us and the boys, it's all we want, we don't need his past like a millstone, though as I said, you're entitled to see him away from here. I wouldn't prevent that. I hope you think I'm being fair to you?'

Another sudden smile, a quick flash of white enamel, her earrings catching the overhead light, and to Olivia in that second, she turned into some glittering, poisonous insect. She dodged out of the kitchen, used the lavatory, and then followed her father to the car, the shiny new Mini that was too small for his big frame and long legs, and he drove her home through the sleet, and only when they got to the house, did he speak.

'I'm sorry, Oli, but you do see? You understand? It's difficult – for me. And for her. of course it is, she's very young. Do you get what I'm trying to say? Oh, and . . .' He reached into his jacket, took out his wallet, found three twenty-pound notes. 'Here.'

Olivia looked at the money and almost pushed it away, but in the end, took it, folded it tightly in her hand, and said, 'Thank you.'

She got out of the car and went down the path without looking back.

Twenty-Four

Chief Constable Kieron Bright sat at his desk with his strapped left leg up on another chair. Cat had bandaged it, and put on a knee support, was taking him for an X-ray later that afternoon. Meanwhile, he was in his office, with Serrailler and DCI Helena Blades, newly appointed, and moved from Bristol. She was pretty, Simon noted, but doing her best not to let it show, with hair in a tight ponytail, face bare of any make-up. She looked tense.

'Before I get to the details, welcome, Helena – we know one another of course and I'm very pleased you're here. I wanted you in today mainly so that you can get up to speed on this case. I know Simon's filled you in but it has moved rather fast in a direction we didn't anticipate –to start with it looked open and shut, and perhaps it will turn out to be so, but perhaps not. We'll see. Sorry, I just need to shift my leg.'

He tried but the chair it had been resting on shot forward. Simon got up. 'Think you need to wedge it. You don't look comfortable.'

'Cushion would help . . .' The Chief looked down mournfully at his knee.

'I'm not sure the station runs to soft furnishings – you know how our resources have been cut to the bone.' Simon did not meet his brother-in-law's eye as he looked round, spotted three or four heavy files and settled the leg on the top of those on the now stable chair. Kieron looked doubtful and adjusted his leg this way and that.

The DCI waited, apparently distancing herself from the whole scene.

'That seems better.'

'A bit. Thanks. Right, let's get to it. Liam Payne's body was found in the flat above the Chinese herbalist's premises in Starly. The PM was conducted by Professor Shenfield at Bevham General Mortuary and he recorded the expected cause – self-administered OD of heroin. No note or anything else indicating that it might have been suicide, so the body was released to the family and the funeral took place on the 24th at St Vincent's Roman Catholic Church, with burial in Fuller Road municipal cemetery. Case closed. Meanwhile, the Chinese herbalist, Mr Wang, has been under observation. Anything new on that by the way?'

'No. We've had a patrol checking the place every night but there's been no sign of anyone at all, and no vehicles. You've had my report of the single sighting I made but nothing since.'

'I don't want too much time wasted on patrols hanging about doing nothing in Starly. We're stretched as it is.'

'I've asked for them nightly until this coming Friday and then once a week?'

'No point, until Friday only, then call it off. Once a week is needle in a haystack time.'

Simon disagreed, nodded, said nothing.

'So, what about this Professor Shenfield?' the DCI asked. 'I read a paragraph about it but it didn't seem to add up to anything.'

'I've asked for a fast track on the Payne post-mortem, closest scrutiny. If everything adds up –'

'He must have known he was losing it.'

'Not necessarily. It was very early stages . . . small blips can be put down to tiredness or . . .'

'Or?'

'This is not about apportioning blame,' the Chief said. 'It's about a single case, at least so far as we're concerned. I have to be convinced that the PM was conducted properly and that the conclusions were accurate, allowing for the usual areas of doubt.'

'Which would be?'

'There's always difficulty with ascertaining drug quantities,' Simon said. 'Everything changes on death, the body behaves differently, estimates can be out by quite some degree, but it's still medically OK to say that the quantities found in tissue were, or were not, sufficient to cause death. A lot of work was done on this at the University of Dundee about fifteen years ago. Look it up.'

'That's not the only area of concern,' Kieron came in, 'or even the main one. I need to be certain there was no possibility that Shenfield could have been wrong about self-administration. If there was the slightest chance that someone else injected Payne with the drug, it changes everything.'

'Then what?'

'Then we're looking at an exhumation. An exhumation is a rare event but if they are not one hundred per cent sure that means I'm not either, so an exhumation it will have to be. Have you ever attended one, Chief Inspector?'

Helena Blades nodded.

'Chief Superintendent?'

'Once, when I was a rookie in the Met. I found it traumatic and exciting in about equal parts.'

The DCI looked at him in what he was sure was amusement with a touch of disdain.

'I have been present at several, you may be surprised to hear, given that it is, as you say, a rare event, but the Bristol force went through the era of a serial killer not so long ago.'

'Arthur Lyscom? You were at the sharp end. A functioning psychopath, as I recall.'

Lyscom, a low-ranking council clerk posing as being someone high up in social services, had eventually been charged with the murder of eleven elderly women, six of whom had been buried not cremated, and therefore the subjects of exhumation.

Kieron began to move his leg slowly off the chair.

'If that's all, Chief, I need to go and acquaint myself with the rest of CID.'

'Thank you, yes, you do that. Simon, can you . . . ?'

Serrailler went to help him stand up.

'Where are you heading?'

'I need a catch-up with my secretary, then I'm off to Starly. You should walk about a bit now, you've had your leg up for a while, you don't want a DVT.'

'Has my wife been talking to you?'

'As if. Now, since the demon DCI has left us . . .'

'I'm not listening to that, Simon, she's an excellent appointment, I've a lot of respect for what I know of her work.' He stood, finally, wincing.

'Painful?'

'Yes. Can you get the ibuprofen from my coat pocket?'

Simon did, with a glass of fresh water, then he said, 'Wheels in motion?'

Kieron nodded.

'You should make DCI Blades attend. She's clearly an old hand at exhumations.'

Twenty-Five

'There's a hairline crack, here and here – but otherwise it's a soft-tissue injury.'

The radiologist sat back to let Cat have a closer view of the X-ay.

'Is that bad? How bad?' Kieron asked. 'Those pictures look like a map of the moon to me.'

'Hairline cracks aren't a problem, they'll heal themselves, though nothing ever happens quickly once we get older.'

'I'm forty-eight!'

'You need to be eighteen to see anything really fast. But it isn't those that are causing your pain, it's the ligaments.' He switched off the viewer.

'Your wife here will explain, if she hasn't already . . . torn ligaments and tendons are what cost footballers their careers.'

'Good job I'm only a plod then.'

'If you were still plodding, you'd be looking at a desk job for a while. As it is, ice packs, strapping, pain relief, then some physio. Are you happy, Dr Deerbon?'

Cat was about to say something when her phone buzzed. 'Sam,' she mouthed. 'I'd better take this. Sammy? Hold on a second, I'm in radiography. Don't switch off.'

She gave the radiologist a thumbs up, and went ahead of Kieron towards the waiting area. By the time she reached it, the phone had gone dead.

'Damn. I'm getting a wheelchair for you, darling, you're strug-gling, you can't walk to the car park again. Sit down here. Do you want a coffee?'

Kieron glanced at the vending machine. 'I think just water. Am I due any painkillers?'

'Another half-hour. You'll just –'

'Thank you, do *not* tell me I'll just have to be brave, lump it, endure, whatever. Why don't you give me your phone while you hunt down my transport? If Sam rings again I'll answer it and keep him on the line till you get back.'

A spare wheelchair took twenty minutes and a tour of Bevham General's east wing to locate but when Cat returned, Sam had not called again.

'What is the boy playing at?' Kieron said, sitting back in the chair with relief. 'He's worrying you with all this messing about, and I've half a mind to tell him so.'

'Maybe wait for the reason first?'

He sighed. Cat had never once in their marriage been troubled by the way he behaved with her three children. Kieron had always deferred to her, always been cheerful, accepting, ready to listen and help out if asked, equally ready to stand back. Felix loved him, Hannah did not know him well, simply because she was away, either at her theatre school or in various musical productions, but they had a relaxed, rather bantering relation-ship. Only Sam had sometimes been touchy but he too was now away more than he was home, and when he had leave he was usually with Rosie.

She tried ringing him a couple of times before giving up and setting off for home.

'I'm on call from lunchtime tomorrow, for two nights and two days solid, so tonight I'm having a large gin and two glasses of wine and sod my own health advice.'

'You're wondering what next, aren't you? Poor Cat.'

'One damn thing after another, but that happens, I should deal with it.'

'I haven't helped.'

'You didn't hurt your knee on purpose.'

'Sam will be fine. Either he's got a dodgy phone or he's messing you about.'

'He isn't like that . . . or he never used to be.'

'True. But then, Wookie has never run away before.'

'Oh God.'

'You can't worry about everything at once, love.'

'I just want to know . . . if he's been killed on the road or . . . I want a body not a black hole.'

'Talking of . . . have you ever attended an exhumation?'

'Have I *what*?'

'Careful . . .' Cat was on the bypass and overtaking fast.

'Well, if you toss out that sort of remark . . . but since you ask, no, I haven't. I doubt if many GPs have. Why?'

'Just wondered.'

'You've got one coming up? Sorry, I shouldn't ask.'

'It's OK. The honest answer is that I don't know for certain yet. Shall I get that?'

'Please.'

'Dr Deerbon's phone . . . You can't, I'm afraid. I can take a message . . . No, I don't think she will tonight, she's not on call . . . Yes, I'll tell her.'

'Now what?'

'Sister Odewe on Fleming Ward about Mr Lionel Brown – she says he keeps asking to see you.'

'That poor man. I'm surprised he's still alive, and he's got nobody. I'll settle you in at home and then –'

'No, you're not going back there, you're exhausted and you need a night off.'

'Sure, but –'

'But nothing. Come on, love, you can't look after the world.'

She did not reply but he was right, she was exhausted, not with the day job but with everything else on top of that. Nevertheless, if she could muster just enough energy after supper, she ought to go into the hospital. The only other person who might have visited him was the warden of the almshouses and she had the other residents to look after. To have no one in the world to see you or care about you except a sheltered housing warden and your doctor was a fate she would not wish on any old person but she knew it was the situation for too many.

'Sleeting again.'

'I wish it would snow or not snow – this freezing rain and sleet and greyness is getting very tiresome. Three feet of snow for three weeks is what we need.'

'You don't mean that. Night calls? Car breakdowns?'

Cat laughed, and turned into the drive.

'Is that a motorbike?' Through the sleet driving against the windscreen Cat could make out little, even with the headlamps on, but as she pulled up at the front door, she saw the bike and then someone huddled in the porch.

'Sam? Sam! What in heaven's name are you doing there in this cold? Haven't you got your key? What –'

'Can you help me out?' The voice was plaintive.

'Wait a minute.'

'You left the car door open, I can't reach to close it and I'm frozen.'

'Oh for God's sake, Kieron, you're like a small child, me me me. Here, hold on . . . put your good leg down first – don't slip.'

'I'm trying not to, aren't I? It's extremely painful. What's Sam doing?'

'Right, hop if you can't weight-bear on that leg. Sam, can you give me a hand please?'

But Sam shook his head. He was standing now, his coat over his head, arms folded round in front of him.

Somehow, she got the door open and helped Kieron over the step and inside. 'Sit there a minute. Let me . . . Sam? What is it?'

Her son stood just inside the door, arms still folded. He opened his jacket.

'I found him on the doorstep. I left my key in London, sorry. I didn't know where you were and my phone was out of battery. I've been trying to keep us both warm but he's not in a good way, Mum.'

Sam and Cat sat down on the kitchen sofa with Wookie lying between them, one paw in Sam's hand. His coat had small clumps of frozen snow matted into it, he was shivering and there was blood on his front leg. His pads were cut and the claws on all four legs torn and ragged.

'Poor little dog, you poor little thing. Where do you think he's been?'

'Down a rabbit or badger hole, I guess, then scrabbling for hours trying to get out . . . or locked in someone's shed maybe.'

'No, he's obviously been outside for a long time, he's frozen. What are we going to do, Mum?'

'Ring the vet. Just keep him wrapped up close to you, Sam, he needs warmth.'

Kieron was leaning on the worktop. 'I think we need a drink. What do you want, love? Sammy?'

'What have you done to your leg, K?'

'Torn something. There's a beer in the fridge.'

'I'd rather have a coffee. I'm frozen as well.'

He was cuddling the small body close to him. Wookie made slight whimpering sounds. They heard Cat talking in the hall.

'Your mother has had the day from hell, Sam – just letting you know.'

'Well, I'm not about to make it worse.'

'What was all that ringing her and ringing off about? Can't have been low battery.'

But Sam bent his head to Wookie, murmuring, stroking his ears and did not give Kieron an answer.

'We have to take him to the emergency vet in Bevham. Come on, Sammy, you can hold him in his blanket.'

'I won't let you drive back to Bevham again, Cat, you're not fit.'

'I haven't had a drink yet, of course I'm fit. I'll grab a bar of chocolate and go.'

'Let's both have a coffee, Mum, then I'll drive.'

'Are you insured for my car?'

'Erm, probably.'

Kieron shook his head. 'Nice try, Sam. '

Wookie was whimpering. Cat sat beside him and looked at his paws, then his leg. She noticed now that he had two puncture marks on either side of his nose, and that the tissue around it was swelling.

She fetched a basin of warm water, a towel and cotton wool, and bathed his face gently while Sam held him. Now and then he shivered but did not try to get away or stop her.

'His ear has one of those puncture marks as well, look.'

'Rat,' Cat said. 'He's been in some back shed or stable then dragged himself home, but how long has he been like that? Poor little chap. Silly little Wookie.' The end of the dog's tail stirred slightly, but wagging it was beyond him.

Twenty-Six

They did not meet, it was all text messages, very occasionally phone calls, from phones that were used for a month, sometimes less, before being wiped and destroyed. One man would know another, maybe two, but never more. There were levels. Top level were the ones nobody else knew, nobody, not even their names, nobody had ever seen them, the brains and the planners. Below them came the ones only known to those on the level above, by name and contact numbers, then came the one below that and the same again. It was several rungs down to the bottom level, the ones who thought nothing, planned nothing, took orders, worked their own patch, found the kids.

The rules were strict, and nobody flouted them, knowing what the result would be – or rather, not knowing, not exactly, leaving everything to the imagination, and so to fear. Rule one was no photographs, of anyone, ever. Two was that anything written and sent was immediately deleted, three that no numbers were shared. The barrow boys knew their own, and that might be three or four or a dozen, like Fats knew Brookie, Liv and five more, though seven wasn't enough, he'd been told that twice recently, and he was trying, like the rest of them were. The ones above knew nothing about it, whether it was hard or easy, they just stuck their hands out, sent the packets, took the money., a lot of money, and they wanted more, and though money came back down the chain again, it was in very much smaller amounts.

There were others, connected to one another and with links to the top, but engaged on different business, in knocking on doors, ringing bells, making phone calls, threatening, talking tough, issuing ultimatums. Travelling further. Some met up in twos, to make visits, deliver and collect, like Mace and Fats to the Chinese pharmacist.

Money moved up, down and sideways in various directions, by various methods, which changed frequently, according to what messages were received. Petty cash bought things. Phones. Shiny toys. Fish and chips.

Bribes. Retainers. Blackmail. Dirty money that went from hand to hand just as the packets did. The higher up the level, the more the money. Below, it was split into smaller amounts, moved about between businesses, currency-exchange booths, pawnbrokers, bookies. Five hundred pounds could be deposited in banks and post offices without questions being asked, not more, too risky. Up into the thousands, it was different again, it was cars bought and sold, it was casinos, it was diamonds and gold, and after that, Bitcoin, though only a few of them understood virtual currency and none really trusted it. Cash was best, carried in body belts and hidden compartments, built into luggage that was loaded on planes, ferries, cruise ships. Cash could be easily transferred, then laundered, cash bore no ID.

The Chief was talking to a full conference room at HQ, mainly standing but from time to time walking about, stretching his leg, wincing slightly, standing with the weight on his other one.

'It's all worked out, it's sophisticated, it moves like mercury. It's not ten steps, it's miles ahead of us and it's bloody clever, it's better organised than a brigade of guards. And it is everywhere, it's on our patch and the patch next door and every patch in the country. It's the biggest threat we have faced in my time as a cop, and all of yours. County lines isn't about the small fry, we've mopped up plenty of them, but they're like that . . . classical mythology. What was it called.? Cut off its head and two grew in its place, and so on . . .'

'Hydra,' Serrailler said.

'Thank you, Chief Superintendent. Every ACPO meeting I have been to in the last year has been, to a great extent, about county lines, their growth, their spread and the threat they pose to every aspect of life in the communities we police. They are a particular threat to our young people, on a par but becoming more widespread than paedophile rings and grooming gangs. And when I say young, I mean they target not just teenagers, but children – we know instances of children as young as nine being recruited to collect and deliver drugs. They are cleverly bribed with gifts – new phones, tablets, bicycles, designer trainers and other gear. Young kids are susceptible, of course they are, and these are generally children from poorer families, deprived kids, kids without all the treats they know others get. It's for the sake of these children that we have to make county lines our main focus from now and going forward. We want drugs off the streets, out of circulation – drugs destroy lives. It's as simple as that. Kids start by being messengers, seems harmless enough, but then they're tempted to try drugs themselves – nothing too strong, just a bit of weed to start with, and if they've got a bad home life, where they're knocked about or bullied or the parents have split or one is in prison, then a spliff takes the edge off the misery. And so it starts, and maybe the kid gets further into more serious crime, because by now he or she has a habit and the habit has to be fed. Not every kid they use comes from a bad background. Some of what you'd call nice middle-class parents find out they have a child who's a drugs mule – where did the shiny new watch come from? Who bought the gold pendant? The Xbox and the expensive games? It spreads, the bad parents don't care, and their kids know that – but someone out there loves them enough to buy them nice gear. Of course, the well-off recreational drug users, people in top jobs, who think a spliff to relax with, a line of coke after a dinner party or at a social function helps to make things go with a swing, don't care. They'll argue that drugs are no worse than alcohol, and often a lot less harmful, in the right hands – which of course are their hands. But none of these people trace the drugs they've bought back to the criminals, the youth gangs, and so on down to the exploited kids.

'So, everything we do from now on, everything, we bring it back to that. Yes, of course there's all the other business of policing, the usual major and minor crime, all the accidents and incidents we continue to have to deal with every day, but I want this at the front of everybody's mind. We're not on our own here – every other force is grappling with it and there is full cooperation between us, no point-scoring, no rivalry, no borders, we share information, we share names and addresses, we share whatever we have with whoever needs it. County lines spread out from the big cities to reach us and the forces like us, and we have to stamp this out and we will stamp it out. Whatever it takes, and between us all. We are not going to let them win.'

'Didn't have the Chief down for a rallying cry before battle sort of guy, did you?' Fern Monroe was walking out of the conference room beside Serrailler.

'Not his usual style,' someone else said.

Simon manoeuvred himself through the press of bodies, pleading urgency to reply to a call, conscious that DC Monroe was blocked in behind him. He didn't know how to deal with her, thought avoidance and escape were his best MO.

He was halfway down the street to the Cypriot cafe when his phone buzzed.

'Chief?'

'Where are you?'

'On my way back in?'

'Sorry, Simon. I'm in your office.'

The stairs and corridors had cleared, everyone had gone back at work, and Fern Monroe was nowhere to be seen.

'Chief.'

'Didn't mean to deprive you of the best coffee in Lafferton but some new stuff has come in about Professor Shenfield. Can I sit here? – I can prop my leg up.'

'Of course. What's going on?'

'Two pathologists have now gone over his PM on Liam Payne – your friend Adam Iliffe and a Dr Kendra Murray from Edinburgh as the outsider. In a nutshell, Shenfield made a few errors – not grave, just oversights, and certainly nothing criminal, but apparently ones a very junior pathologist might have made.'

'Rookie errors.'

121

'Yes, though they note that rookies tend to over-examine rather than make accidental omissions. By the time the body reached his table, the syringe had been either accidentally or deliberately removed from the vein in the arm where it was found though it was bagged and labelled quite correctly, and the police photographs showed everything in close-up. Shenfield took those as being accurate and did not do any tests, for example by replacing the syringe into the vein – he signed off on the photos. That's not a criminal omission but it's the sort of thing a meticulous path like Shenfield would never have done. He also estimated the levels of heroin left in the system by the usual calculations, but apparently there is a recent and more accurate way of measuring those which takes different factors into account – not just time since injection, time since death, any visible effects on the liver and other tissues. Shenfield knew about the latest one because he had been asked to advise and comment – in effect he had done a peer review. This method is slowly taking over from the old one, though there is no suggestion that anyone abandon that completely – the calculations have proved reliable for forty-odd years, but in some circumstances they can be verified and backed up by the second method, and apparently the PM on Liam Payne was just such a case. They were somewhat surprised that, so far as they can tell from the report, Shenfield used only the old method of calculation.'

'Couldn't he have used the recent one as well and simply not noted it?'

'Possible but very unlikely, and remember, he was known to be a stickler for detail. His path students were terrified of making so much as a slip-up in grammar let alone a scientific error.'

'What's the conclusion?'

'That there is room for doubt. About the way the syringe presented in Payne's arm, and about the amount of heroin in the system, in terms of whether it was certain to be fatal, likely to be fatal or unlikely ditto. The margin for error is there but in this sort of case – well, if we were looking at another party being involved, perhaps even administering the heroin, and if we had that person in our custody and were looking to charge him or her . . .'

'Their brief would have a field day.'

Kieron nodded.

'What do Adam and Dr Murray recommend?'

'They don't – they weren't asked to, it wasn't in their remit.'

'Over to us then.'

'It's not a difficult decision, Simon. We have a duty towards the deceased, to his family and to the public, in that we may – or of course may not – be investigating a crime.'

'So, you'll apply to the coroner for permission to exhume the body?'

'Yes, and thank God it was a burial.'

'Depends which way you look at it,' Serrailler said.

'Right, I just wish I could move faster. I'm off to get this show on the road and then I've got a meeting with the Commissioner.'

'Bad luck. On what planet were the government when they thought PCCs were a good idea? Not to mention, why are they voted in not appointed so that we get lumbered with dolts like Axby?'

'I didn't hear that. Oh, and Cat messsged . . . Wookie is having surgery, and according to the vet, his life hangs by a thread.'

Twenty-Seven

Brooklyn had been almost asleep when he remembered, and sat up. Connor was talking in his sleep as usual, Alfie was turning and twisting about.

He had left the phone downstairs, in his bag or maybe in his pocket. Either way he needed to get it, because messages had started coming in during the night.

Hi Brookie.

You awake?

Do you want an Xbox? I got one for you.

What you playing at, Brookie? Don't want trouble, do you?

He wished he didn't have the phone, he wanted to give it back, only he hadn't seen Fats to do that. He slithered out of bed, avoiding the protruding springs, stepped over Alfie's outstretched leg and went down. His bag was at the foot of the stairs but the phone wasn't in it. His jacket wasn't in the pile, or under the other bags, and though he didn't remember hanging it up, maybe he had.

The hall light snapped on. 'You looking for this?'

Brookie swore his heart actually stopped. What was Dad doing back when it was the middle of his shift? He was standing in the kitchen doorway with the phone in his hand.

'Get in here.'

There was a bowl with tomato soup in it, tin on the table.

'What are you at home for?'

'Never mind me.' His dad held the phone up again. 'Where'd you get this?'

'Found it.'

'Where?'

'In a skip.'

'What skip?'

'Outside a house.'

'What house?'

His head went to mush, he couldn't think of any street names at all, not in Starly, not anywhere.

'Sit down.'

He couldn't work out what his dad was like, raging mad, cold mad, puzzled or just fed up with him.

'Whose is it, Brookie?' He tapped the phone screen. 'And don't say "Dunno".'

But he couldn't think of anything else to say.

'Come here . . . sit down. You want a drink? I got some of those packets of hot chocolate.'

Brookie nodded.

'Sorry? Must be going deaf here.'

'Yes please.'

'Better.'

Vince filled the kettle and put the chocolate powder in a mug, while Brookie sat staring at the table. He wasn't sure whether to be worried or scared or nothing. Their dad never ever hit them, he never had, though he yelled and bellowed and chucked things at them all the time. He put out their food and yelled at them to come and eat it, shouted at them to get in the bath, get their clothes off the floor, get upstairs, get downstairs, get out, get to school, get from under his feet, stop making such a bloody racket.

'Here. Don't just drink it, numpty, it's boiling, stir it.' He put sugar in a mug of tea while watching Brooklyn.

'You going to tell me or what?'

Brookie stirred and watched the beige-coloured bubbles swirl round and round like soapsuds.

'Where did you get this bloody phone? You've got no money, it's not been your birthday, Christmas came and went. How long have you had it?'

Brookie shrugged.

'Come on – how long have you had it? A day, a week? A month?'

'Not as long as that.'

'Getting somewhere at last, somewhere but not far enough. Listen, kiddo . . . something's gone on, and you know what it is, and we can sit here all night far as I'm concerned.'

'Dad . . . you know my bed?'

'What about it?'

'Only the springs are all poking through the holes in the mattress and they stick in me, I can't make them stay back.'

'We're talking about this phone.'

'Just saying. Only I thought maybe you didn't know about it.'

'I've got to sort a lot of things out, Brookie, I do my best. You not happy?'

Brookie looked at the floor. 'I'm all right.'

'You're a lot better off with me than with your mother, you know that, don't you?'

'Suppose.'

'Do you remember what it was like with her? Maybe you don't.'

'A bit. I'm all right. I need to go to bed now.'

'You need to tell me where this phone came from first. Quicker you do, quicker you'll be up there. Come on, I wasn't born yesterday. You nicked it.'

'No! I swear to God I never nicked it. I never nick anything, only get stuff off skips and that's not nicking.'

'You didn't get this off a skip.'

His dad stood up suddenly and leaned over him. He was big. He wasn't a bouncer and a security man for nothing. Brookie shrank back.

'Listen to me, Brooklyn – you tell me where you got it now or I'll turn your neck round 180 degrees.' He held his hands out. Big hands. 'Now, let's start counting. One . . . two . . .'

'Fats.' He shouted the name.

'What do you mean, fats? What's fats?'

'A man. That's his name. He says it is anyway and I don't know any other, only it's funny because he's actually really skinny, AND he's a ginge, anyway he gave me a lift from school one time when I'd missed the bus, he was coming out this way and he dropped me at the corner, and then he did it again, when I was running for the bus. He gave me a bag, a rucksack thing when my stuff spilled out all over.'

Vince sat down and pulled the chair over until his own knees were touching Brookie's.

'So, maybe we're getting somewhere or maybe you made all this up. I don't have lying, I've told you all that how many times? Your mother was a liar, lied her way through every bloody day of her life. So no lying. What kind of a car has this Fats got then?'

'Van. It's ancient.'

'He's brought you home in it twice and never told you a real name? Why'd you think he did that, Brookie?'

'Dunno.'

'So he gave you the phone, right?'

'He bought us all fish and chips once. I was going to the chippy with enough money to get scraps and the ends of the chips and he was in there and he bought fish and chips for all of us and peas. He's all right if he did that.'

'Is he? How'd you know?'

Brookie stared.

'Listen, son . . . a bloke who gave you a lift home twice, and didn't even know you – what was he doing hanging about your school anyway? He could have been up to any sort of trouble, he could have been a nonce, he could have been a killer, how would you know?'

'He isn't.'

'Then he gives you a new school backpack, spends twenty-odd quid on fish and chips for four of you, then gives you a bloody mobile phone – for Christ's sake, boy, where's your brain? You're not stupid. You can't think that's normal. Why didn't you tell me? Did you tell the others?'

'No.'

'Why? Afraid they'd get the stuff instead of you?'

'No.'

'What then? They might have told me? Ah, all right, that's it. Pity they didn't do that before you were sitting here in big

127

trouble. Taking a phone off a bloke, you don't know who he is, you don't know his name or where he lives, you just took it? And then he starts messaging you. What do you message back?'

'Nothing.'

'Liar – didn't you hear what I just said about that?'

'I don't say anything back, I don't answer.'

'And how long do you think you'll get away with that?'

'What do you mean?'

'Jesus wept, Brookie, what do I have to say? How do I get this through your thick skull?'

Brookie's eyes were smarting with tiredness and the tears he was holding back. His dad looked at the phone then back to him, back to the phone again, for what seemed a very long time, saying nothing, shaking his head.

'All right, son, this is what's going to happen. I'm keeping this.' He held up the phone. 'If there are any messages I'll answer them, pretending I'm you. Any calls, I'll let alone.'

'He doesn't, he only texts.'

'I'm going to find out who he is and get to him.'

'No! You can't do that, he said if I told anybody, he said –'

'Whatever he said you can forget it. I'm sorting this now. If he's waiting for you anywhere, you dodge him. No going in the van, no lifts home, nothing. Got that?'

'But he . . .'

Dad reached over and circled Brookie's skinny wrist with his finger and thumb. 'He won't. You forget all about him, you get on with your schoolwork and stay near the others. No wandering out by yourself, understand me? Because he's a bad 'un, and you're eleven and you're not safe to be out on your own. But from now on, I handle this, OK? Now get to bed.'

When he was at the door, his dad said, 'What was all that stuff about your bed?'

'It's . . .'

'Never mind, get up there, I'll look at it tomorrow. Scoot.'

All the way up the stairs and along the landing, Brookie was in a flat panic, and as he stepped over Alfie, lay down and pulled up the covers, automatically moving away from the springs. But then his panic thinned and floated away as he closed his eyes and did not trouble him in his sleep. In the morning, he woke and remembered that the phone wasn't his any more, his dad was sorting it. He felt better.

Twenty-Eight

'This is Sister Odewe on Fleming Ward, Bevham General Hospital, for Dr Deerbon. Please will you ring me back or come in, Doctor, regarding Lionel Brown? Thank you.'

The message had come in at six; it was now twenty past seven and Cat already had five calls listed. It had snowed, thawed a little, frozen again, making roads and pavements lethal, so that A&E was packed with fractures, pneumonia, hypothermia cases and the various victims of RTAs.

'Felix, there's a text saying choir practices are cancelled today but I still want to set off early for school because of the roads. Don't pour the milk onto your cereal from three feet up, it splashes everywhere.'

Felix grinned. 'Sam's still asleep, did you know that?'

'Ta-dah! No, Sam isn't,' his brother said, leaping into the kitchen. 'Bet you haven't left any of that.'

'New box in the cupboard.' Cat waved her arm vaguely, looking down at another message about an elderly patient.

'Mum, you haven't rung about Wookie! You just forgot him.'

'No, I'll do that later, the vet won't have any update on him yet.'

'He might and Wookie could have taken a turn for the worse, he might be in agony, the vet said his life was hanging by a thread and the thread might have snapped in the night.' Felix's face was contorted with distress, his eyes huge. It was not long

130

since he had sung 'Morning Has Broken' at the garden burial of the old cat Mephisto, part of the family since before Felix was born, and he had immediately transferred all his love and concerned attention to Wookie. Cat had recognised when he was less than three that Felix needed something with which to bond and about which to worry. Where his generalised anxiety came from she had never been able to work out but it was very real and she took it seriously.

'Mum, listen, I've had a good idea. Why don't I be your chauffeur today? We can drop Felix, then go to your calls, I can take any messages while you're seeing patients, and ring the vet and whatever. You can relax a bit and just focus on the job. And don't open your mouth to object. I haven't got any other plans.'

'Aren't you seeing Rosie?'

'No.'

'I don't know, Sam, the roads are pretty treacherous.'

'I'm a careful driver. And I'll do that insurance app to put myself on your car, takes five minutes, then just think, you get to spend quality time with me, as a bonus. Felix, if you poke the end of a knife in the toaster while it's on, your hair will catch fire and you'll be thrown across the room and hit the wall and it won't be funny. Switch it off first!'

Cat went upstairs to see if Kieron needed help. His knee was still painful and he couldn't bend it to put on his shoe, though her own observation was that it had improved rather more than he was prepared to admit.

The country roads were difficult but once they were nearer the bypass the surfaces had been well gritted and traffic was flowing normally. Sam's driving was good, careful but not overcautious and by the time they dropped Felix at school, Cat had relaxed.

'First call is out towards Highnam – about seven miles.' She had already programmed the satnav. 'You're right, Sammy, it's good to have a driver. I'm sorry last night was crazy and we didn't get a chance to talk . . . How are you liking midwifery?'

'All right.'

'No better than that?'

'Sorry . . . yes, I mean, it's fine. It's . . . yes.'

'Sam, if you're finding it isn't what you expected or you're not as keen as you thought you'd be, that's perfectly OK. There is no branch of medicine at all which you could spend your life in, loving every single minute. Every area has its downside and midwifery isn't all joy and delight.'

'Not that. Hang on . . .' They had turned into a side road and now Sam was slowing to a crawl behind an L-plated scooter which was skidding and sliding. 'He's not safe.'

Cat waited while Sam negotiated the tricky overtake, and glanced in his rear-view mirror to check that the scooter rider was still on the road.

'I am so relieved you never once thought of wanting a scooter, even if you did have a flirtation with the idea of a souped-up Harley-Davidson. Your present motorbike worries me enough as it is.'

'Mum, I was fourteen.'

'What's happening with Rosie?'

She had always found it best with her elder son to attack a potentially touchy subject when he was off guard.

'Nothing.'

'Listen, you don't have to tell me, but I don't believe you. You kept ringing me and hanging up, you've barely mentioned her, you said you –'

'OK, OK. Get off my case, Ma.'

'Fine.'

'And don't get in a huff, and yes, I do know I can talk to you at any time blah-blah.'

'No, you turn left.'

'Not what the satnav says.'

Cat was silent. The road he had turned into was a cul-de-sac which had not been gritted, so that reversing down it and round the corner took all Sam's concentration.

'Well done.'

He grunted but there was no more conversation for the next ten minutes, until they pulled up outside a large detached house, one of four, very new and spaced well apart.

'Ah, the luxury of private medicine,' Sam said.

'Will you ring the vet while I'm inside? Number's on the sticker.'

Sam rolled his eyes. In spite of being a long-time and efficient smartphone user, his mother still insisted on having various coloured Post-it notes, scrawled with vital numbers, stuck to the dashboard.

A text message came in with a name and address, and *Girl, 4, high temp and rash*, a second followed immediately with an address and *Mr Curtis's headaches again*. There was a pause and Sam was about to call the vet when he saw a missed call. Listened to the voice message.

'Dr Cat, this is Sister Odewe, Fleming Ward at Bevham General. I've been trying to get hold of you. Please contact me about Lionel Brown.'

Sam called the vet's before anyone else could jump in.

'Oh yes, poor little Wookie . . . Michael is in charge of him, hold on.'

There was a long wait while the phone played 'The Skaters' Waltz' on a loop. Sam held it away from his ear. There was no one about, the close was like a deserted village, though presumably a few people were behind the shiny new front doors and swathes of icy gravel, the CCTV monitors, the security lamps. Beside the front door of the one Cat had gone through were two tubs containing small bay trees, which had been covered with fleece against the frost.

'Michael Farmer.'

Sam's mouth had gone dry and his stomach was tight. Please, he said silently, please.

'It's Sam Deerbon.'

'Hi, I've just been in to see him again actually. He's holding his own but it's still too early to say if he'll make it, Sam, he has a nasty infection in his wounds and the vital thing is to stop that becoming systemic. I had to put stitches in three of his pads, and his ear had to be stitched as well, he tore that on some barbed wire. He's been warmed up gently and we've got him under a lamp, so I'm not worried about the hypothermia now, but he's been through a hell of a lot, and he hasn't got much energy to fight it all. I think it would be a good idea if you or your mother came in and saw him – he might buck up if he heard a familiar voice. They get very bewildered and then they lose heart when they're away from home for any length of time, and so ill . . . just like people.'

'Do you think . . . I mean, does his life still hang by a thread?'

'Did I say that? OK, let's just the thread is holding.'

'But might it snap?'

'I hope not. If he gets his spirit and the will to live back, it might hold. He's a small dog and they often do better, just as they live longer.'

Cat was coming towards the car.

'Thanks,' Sam said. 'One of us will come and visit.'

As he ended the call another text message came in.

Child 4 with temp and rash is worse. Will Dr Cat please make it her next call?

He handed it to her.

'Right, that's out at Meacham Green – I'll direct you. Take the bypass, it's safer and we can move faster.'

Sam focused on driving while Cat scrolled through the messages, occasionally giving him a direction, but otherwise, conversation was on hold.

He was glad of it. Rosie, his course, his future – he wanted to keep it all to himself now, he needed to think everything through, not once but many times, turn it over and look at it, though he had been doing that for the past three weeks without coming to any conclusions. His mother was a good listener, she wouldn't push solutions at him, but she would still be his mother, worried, trying to help, asking too many questions he couldn't yet answer.

The roads were getting easier, and the temperature had risen to plus two on the panel. He had to slow down as he turned into the twisting village street, and Cat looked for house names and numbers. When they saw Ferndale, she was out of the car before the wheels had stopped turning.

There were no more messages so Sam turned on Radio 2 and a strange, wild singing voice he didn't recognise, though his mother would have known from the first couple of notes that he was listening to Kate Bush.

He slumped down in the seat, folded his arms and went to sleep.

He surfaced twenty minutes later when the band was the Raconteurs, their song 'Help Me Stranger', and the blue light of an ambulance was turning in front of his eyes.

'Serious then?' he said when it had moved away, siren winding up and Cat got into the car.

'Meningitis. They should have called the paramedics, not me.'

'Will she be OK?'

Cat shook her head, saying nothing.

'Not sure what order you want to do this but a sister at BG rang about a Mr –'

'Lionel Brown. Oh God, yes, and I haven't called her back.'

'And the vet says one of us ought to visit Wookie or he'll think he's been abandoned and lose the will to live. I'll do that. Hospital?'

'I ought to look in on Mr Curtis first – five minutes.'

It was twenty before she escaped.

Twenty-Nine

Friday night and there was never time to talk to anyone, the queue stretched round the block, even tonight, with a freezing wind off the canal and sleet underfoot. They didn't seem to notice, in skimpy frocks made of tissue paper, skirts up to thighs and beyond, only one in twenty wore any sort of jacket or scarf. Vince walked up and down the line. You'd expect them all to catch their death, their lips to have gone blue, but they'd be back the same tomorrow. He dreaded the day when his own started wanting to join the clubbers. Tommy. Connor. Brookie. Alfie.

Brookie. He clenched his fist before he went to the back of the queue and started. 'If you've got anything on your person, hand it over to me now please. No drugs, no knives or other weapons. Spot-checking. Turn out your pockets please, sir . . . Thank you. Turn out your pockets please, sir . . . Because I'm asking you nicely and you know the rules . . . That's fine, your right to refuse, my right to refuse you entry . . . Not accusing you of anything, sir . . . You, less of that . . . Handbags open ready for checking please, young ladies . . . no drugs, no weapons, knives, scissors . . . Thank you. I don't know how you're not freezing to death.'

On down the line which moved slowly forward to the outer door, first check, inner doors, second check, then either in you go or out on your ear.

Vince had a walkie-talkie earpiece and a padded jacket, but they weren't allowed any sort of headgear, and nights like this

136

he wished for his hair back but he still preferred to be outside, cold or not, because the noise in the club made his ears bleed. They'd all be stone deaf by forty but that never seemed to bother them either. Live today.

'All right, moving in now, nearly there . . . Handbags ready for checking . . . Plenty of nice hot cocoa inside for you.'

Behind the sooty spider-lashes and the glitter patches, the red lips, the pink and purple hair, they were children. If he worried about his boys, what would he have been like if they'd been girls?

The queue shortened and shortened. Ten minutes and he could go round to the back room for his break.

There were four of them working the queue and the doors in rotation, and then inside and on the cameras and Vince saw himself as the lightweight, given the others were all six foot six and more – in Mo's case, six eight, and twenty stone of solid muscle. Nobody took on Mo unless they were off their heads and couldn't see straight. But Vince was fast and light on his feet, a one-time middleweight.

Not that he ever wanted to get into a brawl, he wanted a regular life, hold down his job, retire in safety. He had four boys, one of them wading in troubled water, and if he, his dad, didn't sort it out, it would be over his head.

He was first into the back room, his job to put the kettle on. The cupboard was kept well stocked, he had to say, they never needed to scratch around for tea, coffee, Cup-a-Soups, decent biscuits, sarnies and cans from the fridge. The pay was as usual, tips didn't exist, but the extras were handy.

He was sitting with his first brew when Odd came in. It was the name that gave him a nudge. Odd. Fats.

'All right, Vince?'

'I am. Where were you last week?'

'Shocking cold, coughed as if I was a two-pack-a-day man, retched my guts up.' He held up the kettle.

'I'm all right for now thanks.'

He read a page of sport, boxing, darts, turned over from cricket in Australia. Looked up. Odd was back in his chair, legs splayed.

'Missus all right?'

Odd snorted.

'She still working the market?'

'It's an addiction, man.'

'Selling knickers is an addiction?'

'Has to be, she and her mother.'

'Brings in the pennies.'

'Not in this weather.'

'You know a few about the place, Odd. I'm trying to get hold of a bloke.'

'Sort of a bloke?' Odd was still crashed back, but he was listening.

'Don't know much else. Goes by his stupid nickname.'

'Sort of stupid nickname?'

A door blew open and a blast as loud as a bomb exploded into the room from the club. Died again. In the inner room the bank of small screens flickered, watching the dancers, the standers, the drinkers, watching, watching, never blinking. Cooper, the deputy manager, was on the screens tonight. Any minute, he'd put his arm up for black coffee, three sugars.

'You ever heard of someone called Fats?'

Vince kept his eyes on Odd's face but there was nothing.

'Fats what?'

Vince shrugged.

'Don't ring no bells. What's it about anyway?'

'Something and nothing, to do with one of the lads. Don't suppose it's much.'

'Fats. Nope. Still, if I do . . . not a name you hear every afternoon.'

'Like Odd.'

'Summat like that.'

The arm requesting black coffee three sugars came up at the window.

Saturday nights were not often as full-on as Friday and on this one there had been heavy rain all day, turning to sleet later, and the pavements were awash. By peak time, around eleven to half past, there were probably half the punters of the previous night and they moved them off the street and into the club fast. It was

Odd's turn on the screens and when Vince took in his coffee – white, no sugar, no biscuits because of his diabetes – Odd took it, drank it even though it was scalding hot, set it down, all with one eye still on the heaving mass of dancers.

'Got something for you.'

'What's that?' Vince pulled over a tatty plastic-covered stool. There was no one else in the office and somebody had already nicked the paper.

'Funny how things come up again, once they're in your head. That bloke – Fats.'

'You do know him?'

'No, but I met a mate outside the dogs, he's a regular, owns half a back leg of one or summat, and he said he'd had a lot of luck the last few weeks, won a pot, and it was through someone he'd met on the track, who'd given him a couple of tips and then said if they came good he'd come back and ask my mate to do him a favour. As luck would have it, they both did the business, long odds and all, Derry was well up – getting on for a grand, he said, so when the other bloke found him he was happy to do the favour.'

'As who wouldn't. He must have had plenty to put on.'

'Yeah, well, Derry always seems to have money tucked up somewhere, God knows where he gets it, I don't ask.'

'What did he have to do then?'

'Take a wallet of cash and put it all on a dog in the last race.'

'How much?'

'He didn't know. Wasn't to open the wallet, just go to the one bookie, hand it over, name the runner and get his slip, but he reckoned it had to be a good wodge, the wallet was thick as a bog roll with it.'

'That it?'

'That was it. He waited till the last and the bugger won, only he hadn't put anything on, thought he'd quit while he was ahead.'

Vince finished his coffee, and then opened his mouth to ask what the dog story had to do with anything, when Odd was up on his feet, hand on the alarm button beside him. On the screen a space had cleared in which three or four youths were fighting, girls were pushing back and screaming, the music went dead and as Vince followed Odd at a run, out, down the iron staircase and through a back way onto the floor, the other bouncer was in from the street, and onto the pile-up as Vince yelled at him to get away, get back, as the knife appeared from somewhere in the heap of bodies, flashing in the turning light of the glitter balls.

The fire doors were opened, girls went tottering outside clutching one another, their faces turning neon blue, as two, then three police cars came wailing down the street.

It was only at the end of the night, when they'd hung around giving statements and calling the cab ranks to send every car available to ferry the kids home, getting on for three o'clock, the last coffee brewed and drunk, the place locked up and dark, the cops waiting for them to leave in their own cabs, that Odd said, 'Cheers, Vince, we done well. Don't miss the eight o'clock mass at St Gregory's now.' And Vince thumped his arm and remembered. 'What was that all about – your mate and his win at the dogs?'

'Oh, right – I was getting to that.'

'You were?'

'Derry said the man he got the tips off wouldn't tell him his name, just said the bookie would know who the wallet had come from, and when he took it the bookie said, "Is this from the Cabby or Fats?"'

Thirty

The cars crept along the paths, crunching on the gravel, and the gravel sparkled like the sea under a heavy frost and the dawn sky was sea-blue, with a fading half-moon. When they stopped and people got out and stood waiting, breath plumed up like smoke.

Simon stamped his feet, the Chief banged his hands together. A robin stood on the white grass beside the white tent, bright-eyed, watchful, head cocked.

The van was already there, parked on the far side of the tent, invisible from the paths and shielded by a high wall. The ghosts in white suits, white hoods pulled up, bent over bags of equipment.

The black police Range Rover was by the tent on the near side, the unmarked van as close as it could get to the entrance flap.

It had been the right of the family to attend but no one had wanted to.

When Serrailler had been to see Lynn Vines, she had stared at him in shock, her face pale blank of expression for a several moments, before she said, 'Oh God, not this, please not . . . we've had enough. He's had enough. Can't you let him be?'

He had explained carefully, gently, stressed that everything would be done with great respect, very early in the morning so that there could be no gawpers, and no funerals taking place at the same time.

'I totally understand how you feel, and if you don't want to be there – and I think you're right, you've had enough and it wouldn't serve any purpose – then you needn't even know the date and time.'

'I wouldn't want to know that, I'd think of nothing else, I'd . . . Do I have to tell Mum and Derek?'

'They ought to know, but if you'd prefer it, I can go and see them and explain.'

'No. It ought not to be a policeman. They wouldn't want . . . sorry, I'm sorry.'

'Please don't be. I understand everything you're saying, I really do.'

'Where will he go?'

'Liam's body will be taken to the hospital mortuary and it will be examined by two pathologists – neither of them had anything to do with the original post-mortem, though one is from the same hospital. This has to be got right and it will be. If Liam didn't die of an overdose, or if he did but the drug was not self-administered but injected by another person, then they will find that out.'

'Then what? What if the first report was right all along? It could be, that's what everyone said, it's what you said, Mr Serrailler.'

'I did and if that turns out to be the truth, then our investigations will be at an end and you and your family will have closure, which is what you deserve, and Liam can rest in peace. But if there was something else, then we need to find out what, and if it involves another person we will find them.'

Listen to me, Simon had thought, listen to the patter, I could be standing in front of cameras reading from a prepared statement in the usual robotic manner, as if it didn't really involve or concern me. I'm turning into a cop who sounds like cops sound and says what they say and who switches off at the end of the day. I tell my sister it's what she should do and a lot of the time, when things are routine, she can and does, but at other times, she can't, she takes it home with her and carries it about with her because she cares for people, not patients. It's why she was never going to fit into being a manager or a team leader.

142

She made a good fist at it but she wasn't happy or fulfilled and now she is. And it takes it out of her, always has. Can I say that?

'Mr Serrailler?'

He had come to.

'Can I make you a hot drink? It's such a bitter winter we're having, my kettle's barely off. Coffee?'

He'd glanced at his watch. He ought to go back to the station but there was no urgency.

'I'd like that. I didn't have my usual top-up this morning. Strong black, no sugar please.'

She'd seemed pleased. She wanted to go on talking about her brother because it was what people did, it helped them. He was a detective chief superintendent acting as family liaison officer, for the first time in many years. Too many. It ought to be a permanent part of the job, a skill they never forgot.

Someone tapped him on the arm and when he looked up he saw that the Chief was moving forward to join the forensic team and the undertakers. Cold as the grave. It carried real meaning. The opaque white sides of the tent let in the morning light. The sun would be up in half an hour but the temperature was minus five.

The grave had been opened, the earth piled on either side by the digger, handled as carefully, accurately, as if the bucket were a teaspoon. But it was man not machine power that took over now, six feet below the ground they stood on, securing the coffin to be lifted up, as respectfully as it had been lowered so recently into its resting place. Later, it would be returned there, in the same way and with the same respect.

At ten minutes to ten, Serrailler was sitting alone in the coffee shop with his double espresso and a pile of cinnamon pancakes, attending to his hunger and thirst but struggling to get warm, though the place was small and there was already a fug inside and steam on the windows.

He had felt no particular emotion during the exhumation, other than a renewed determination to get to the truth about Liam Payne's death quickly. He was glad the family had not been there. It was not a scene they could have borne easily, nor ever have erased from their minds.

He gestured for more coffee and pancakes. Drugs. Damn drugs. He had changed his mind about almost everything to do with them in the past couple of years, as they had moved from being a peripheral nuisance to a dark presence lurking behind everything, and most of all the vulnerable young. Drugs had been common when he was in the Met, but he had rarely encountered them when he had first come to Lafferton. That had been before the men at the top had realised the cities were becoming saturated – too many dealers, too little profit – so they'd worked out ways of spreading it. If the big cities, why not the smaller ones, then the market towns, and even the villages that had been growing, new estates everywhere, for the last five years? Plenty of scope there to recruit some new users. But where were the pushers to come from? If you hung about in underpasses or up alleys or in shopping streets after dark in a big city, you were never noticed, and anyway, you could get away and vanish PDQ. Not so easy in a smaller town, or a prosperous suburb. Pushers would stand out a mile. So, switch to phones. Then someone came up with a bright idea. They thought of it as recruitment – target locals, and so as to be another step away, target young ones. Teenagers. Even younger? Why not? It was cheaper too. Pushers and dealers were getting greedy, wanting a bigger slice of the profits – kids wouldn't have a clue. Give them a new Nintendo and a couple of games and they'd be happy. Serrailler had watched it all escalate. He had always treated drugs ops as a bit of a diversion, certainly a waste of resources, achieving little. Not any more. The picture of the young man's body lying on the bare boards of a bleak, empty flat would be with him, along with all those other images from his police years, because nothing went away – it might fade but it was there somewhere, ready to leap out at him without warning, at some faint reminder, another incident, or else for no apparent reason at all. When he had been in hospital after losing his arm, he had had nightmares and hallucinations in which too many sights and scenes rose to the surface of his mind and bobbed about, scummy and horrible. Bodies. Faces. Mutilations. Blood. Guts spilled onto pavements, eyes going dead in agonised faces, gunshots, screams, running footsteps, the screech of tyres, women wailing in grief, men crying silently, children too traumatised to cry. The stench of burning flesh. They would always be there, the pictures, the sounds, they were there now, as he poured maple syrup onto his pancakes and topped it with a sprinkle of cinnamon.

Kieron had gone straight from the cemetery to London for an ACPO conference, his left leg carefully propped up on the back seat, a stream of files to read on his iPad in advance of the day's meetings. Simon would send him the post-mortem results as soon as they came in. What they might reveal, anything new or nothing, he had no hunch about, he only knew what he was hoping for.

The door opened, pushing in a blast of freezing air, and in the moment, he was reminded not of any terrible scene from the past, not of what he had witnessed earlier that morning, but of sitting at the table adjacent to the one he occupied now, with Rachel. His sense of her was immediate and vivid, so much so that he glanced up, half expecting her to be there, sternly but at the same time amusedly reminding him not to dash across roads in front of oncoming traffic, holding her coffee cup in both hands, looking at him over the rim, with an expression he could not read. She had been friendly enough, there was certainly no embarrassment, but there was no warmth either. She could have been Cat, or another plain-clothes cop, an old friend, anyone but a woman who had been his lover. There was no flicker of that awareness, no nostalgia, nothing remotely intimate in her voice, her gestures, her expression. Her eyes.

He had finished his coffee and wondered whether to wire himself up with a third, but his phone started to buzz. The day had begun once already but now it seemed to be doing so all over again.

Thirty-One

Lionel Brown was in a side ward which was made for four patients but held six, beds too close together so that Cat could scarcely get between the last two. She had expected the curtains to be drawn round him. He was turned to face the wall, his eyes closed and he looked not to have been attended to that morning. She managed to wedge herself onto a stool pushed up to the bed. On his right, an old man was propped against a back rest but he had slumped over with his pillows sideways on, though he seemed not to be aware of anything. Opposite, another old man, and then two much younger patients, who spoke intermittently to each other, then stared out of the window onto the buildings opposite. A trolley was by the entrance, trays containing half-eaten breakfasts slotted into it, a trolley that should have been cleared away a couple of hours ago and which was partly blocking the exit. Cat's instinct was to move it herself, out of the ward area altogether, to the lobby beside the lifts but she had come to see Lionel Brown not to be an extra pair of hands.

She touched his arm and his skin was dry, pale, papery. His nails needed cutting, his hair needed a trim, he was unkempt and not particularly clean.

He made small noises in his throat as he breathed shallow breaths, but otherwise there was nothing, no response to her touch or any apparent awareness of his surroundings.

'Are you a relative?'

146

The nurse was wearing Scholl sandals with wooden soles that clattered as she came in, clatter clatter, clack clack.

'No, I'm Dr Deerbon, Mr Brown's GP. Sister rang me to say he'd been asking for me.'

'Hmm. Not really visiting time, you know.'

'Is Sister about?'

'Why?'

Cat took a breath. 'I'd like to see her – she rang several times so she probably wants a word with me.'

'Right.'

The girl tweaked the end of the bedclothes, picked up Lionel Brown's chart, looked at it and put it back.

'Has he had a wash this morning? He could do with it, and really his bed ought to be made a bit more comfortable.'

'We're overloaded and understaffed, we haven't even got the meds round finished, never mind the laundry. You could do it.'

'Yes,' Cat said, 'but it is very much not my job. I tell you what – you do it, while I go and find Sister Odewe.'

The main ward was chaotic. Cat stepped round trolleys, avoided oncoming posses of doctors trailing medical students, waited until someone was wheeled round her and away, saw a group at the nurses' station, heads together staring at a computer screen, a drugs trolley standing beside the desk with the key dangling from the lock.

'I'm looking for Sister Odewe.'

Nobody looked up. Someone said, 'On her break.'

Someone else said, 'No, she's not. Who are you?'

'Sister Odewe?'

'I am and these are not visiting hours.'

'Dr Deerbon. I've –'

'Ah yes, Mr Brown. Have you seen him? He's on the way out, you know. He was asking for you half the night but he's sinking.'

'He really doesn't look very comfortable, he needs a wash and his bed making. He deserves some attention, however he is.'

'Have you seen what this ward is like? Fine for you GPs, you've all forgotten what it's like inside a hospital.' She was marching towards Lionel Brown's ward, not turning her head.

'I certainly have not and I know when a patient needs some attention.'

'Sister, can you –' She ignored the call and did not break stride. The breakfast trolley was still in the doorway.

'Now, Lionel, here's the lady you've been shouting for all this time. Let's sit you up and get you sorted.'

She bent over the bed and froze for a second, before whipping the curtains closed.

Lionel Brown had slumped to one side. His eyes were still closed and there was no longer the rasp of his breathing.

'Pity you didn't get here sooner,' the sister said.

Cat's car was in the visitors' car park but Sam had left a note. *Quick catch-up with the porters. Text when you're good to go x*

To angus.flynnCEO@bevhamgeneralhospitaltrust.co.uk
Cc karen.mayseyCNO@bevhamgeneralhospitaltrust.co.uk
From cat.deerbon@conciergemedical.co.uk

This morning I visited my patient, Mr Lionel Brown, on Fleming Ward. The ward sister had phoned to tell me that Mr Brown had been asking to see me and was in a poor way, so I visited him this morning as his doctor and his friend. He had no family living.

Mr Brown had not been attended to in any way this morning. He was in a very poor state and he died within ten minutes of my arriving. It was my impression that his death might not have been noticed for some time. The entire ward appeared to be in chaos, and every aspect of the daily routine needs attention. A drugs trolley had been left un-attended with the key visible. The general level of hygiene and orderliness was below standard.

This is an informal complaint but I would like to meet you to discuss this matter as soon as possible, otherwise I will be obliged to make an official complaint to the hospital board of trustees.

An auto reply pinged in telling her that the CEO was on leave and enquiries should be addressed to his deputy.

She told Sam that she was waiting, and by the time he appeared, four calls were lined up, scattered in four different areas of her patch. Sam turned out onto the road, only saying 'Fine' when asked about his reunion with the hospital porters. Work took over until well after four o'clock, they had only a quick stop to pick up drinks, fruit and chocolate, and no time to talk. The final call of the day was out to the Burleigh hotel where a well-known actress was staying while filming nearby, and had been taken ill with what she, the hotel manager and her assistant told Cat was a coronary thrombosis or a heart attack, but which Cat assessed quickly as a panic attack, much to the woman's displeasure. It took some considerable time to persuade them that the air ambulance was not required and leave her with a mild sedative and some breathing exercises to practise.

She went down the stairs from which she had a view of the bar area, and of Sam, this time sitting in a comfortable chair with a glass of Coke and ice, bowls of crisps and olives. He jumped up when he saw her.

'You'll say it's too early but I say you need a drink, Ma.'

'I'm not going to argue, a vodka and tonic please, and don't call me Ma.'

She leaned back in the armchair, took some of the deep breaths she had just prescribed and checked her messages, but there was nothing new and her working day was done. She handed over to Luke, filled him in on a couple of patients, and put her phone in the bottom of her bag.

Sam returned with her drink, settled into his own chair, and said, 'I'm not going back to midwifery school.'

Thirty-Two

'Simon?'

'Adam . . . hi. News for me?'

'I haven't written it up yet but I know you need this asap. Liam Payne. There looks to have been enough heroin in him to kill him twice over, even though he was a long-time user, so his tolerance would have been pretty high. That in itself doesn't tell us any more than we knew, except that Shenfield had estimated a lower dose. But the way the syringe was inserted, the way it was positioned when the body was found . . . we started asking a few questions. Tentative, mind you, but worth putting to you. This is a bit speculative but we tried a mock-up and for my money the stuff might have been injected with another, different syringe and into the opposite arm.'

'What?'

'The veins in both arms were in a poor state but those in the left arm were pretty much shot to pieces, he'd have had a job getting the needle to hold. They were a bit better in the right but there were clear signs of very recent needle penetration in there. Now it would be difficult to inject your right arm efficiently with a syringe held in your left unless you were left-handed.'

'He wasn't.'

'Certain?'

'It was one of the questions his sister answered.'

'Then maybe someone else injected him and possibly it was done elsewhere and he was brought to the flat and dumped there.'

'Someone shoved a needle in to make it look –'

'Self-inflicted, yes. But I know your guys found no indications of a body being dragged in.'

'Nothing. So the floor could have been cleaned – the staircase as well. Shit.'

'Listen, at the end of the day, I don't think I could put my name to a cast-iron conclusion. I can't say it is certain that Liam Payne did not inject himself with the overdose of heroin and overwhelmingly likely that someone else killed him. But the exhumation was justified because, in my opinion, there is room for reasonable doubt. Whether that's enough for you to start a murder investigation I can't say.'

'But meanwhile, there are more question marks over Shen-field's conclusions.'

'I'll type up my report – it has to be checked and signed by my colleague because of the circs so it won't be with you until very late tonight, maybe even tomorrow morning depending, but I'll do my best.'

'And no authorisation for reburial yet.'

'No.'

Which meant he would have to tell the family, though not until he had read Adam's full report and the Chief had gone over it in turn, then decided whether or not to open a new case. Adam Iliffe had raised suspicions, with a certain amount of . . . of what? Evidence? Simon doubted it. Suspicion was not proof. Opinion was not evidence.

It was a quiet morning. Most of CID were out on their own jobs, there was a planning meeting for uniform after news had come in from the underground network about a rave due to take place that Friday night, plus rumours of a demo somewhere in the force area, though what sort of demo and by whom and exactly where was unclear. The problem was always sorting out genuine info from false, and in the case of the rave, trying to second-guess whether it was really taking place at the site mentioned or if this was a deliberate red herring.

Simon picked up his pen and started jotting down thoughts about how he would proceed on the Liam Payne case in the

151

light of Adam's call. Nothing was obvious, nothing was new, everything was up for grabs, but so much was still vague and unconnected. There was only one way to tackle it – start over, pretend this was the morning he got the call to Starly and drove over there knowing nothing whatsoever except that a body had been found.

And then his phone rang.

'Guv, there's a man at the desk asking for you, well, not so much by name but wanting the bloke at the top, in his words.'

Serrailler had always taken his own particular view of such visitors, once the desk sergeant had gone through 'drunk, mad, dangerous' or simply 'elderly confused'. Most senior officers would rarely meet random visitors at the front desk, they would fob them off with someone down the line, or with the usual excuses about being out on a call, in a meeting, on the phone, not on duty. But Serrailler had had many a good lead from mystery visitors in the course of his career, and several of them had turned into valuable, long-term informers for the force. He had never discussed snouts with the Chief, though his prede-cessor had approved of them, believing that, properly handled, they could only be useful and that the police needed all the help they could get. Something made him doubt if Kieron took the same view.

'What's his name? No, don't tell me . . .'

'I've tried, guv, believe me I've tried, and I confess to you that I have totally failed.'

'I'm in bits. All right, Sarge, will you send him up with one of your finest, tallest, broadest, most silent men?'

'PC Welby's just coming through the door.'

'Perfect.'

He was not trying to intimidate the man, whoever he was, but a show of strength at the beginning sent the right message.

Ex-military. Security guard. Bouncer. Boxer? Not a man to be intimidated by PC Welby's six feet four in his socks. All the same, he was nervous, not sure of his surroundings, looking round cautiously, checking this and that, before eventually meeting Simon's eye.

'I'm Detective Chief Superintendent Serrailler, and I'm told you want to see me but otherwise I know nothing at all about you.'

'Is this . . . ?' He looked round again.

'Safe? Yes. Bugged? No. Are we on our own? Yes, except for my secretary and PC Welby next door, and whoever might be walking down the corridor. There's always someone. Sit down?'

He was bald, having shaved his head so often the hair had eventually abandoned hope. His was not an ugly face, nor a pretty one – dark brown eyes. Large ears. They always had large ears. Maybe it was a condition of employment in his trade, if some form of security was indeed his trade. He was still wary, still unsettled, but gradually he stopped sussing out the room and relaxed. A bit. There was something about him that Simon liked, though, as ever, he could not have explained why, any more than he could ever explain why he sometimes suspected, disliked, did not trust any particular individual.

'Can I get you anything? Tea, coffee – they're better here than from the machine.'

'I'm all right, thanks . . . You know, maybe this wasn't such a good idea.'

'Coming into a police station?'

'Look, I'm not here to confess anything – anything criminal, I mean.'

'Glad to hear it.'

He was silent. Serrailler waited a moment, then sat down in one of the two chairs in the middle of the room, not behind his desk.

'You don't have to give me your real name Invent one if you like.'

'Why would I do that?'

'People do, and if you prefer not to sit down, I'll stand up.'

A silence. The man was clearly uneasy.

'Listen, would you prefer it if we went for a walk?'

'Right. Yeah, that'd be better.'

'Still as cold out there?'

'Brass monkeys.'

*

153

Five minutes later, they were walking down the street in the direction of the industrial estate and the cemetery. No one was about, though the roads were busy.

'I'll make a guess. You're in trouble and someone's threatening you and you don't know what to do.'

'No. Well . . . not me. I've got four lads.'

'One of them then?'

'In a fashion. Yes. My name's Vince Roper. I mean, really.'

'Thanks.'

They reached the corner and turned down the long drag past the sheds and warehouses, garages and bays. A dozen firms had premises on this industrial estate and there was plenty of activity.

'Next left there's a cafe. That all right with you?'

Joe's Eaterie was empty apart from one man, reading the paper over a plate of beans on toast, and he did not look up. Serrailler got tea and flapjacks. The place was a functional provider of all-day breakfast, sandwiches and cakes from six in the morning to three in the afternoon. It was warm, cheerful and impressively clean.

'It's a bit of a story.'

'I'm listening.'

He listened for a long time, to the story of Vince's marriage to a violent narcissist, the divorce which gave him custody of his four sons, and his efforts to do as many jobs as possible to bring in enough money and keep an eye on them.

'I did long-distance lorry driving for a bit when she was there but I can't do that any more. Now it's the nightclub job and a bit of relief security but it doesn't pay. I'm always looking for something daytime.'

Vince put a small black phone on the table. The story of Brookie and the mobile came eventually and it was clear that the Chief had been right, the county lines dealers had infiltrated all corners of the force's area, and Starly was high on their list for several obvious reasons. That a boy as young as eleven was being groomed, with a new school bag and then a mobile, and was now being sent streams of messages, was shocking but true to their form – whoever they were.

'How often had this Fats guy given your son a lift home from school?'

'Two or three. He didn't seem to think it was anything to bother about, but he still made sure not to say much to his brothers.'

'They're not involved?'

'No. He'd have said. It's just Brooklyn. And it makes me bloody mad.'

They had more tea while Serrailler heard the story of the greyhound track and the man who might be the same Fats.

'I'm going down there on Wednesday'

'What's your plan – if you've got one?'

'Not got it completely worked out yet.'

Simon waited. A lot of talks with stray blokes like Vince Roper were spent waiting patiently, not pushing, not probing, waiting until they got it together and trusted him enough.

'I read in the paper about these county lines . . . what the Chief Constable said, the usual about anyone with information . . . only I didn't have . . . maybe I still don't and won't, but if I do . . . I could be useful, couldn't I?'

'Possibly.'

'I wouldn't do anything risky. I've got four lads, like I said, only it's funny what you hear when you hang about and I could do that.'

'Tell me.'

'Listen, I was never bothered what anyone got up to, I mean outside of my job . . . let them get on with it. Only this is different. They're having a go at my son, and how many other people's kids? That's what they are, not even teenagers, they're kids. I could bloody strangle him. No, sorry . . . I'm not like that, I wouldn't, only it's got to me, you see.'

He looked directly at Serrailler, who saw anger in the man's eyes but not the sort that worried him, this was different, there was a good reason for his fury.

'I don't suppose I was the best to live with, but I did as well as I could, I never left her in want of anything, but she's rotten, rotten to the core, I saw that pretty soon after Tommy and Connor were born, she wasn't a proper mother, she left them alone, went off, she never sees them now, isn't interested . . . how can you give birth to four kids and not be bothered with them? Never understood it. If she knew what this bloke was doing, trying to hook a kid of eleven into drugs, I'm not sure she'd give a toss. Well, I give one, I know what they do with them at that age, get them to carry stuff and deliver it, they reel them in with nice things, and then to make sure they stay, they threaten them with all sorts. I've read about it . . . only I never expected it to happen around here, I never dreamed one of mine . . .'

He slammed his fist on the table suddenly.

'Oh, don't worry, I've thrown a few out of clubs in my time, their feet didn't touch the ground till they hit the pavement, but that's my job. I'm not a violent man, and I've never lifted a hand to the boys. I don't need to. I've got a loud voice when I want to make them jump.'

He finished his tea.

'Sorry, I'd no business getting carried away. Sorry.'

'That's all right. But I wonder where I – the police – fit into all this, Vince? You don't really know anything yet. Anyway, this Fats is small fry and the small fry are no good to us, they never lead us to the big boys at the top because they don't even know those big boys, it's pointless bringing them in. That's why we stopped doing drugs ops, hanging about in underpasses, sweeping up the odd guy handing over gear on a street corner. It's a waste of time.'

'What I thought.'

'So what else did you think?'

'That I could hang about, get in with this Fats, or try to, hear things, get led to his mates, get trusted.'

'Start dealing?'

'Shit, no.'

'How else would they trust you?'

Vince looked deflated.

'I'm listening, don't worry, and possibly you can help us – and we need all the help we can get – but it's not straightforward, you know – get yourself in too deep and we can't necessarily pull you out.'

156

'Understood. Only I want them stopped as much as you do, Mr Serrailler, can't you see why?'

'I can. But this is a long game. It could take months. You're not going to be told the names and addresses of the godfathers the first day you meet up with Fats on the dog track.'

'What should I do for now?'

'Finish your tea.' Simon stood. 'I've got to get back and I need a contact number. Does anybody else have use of your phone?'

'Occasionally one of my boys.'

'Girlfriend?'

'I'm done with women.'

'If I get in touch it will be a text giving you a number to call and my initial. If you've heard nothing by this time next week there'll be nothing to hear. When we get outside, we take the opposite directions.'

'It's like the bloody movies.'

'No,' Serrailler said, walking out, 'actually, it bloody isn't.'

He walked into an almost empty CID room, with just one DS head down and typing furiously at what was probably a very late a report, and who did not even register the DCS's presence, and, at the far end, DC Fern Monroe, reading a printout. She looked up to meet Serrailler's eye.

'Ah . . . everybody else out?'

'I'm free, guv.'

'Well, you shouldn't be. Where's DC Sandhu?'

'No idea . . . out on something or other.'

'All right, have him find me when he's back.'

She caught up with him in the corridor. 'I just finished the arson report, I'm happy to mop up something else.'

'Thanks but it will be good research experience for Bilaval.' He went towards his office.

'Hold on a minute, Simon . . .'

He stiffened and took a step back.

'One minute you're taking me out dinner, then I'm not even good enough to do a piffling job for you. I realise this is a bit awkward, but –'

'I don't think so. Let's drop the subject now, shall we?'

He turned away quickly, loathing confrontation of this sort, as he always had, and as his sister had commented on enough times. But Cat knew nothing about Fern Monroe and never would.

A DC passed him. 'Sandhu – the very man.'

'I was –'

'Going off on job? The canteen?'

'What can I do for you, guv?'

'In here.' Serrailler closed his door.

'OK, before we start, I don't suppose in a million years you've came across someone called Vince Roper?'

'Don't think so. What's the context?'

'That's what you're going to find out. I've no reason to suppose he's got a criminal record but start there and if he has you can stop there, but otherwise whatever you can get.'

'Will do. How urgent is this?'

'You can get your coffee and doughnut, if that's what you mean.'

'Ah, there you are.' His secretary looked relieved.

'Sorry, Maggie, I should have let you know.'

'You should.'

'What's happened – something has, you've got that look.'

'A call for you from Lafferton Vets a few minutes ago.'

'It's my sister they want.'

'They can't get hold of her and it's urgent apparently. I said to try your mobile.'

'Oh God. Right, I'll –' His phone rang. 'Serrailler.'

'Michael Farmer, at Lafferton Vets. I've been trying to get hold of your sister but it's always voicemail. I'm sorry to disturb you but I need permission to operate on her Yorkshire terrier again.'

'Can I give that?'

'She has you down as next to contact.'

Simon sighed. 'Right. What's up?'

He listened to a long description of Wookie's state, which had worsened.

'If I don't do this now he won't survive, the infection from the rat bites has got a grip and I need to cut out some tissue. He's on intravenous antibiotics but it's not enough.'

'Operate, it's what my sister would say, she loves that little mutt – everyone does. Even me.'

'Thanks. If you get to speak to her first would you tell her and I'll call her with an update later? Do you know when she might be available?'

'Not a clue but I'll keep trying her as well.'

He stood up. His back had been painful all day. He lay on the floor and drew up his knees, rolled carefully to one side, paused, then the other, following up with the other exercises he had been taught years ago. He should do them daily but when he was out of pain he skipped them, and cursed when he paid the price. He had been warned by the physios when his arm was amputated that once the first week or ten days was over he should not let himself depend on painkillers, but take them very occasionally if he was having a particularly tough day, and he had been religious about following the advice. It was the same with his back pain, though to get him through some long and exhausting days he kept a small supply of co-codamol about him. He was nowhere near that point now.

He had a long weekend's leave coming up, though late winter was not a great prospect for a relaxing break and it was not long enough to get away to guaranteed sunshine, but just to be away from the office, the job, everything and everyone, would help. It was a depleting time of year and the icy weather didn't help. Everybody was burning on a short fuse, impatient and irritable about nothing very much.

He opened up his laptop and went to recent messages but it did not take long to gather the general situation – nothing urgent, no new major incidents. If things would just stay that way until the following week, he had his leave in the bag.

Thirty-Three

Greta Tonks started work as soon as Olivia had left for school, had a short coffee break and half an hour for lunch, then continued until Liv got home around five, though if something urgent had come in she might go on until six. There was no shortage, a good legal secretary and typist would always be in demand, and she enjoyed the plain, meticulous prose she had to copy up.

This week she had taken half a day out, to have her check with the GP – more a formality than anything now, as it was eight years since her breast cancer and he had told her that she could make the checks every two years from now on, all was well. But the relief was always huge and she walked on air back to her car. It was only ten past three. She would go into town to buy her sister's birthday present and a new wallet for herself – her present one, which Jeff had given her a very long time ago, was falling apart.

After that, a cup of tea and a scone, a quick call into the book-shop to collect her order, and home around the same time as Liv, who had her own key, but going into an empty house was a bleak thing at the end of a long school day, and Greta had always tried not to let it happen.

It was still very cold but the sleet and dark clouds had given way to a brilliant blue sky. Her relief at coming through the latest health check uplifted her spirits so much that she spent more than she had meant to on Nadine's present and splashed out on a red Italian leather wallet for herself, larger than her old one with more sections. She also bought Olivia a small yellow rucksack, and a copy of a Maya Angelou novel, when she picked up her own book. In the tea shop in the Lanes she decided on a thickly buttered teacake with her Earl Grey and bought a ginger slice to take home.

Drinking her tea and looking out on the street, it occurred to her that not only had she enjoyed every minute of her afternoon but that she had not felt any need for company, certainly not that of her ex-husband, who hated shopping, hated tea shops, hated what he would have regarded as time-wasting. The thought of how much of his time was going to be eaten by a young wife who would probably love spending his money, and twin boys who would gobble up even more of it for the next twenty years, was a pleasing one.

The front of the house was dark when she got home, which meant that Liv would be in her room at the back. The porch light came on so that she could see to get her key and unlock the door before it snapped off again as she moved inside.

She set down her shopping and switched on the hall light.

'I'm back, Liv. Come on down and see what I've got you.'

There was something about the silence.

'Olivia!'

And then.

Greta's hand went to her face. She was cold. Hot. Cold. Wanted to faint but did not, to run but could not. Scream. Cry out. Vomit. She could do nothing but stand completely still.

But there was a sound, odd, like no sound she had ever heard, surely coming from the hanging body of her daughter, suspended from a rope tied to the banister above. Greta could not go closer but she strained to hear it, the ugly, peculiar sound of life. But it did not come again.

And then she backed out of the door, stopped in the middle of the dark pathway, and began to scream.

Thirty-Four

'Vincent Paul Roper, guv. Squeaky clean, not so much as a minor traffic offence. Employment record clean . . . was in the army, then done all sorts of security jobs, bit of long-distance lorry driving, been a bouncer for six years. Good council tenant. His ex walked out, lived in several places with several blokes, social services were involved with her when she looked after the kids but didn't, as you might say. No probs since he had custody.'

'Mates?'

'A few – mainly from work, a couple from army days but it's just the occasional meet-up in a pub. One time he and an ex-squaddie and his missus took all their kids to a holiday camp – seven lads but no probs there, which is hardly credible but there you go.'

'All looks good. Thanks for getting that done in quick time.'

It was looking good. Vince Roper wanted to be a snout and Serrailler had often mistrusted the breed because of their motives, though he was not too worried if that was chiefly money. Trouble came when it was, as so often, about revenge, wanting to pay someone back, get even, which was understandable but it meant the snout was harder to control, to keep walking the line marked out for him, not veer off onto one of his own.

But if he'd been speaking the truth, Roper's motive was good, and though some desire for revenge was in the mix, it was straightforward – he wanted the man who was trying to groom his young son and rope him into being part of the drug scene,

162

a lowly postboy carrying gear from A and delivering it to B. How many kids like him were now in their clutches? If Roper could infiltrate even a single section of the organisation and pass on some sound information, he was going to be worth signing up and nurturing.

The Chief, with several of his opposite numbers from adjacent forces, was planning a conference for senior officers, in both uniform and CID, on coming up with new strategies for getting on top of it all. Simon thought privately that such meetings often produced a lot of hot air, a cluster of hopeless suggestions, and maybe a couple that had legs. He would attend, of course, he had to, but his faith in the old-fashioned method of handling a good snout was resolute, because he had found them too useful too often to believe that they might become obsolete.

If Vince Roper was on his mind, Roper led back to Starly, and the reopened inquiry into the death of Liam Payne. He needed to look at the scene again from the fresh perspective the second post-mortem had given him. It was now possible someone had been with Liam and either injected the overdose of heroin there or done so elsewhere and then taken his body to the flat – which seemed to Simon, as he brooded on it while getting ready to leave, an unlikely scenario. It was half past four, so he should get to the Chinese pharmacy while it was open.

On the outskirts of Starly he was overtaken by an ambulance on blues and twos, a paramedic car driving very fast, and a police car, all of which were causing a backup of traffic. If it was an RTA the road would be closed and he would have to take the diversion which wound round the country lanes to get into the village from the far end, but after half a mile it was clear and he entered the square without a hold-up, parked in the side road and walked down to the shop. The pavements were no longer icy but the gutters were still rutted with dirty frozen snow, and as he stepped over it, Simon felt suddenly weary of this winter, of cold and sleet and skies like the inside of an aluminium saucepan. He longed for warmth on his face and the smell of the first spring flowers. Greece? Could he get out there, even just for a long weekend? He hesitated outside the chemist's, basking in a bubble of sunshine and clear turquoise sea, before opening the shop door. The pharmacist had his back turned and spun round, startled when he heard the bell – more startled than he ought to be at the arrival of just another customer.

'Good afternoon, Mr Wang.'

The man was trying to compose himself, smiling a brief, stiff little smile which came only from his mouth while his eyes were wide with alarm.

'Detective Chief Superintendent –'

'Yes. Yes, I know, I remember, and what do you want? There has been no trouble, no problem at all with anything since the . . . the very sad event of the young man in the flat . . . everything is all back to normal now. I am going to close soon, I have to get home.'

'There's nothing to be alarmed about, Mr Wang, I just need to give you an update. Maybe you can close the shop now and we can talk without risk of being interrupted?'

'But it is not exactly closing time and a late customer may come in at any minute.'

'I think we'll risk that.'

Serrailler went to the door, dropped the latch and turned the sign to Closed.

'Is there somewhere we can go to talk? I think you have a back room.'

Wang sighed. 'We can go into the office.'

'This is all very orderly, Mr Wang,' Simon said as he looked around the tidy room.

'It has to be. My storeroom is too . . . would you like to see? Just here.'

He had changed from a frightened man into one full of pride in his work, who, as he relaxed, would be far easier to interview, though this was one of the times when Simon preferred 'talk to'.

'I'm interested . . . you have a very wide range of medicines. All they all herbal?'

'In the widest sense, yes. Apart from whether we would wish to use them, we would not be allowed to give any conventional prescription medicines.'

'Do you give treatments here? Acupuncture and so on?'

'No. I am not qualified but I have a colleague I refer people to if they wish. Why, is this something you need? He is the best, very highly trained.'

'No, but I have heard good reports of it so I'm glad to know where to come. Do you have many customers?'

'This varies every day of course. It is quiet now, busy in the mornings, and the bad weather doesn't encourage people to go out. They come if they need anything. I have many regular customers. They recommend.'

'So business is good?'

'It is certainly not bad. I would always welcome more of course because I like to provide a service to people who have had no help elsewhere, to see that I can make them improve . . . not always of course, I know my limits. I would never hesitate to refer to a doctor. But I am quite happy with business. Why do you ask?'

'Do you come into contact with illegal drugs, Mr Wang?'

The man's expression changed, tightened, he became cautious in a second.

'What drugs do you mean? Everything I use is licensed, perfectly legal.'

'Heroin? Cocaine? Hallucinogenic drugs?'

'No, no. Of course I would never give these or stock them. These are very dangerous, these ruin lives. No Chinese pharmacist would have anything to do with any of them. The young man who died upstairs – please, I have nothing to do with this, I did not know him, but it was shocking that he found this place and overdosed himself here. It is not my flat, I do not own it, it has –'

'I know. Don't worry, that was all checked out. You rent this shop only.'

'Yes, yes. Mr . . .'

'Serrailler. '

'So why have you come here again?'

'I need to ask you one or two more things.'

'What has happened? I thought it was all decided, case done. I was told so.'

'There is new evidence that suggests Liam Payne didn't self-administer the overdose, it might have been injected by another person, and probably it was not done in the flat but somewhere else – we don't yet know where – after which the body was brought here, either already dead or dying – again, we aren't yet sure. So it must be obvious that there were at least two people in the flat . . . and dragging a body across bare boards, or dumping it down onto them, would have caused a certain amount of noise, the sound of footsteps, bumping about, movements up and down the stairs.'

'This is not something I ever heard. And it would not be my business – when people rent a place, they do what they wish. But I did not hear anything, at any time.'

'Cars parked?'

'I can't see the side road from in here, people could come and go, I would not know – as I have said, this has nothing to do with me. Now, I have to go home, I am sorry, I can't be of more help to you.'

'Do customers have access to this store? The office?'

'Of course not. That would be quite wrong, the drugs I keep are not sweets and chocolate, Mr . . .'

'Serrailler. So you are the only person who ever comes in this area behind the counter?'

The flicker of alarm, the worried eyes.

'Yes.'

'What about deliveries?'

'They bring into the shop, I sign, I bring them here.'

'Have you ever been burgled, Mr Wang?'

'What is this? Why are you questioning me as if I am in some court of law? I have answered everything, I know nothing. Please leave now.'

'Yes. Thank you for your patience. One thing, Mr Wang – if you do hear anything from the flat from now on, it's very important that you let us know. The landlord can't let it at present until it ceases to be a crime scene, so there should be no one up there at all except forensics teams and the police, and we will always let you know we're there. If we haven't and you hear anything, or see anyone, please call the station immediately, on this number, or call me direct. It's very important.'

'Yes. Now please –'

'And if anyone comes into the shop, and you're worried for any reason at all, then ring us about that too. If they start asking odd questions or it just doesn't feel right, we must know.'

'I will do that but I am sure there will be nothing. Now please . . .'

Serrailler left.

Thirty-Five

Kevin Astley jumped up from his desk and ran out of the house when the screaming began, so loud and anguished, like the howling of a trapped animal. Greta Tonks was standing in the path, her front door wide open, and when Kevin appeared she only managed to point, but not to stop the noise that seemed to be issuing from her with a force all its own.

Later, he did not remember exactly what he had done, or how, let alone how he had known to do it. He had raced into the house, seen Olivia's hanging body, shouted 'I need something to cut with' and held her, taken her weight, until Greta grasped what he was saying and needed and brought a carving knife.

After cutting the rope, he laid her on the floor, saw that her chest was not rising and falling with any breath, but that there was the movement of a pulse in her neck, and then he heard urgent words, phrases, people talking to him in his head, saying things he remembered from films and television, a confusion of voices. 'Chest compression.' 'Mouth-to-mouth.' Raise her head.' 'Don't raise her head.' 'Lift her legs.' 'One hand over the other and One-two-three-four . . .' Hours passed and nanoseconds, during which he was following the instructions one after another even though he thought that he was paralysed, was pumping, pressing, listening, trying again, and then the sirens and footsteps running down the path. Greta Tonks was no longer screaming, just standing, chalk white and speechless, her hand jerking towards Olivia on the floor, Kevin Astley on his knees beside her.

'You cut her down?'

'It was just instinctive, it seemed like the right thing to do but maybe . . .'

'It was. I'll take over now, thanks. What's her name?'

After watching the paramedics work together, saying little, Kevin got up, meaning to leave, feeling suddenly shaky, needing fresh air, but Greta was in his way, and looked at him in desperation, panic, and also bewilderment, as if she could not make out what had happened, and who these people were, what they were doing to Liv and why she was lying on the floor.

'They'll take her to hospital as fast as they can.' He touched Greta's arm. 'You'll need to go with her, you can leave me to lock up and I'll keep an eye on the house. Can I get you anything now? Would you like a glass of water? I've got some brandy, I could –'

'Jeff,' she said, as if coming out of a deep trance. 'I have to tell Jeff. I don't know . . .'

He led her to the hall chair, sat her down, found her phone, her husband's number, rang it. Greta was trembling violently.

'I'll hold it, you just talk to him.'

'Jeff . . . you have to come, now, Liv tried to hang herself, the ambulance is here, just get here.'

Kevin heard the terrible silence at the other end as the man tried to take in what he had been told, a man he didn't know – Greta's husband had moved out a month before they had arrived next door. She thrust the phone away from her and was getting up.

'Hello . . . Greta? Greta, I don't understand.'

Kevin took the phone, gave his name.

'Your daughter was hanging from the banister. I cut her down and they're working on her now, they're putting tubes in . . . I think she's still alive. I don't know any more. I'm sorry, I can't answer any of your questions but you should come as soon as you can.'

They had put a tube down Olivia's throat, were listening to her heart, taking her pulse. One said, 'Abnormal posturing.' The other nodded. 'GCS low.'

Greta stood staring down at her daughter, lying oddly on the hall rug, wires and tubes, already attached to her. One of them lifted her eyelid briefly and shone a torch.

'What's happening? She's unconscious but she's going to be all right, isn't she, she's going to live, once she gets to the hospital they'll make sure she's all right, and you got here in time?'

'We're doing everything we possibly can for her and the HEMS team are on their way – that's the air ambulance, they'll have a specialist emergency doctor on board. Best if you sit down, you're quite pale. I'll look at you in a second.'

'Let me get you some water – or some brandy, I've got brandy in the house,' Kevin Astley said again. Greta shook her head and went on shaking it but he fetched a glass of water from her kitchen and held it while she drank.

'Jeff should come, Jeff should be here.'

'He will. I told him what was happening.'

'It's his daughter and she won't dare to stop him, she has no right. Olivia comes first, we come first.'

She burst into sudden harsh sobs that came from her throat, as if they had been forced up by something deep down within her.

Kevin felt helpless, frightened, repulsed, he wanted to run out of the house and back into his own, back to his work, back to the normal place he had been in ten or fifteen or how many minutes ago, but he stayed because he was too embarrassed to leave, and perhaps his presence was useful in some way. He had done one thing right, he had held the girl, taken her weight, he remembered the feel of her, so light and thin, and cut the rope and laid her down. He had done that.

A helicopter was near, and then the noise of the engine and the rotating blades were right overhead and descending, to land on the green in the middle of the horseshoe of houses, lights brilliant, and seconds later, the sound of people running, running, running.

Thirty-Six

Cat leaned over and stroked the dog's head gently but he was too deeply asleep to respond, full of anaesthetic and painkillers after a long operation.

He seemed even smaller now, his body was bone and fur with so little flesh to be felt.

'Goodness knows what happened out there,' the vet said, 'and I guess we'll never know, he's had a tough time, been through a couple of wars, but I'm happier about him than I was.'

'You think he's going to pull through?'

'There's some hope, whereas yesterday I didn't hold out any at all, I was weighing up whether to suggest that we let him go, but something about him just tipped the balance, maybe something in the look he gave me. He's a tough little dog and it didn't seem to me as if he was wanting to give up, so it was worth a go. I'll keep him in, not sure yet for how long, and we're monitoring him all the time, but the signs are pointing the right way.'

Through the usual tiredness at the end of a packed day, Cat felt a rush of energy and optimism, as Wookie's heart beat strongly under her hand and he gave a small snuffle.

A nurse put her head round the door. 'Dr Deerbon's son is in reception – he wants to know if he can come in and see Wookie.'

But Sam wasn't waiting for a reply, he was in the room.

'It's good for him to hear another voice he knows.'

Sam stroked the dog's head, then bent and spoke in his ear. 'You're doing fine, Wookster, you're winning. Hang on in there.'

In the car, Cat looked at her messages, replying to one or two. Sam had tears in his eyes and he needed to wipe them away while she was occupied, though he had never been ashamed of being a boy who cried readily.

'Home,' Cat said eventually. 'Nothing else today. Thanks for chauffeuring again, Sambo.' She did turn to him then. 'How long are you staying, by the way – because you might find yourself with a permanent job. I quite like driving but this makes a big difference to my working day when the weather is foul and I'm stressed.'

Sam started the car. 'Wookie's going to be fine,' he said, 'I could tell. Is K in tonight?'

'Not till very late and Felix is at the Dills'. We repay the favour by having Marcus on Friday for *Super Mario*.'

'Good.'

'We could pick up fish and chips if you like? And you can tell me about your decision to leave midwifery. They'll keep hot if you put your foot down.'

'Is that a challenge?'

Thirty-Seven

So, where next? He had pulled into the side of the lane for a car coming the other way, and sat on, trying to decide. Home? But he felt the need to talk – about what though? Whether he should have a long weekend away? Where he might go? Who with?

He wanted to talk about the state of things, his strange sense of being rudderless and slightly adrift, of his life having no focus. It was not unhappiness, frustration or even boredom though there was a kind of staleness. Maybe he needed to consider moving to another force, larger, more challenging. But he had come from all that, and besides, although Lafferton had its quiet spells those were becoming fewer and now his job was as big as he wanted. The Met had been an exciting place for a rookie PC and then for one climbing the first rungs of the CID ladder, but he had no wish to return. London was a young man's game, unless you wanted to gain top rank and be stuck at a desk.

Perhaps it was the flat. Perhaps he had spent long enough living in Cathedral Close in the centre of Lafferton. Perhaps, as he had occasionally fantasised, he was ready to move right out of the town, into a cottage in one of the surrounding villages which had not yet been spoilt by developers. There were still a few of those left, if you knew where to look.

An ambulance went past, but not in a hurry, no lights or sirens.

His restlessness had even affected his drawing, and the books he read. He had finished the series of sketches, of the gargoyles in the cathedral roof, which had taken him eighteen months, they had been framed and put on display in the crypt, and now were being reproduced in a book, together with a commentary, though goodness knows how long that would take to be ready. Since then, though, he had done little, and been nowhere very interesting from an artist's point of view. At times when he was particularly busy, he usually read a classic novel or a biography, followed by something contemporary, interspersed by a favourite P. G. Wodehouse if he was especially tired at the end of the day. Now, he was halfway through rereading both *Bleak House* and Martin Amis's *London Fields*, but they sat about the flat with markers stuck between their pages, and when he picked them up, he often lost focus after half an hour. He did not altogether know himself.

A sudden wind had got up, rain was lashing the windscreen, and as ever when he felt like this, he turned in the direction of the farmhouse, knowing he was likely to find someone, if not everyone, at home, a drink and food and talk.

Kieron's car was not in the drive, and when he was out Cat always kept the doors locked, but as Simon had a key, he let himself in, calling out from the hall, although she would have heard his car. No one responded but there were voices in the kitchen.

The remains of a fish and chip supper were on the table, Sam had his head down, his mother was sitting beside him, and when she looked up at her brother, he saw that he had interrupted something serious.

'No,' Cat said, seeing his face, 'it's fine. Sorry, there's no supper left but you can make yourself something.'

She got up and started to clear away. Sam had not moved.

'Good news about Wookie, by the way – all being well he can come home in a couple of days. He's extremely lucky.'

'Great. As I came in it seemed very strange not to have a whirling dervish round my heels and no cat either. Can I get you a drink?'

'I'd like a coffee but have what you want.'

Simon looked at his nephew but Cat frowned and shook her head.

'What have you been up to?'

'Starly . . . the Chinese pharmacist. There's something but I don't know what, I can't put my finger on it. I don't think he's up to anything but he knows something, or –'

Sam got up, averting his head as he said, 'I'm going to have a shower. Hi, Si.'

'Hi back. You OK?' But his nephew was gone.

Simon turned on the coffee maker.

'Shall I get a mug for Sambo?'

Cat shrugged.

They sat without speaking, Cat leaning her head back in the chair, eyes closed. Simon thought she looked exhausted. She seemed to have taken a lurch forward into middle age Did she look at him and think the same? Perhaps this was why he had been feeling itchy. Age. Just age.

'If that was private, between you two, just say.'

Cat sighed and looked at him over her coffee. 'No, he might easily have told either of us – maybe you more than me actually.'

'Kieron?'

'No. They're fine but – no. Are you staying?'

'No, I've got to do early stuff. Besides . . .'

'Social call?'

'Not entirely, but I'm not going to join the line of those wishing to unburden themselves. Well – maybe one thing. I was half wondering about moving.'

'What, from the Lafferton force?'

'Not the job, no – just, you know, from a top floor in the middle of town to somewhere with a bit of space – garden, something that's mine.'

'I can't see you anywhere but in that beautiful calm white space. I can't see you in a cottage with beams and an inglenook.'

'Who said anything about all that? But yes, I might like a cottage, not too far out, but quiet. Country.'

'Like here.'

'Smaller.'

'Why?'

Why? He couldn't give her a sensible answer.

'Just . . . you know.'

'Not really. Makes sense to buy a property instead of renting the apartment for the rest of your life of course, but financial prudence is not why you're thinking about it.'

'Didn't cross my mind.'

'Money's never motivated you, has it? I mean, you like enough to keep your life comfortable but that's it.'

'I rarely think about it. Is that irresponsible?'

'No idea. Si – is this just about bricks and mortar and a patch of land?'

'Seems to be.'

She knew better than to press him.

'Is Sammy OK?'

'Not altogether. Bit of a life crisis – crossroads, whatever. I don't want him to hear.'

Simon opened the door into the hall and listened. From above, the sound of rushing water and loud music.

'If he wants you to know, he'll tell you himself, but essentially, Rosie's behaving badly and midwifery isn't for him.'

'So what is?'

'No idea. He hasn't either.'

'Do you mind? Are you worried?'

'No. Better to find out now. He'll get there – not everyone finds the right career straight away, as you should know . . . but he will, he works hard at whatever it is, he just needs to relax about it.'

'I thought he and Rosie were all good. I like her.'

'I do too – or I did, but not if what Sam tells me is true. My view in this sort of situation is that you either stay or go, you don't mess about.'

'With someone else?'

'He thinks so.'

'But he hasn't been around.'

'No, but there's always a kind friend thinking you ought to know . . .'

'He needs to make sure.'

'Yes, but he's only twenty, Simon, and how were you at twenty? How was I?'

'You? In your second year at med school having just met Chris.'

'Yes, well, I'm not representative. I'm going to watch the news.'

'More murder and mayhem.'

'You don't have to watch.'

But rather than hang about in the kitchen looking as if he was trying to corner Sam when he re-emerged, he went into the den.

'You see?' he said after three minutes.

'Wait for the local news, it can be quite soothing.'

'A fourteen-year-old Starly schoolgirl has been taken to Bevham General Hospital by air ambulance, after she was found by her mother unconscious and unresponsive at her home earlier today. She is said to be in a critical condition. Her identity and any further details have not been released.'

Serrailler felt the split second of something like an electrical charge go through him that he always received when hearing a piece of news which was or soon would be relevant to him.

'Unconscious and unresponsive?' he said.

Cat shook her head. 'Could be anything – an accident, fallen downstairs? Doesn't sound criminal.'

'Starly. I get bad vibes.'

'The junkie, the Chinese herbalist?'

'Thin end of the wedge. Much nastier things are going on in and around Starly, which is why this newsflash came with a red alert.'

'Can you find out?'

'I have a horrible feeling I'm going to.' He got up. 'Have you thought any more of what I said about me moving?'

'Well, I've hardly had time or headspace. I didn't know my thoughts were urgent.'

Her brother shrugged and went out into the kitchen. He wasn't going to wait for them to call him.

He hadn't expected to get much more detail beyond the girl's name and address.

'Is it one for us?'

'Don't know at this stage, guv, but probably not. Looks like a suicide. Parents are at the hospital.'

'Can you try and get a report from the HEMS? We need to be told now if they think there's anything for us.'

'Will do. I'll call you. Do you want a bod posted at the house? Nobody's there at the moment, but apparently a neighbour is keeping an eye.'

'Have we got someone at the hospital just in case?'

'We had but she's had to leave, it's kicked off big time at the Moon Cat Club, they called for all the backup we can send.'

Thirty-Eight

The emergency area to which Olivia had first been taken was out of bounds to them, once they had seen her briefly and been allowed to kiss her forehead, and the space was already crowded with a frightening number of people, each doing a separate job while working as a team, a consultant calling out instructions among trolleys, wires, poles on wheels, instruments, dials, machines beeping and blinking.

To Greta every word was in a foreign language and the sounds made a terrible, tuneless music.

'I'm sorry, I have to ask you to leave here now but someone will show you to the relatives' room.'

Instead, they stood outside in the corridor under the fluorescent lights that drained their faces of all colour and people went quickly past on screeching shoes and then other people, going the other way, and no one noticed them, so that after a few minutes Greta knew that she was invisible, she was not here, not in a hospital corridor, because what she had seen she had not seen and what had happened had not happened. Nothing had happened, there had been no opening of the front door, no seeing a body suspended, the body of Olivia, her daughter, and no screams, no cries, no neighbour, no blue lights, sirens, people in green carrying huge nylon bags, no deafening helicopter right overhead. No phone call to Jeff nor a terrible, unimaginable, lifting, swaying, swooping journey across the sky, no nausea, no weird sensation of landing on the ground and, after that, no

179

Olivia with a mask over her face and pads and wires and tubes attached to her slight body. None of it. Nothing. There had been nothing.

A man walked past quickly, pushing a trolley and tutted them out of the way.

'I'll go and find someone. Or should we just look for this room? I don't know.'

Jeff did not move.

'What should we do?'

'Mr and Mrs Tonks, will you follow me? So sorry.'

They did not know how to sit as Mr and Mrs Tonks, not having spoken to one another in any civil way, for two years. Together and not together. They were both.

In the end, they sat with one chair separating them. The chairs were orange and bright blue. There was a pot plant that needed water. Water was in a dispenser. Water to drink. Greta wanted to give some to the wilting plant but did not dare and anyway could not move. She felt desperately sorry for the plant. The plant was suffering.

Life went on noisily in the corridor outside. Olivia was alive. She had not looked alive at any point but they had told her that she was alive.

'What does it mean? Alive?'

Jeff stared at her.

Someone opened the door but did not come into the room, backed away.

'What were you doing? When I rang you, no, I didn't ring you, it was Kevin who rang. What were you doing?'

He stared at her again. Greta wondered if her voice was not emerging from her as a voice, as if she knew what she wanted to say and had said it, but in some way had not.

'When I told you. What were you doing?'

'Holding Noah. Or Isaac. I don't remember.'

'I heard crying.'

'Yes.'

'Do they cry a lot? Olivia never cried.'

'She cried.'

'Not very much.'

'Was there anything at all, Greta, something written down or a message on the answering machine? She must have left something. Did you even look?'

Now Greta stared at him.

'Or her phone. Did you check her phone?'

She was going round the house in her head because she hadn't done that, she had stood waiting, she had screamed, she had spoken to him when Kevin Astley had rung for her, but she hadn't gone into every room or looked everywhere. She should have done that and she hadn't.

'I didn't see it.'

'On yours then. She left a message on your phone.'

'Did she?'

'Jesus, I am asking you, Greta.'

She picked up her bag and felt around in it for her phone and found it and it was switched off.

'Christ, Greta.'

She dropped her bag back on the floor.

'What will they do? They tried to bring her round, but maybe they didn't have the equipment, you know, the machinery or all of that, of course they didn't, so they're trying now, here, and they can make it happen now. How long will it take?'

A single great explosive sob burst out of him. Then nothing. His head was bent, hands hanging between his knees.

'It's not your fault,' she said.

He did not look up.

'Shall I get a drink? There was that machine.'

'If you want.'

'Do you?'

'No.'

In the end, she just got them a paper cup of water each.

'What time is it?'

'I don't wear a watch. Have you forgotten that I don't wear a watch? There's a clock on the wall behind you.'

They both turned and looked at the clock.

'Ten past ten.'

'Oh my God, I haven't rung Madison.'

'Why do you have to ring her? This has nothing to do with her.'

'She'll wonder where I am, she'll want to know what time I'll be back, she's on her own with the twins.'

Now Greta stared. What Jeff had said made no sense.

'Oh God.'

'They would come and tell us, wouldn't they, if she . . . they wouldn't just . . .'

'Of course they would.'

The door opened and a doctor came in, a doctor wearing thick glasses and an expression of wariness, exhaustion, distress, a face that did not beam good news.

'Mr and Mrs Tonks?'

'No. Yes.'

He blinked. 'I'm sorry, I thought . . .'

'I am Jeff Tonks, this is Greta Tonks. We're not Mr and Mrs Tonks, we –'

'We're Olivia's parents.'

'Right. I see.'

He looked at the arrangement of chairs, hesitated, pulled one over to face them, looked at it, at them.

'I'm Matthew Green, I'm the neurological consultant in charge of Olivia's case.'

Not Olivia, Greta thought, Olivia's 'case' or the case that was Olivia. She was a 'case'.

He wore a lanyard with his photograph and name on it.

'What's happening? What's going to happen to her? I know she's going to be all right, they got to her in time, I know, they saved her life, the helicopter was very quick, but what happens now? Where will she be? How long will it be? What –'

'Shut up, Greta.'

An alarm bell, a fire alarm, an emergency alarm, screeched outside.

'It's OK,' Dr Green said. What was?

'So . . . who was it found Olivia? One of you?'

'Yes. I'm her mother. She lives with me.'

'OK.' He looked embarrassed. He pulled his pager out and checked it, though it had not made a sound. 'Right. Have you any idea how long it was that she'd been hanging there? Even approximately, a rough guess?'

'I don't know. I was out. I wasn't there. How would I know?'

Could he not tell? Why didn't he tell them, not the other way round?

'It can't have been very long,' Greta said, 'because . . . I know she wouldn't have been home more than . . . but she was alive, wasn't she, she was breathing when they arrived?'

'Mr and Mrs . . . The thing is, when the paramedics first checked her, she wasn't breathing, no, but she did have a pulse.'

'So she was alive.'

'Technically. She is – was . . . she's very slim, very light. If she'd been a full-grown adult or much heavier, then the – she would have died pretty much straight away, the rope would . . . she wouldn't have . . .'

'I'm lost,' Jeff said, 'I don't know what the hell you're trying to say.' He was annoyed, angry, irritated, all of those. Greta still knew him.

'Olivia is technically alive, because we are keeping her alive – the machines are. They are breathing for her, making the blood pump round her body, but her brain was starved of oxygen and as you can't say how long it was that . . . you see, the brain can only be starved of oxygen for minutes, five or six, give or take . . . before it dies. Hypoxia – when the brain isn't receiving oxygen. That's the state.'

'Are you telling me she's going to be brain-damaged?'

'Us. Telling us.'

'No, what I am saying is that she already is brain-damaged . . . damaged beyond repair. That's what happens.'

'So, she'll be . . .'

Each one waited for the other to say it. Or for him to say.

'I don't think you quite understand. We are keeping Olivia alive with machines . . . if we switch those off . . . when we switch them off, then she will die. She can't do anything else. She isn't keeping herself alive. If you follow me.'

They did. They did not.

'What will happen to her?' Greta stood up suddenly and shouted at him. 'WHAT IS GOING TO HAPPEN?'

'Greta, sit down. Greta . . .'

183

He put his hand on her arm and kept it there, and eventually, she felt it, turned in surprise, because he had touched her.

'Sit down,' Jeff said quietly.

She sat.

'We'll wait. We've done some initial brain-function tests but we want to wait . . . hypoxia can take different forms, different . . . she's young, she's healthy, so we wouldn't make any changes, any decisions . . . not yet. Not for perhaps twenty-four hours.'

'But then what do you do?'

'We perform all the tests again, very systematically, we check absolutely everything we can check. It may be . . . it could possibly be –'

His pager sounded and he leapt up and rushed out of the door looking at it, desperate to get to whatever it was, desperate to get away. That was the clearest thing of all, how desperate he had been to leave the room, leave them.

'They don't have any idea,' Jeff said. 'No idea at all.'

'What do you mean?'

'He didn't. So now what? Do we wait here or . . . ?'

'Someone will come and tell us.'

'Yes. Though I suppose it depends, how much – how busy they are and what else is going on, it all depends. But someone will come.'

After a long time, Greta said. 'Hadn't you better ring . . . her? She'll . . . she hasn't rung you though. You'd think . . .'

'Shit. It's in the car. I just left it and ran. Shit.'

'I wish you wouldn't swear like that, Jeff. What is?'

'My phone. It . . .'

She didn't hear more because the door had closed behind him.

Hospitals were never quiet but suddenly it was silent, in the corridor outside, in this room, so that Greta realised it was because Olivia had died. Death is the greatest silence.

Soon, someone would come to tell her and take her in to see her daughter. No one came.

Where was Jeff? She needed him, they were parents, they should be together, she couldn't do this on her own.

It seemed so unlikely that she and Jeff were divorced and he was with another woman, that he had twin boy babies who were always yowling, it was ridiculous. She and Jeff were married, they had always been married, they were Olivia's parents.

The usual noises started up again outside.

'Mr and Mrs Tonks? Oh . . .'

'He had to go and phone . . . somebody. Mr Tonks. Jeff. Sorry.' The nurse looked desperate.

'She's dead, isn't she? Olivia? My daughter's dead. I heard her die. I heard – nothing, I just heard the silence.'

'No, no.' As she came into the room, Greta saw that the woman was pregnant, probably almost due.

'I was only pregnant once, that was with Olivia. You're here to tell me that she died, aren't you?'

'Mrs Tonks . . .' She came and sat down next to Greta. 'I don't know if that's better or worse, sitting down.'

'I found standing up the worst.'

'I think it's all the worst at this stage.'

'When is it due?'

'Oh, ages yet – seven more weeks – yes, I know – God knows what I'll be like, a beached whale I should think.'

'I don't know how long he'll be. My husband . . . he . . . he isn't my husband. If you want to tell us both.'

'Mrs Tonks, I have to apologise, but tonight we're absolutely bursting at the seams here, every cubicle, every corner . . . and there's only this one relatives' room, you see, and it's disgraceful, there should be more, at least two more, this isn't the first time.'

'What isn't?'

'I have a family waiting to . . . to be on their own, and they're in the corridor by the entrance, they shouldn't be there, they've a right to privacy, but . . .'

'Why aren't they in here?'

'But how would you feel about that?'

'Of course . . . of course they must come in here, I'll go out, we can sit in the corridor, it's fine.'

'Mr Tonks . . .'

'He'll sit there with me.'

'The trouble is this isn't a very big room, is it, and there are five of them, but if you want to stay as well then that's your right, please say, I can find some more chairs or –'

'What's happened to them?'

But her face said, don't ask me that, you have no need to know, no right to know, I can't tell you that.

'Poor things.'

'Yes. Difficult.'

Greta stood up, Jeff came in, another nurse behind him, beckoning to the first nurse, making faces.

'What?'

'The on-call room is free for now, I've put them there.'

'Oh –'

'What's going on?'

'I'm so sorry, Mr Tonks, Mrs Tonks . . . can I get you anything?' She went. Jeff stood. He had been crying.

'I'll get us something,' he said. 'Tea or –'

'What did you tell her? What did she say?' Greta could not use his new wife's name, no, not his wife, the girl, young woman.

'They've probably got cold drinks. The tea and coffee won't be up to much. Greta?'

But someone else came in.

Thirty-Nine

Serrailler had managed to stop a doctor coming out of resus, and shown his ID card.

'No one goes in there, sorry, but she's not conscious, she wouldn't be able to tell you anything.'

'What's the outlook?'

'Not sure you've a need to know, Chief Superintendent.'

But he looked drained and blank-eyed and it did not occur to Simon to argue with him.

'Understood, but if she does come round one of us will need to talk to her at some point.'

The medic leaned against the wall, then slid down it and sat on the floor.

'You all right?'

'Yes, I just need a break and some fresh air – come out there with me.'

At the entrance, they went a few yards from main doors, before he got out a cigarette, giving Simon a look as he did so. 'Don't even go there.'

'As if.'

'I'm a hypocrite.' *Dr Ivan Lloyd, ITU Registrar* it said under the bad photograph on his lanyard. He smoked for a few seconds before saying, 'Off the record – though there's no disagreement – the kid hanged herself but quite inefficiently, so she still was alive when she was cut down, and even when the paramedics got to her – just not alive enough.'

'Hypoxia.'

'I forget cops know stuff.'

'Plus I did three years at medical school.'

The doctor raised an eyebrow. 'Feel like swapping?' He threw his cigarette down and stamped on the butt.

'Anyway, she's brain-dead. You want to see the parents?'

'After you've told them everything and they've seen their daughter again. I have to ask them a couple of questions.'

'Is this the right time?'

'There's no right time.'

'Shit, this is the part I'd give away to whoever would take it.

'When are you going to break it to them?'

'As soon as the boss gives the word. I'd have given it before now because where's the point, but Matthew's in charge.'

'Every last door must be closed, every last avenue explored, and every last hope is like a candle that must be allowed to run its course until it flickers out.'

'Who said that?'

Serrailler shrugged, not wanting to tell him that it was his sister.

'I'll hang around . . . probably get a coffee. Here's my number . . . call me when you can. I do need to see the parents.'

The canteen was quiet and the shutters were down on the hot-food counters. He got a coffee and went to a far corner of the Staff Only section, counting himself as that for the time being, and because it was empty. When he needed to think hard, he did so with a pocket notebook and pen, which helped him focus. He also made lists.

Sam?

Move house?

Weekend break.

R

He started a new page.

Wang. Search?

Flat. Forensics.

Roper.

Olivia Tonks.

Reasons? Parents. School. Friends. Boyfriend?

Starly.

He underlined it. Wrote it again and double underlined it.

He sat for an hour and twenty minutes, drinking coffee and water. Waiting. Thinking.

Thinking that medics could be wrong, machines could give false readings. Maybe it was all to play for.

His phone buzzed.

Forty

Everything was the same and no time had passed, but then Greta realised that there were not so many people in the room and around the bed. Olivia looked the same, but then she also realised that there were fewer wires attached to her, fewer machines humming and beeping. Why was that?

She did not look ill and there was no mark on her, though there was a sheet up to her chin now, they could no longer see the red line around her neck.

If she spoke to her, Liv she would hear and wake, open her eyes, smile. She looked as she had looked that morning, which was in another time, but she also looked as if she had nothing to do with this world and had no place in it. Certainly she did not belong here.

Jeff was crying. Now and then he wiped them away but otherwise the tears ran down his face and were followed by more which seemed to disappear before they fell, giving way to the next. He looked at Olivia helplessly, and in what seemed like bewilderment, as if he too did not understand why she was where she was or what was happening, or even if he knew her.

A nurse stood beside them. The consultant had explained everything, and guided them with great patience towards their agreement with his decision. He stood on one side of the bed, next to the machines. Olivia's chest was lifting and falling, lifting and falling.

'But that is the machine,' he said now. 'The machine is breathing for her perfectly and it could go on breathing for her for a very long time but that's all it can do, it cannot restore her to life as a functioning human being, it can just breathe for her in this mechanical way. It can't feel for her, see for her, hear for her, know anything for her, or make her conscious. It can't reach or affect her brain. She has no function there now. She can never have that again.'

Jeff's tears fell and fell and to Greta it seemed that he was crying for them both, he had taken over like the machine, because she could not cry. She might never cry again. This was something far beyond anything that tears were for.

'I know how hard this is. But please tell me that you understand everything I've explained to you – if you don't I will explain it again, as many times as you need me to. There is no hurry now.'

No hurry now.

'Please . . .' Greta felt as if she had been dried up, dried out inside herself, so that she could not even moisten her lips. 'Jeff?'

But Jeff was beyond words as she was beyond tears.

'Just nod,' she said to him.

After a moment, he did so.

'Yes,' she said, 'I understand. We do. Thank you. You've been very clear and kind, very kind. Please do what you have to. She isn't here now, is she?'

The nurse beside her took her hand.

And then everyone in the small space looked at the girl on the bed. The doctor reached over to the controls on the machine. Nothing happened. It went very quiet but nothing else happened, nothing happened to her daughter or would ever happen again. Greta saw that the rising and falling had stopped and at that moment joy flared up within her because nothing could touch or harm Olivia ever again, she was free.

She looked different, changed in a moment, further away, a wisp on the bed.

Jeff made a terrible sound, an animal sound, a sob and a howl of anguish together, and blundered his way out of the room.

Greta went closer to the bed and touched Liv's hand. Two nurses were swiftly unclipping wires, gently removing the ventilator tube from her, so that within seconds Olivia was stripped of everything that had come between them. Only her child remained. Greta bent to kiss her cheek and her forehead, stroke her hair. What or why were not questions she bothered with, not now, not yet, those would come, like everything else, but here and now, nothing came, not even grief, and the quiet room was filled only with love and acceptance.

'Thank you,' she said.

The doctor nodded. 'I'm so very sorry. If I could have done anything else for her . . . Please stay with her, there's no hurry, you can sit as long as you want to.'

She looked again at the bed and then turned away, knowing that she did not need to stay now. Olivia was no longer there.

Forty-One

'I'm really sorry but I can't face that relatives' room again.'

Serrailler had his hand on the door but dropped it. 'OK, I understand.'

Jeff was leaning against the wall, his face white, shaking his head.

'I'll take you both home and you can collect your car tomorrow, Mr Tonks, you shouldn't drive tonight. I have to ask you a couple of questions – we can do it there or I can come back tomorrow morning.'

'I don't . . .'

'Jeff doesn't . . . we're divorced. He lives in Bevham.'

'I'll come back with you, Greta.'

'What about . . . you should be with your family now, Jeff.'

'I'll come with you.'

Greta's head was clear, as if it had been rinsed through with cool water, she was calm, she could make decisions, she could deal with everything. Jeff was the wreck. Jeff was no use to her. Best get it over with.

'Shall we go then?'

Greta moved past Serrailler, to get out of the room, leave the hospital. She turned away from the thought that it was also away from Olivia.

At the house, she walked through the hall quickly, looking at the floor, only the floor. The kitchen was just as she'd left it.

'Can I get you something to drink?'

'Water will be fine.' Simon sat down while Greta filled a glass, made two cups of tea. Jeff stared at the kitchen tiles, head down, saying nothing, trembling. Greta wanted to slap his face, tell him to pull himself together and get home to face his responsibilities, tell him he'd made his bed and he shouldn't let anyone else down.

'I'm recording this on my phone because it's quicker and it's accurate, but I'll play it back to you when we've finished so that you can add or correct anything you've said. There's no rush.'

'Start,' Jeff blurted out, speaking to the floor. 'Get on with it.'

Greta looked at Serrailler to apologise, as he switched on.

'Mrs Tonks . . . I know what happened when you found Olivia and afterwards, but it's before that I would like you to try and remember.'

'I remember everything.'

'When did you last see and speak to your daughter?'

'This morning . . . eight o'clock ish.'

'And were things all right between you?'

'We didn't have any argument, if that's what you mean. Things were – normal. Yes. Just normal.'

'Had you had any kind of disagreement in the previous days – weeks even? Not about leaving her things lying around, where she went, her friends, her schoolwork, all of which is usual, I know that, but anything more serious, maybe something that had flared up, or else perhaps been an ongoing issue.'

'No. We didn't have anything like that. We were close. We had to be.'

'Mr Tonks?'

Jeff started. 'Yes?'

'When did you last see Olivia?'

He seemed not to understand the question, took minutes to react, more to reply. 'Oh . . . the other day. She came to my house.'

Greta looked at him.

'Just turned up. The twins were a bit colicky . . . my wife . . . well, it wasn't the right time, we told Oli she should phone in advance. My wife . . .'

'Can you tell me which day this was?'

'Saturday.'

'What?' Greta sat forward.

'Didn't she tell you? she said she'd asked you first, she said . . . anyway, she came from town, in a taxi, fourteen pounds that cost me, and then her phone woke the boys, we'd just got them to sleep. My wife . . .'

'You mean Saturday? Last Saturday? Jeff? And if fourteen pounds for your daughter is too much, don't worry, I'll give you your fourteen pounds.'

'Mr Tonks, would you say that you had a quarrel, you and your daughter?'

'I don't know. No. It wasn't that serious.'

'Had this happened before, that she turned up at your house unexpectedly?'

'No. She never had.'

'So were you surprised?'

'Yes. It was the usual chaos, the boys are only a few weeks old, it wasn't the best time.'

'Maybe she felt she wanted to get to know her brothers.'

'Half-brothers,' Greta said. 'We knew nothing about them, didn't know they even existed, it took a friend to tell me, she'd read it in the paper, he didn't even tell Livi.'

Serrailler nodded but continued to talk directly to Jeff.

'Did you see or speak to Olivia after you'd brought her back home that afternoon?'

He shook his head.

'Had you been in any sort of touch with her between then and this afternoon?'

'No.' He could barely be heard.'

'Thank you. Can either of you tell me about Olivia's friends? Any who were specially close to her?'

'They were a gang – no, that's not the word . . . group. Four or five of them, one might drop out, another might join, but not a gang, no.'

'Was this both girls and boys?'

'I never heard of any boys. Olivia was fourteen.'

'She was at a mixed school?'

'Sir Eric Anderson, yes . . .'

'And she didn't mention falling out with anyone?'

'No.'

'If you remember anything, any chance remark she may have made, will you let me know? I want to find out if there was something that might have particularly upset your daughter.'

Jeff looked at her. 'You're the one who knows all that.'

'Well, you're certainly not, not any more. Mr . . . please I can't think straight, not now, I can't remember anything. I'm exhausted, I'm a mother who found her daughter hanging from the stair rail and watched her pronounced dead, I saw her stop breathing. I don't understand it and I'm beyond explaining it and I am beyond crying but I realise you need to know.'

Serrailler had been in numerous emotionally stressful and difficult family situations. It was never easy and, surprisingly often, it was embarrassing.

'I'm sorry, of course you're beyond answering or even talking any more. I'll call you tomorrow, and if you feel up to sparing fifteen minutes at some point I'd be grateful because I'm sure you understand we need to cover everything and do it as soon as possible. But not tonight. Try and get some rest . . . and this card has the station contact details and also my own mobile number. That gets me or a voicemail, no one else, and if you need anything, to ask questions, to talk it through, please ring me, doesn't matter when, and if I'm not available, leave a message and I'll get back to you the second I can.'

'Thank you, but I won't trouble you. I'll think of anything I can to answer your questions tomorrow.'

'But there's really nothing to say, is there?' Jeff Tonks said. 'Nothing to know. Liv hanged herself, God knows the reason, but why is it a police matter?' For the first time, Jeff was in control of himself, and he was angry.

'Firstly, there has to be a coroner's inquest, Mr Tonks. The coroner will need any information you or others can provide to help him – though the initial inquest will be held as soon as possible and it will be opened and then adjourned straight away, while we make inquiries. There's one other thing I need to tell you. At the moment, because there is no note or any other communication from Olivia to you or, so far as we know at the moment, to anyone else, we can't rule out other possibilities. Someone else may have been involved.'

'How can they have been? No one else was here.'

'It seems not but we can't be certain until the forensic investigators have been in. This means they will come here, they will take your fingerprints – and yours, Mr Tonks – for elimination purposes and then they'll do a full sweep of the scene and of the other rooms, of all the doors and windows, in case there are anyone else's prints. Can you tell me if you have another person in here regularly – a cleaner, for example?'

'No. There's no one.'

'No friends, family, neighbours, workmen – no one has been here recently, especially in the last few days?'

'No.'

'If you do think of anyone please let me know because that person will have to be fingerprinted too.'

'She said nobody, didn't you hear her?'

'Jeff . . .'

'It's all right, I understand. You have to say whatever you need to.' Serrailler got up. 'Mrs Tonks, is there anyone you can ask to come and stay with you tonight? You shouldn't be on your own.'

'I'll be all right.'

'I'll stay,' Jeff Tonks said. 'This is about our daughter. Hers and mine. Of course I'll stay. What do you take me for?'

Simon's phone rang a few minutes after eight the next morning.

'You can come and ask whatever you like, I'm all right now.'

'Did you get some sleep?'

'No but that's not the point, as I said. Just let's get it over with.'

'Is your hus—'

'Jeff's gone now.'

If anything, Greta Tonks looked worse, when she opened the door, her face grey, and aged twenty years overnight. She offered him coffee but this was a time for getting on and getting out, though he sat down, to help her relax more than to settle down.

He asked the questions tactfully but more formally now, feeling this to be another day, separated in some way from the one in which it had all happened. However sleepless it had been for them, the night had moved them one step on. Now they would say 'yesterday' instead of 'today'.

Greta had precious little to tell him. She knew Olivia's close friends, gave him names and details, but she could tell him nothing else about how matters had been between Liv and any of them. She talked about school, where the girl seemed to have had no problems, about her dance classes, her sports, her possible GCSE subjects. A bit more about her relationship with her father. But if Olivia had had secrets, they had been exactly that.

It was over in half an hour.

'Just one last thing, Mrs Tonks. Do you know where Olivia's phone is? We need to check it – I'll have to take it away but of course it will come back to you as soon as we've finished with it.'

'It'll be in her school bag, though she sometimes emptied that out and put things in a drawer.'

'May I come up? This is about my just – this may sound strange to you – just standing in her room and getting a sense of your daughter. An idea of her in the place she spent a lot of time.'

They stopped outside the closed door. Greta pushed it open, but as she took a step forward, she let out a couple of choked little sobs. 'It smells of her. You wouldn't know that.' But then she went across to pick up the school bag from the floor beside Olivia's desk, and held it out.

'Thank you. I won't be a minute. But she was a very orderly girl, wasn't she, tidy and careful. She must have loved her room.'

'Yes.' Greta smiled slightly. 'She did. She'd had a much smaller room since she was a baby but last year I turned out everything from when this was the spare bedroom and had it decorated as she wanted – she chose it all. Yes. You're right about Liv, Mr Serrailler.'

He had taken out textbooks, a file full of notes, neatly made, separated by colour-coded dividers, pencil case, a timetable in a clear plastic wallet, a tube of fruit sweets, a stick of lip salve . . .

and the girl's mobile phone, a smartphone but not the latest model, with a well-thumbed screen. He put it into his pocket and dug around the bottom of the bag, and felt something in a side pocket.

The second phone was a burner, black, small, probably only for texting. Like all of this type, it had plenty of battery left because the occasional text and nothing else used up very little power. He clicked it on. The screen lit up and he clicked again. Most phones, especially those belonging to teenage girls, had a long directory full of names and numbers.

But this phone had one mobile number stored, and only one.

He knew what it would be before checking. Olivia had been given the phone by the owner of the number, so that he could text her whenever he had a job for her. She would reply when she had picked up the packet and again when she had delivered it. And then the phone would be silent until the next time her county lines runner needed her.

Forty-Two

Vince had never gambled, apart from buying a National Lottery ticket every so often, and he had never been able to see the charm of it, given the number of people he had known who had ruined their lives via the racetrack or the casino, but when he walked into the Bevham Greyhound Stadium he caught the excitement and the buzz of the place.

He had once been to horse racing, at a course on the outskirts of a small town. There had been hardly any spectators and no buzz at all.

For a while, he wandered about, looking, listening. It was packed in spite of the cold and no one took any notice of him. He bought a programme and a lager and stood at the bar, studying faces, the way men walked, what they were wearing – the crowd was ninety per cent male – listening to talk about dogs and statistics and chances, odds, physique, which one liked to break late, understanding nothing much, but feeling the energy of the place get to him.

But he wasn't here for the energy, he was here to find Fats, and where the hell did he start? He looked over to the bookies' enclosure, at the small queues in front of each one, at the windows of the large firms who had permanent sites and longer queues. Fats. Any one of hundreds could be Fats. Fats might not even be here.

Race 1 and he was at the rails jostled from behind as the dogs flashed past.

Races 2, 3, 4 came and went and then he edged nearer to the bookies' enclosure, looking at the programme, the names of runners, the pedigrees, the chances. A fiver, no more.

Runner 7. Connor's Milady.

Runner 4. Delia Frances.

One of those. A fiver. Toss a coin.

Four in front of him. He glanced left to see if the next queue was shorter and was about to join it, because one man moved off, tucking his betting slip inside his watch strap, and the last took his place, a skinny, weaselly bloke, a bit ginger. He handed over a tenner, said something, no more than a couple of words, out of the corner of his mouth, and the bookie passed over a the betting slip and a small canvas bag. The man took it, and slipped sideways into the crowd.

The name of any dog he might have picked to carry his fiver vanished from Vince's mind as he went after him.

He got held up in the crowd at a couple of points, but then he saw him, heading towards a hot-dog stand, the same bloke, no doubt about it. The tannoy had begun shouting out the preliminaries to the next race, so the queue at the stall was small. Ginger was second in line, Vince fourth, before the front man took his hot dogs, folded into a thick napkin, and squirted a vivid yellow worm of mustard down the middle.

Ginger gave his order and Vince nudged himself up to his shoulder. The canvas bag wasn't visible so he had either hidden it inside his leather jacket or passed it on, but there hadn't been time for that. Or had there? Maybe the next man had been standing in a given spot, Ginger had edged past, the bag had changed hands in one, swift movement. Which?

The hot dog was folded into a napkin, Ginger reached out, and someone shoved Vince hard in the back, making him spin round, shouting out to whoever to watch it. It took a few seconds during which Ginger had disappeared and the hot-dog guy was apparently slipping something under the serving counter, but he came upright again with a fresh cloth and was putting it over his shoulder.

'Next?'

Vince shook his head as he moved away from the van, the crowd began to roar the dogs on as the tannoy commentary started up, and Ginger was nowhere.

But he had something for the Chief Superintendent now, though he wanted to kick himself for not taking out his phone and getting a quick photo of the man he had convinced himself was Fats, Fats moving money from here to there, Fats who had sucked Brookie in, Fats who deserved . . .

Only that was not the way to go, don't even think it, he was here to sniff something out and report back, let them deal, which they had a reason to now, short of money or not.

Delia Frances had come in, the lines of people with winning slips were forming at the bookies; if he'd put his fiver down it would have turned into forty plus his money back, but Vince wasn't bothered. He hadn't come here to start gambling, win or lose, he had had a better reason than that. More important.

He headed for the exit.

Forty-Three

Ginger was approaching a small beaten-up van on the far side of the car park. If the stadium had been emptying out at the end of the racing, Vince would never have spotted him, but not a single other person was there, so that he managed to reach his own car, keeping Ginger in sight, and staying behind him at a safe distance, onto the main road and away. What he ought to do was call the DCS but he had to stay in pursuit now – if he found out where Ginger lived, he would have much more to tell.

Outer reaches of Bevham was what he guessed and for a couple of miles that's what it looked like but then they swung left so maybe he was heading for the motorway and he came from somewhere much further off. The roads were quiet. Another left and the Lafferton sign. Another three miles, skirting it, along the canal road. This was his own way home.

Starly.

Nothing else came between them and Vince had to slow a bit, not wanting to look as if he was following. He was on sidelights only now. Forty, fifty miles an hour for a bit, then the lanes twisted about from here, the road climbed, and Ginger was driving carefully. There were no speed cameras round here but police patrols had been more active lately, stepping up the surveillance, the random pulling in, making their presence felt.

Starly was at the top of the hill but it had low-level street lighting, night-sky-friendly, the village had been noisy about it, like so many other eco things, nagged enough to get their way. At nearly half past ten, the place was empty and quiet. They had illuminated the church tower for a while until there had been another protest, to save energy and the planet, and the compromise had been lights on the facade only at Christmas, on Remembrance Day and national events like the Queen's birthdays, jubilees and anniversaries. Vince had voted for keeping the lights on full-time, knowing that his side would lose. But you had to try, you had to speak out, just as you had to vote because if you didn't you'd no right to complain afterwards.

Ginger had slowed right down after turning into the square, and Vince decided to stop, and continue on foot. The van pulled up outside the Chinese pharmacy, switched off his lights. Then, nothing. Vince slipped into a doorway further along.

Two minutes. Five. Ten. He was frozen, he had to clench and unclench his hands and play keyboard with his fingers, pull his collar up and his fleece hat right down.

It was getting on for twenty minutes before another car turned into the square and slipped in behind Ginger, and the men were out, and up to the door of the pharmacy, the second man, much taller and bulkier than Ginger, with a key ready in his hand. Vince edged his way along the row but stopped three shops down. No light went on inside the shop, but after a few seconds, he could make out a thin torch beam moving quickly down to the counter area.

They were just thieving, then? Casual thieves had keys, did they? And unless they were just after money, how likely was it they'd want herbal toothpaste and Chinese vitamins?

He edged forward one shop. Dreamcatchers, crystal balls, tarot packs, Wiccan gear, all both weird and dusty. Vince remembered it first opening and the incense smell that always got at you from six doors down.

The torchlight inside the pharmacy disappeared but no one came out. He edged right up to the side window and cupped his hands against the glass. At first he saw nothing but then the thin beam of light again, moving about right at the back. they had obviously been here before and knew their way round. He should wait until they did emerge, see if they were carrying anything, maybe follow Ginger again, in which case he should make a note of the other car number plate, pass it over to his cop. He turned but the plate was hidden and he could only see part of the car registration. Could they get anything from a description and half a number plate?

'Who the hell are you?' Two men had come out of the shop fast and one had cannoned into Vince.

Vince shook his head. 'Here, watch it, come out of there like a charging bull. No reason I should give you my name that I know of.'

But the ginger one was waving a torch in front of his face.

'Don't know him. What you doing here?'

'None of yours.'

'C'mon, let's get out of it.'

'He's seen us, he'd know us.'

'So? What's he going to say to who?'

Ginger shone the torch again, this time directly into Vince's eyes. 'Listen up, shitface. You weren't here, we weren't here, you didn't see nothing.' He made a dive for Vince's phone but missed.

'Back off.'

'You stop there until we're out of the way and you don't hear us no more and then you bugger off home.'

And their car doors slammed and they were gone.

Forty-Four

It never took long for the quiet and calm of his apartment to smooth Simon's frayed edges and restore his mood. Now, he stood with a vodka and tonic looking out over the empty Cathedral Close, relishing the prospect of an evening by himself. The last of the snow had thawed, but the grass was still frosted over and sheened silver in the moonlight. A Bach cello suite was playing, he had a sirloin steak to move quickly round a red-hot pan, and John le Carré's *Tinker, Tailor, Soldier, Spy* to reread. Crime writing had never attracted him, even the old-school classic detective story, being too close to the day job, and he had come late to spy fiction, but had been hooked by the first he had read. The only trouble was that whereas crime novels had spawned by their thousand during recent years, spy stories were still thin on the ground, but rereading the master, along with an occasional replay of the televised versions, was fine until a new genius came along, and he was keeping a close eye out for another episode from Mick Herron's anti-hero Jackson Lamb in his run-down department of espionage situated on the wrong side of the tracks.

He took a deep breath and released it slowly, relaxing even further, and glanced round at the white walls of his room, his own framed drawings of his mother and his young sister, Martha, a very small Hockney of tulips in a vase, then at the eight-foot-long old elm table. He loved it all, each item gave him joy. How had he ever thought he should move out of Lafferton and into some dark, beamed, spider-infested cottage? If it made sense to buy a property for investment, as very occasionally crossed his mind, then he could do so, and let it to someone who needed a long-term rental at a fair price. Lafferton was becoming unaffordable for most of his police colleagues, and for many young people making a start in life and work. He enjoyed comfort, he could buy the best steak and a good bottle of wine and new books, take a holiday wherever he wanted, and those were things he appreciated, but he was not otherwise motivated by or interested in money or in accumulating it. It made no sense to continue renting this flat and not owning any property but otherwise he was reminded how happy he was and always had been here. He watched the light on the grass and paths change from silver to an amber gold as the moon slipped behind clouds and the lamps round the close glowed. A moment later, his sister's car came in sight.

There were very few people he would have been pleased to see, hungry as he was and looking forward to his quiet evening, but Cat was one of them, tonight as ever. He pressed the intercom.

'Hi, sis, come up.'

But it was not Cat who appeared.

'Is this OK?' Sam stood in the doorway looking uncertain, a young man now as tall as him and having to duck his head.

'Hey.' He bit back 'Hope you've got your mum's permission to take her car', partly because Sam looked miserable and troubled, and because he was no longer the teenager who had passed his driving test at the first legal moment.

'You can't have a beer – coffee?'

'I know I can't have a beer, thanks, I wouldn't drink drive any more than you would.'

'Sorry.'

'Got any Coke?'

'Sorry again.'

'OK, coffee then. I'll get it. You?'

'No, I'm off so I'm having a beer.'

They got their drinks in a silence that should have been companionable but felt tense.

'Have you eaten?'

Sam nodded, and took his mug into the big room and flopped down onto a sofa, head back, eyes closed.

Simon gave him a few moments.

'Quieter here than at home,' Sam said eventually. 'I love that.'

'Best in winter.'

'Mum said you might move, get something in the country.'

'Might. Might not.'

'I wouldn't want to leave here.'

'No? I've been renting this for over ten years – really doesn't make financial sense.'

Another pause. A wind had got up. If it increased and came from the North-East down the close it would batter at the flat all night.

'February,' Serrailler said. 'Feels as if it's been February for about a year.'

'January another year before that.'

'Haven't heard from Hannah for a while . . . how's she doing?'

'Good . . . I think. Understudying the lead – hasn't actually gone on though, she's just in the chorus She sends crazy texts. Honestly, I don't really know my sister any more, she doesn't belong in my world.'

'Not true, just that she has another as well.'

He looked at Sam but the look was evaded. Simon waited on a count of two full minutes, reminded as he did so how endless that two minutes always seemed on Remembrance Sunday when he was standing in aching cold.

'OK, spill, Sammy. What's up?' he said.

Sam was looking down at his left shoe on which the lace was broken in half and did not reply.

'All right, I'll start. How's the course?'

'Come on, Mum will have told you, she tells you bloody everything.'

'She doesn't actually.'

'Yeah, right.'

'Sam, listen to me. Other than the inevitable and essential lies about is there really a Father Christmas, when you were five, I don't think I have ever not told you the truth. I may have said

208

nothing, but that can be necessary. So, no, she hasn't said anything and you don't have to. Tell me to mind my own.'

'Sorry.'

'That's OK.'

'I've quit. At least I think I have. Now say it.'

'What? I quit medicine after three years which was a lot longer and caused a lot more problems but it was the right decision. You're not a quitter so I guess yours is too.'

'It just . . . I dunno.'

'Man in woman's world?'

'No, wasn't that, they were great, and there's plenty of men about anyway – obstetricians, anaesthetists . . . just not many midwives. It wasn't funny looks, it wasn't that I didn't seem to fit in, it wasn't the mothers or the dads and it definitely wasn't the babies.'

'So, what?'

'It was one moment . . . watching a woman who'd just had her baby, everything fine, no probs, everyone laughing and congratulating, and she started to haemorrhage . . . and it was panic – controlled panic but the whole room changed, the whole . . . everything. The dad was crying, doctors came out the walls, bells went off . . . and it was sorted, really, really quickly, they stopped it, she was OK, they'd got a theatre alerted in case but it was all right. Only I thought – if it hadn't been and if it had been me in charge? What got to me was the responsibility, you know? The pressure of that – never mind if you know what to do . . . it shook me up. I had a couple of days out, said I had a stomach bug . . . so what kind of a wuss am I?'

'No kind, Sambo. The point is, you hit the wall early on . . . and maybe you'd have climbed over it.'

'I didn't want to.'

'Exactly. So, you haven't failed – you tried and it didn't work out, it wasn't for you and you didn't wait three years to learn that. It's fine. And I bet your mother said exactly the same.'

He nodded.

'So. Look, Sam, there's no rush and no point in going into the wrong career because you think you've got to make a quick decision. You can get a job and work on things while you do it. What does Rosie think?'

He could tell everything from the boy's face. Sam looked like a ten-year-old again, discovering his name had been left off the first cricket 11 list.

He looked down but not quickly enough for Simon to miss the tears in his eyes, controlled, not falling, but visible.

'OK – suggestion. I was about to cook a steak when you arrived and I'm very hungry, so I'm going ahead with that, you say you've eaten but you can either stay in here or come in there and watch *MasterChef*. You can talk or not, whatever, I'm not going to probe.'

He got up and went into the kitchen without waiting for a reply and put Dave Brubeck on low. Then he got on with his cooking.

Sam did not join him until it was almost done, mushrooms and tomatoes ready, but glancing through, Simon saw that he was at the window. Everyone who came here went to the window, the long view of the close drew them, caught them up in itself and worked its own magic. Whatever he decided about buying somewhere else, he knew the one thing to hold him back would be this.

He had started to eat when Sam wandered through. Simon pointed to the coffee machine.

'Another? Make one for me too.'

'Better not. Mum isn't on call but you never know, she might have to go somewhere in the middle of the night even so.'

'How's chauffeuring for a career?'

'I'd only do it for her but it makes me feel quite useful.'

'I'm sure you are.'

'Wouldn't mind going back to portering for a bit. I really liked that, it's another useful job, in spite of what Grandpa said.'

'Oh, I can just guess what he said. Portering is fine and necessary, just not for his grandson. Ignore him. If you're not going to make the coffee, will you sit down, you're giving me indigestion.'

'Sorry. You got any peanuts?'

'I never have peanuts. There's cheese, got it today on the way home. Good cheese shop that new one.'

It went on, chit-chat, about the merits of Brie versus Camembert, Wensleydale versus Cheddar. Sam found the crackers and ate in silence, demolishing the Brie, digging deep into the butter dish.

'More in the fridge.'

'Thanks.' And then, his mouth still half full, he said, 'Actually, I went into BG to see them when I was waiting for Mum. Portering is camaraderie, people stay. Only one of the guys I worked with had left.'

Simon ate slowly.

'Saw Rosie there.'

He crammed his mouth full again, head down.

'Ah.' And it was all clear.

'Some junior doc, never seen him before. Well, I wouldn't have. Bastard.'

He jammed his knife hard into the cheese, and it hit the plate below with a screech, making them both wince.

'You could have read it wrong. You know hospitals, everyone is under pressure, you need friends.'

'Oh sure, absolutely.'

'More than friends?'

'Seemed like it to me.'

'Did she see you?'

'Yeah, and looked right through me. I wasn't there, I didn't exist.'

Serrailler pushed his plate away. 'I'm sorry, Sam, I really am. Nothing else to say. It's a bugger.'

'Yeah. And don't tell me I'll get over it, plenty more fish in the sea, she's not worth it, blah-blah.'

'Does Cat know?'

'No and –'

'Don't even say it. Of course I won't tell her. We're a close family but I've never wanted the "everyone tells everyone else everything, no secrets" thing. Your life is yours, you talk or not, to whoever you choose. Or not. Cheese seems to have vanished.'

'Plenty of that weird Cornish stuff with nettles round it.'

'Yarg. You don't know what you're missing. But if you go back to portering, you risk seeing Rosie every day and that might not be the best idea?'

211

'She qualifies soon.'

'Still.'

'And it's a big place. What do you do, Si?'

'When?'

'When it happens to you. I mean, when you get dumped.'

But he did not wait for an answer, probably, Simon thought, because he did not really want to know.

Sam did not make any coffee, he put his cheese plate in the sink and was away, thundering down the three flights of stairs, embarrassed, upset, annoyed with himself – probably all three.

Simon went back into the sitting room and stood at the windows. There was an icy drizzle in the air, blurring the edges of the lamplight as it fell in soft circles on the grass, the paths. He felt for Sam. What had happened was the worst way to find out about the other person's love affair, apart from being told about it by a gloating friend. But Sam was twenty, he had life ahead, and loves. Love.

Forty-Five

Greta went straight back into the kitchen, because the house was cold and she needed to switch the heating timer back on, and because she could not bear to linger for a second in the hall.

'Do you want more tea? Have you had anything to eat? Jeff?' No reply. She called his name out again. 'What are you doing?'

He came to the doorway, his face like a death mask, lines and furrows, sunken flesh seeming to have formed and settled themselves over a few hours when they should have taken years. Nothing would restore youth and hope to him, nor ever return him to the deceitful happiness he had known briefly.

Greta did not want to look in the mirror at her own face, knowing that it would have aged and crumpled in the same way.

'I can make us something.'

He went on staring round him as if trying to work out where he was, in this house that was so long familiar and yet strangely unknown, unrecognisable.

'I haven't made up the spare bed, I use that room for my quilting stuff now.'

He shook his head.

'Jeff, you should go back, go to your wife and boys, your own home. Ring a taxi. You'll be needed there.'

'I'm needed here.'

'No,' she said quietly. 'You're not. You were, you were needed by me, and by Livi, you will never ever begin to know how much we needed you, but that's over.'

'I can't go back.'

'You're a coward, Jeff.' She filled the kettle.

'I looked but I couldn't picture her.'

'What?'

'From the banister. She was so skinny, Greta, she was so small, she weighed nothing, it ought not have worked.'

'Well, that's what happened, isn't it?'

She did not look at him, just got her phone, rang the cab firm. Poured tea.

Jeff sat down at the table, his shoulders hunched over, rising and falling as he sobbed.

So many sentences slid across Greta's mind but left no trace and she knew she had nothing else to say to him and never would.

'You're a coward' had been all, and it was simply the truth and not an accusation.

Forty-Six

Vince's text came in as Serrailler was going into a CID round-up. *Need to see you. V.*

But the round-up, estimated to last under an hour, went on for two and a half, interrupted by DC Lola Smith fainting, being sick and having to be taken out. By the time they had decamped to another room, and an extra item had arisen, it was almost noon.

Simon texted back *Bit pressed. Urgent?*

Urgent.

Sportsman's Arms, Cotton Street, 1.30.

It was surprising the pub was still standing. It had been popular with workmen building a new estate, and then with those constructing the bypass, but the caravan had long since moved on, and the Sportsman's was now washed up like an abandoned ship in the middle of a wasteland alongside a couple of repair garages and a betting shop that had closed. But the pub was open, and for those in the know, it kept decent beer though appalling food, chalked on a blackboard behind the bar. Serrailler borrowed a parka and a baseball cap, and went in one of the beaten-up but fully serviced cars used for exactly this sort of job. He felt a prickle of anticipation, a shadow of some past undercover ops in earlier days. There was nothing quite like it.

Vince was in the half-empty bar with a pint, but Simon nodded to another table, in view of the door.

215

'Didn't know you.'

'Good. You OK?'

Vince nodded.

He drank down half his glass and then started on the story. Serrailler had to lean close, arms on the table, to catch everything, and when it was finished he drank his shandy and said nothing for a moment. The door kept swinging open to let in new customers, utilities crew, oddballs, a bleary old man who smelled of manure, wearing a matching dung-coloured raincoat, garage men who smelled of oil.

Serrailler leaned back, turning his head to one side. He didn't expect anyone in here to know him, or to get the whiff of a cop, which was always hard to lose, but you never knew and it was Vince who need protecting.

'You're an idiot,' he said at last. 'What made you think going off on some sort of chase on your own was a good idea?'

'I thought you wanted me to find out stuff.'

'I did. Do. That doesn't mean playing cops and putting yourself in danger. As you said to me at the start, you've got four boys. Didn't they cross your mind?'

'Christ sake. My lad is what this is all about – him and for all I know a load of other local kids. Why else would I be here?'

'Fine. I want you to go over two key things again. The handover by the bookie and then up at Starly, from when you saw the two men arrive and go into the shop to when they scarpered. Rewind it in your head, slowly. I want everything.' He picked up Vince's empty glass and went to the bar.

Forty-Seven

'This is a big spend,' Kieron Bright said. 'Our overtime bill has been way too high for the last year and I need to get it down. This wouldn't help. Excuse me.'

He got up stiffly and came round to the other side of his desk. 'If I don't do these half a dozen times a day, I pay for it.'

He performed a series of exercises with his left leg, standing on his toes and down, up, down, bending and stretching. Serrailler watched impatient with the fuss the Chief continued to make about his injury, minor in Simon's opinion, and because he was ready with his package of arguments and the pause in the conversation was unhelpful.

'Has the physio said how long you have to do those for?'

Kieron winced as he rolled his leg sideways. 'Until she tells me to stop I imagine. I daren't give up yet, I don't want to go back to square one.'

'You probably wouldn't.'

'Well, I'm not about to put it to the test. Right, that's it for now.'

He hobbled back to his desk.

'I can't authorise this now, Simon, you just don't have enough reasons for me to justify the expense.'

'I have as many as I'm likely to get without moving this forward now.'

'Really? You don't think keeping your snout going, maybe provide one bod to follow up at the dog track, would give you a breakthrough?'

'No, I don't. In any case, his cover might be blown.'

'Only to a couple of small fry.'

'Who report up. Come on, you know how it works. I can't risk him hanging around the track now, I've got to stand him down, for a time anyway. He's a bit too gung-ho, understandably.'

He leaned on the Chief's desk. 'This is the first breakthrough of any kind that we've had. Evidence of money being handed over.'

'You can't prove it's for criminal purposes – could be just a good night's takings for one bookie being sent off for safe-keeping.'

'They don't work like that.'

'How much time have you spent at the dog track?'

'None – plenty at horse racing though.'

'Did your snout get a photo of Fats, or the bookie, or the other man up at Starly? No? Thought not.'

'Fats is the one we need to put a watch on.'

'We've had a man on this Chinese pharmacy before, haven't we?'

'That was to do with finding the junkie in the flat . . . and it was one bod.'

'You want two round the clock for what could be weeks?'

'I don't think it will be weeks, but yes, I want to have that option.'

Kieron leaned back, going over it in silence.

It had been a surprise to them both, Serrailler thought, that they had managed to have a professional relationship quite separate from the family one, able to encompass serious disagreements, occasions when the Chief had to talk him down, argue against and finally overrule him, to refuse a request, without it affecting them outside the station. Simon had learned to get over the few frustrations, sometimes acknowledging later that the Chief had been right. But this time he was not about to swallow a judgement he was sure was wrong.

'I understand about resources and I appreciate your position, but as so often, this is not only about money, this is a chance we may not get again, or not for a long time, during which they will have moved in closer, got their pincers tightened, and ruined the lives of more kids. Come on, Chief, you know that. Yes, they're the minnows, near the bottom of the food chain, and generally those guys not only don't squeal on their masters, they haven't a clue who those masters are. But we can't be certain of that. They might lead us two, three levels up, and from there . . .'

He stopped. Kieron knew what he was saying.

He went to the window and looked down on the back of the station, the secure entrance for the newly arrested who came stumbling out of police vans, the place for off-duty cars, the fuel pumps, the bicycle racks. Beyond, a fringe of trees and, behind them, the tower of St Michael's Cathedral, to which the eyes of people going about their daily business were so often, unconsciously drawn, the focus of Lafferton, a beacon for miles around. Simon suddenly imagined a space where it had once been, and the vision shocked him.

'Sorry, but it's not enough. We'll have patrols take a look when they're in the Starly area and if you get any better info you can have your search but I'm not authorising one now.'

Forty-Eight

'Sam, are you still in the attic?'

She could just make out a 'yes' from above.

'Can you come down?'

'Hang on,' she heard, as if shouted through a layer of felt.

'What?'

'Can you leave that for a bit? The vet just rang – we can collect Wookie.'

'Yaay! But why don't we wait till we get the boy from school and take him?' He had started calling Felix 'the boy' a year or so back, and because it had annoyed his young brother, Sam had gone on with it. Now, it no longer bothered Felix but it had stuck all the same.

'Good thinking, he'll love that and he hasn't got anything after four o'clock on Thursdays.' Cat had a day off and spent most of it trying to write a letter to the Health Secretary about the serious shortcomings on Bevham General's wards and the lack of response from the trust to her complaints. She needed to phrase it carefully, making sure that she praised other areas of the hospital and did not point too many fingers while at the same time going into detail about the failures she had observed in nursing care. When neither of her emails to the hospital management had been answered, Luke, her partner in Concierge Medical, had urged her to go to the top.

'The government will have to look into it and BG will have to get their act together and investigate properly. No point in trying to get them to answer, they'll have ignored you in the hope that you'll go away.'

'I'm going nowhere on this one.'

But she had spent too long writing and deleting, starting again, trying to get her tone right. It had been a relief to be interrupted by Michael the vet.

'I'm starving,' Sam said, swinging into the kitchen. 'Can I make a bacon and egg sarnie?'

'Not sure we've got bacon. I have to do a shop. In fact we –'

'No. N.O. to the bloody supermarket – get a delivery. There are two sausages – they fit for human consumption?'

Sam started frying and slicing doorsteps of bread, while Cat put on coffee. It felt companionable, he seemed better.

'Ketchup?'

'On the shopping list. How much of that stuff do you get through, Sam?'

'Tomato contains ly . . . something. Cures cancer.'

'Lycopene, and it doesn't cure but it may help prevent cancer.'

'And what's a fry-up butty without it?'

'Put the fan on and open the window, you've got that pan on far too high.'

'Dropped in on Uncle Si the other night.' Fat spurted up and Cat opened the window herself.

'Haven't heard from him for a day or two – they've got some big drugs op going.'

'Yeah, nasty stuff.'

'We've got some real tomatoes, you could cremate those as well.'

'Not the same and don't start on about healthy eating. I do that already.'

'So I see. How was he?'

Sam stood back from the stove as a sausage broke open. 'You know . . . I never really get Si, not really, and I've been with him on his own all over the place enough times and we talk a lot, you know, but he's an oyster. I love him to bits but I don't think I know him.'

'He's not actually that complicated, Sammy. He likes to play the mystery man but he's not all that difficult.'

221

'Go on then, do your Freud thing.'

Cat shook her head. 'You try.'

Sam was silent, basting his sausages, turning to butter the slabs of bread, cracking an egg into the pan. Cat watched him without appearing to watch, saw a very young man who was hoping to pass as older, a competent, easy-going person trying to work out where to go in life and worrying too much that it wasn't as straightforward as he had expected. He had been messed about by a girl who should have behaved better but who, also, had not found things going as smoothly as she thought they should, a clever, ambitious, potentially excellent doctor who had met Sam far too soon. Cat had liked Rosie, inevitably been angry about the way she had treated Sam but at the same time understood it and did not want to blame her.

Sam. He laid sausages and egg carefully onto the buttered bread, salted it all too much, put it onto a breadboard not a plate. Cat smiled. She had been thinking how like his uncle he was, and that was partly true, but Simon was a careful and fastidious cook who ate well, and would never have let the fat spurt out over his immaculate kitchen or larded his bread with so much butter.

'He's messed up, hasn't he?'

'Don't talk with your mouth full. In what way? Certainly not career wise.'

'I don't mean that and you know it.'

She drank her coffee and waited.

'Women. I mean, what is he like? Commitment-phobe.'

'I suppose so. He loves his own life, his own space, his little world, and nothing wrong with that, but he's never learned how to give a bit, how to share, how to understand that by letting someone into his life, himself, he would actually be able to have what he's already got plus a whole lot more. He doesn't see what he's missing, and after all these years, I really can't find any way of getting through to him or changing him – no, that's wrong, you can't change people and you shouldn't try but you can help them modify their behaviour. I've definitely failed there.'

'He's too old and set in his ways.'

'Thanks. He is my age. Exactly.'

'Yes, but you change, you take up challenges, you do new stuff, you'll never get stuck in a rut. You married K. You joined Concierge. What's Uncle Simon going to do when he's old? What will he be like?'

Cat poured herself more coffee. 'God knows. Right, I've got to finish a difficult letter and do a bit of admin before we get Felix, and after him, Wookie.'

'The Wookster! I was really afraid we wouldn't get him back, you know, and after Mephisto that would have been the worst thing, like the family was falling apart.'

Forty-Nine

Black Cat, Spenser Street. Fats alone. You can't miss him.

Serrailler replied at once.

You there?

Not now. He might know me.

Thanks.

He took off fast. Fats had probably gone but it was worth taking the chance. He had grabbed the old parka as he left and now he pulled the hood up. It was cold but dry and bright and Simon felt an upsurge of the old thrill of the chase, which he rarely got these days. He felt twenty years younger, and mocked himself.

He was still there, still on his own, and unmistakable, skinny, thinning ginger hair, weaselly face.

Serrailler got a mug of tea, keeping an eye out for him to leave, but he was staring into his own mug, a cleared plate at his elbow.

Simon pulled out the chair opposite, set his tea on the table and sat down, not asking permission.

'Do I know you?'

Serrailler shook his head.

'Then there's other tables.'

'Waiting for someone?'

'Are you deaf or what?'

'You want another of those?'

'What?'

'Tea? Bovril?'

Fats made retching noise.

'Tea then. Sugar?'

'Why would you be buying? No thanks.' He made to get up but Serrailler put his leg out, ready to trip him up.

Fats's eyes narrowed. 'I get you.' His voice was lowered. 'Manchester,' he said.

'What about it?'

'Are you or aren't you? They said I'd be waiting a week, and it's two days. Why the change of plan?'

'What are you doing in here?'

'Having me lunch, what else?'

'Waiting for someone.'

'I dunno. Who'd know I'd be here?'

'That's easy. You come here.' This was where you played a game and took a punt, and if you were right, everything followed, or at least something did. If you were wrong, nothing. You bluffed. He'd always enjoyed the bluffing.

'You got eyes in the back of your head, you lot. You are Manchester, I can tell, see?'

'Maybe.'

'I'll have that tea off you then.'

'You fetch it.'

Fats hesitated before getting up.

A couple of men from the new housing development came in, hard hats still on, followed by an elderly woman with half a dozen plastic carrier bags, not full of shopping, full of her life possessions. Serrailler recognised her. She came into the cathedral undercroft and sat in the warmth, went up to the refectory and talked to anybody, was bought food and drink, and eventually gathered up the bags and left. She caused no trouble, she had never been found sleeping on the street. She gave a different name any time she was asked. Simon would have bought her tea and a sandwich but he daren't risk Fats darting for the door, he'd have to do it later.

'Never been to Manchester.'

He slopped the tea as he set it down. Drank some, chuckling. Serrailler said nothing.

He was pleased with himself, he was cocky, he was expecting to be patted on the back by this guy from Manchester who was several rungs up the ladder from him, would maybe even give a leg-up there himself if he played his cards right. You stupid little git, Simon thought and almost said aloud.

'What's the next job then?'

'When you're told.' Simon leaned across the table. 'He saw you. Both of you.'

Fats flinched, shook his head. 'We was too quick.'

'Who was he?'

The ginger weasel shrugged. 'Nobody. Pond life. Don't matter.'

'Oh it matters.'

But the note in his voice passed the man by, as everything would for as long as he was blinded by his own cleverness.

'He did see you.'

'No he didn't.'

'How long had he been outside the shop in the dark?'

'Dunno.'

'You see a car, a motorbike?'

'Nope.'

'Torch beam?'

'I was in the back out of sight, wasn't I? He didn't see anything.'

'Chances are he's got your faces photographed on his brain as well as on his phone.'

A flicker of uncertainty in the man's eyes but it was gone in a second. 'Not him.'

'All right. Now finish that, get up and follow me.'

'What you . . . where to?'

'You'll find out.'

Fats attempted a grin. 'Manchester?'

'Move.'

Serrailler went first, and as he passed the table beside the door, dropped a fiver in front of the bag woman.

Fats shook his head and then walked next to Serrailler, docile as a puppy, all the way to the cab rank.

'Get in.' He got in.

Serrailler knew the cabby and the cabby knew him and what the nod he gave him meant.

Five minutes later, they were pulling up at the station.

226

Fifty

There was no way he could keep Ginger beyond three hours and even that was pushing it.

'Anyone free? Bilaval? Donna? Come on, you're not all banked up. Where's Denzil? Ah, on cue.'

'Guv?'

'Don't take your coat off. I've got a guy downstairs and in ten I have to let him go because he's slippery as soap but I want him tailed until he leads you to his place, wherever and whatever that is, flat, house, tent in the woods, I've no idea, but possibly he'll be anticipating a tail so I'm sending Richie out first, making himself easy to spot. You follow on and he won't notice, his attention will be taken up with Rich. Have a bag with you, something better than a plastic carrier, you're on your way into town, do some shopping. Richie will peel off at some point where there are plenty of people about, you carry on. Anything he does, anywhere he goes, anyone he meets, you clock it. If he heads back to the Black Cat in Spenser Street you do the same. I'd advise the tea not the coffee.'

'Smart shoppers are all the rage in there,' Donna said. Serrailler gave her a look.

'If he gets suspicious, back off, but if he leads you to anywhere that looks like his home, get a good look, then go. He's pissed off and he thinks he's looking for a fight but he isn't a fighter. Right, ten minutes, time for me to have a last word and escort him off police premises. Richie, you're hanging about at the front desk, Denzil, on the stairs. Let's go.'

They lost the ginger-haired man just before the square, when he turned suddenly left down one of Lafferton's narrow side streets, and sight of him was immediately blocked by a delivery lorry. Richie dodged across between parked cars and round it, but Ginger was nowhere in sight. That street led to another, beyond which was the site where the new city council building and magistrates' court were going up, behind hoarding and an entrance guarded by a security Portakabin and a barrier.

There was little point in asking if the guard had seen a skinny, ginger bloke but the DC did so anyway.

JCBs, excavators and aggregate lorries were backing and advancing, tipping and reversing so that he could barely make himself heard, but the answer was as expected and the site was impossible for anyone to sneak into without being spotted.

Richie turned and saw Denzil waiting at the top of the lane. 'Bad luck.'

Richie shrugged. 'Not sure the Super will see it that way.'

'Do we even know who he is and what he's supposed to have done?'

'Nope and ours not to reason why. We just obey orders.'

'Not sure I like that way of thinking.'

'Oh come on, let's get an overpriced coffee in the brasserie. Who's to know?'

After forty minutes, Richie sent a message. *Lost him after he ducked and dived in crowd. Nothing to report. Back in fifteen.* Which would make Serrailler think they had tailed Ginger further and for longer than they had.

'I'll treat you to a chocolate brownie with that. Go on, don't look so worried, we're entitled.'

'Are we though?'

Richie winked before turning round to catch the eye of the server.

Fifty-One

Next-door neighbour Kevin Astley and his wife Helen had behaved perfectly ever since the night of Olivia's death, never butting in, never asking too many questions if they met, but sometimes putting a tin with a freshly baked cake inside, or a bunch of the first daffodils with a note. *Ring or come round if you need anything.* Guy, one of their two teenage sons, had cleaned and polished Greta's car without being asked, and taken out her recycling bins with their own as he left for school. She appreciated the help, and the gifts, but even more, she appreciated their tact.

Tonight, she had had to dash out to catch the post office before it closed, and when she got back, there was a cardboard box on her doorstep, with a note. *Reheat for 30 mins at 200. Or freeze straight away. I made far too much for us.*

She unpacked two foil containers containing beef casserole and as she had not bothered to cook properly for herself in the last fortnight, only eaten lumps of cheese or some scrambled eggs, at first the savoury smell made her recoil slightly. But she should eat better, she knew. Liv would have said so – Liv, whose own appetite had decreased as she had become picky about her food, which had to be organic, locally sourced, additive-free. 'You're going to have to do your own shopping if this goes on, Livi, I can't get it right and the supermarket doesn't appear to reach your standards.'

'You shouldn't go to supermarkets, you should shop in Starly. The organic shop has great things.'

'Yes, at great prices. Fine for a few organic eggs but I'm not doing a whole shop there, eco this and phosphate-free that costs more than I can afford.'

She turned off the inner recorder, the one that played conversations at random, and put the foil dishes on the worktop. She would heat one later, bake a potato to go with the meat. She had lost weight but she had had none to lose and, worst of all, she had lost it on her face, so that her eyes looked more prominent, staring back at her own image in the mirror out of hollow sockets. Her cheeks had fallen in.

'Then don't look at yourself,' the voice said. Liv's voice. Sharp, reasonable. Impatient. In Greta's video, Liv turned away and ran away up the stairs.

Eat the casserole tonight? Cooking exhausted her, she would have a piece of cheese and an apple, and tell the Astleys their food had been delicious.

The doorbell rang.

If she thought she herself looked strained, Jeff was a man who had aged twenty years in a couple of weeks. She looked at someone who appeared to be at the end of his life, all energy drained out of him to leave a man with greyish skin, a beak nose protruding from fallen cheeks, dead eyes. He wore an old jacket she thought he had thrown away and at his feet were two plastic carrier bags spilling over with unidentifiable stuff.

He said nothing. Nor did she, just opened the door wider and returned to the kitchen.

He set the bags on the floor, and after a moment, pulled out a chair and slumped at the table as if he had walked a hundred miles to get here.

'I was going to put supper on.'

He shook his head.

'The Astleys think I might starve.'

She stood looking down at the foil dishes and there was an odd silence which neither seemed willing to break.

She did not want to put the food away, or into the oven, she did not want to ask him why he was here, she wanted only to flick a switch and have Olivia sitting between them, fiddling with her hair while she looked at her maths book or her geography homework or a music magazine, waiting for supper, with the table laid and Jeff telling some work story or mentioning an item on the news or complaining about endless roadworks on his journey home. And Liv's bag dumped in the middle of the hall to be tripped over.

Greta let out a single, terrible sob, as the scene shifted back.

'I haven't got anything else much. I was going to put a potato in to bake.'

They looked at one another and each saw how the other was.

'It's taken us as well. It's taken what we were.'

'It,' Jeff said.

'Well, I can't say "she". She.'

'I started it.'

'Don't flatter yourself. Liv didn't do it because she was missing you.' She heard the cruelty in her voice.

'No.'

'We were fine.'

'I know.'

'Now I'm fine.'

'No,' he said. 'You are not fine.'

'Get your head round it, Jeff. We never will be fine again.'

'People cope.'

'Oh, coping. Do you want tea?'

He shrugged and she wanted to scream at him to wake up, get himself together, help himself. Help her.

'You've lost more hair,' she said.

'You mean I'm going bald.'

'Balder. Yes.'

He was balder, the rest of his hair was thinner and greyer, the flesh on his neck was flabby though he had lost weight.

Greta said down beside him and put out her hand to touch his arm briefly.

'What have you done with your life?'

'You mean, if I hadn't left you Livi wouldn't have hanged herself.'

She flinched at the raw words.

'Who knows anything about that? I doubt if we'll ever know. But you have two more children.'

It was his turn to draw back sharply from words and their meaning but he said nothing.

'What are they like? Do they look like you? Do they have different personalities? Identical twins do, I've heard that.'

'They're not identical.'

'Oh.'

'You don't want to know about them, Greta, not really. Why would you?'

'There has to be something from the wreckage, hasn't there? And it would be them. Your two sons. None of this is their fault.'

He turned to look at her and she saw the bruises under his eyes, and the deadness within them, saw utter weariness.

'You love them. You have to love them, Jeff.'

'Will you make that tea?'

'Will you?' He looked round as if he had never been inside this kitchen before. 'Oh for God's sake.'

She made tea and served it in total silence, put the casserole in the oven, and then sat down again, though not next to him now but across the table.

'Can I stay here '

'What do you mean?'

'I can't go back. I can't live there any longer. I love them because it's visceral, isn't it, but I don't like them, I don't like being around them, they cry and cry, they scream, I don't remember Livi screaming, do you? One sets the other off, and it can go on for an hour, two hours. I have to take them out in the car, or walk them in the pram, to get some quiet. The house is upside down with stuff . . . I don't remember Livi having so much stuff, do you?'

'Stop saying that. All babies have stuff. They themselves don't take up much space but everything they need does, it takes over the house.'

'It's a mess. I'm not much good. I tidy up but it's like the tide, so I've given up. It was a lovely house, it . . . I spent a fortune on getting it . . .'

'How she wanted it.'

He sighed. 'I can't go back there.'

'Do you love her?'

'I don't know.'

Greta snorted. 'All right, did you? You must have thought you did. Or was it only sex? Come on, we can have this conversation now, we never did, we just shouted a lot and then you left, but this is a conversation we've started at last, so let's go on.'

'What do you expect me to say? If you want me to feel guilty, don't worry.'

'No. This isn't about guilt or anything else to do with our marriage and your walking out of it. That's done. You have a new life and if you walk out of that, if you leave a very young woman and two babies because you feel guilty, you've decided you're not happy with them after all, you can't cope with their crying, you don't like the mess and the untidiness . . . then I despise you even more than I did. Look at you. You're a wreck and it's not all because of our daughter. Whatever the reason she did it, don't flatter yourself it was anything to do with you. I've made tea, the supper is heating up and you're welcome to some and then you take your carrier bags full of shirts or whatever they are and go back home. Home, Jeff. This isn't your home any more.'

When he looked at her again, Greta saw defeat and misery, grief and despair.

'If she didn't do it because of me – and maybe you're right – then what was it? Why did she do it, Greta? What happened to her?'

Fifty-Two

'I just don't want to go. Not tonight, not any night.'

'Do I have to talk to you as if you were five and say that sometimes we just have to do things we don't want to?'

'OK, OK.'

'Si, I understand, you know that, but you have to go. Dad's old, he's on his own –'

'He's his own worst enemy.'

'It won't be as bad as you think.'

'No, it'll be worse.'

'Just bite on the bullet.'

'Any other platitudes? I rang you for sympathy.'

'Well, you're not getting it. For heaven's sake, it's *one evening* of your life and it's now five to seven . . . Talk later.'

Cat did not quite hang up on him but only paused a second before switching off. She was not on duty, she wanted a quiet evening by the fire with her husband and the last volume of Hilary Mantel's trilogy, not a series of calls and texts from her brother. Richard Serrailler was without a female companion for the first time in Cat's memory, possibly the first time ever, he was nearly eighty and had recovered surprisingly well, but a stroke was a stroke, he had sensed mortality and did not care for it, and he needed them all, without ever being able to tell them so. She dropped by his flat whenever she could, took shopping, stayed to talk for half an hour, frequently brought him to the farmhouse for Sunday lunch. He was as acerbic and critical as ever but there was a new vulnerability about him now, which he would never admit to and concealed beneath his usual brusqueness. She felt sorry for him, but since the end of his marriage to Judith and the fact that his violence towards her was the reason and then his being accused of sexual assault on another woman, she found it hard to feel any warmth or affection for her father, but she knew what she must do, Kieron backed her, and she was annoyed when Simon whinged about going for a single supper.

'He's just spoilt,' she said, taking two mugs of tea into the sitting room. Kieron was on the sofa with his leg up.

'Not by me.'

'Of course not. Have I spoilt him?'

She saw his look and shrugged.

'You'll never be able to do anything else,' he said. 'And he knows it.'

'He needs a bloody wife.'

'So did I but then I got lucky.'

'Thank you. Simon has struck lucky several times but either he didn't know it or turned his back. Oh God, let's not go there.'

'That sounds quite difficult,' Kieron said, listening as Benjamin Britten for oboe floated down from Felix's room.

'It is. He's made one of those sudden leaps people do when they're learning an instrument . . . they chug along for a time on one level and then do a leap . . .'

'Grade what?'

'Five. Meanwhile, his voice won't hold out much longer.'

'He told me he didn't want to go on anyway, he's done with singing, apparently. Will you be sorry?'

'Yes and no, but whatever, it's his choice.'

She picked up her book but as she opened it there was a whimper. 'OK, Wookie . . . come on.'

The Yorkie settled down on Cat's lap with a happy sigh.

'He went trotting across the field OK this morning but I guess jumping onto a sofa is more of a strain.'

Cat rubbed Wookie's ears. 'He's a lucky little hound. I think he still misses Mephisto though.'

'Rubbish.'

Kieron turned back to his iPad, Cat opened her book. Britten had given way to mellifluous Corelli and somewhere in the distance, emergency sirens wailed through the darkness.

Fifty-Three

He should have left the flat at least a quarter of an hour earlier but he had hung about, without an excuse, checking his emails, washing up a couple of mugs, putting his dirty shirt in the laundry basket.

'Seven, for a drink beforehand,' his father had said, 'and I would be obliged if you were not late, my recipe is carefully timed.'

He would be late, not by much but enough to put his father's back up before the evening had properly begun. He picked up his phone, keys, jacket. Left the usual light on. Slammed the door behind him. As he got into the car, he remembered his sister's words, 'he's on his own', and wondered fleetingly if he would ever feel the same. No. Or at least not until he too was pushing eighty.

He was on the open stretch of the bypass, where on a quiet night like this, he could enjoy giving the Audi its head, but before he had the chance, he heard sirens and saw the blue lights coming up behind him. He slowed and pulled over to let two fire engines past, followed by a patrol car, and a minute later by another engine. He was heading off the road to the west, they carried on.

'Six minutes late. Better than expected.'

'Why?'

'I usually give you ten.'

'I was slowed down by emergency fire engines.'

'Always something, Simon. Gin and tonic? Or a sherry?'

'Gin, thanks, Dad, but let me get it.'

'Thank you. It's all laid out.'

'Something smells good.'

'I've braised the pheasants this time, with celery. Too old for roasting.'

'Excellent.'

It had surprised them all when Richard had started to cook, after a lifetime of having done no more than make toast. Simon's mother Meriel had been a decent, plain cook, without taking much notice of what she was doing, his stepmother, Judith, had been better, and there had always been others. Perhaps his taking to careful, recipe-led cooking was a sign that Richard knew those days were behind him.

Simon was carrying the tray of drinks into the living room when his phone rang.

'I hope you will ignore that.'

'Don't worry, I'm off.' But he still glanced at the screen. The station never called on rest days unless it was urgent. 'I ought to just get this, sorry, Dad . . . it won't be anything.'

'Then ignore it.'

But he had already stepped into the hall.

'Serrailler.'

'Sorry, guv, you're needed. Chinese pharmacy in Starly has gone up in flames. Query explosion.'

As he left, Richard was shouting, 'I'll throw the whole bloody supper in the bin, and you needn't expect a further invitation.'

The square had been cordoned off by the time he got there, and four uniform were keeping onlookers back. Four fire engines were on the scene, and the firefighters were both attacking the main blaze and working to keep it from spreading into adjacent buildings. He had always found fires terrifying, to look at, to smell, to deal with, since he had been involved in a massive blaze in the Docklands, in which seven people had died and the whole thing had taken two weeks to burn out. Now, as he dipped under the rope and went cautiously across the square, he felt the heat on his face, smelled the acrid burning.

The fire chief turned and nodded. Serrailler had worked with him only once before and knew him to be very competent.

'Do you know anything at all yet?'

'Not much except that three separate people reported hearing some sort of explosion – one said it was the same sound as an oil drum he'd once heard going up. Whether there was anything inside the shop that was combustible I don't know yet – could have been something electrical.'

'Or . . . ?'

'Or could have been arson, something thrown into the shop, left in there – impossible to say just yet. Anything you know?'

'Possibly. The place has been under surveillance since the body of a young junkie was found in the flat above a few weeks ago. The pharmacy belongs to a man called Wang Lin.'

'He doesn't live above?'

'No, in Bevham. Assuming he'd left around five as usual, there'd have been nobody in the building.'

A sudden shout, and a great spurt of fire burst out of the roof and skywards.

'I'm needed. We have to evacuate this whole side plus all the houses up the hill behind.'

Simon moved back. The square was like a film set, a moving scene of men with hoses, pipes, walkie-talkies, the noise of water under massive pressure pushing into the flames, voices shouting orders. Crackling. Sudden small explosions. Bangs. More shouts. Engines running on all sides.

'Thought you'd have got here.' Kieron had come up behind him. 'Anyone inside?'

'Probably not but they can't get anywhere near to find out yet.'

'Maybe I should have given you that twenty-four-hour surveillance.'

'Hindsight's a wonderful thing, sir.'

'Think it's accidental?'

'No, but there's nothing to say it isn't either. They've got their hands full with keeping people away and organising an evacuation, but I need to ask if anyone reported lights in the shop. This place is dead after six in winter, though, so the chances are nobody was around to see anyway.'

'Is the chemist here yet? Presumably he'd gone home by the time it started.'

'Pray he had but I don't know any more. Someone has to contact him if they haven't already.'

A burst of black smoke went up and some of the firemen were already wearing breathing apparatus.

'Better get further back – a muggy night like this will make the fumes hang about low down.'

There was a warning shout as the shop window fell out and crashed onto the pavement, and, as the glass shattered, the outside air hit the flames inside with a roar.

There had been no reply from Wang's landline, or his mobile, so a patrol had been sent out to his home. Simon stood watching, waiting, anxious, various possible scenarios running through his head. The call interrupted them.

'We're outside 14 Marmion Road, guv, and we haven't been able to raise anyone, there are no lights on, curtains are drawn, there's no car in the drive or parked.'

'Any neighbours come out or look through a window?'

'No, but the house next door is empty with a Sold sign and then it's a corner, with a side road, so chances are nobody saw anything.'

'Houses opposite? Come on, you shouldn't need me to tell you this.'

Half an hour later, they reported that one neighbour was about but was new and didn't know anyone, another said she thought the Wangs were early risers but she didn't know any more.

'I'll be over. Stay where you are.'

'We're supposed to be off in ten, guv.'

'I didn't hear that.'

The patrol car was parked up, uniform in it looking bored.

Serrailler opened the door and beckoned them out. 'And this takes as long as it takes, have you got me?'

He turned his back on them and went up the drive of number 14. The curtains were all drawn together. He pushed open the letter box but there was a felt cover on the inside, so he could not see into the hall; he put his ear to it and heard no sound at all.

'Round the back.' A well-tended garden, even in winter, shrubs neatly trimmed, a path which had no moss or dirt on its surface, a small summer house at the end, locked but with folded deck-chairs and a small table visible through the window. The glass back door of the house that opened onto a strip of terrace was also curtained. They returned to the front.

'We need to get inside.'

'I've got a strong shoulder, guv.'

'Fine, but just before you apply brute force, have either of you looked for a spare key? Under the mat, a plant pot?'

The three of them split up to search and it was only a couple of minutes before the big man shouted. There was a low wall between the terrace and the grass, made to look like a rockery and he was standing beside it, holding up a key in one hand, a grey lump in the other. 'One of them phoney stones with a space inside – you can spot them a mile off.'

'Surprised you didn't then,' Serrailler said.

He stepped inside, stood still and listened. There was the strangely dead silence of an empty house but he still called out, and went on calling, as he entered the two ground-floor rooms, kitchen, pantry, covered walkway with two children's bicycles and the recycling bins. A small wooden sledge was tied to the roof.

Upstairs. Four bedrooms, all curtains drawn, everything tidy and clean and very empty. He opened a wardrobe in the main bedroom, then a chest of drawers, after which he went into the children's and a spare room and did the same. All of the drawers and hanging cupboards were more than half empty of clothes, shoes, toys and both bathrooms clear of any toiletries.

As he stood on the landing he saw that the hatch to the roof space was very slightly out of place. He pulled the ladder down but found only some rolled-up carpet and an old television set and faint lines in the dust.

'They've gone,' he said, running down the stairs. 'Clothes and personal stuff missing, and it looks as if there were some suit-cases in the attic which have been dragged out.'

'So that's it?'

'For now. You can get off, don't want you missing a second of off-duty time. I'll lock up and take the key.'

'SOCO then.'

'As far as we know the house isn't a crime scene, so probably not for the time being. Thanks, guys. Oh, and well spotted on that trick stone – you saved your shoulder and the force a repair bill.'

In the car and about to pick up messages, Serrailler felt as if life and energy had been drained out through the soles of his feet. He had had no sleep, only coffee and a bacon bap to eat, his throat was raw and he could taste the smoke in his mouth. When he breathed in, the lining of his lungs were sore. If he went back to the fire scene there would be nothing he could do, and there would be no more information now until access to the building was allowed. He opened the window and inhaled deeply a few times. Bevham air was not like that on top of a Swiss mountain but still a definite improvement on that in and around Starly now.

He usually ran up the stairs to his flat but now, his legs apparently full of lead, it was three flights of toil. He felt better after a hot shower but when he sat down on his bed, he was swallowed up by tiredness. Three minutes later, he was asleep.

Fifty-Four

'Brookie and Alfie, get out of there and home, now, or you'll feel the back of my hand. I said you weren't to come round here, it's not safe, and that cop has told you to scarper. Tommy and Connor, you should know better. Now come here!'

They went. You didn't mess with him in this mood.

'Get in front of me. What do you think you're playing at? You haven't got a brain between you. Fire. Know what that is? It kills, it burns, it chokes you. Don't you ever sneak out of the house in the middle of the night again, hear me? And look at you, you'll catch your death.'

'Aw, Dad . . .'

'In the house. You heard. Right, I'm getting breakfast, you're eating it, and then I need my kip, and you're staying inside, and there's no Xbox and no –'

'Dad! You can't do that.'

'See if I can't. Connor, get the eggs, and there were four sausages in the fridge, last I knew. Brookie, toast.'

'Dad?'

'Toast I said.'

'I'm getting it. Dad, they said there was a man in there burned to death, is that true?'

Vince Roper paused. He hadn't hung about the square long enough to hear anything, he'd gone with just the one purpose.

'Margarine should be in the fridge, where is it?'

'Dad . . .'

243

'Tomatoes.'

'Noooooo.'

'You heard. You got to eat healthy.'

'Dad . . .'

'Who told you this, about a man being in there?'

'Everybody was talking about it.'

'That all? Just rumour and gossip?'

'Must have been true.'

'No it mustn't, people make stuff up, gives them some sort of buzz – a sick one, ask me.'

He scooped sizzling oil over the sausages, slipped eggs into the pan. Thought. No smoke without fire, ha ha, but why and how did a fire like that start? There could have been a man in the shop, easily, the Chinese, gone back to fetch something, working late. Could have been.

Or someone else.

'Plates! And when you've eaten that, you can go back to bed, stay up, do anything you like, only you stop in, right? I'll know if you've so much as sniffed the air, any of you.' He punched his fork into the egg yolk. They had their heads bent, not catching his eye, scoffing. He wasn't as mad as he'd made himself sound, but then, they knew that, more or less. Just couldn't be quite sure. Vince smiled to himself.

'Dishes,' he said, leaving the kitchen ten minutes later. Brookie was putting more bread into the toaster. Hanging round the fire scene before dawn had given them an appetite.

The whole of Starly stank of it. Vince walked round the far side of the square but the cordon was still in place, police were patrolling and two fire engines remained. Three men were standing beside the Salvation Army wagon with steaming drinks, so he ducked under the rope.

'Any chance I could buy a tea off you? I'm not a firefighter but have just come off nights.'

'You can't buy anything but you're welcome to a tea and a bacon roll if you want one – and if you'd like to put a donation in the tin we'd be very grateful but there's no obligation at all.'

'Thanks a lot.' Vince slipped a pound coin in the slot. 'You people are saints.'

She laughed. 'I don't know about that. Sugar's on the counter.'

He stood next to one of the guys in heavy-duty gear. 'Smell of smoke gets into everything.'

'Takes twenty-four hours and a lot of water to get rid of it, and even then. At least this one's not oil. Oil's the real stinker.'

'Explodes as well.'

'Oil. Chemicals.'

'Looks as if it's out now though.'

'Pretty much. Walls and beams and are still hot.'

'How long will that take?'

'Depends. Few days.'

'So you can't get inside yet?'

'Oh yeah, we've been in but nobody else though, so don't even think about it, mate.'

'As if. Electrical fault?'

He shrugged. 'Not my call.'

'Everyone safe?'

'You a reporter or something? Because if so –'

'Do I look like a reporter? I'm a bouncer at the Moon Cat, aren't I?'

'Right, sorry. How's that for a living?'

'Could be worse. Biggest job is telling kids of thirteen going on twenty to get home to Mum.'

'Right.' The fireman threw his paper cup into the bin. 'Better get back.'

'Ambulance gone, has it?'

'What ambulance?'

'Heard there was someone trapped inside. That not right?'

'If you're not a sodding reporter you're doing a good job of behaving like one.'

Fifty-Five

They had left the house in darkness, and saw few cars until they hit the motorway going north. The car was packed full with every last thing they might need.

'How long will we be there for?'

'Why are we going?'

'Can't we just go in the morning?'

But then they were quiet, then quieter. His wife sat beside him, saying nothing, asking nothing because that was her way, the way their marriage ran smoothly, and for the last year or so, since the men had first appeared in the shop, that was the way he knew was safest. It had begun easily enough, with the occasional letter or small packet left overnight, or for a couple of days, and all he had had to do was leave it alone. They would come to collect. They always did. He convinced himself that he had no idea what the packets contained, and lying to himself had come easily, until the time when they had asked for more. He was a pharmacist, he knew how to do this or that. How to mix x with y, how to cut larger things up to make several smaller, how to grind and crush and turn to powder, his skills were what they needed as well as his storage space. And his silence. He had not known how to extricate himself by then, they had wound invisible threads so tightly, with such intricacy, and that was when he had realised and started to make plans, though only in his head, for what he could do if it escalated. Still, for another six months, it had not. The same two men had come and gone, never with any warning, always with the air of threat hanging round them, one that he could smell and taste and sense. Fear. That was their weapon. They were experts at fear.

He had always been aware that if he had to leave it would be in a hurry and unexpectedly, his plans had been based on that, so that when it came, he was prepared, calm even. And after all, it had not been very difficult.

His wife had turned on the car radio not to news or chit-chat but to soft music. His children were tapping soundlessly on their games. Traffic was heavy for the first thirty miles or so, but when it eased, Wang picked up speed and so the distance between them and home widened, and that between them and safety lessened with every mile.

There hadn't been time to ask if his instincts were correct, if he was doing the right thing, the fact that he had seen the men drive past but not come into the shop, and then later, both sitting in the car parked up the side road when he had gone to get his coffee, had frightened him. They had always just appeared, gone into the storeroom and out again, so different behaviour was troubling, though he could not have said exactly why, and the next time he had looked out across the square, the car had gone. He had worried about it all afternoon, which had been quiet, so he had had time. He had checked the store but there was nothing.

Then, he had locked up an hour earlier than usual, his mind made up, his sense of unease stronger than ever.

They had spent the evening sorting out and packing, loading the car. His wife simply did as he asked, apparently untroubled. They were going to his family, and to see hers, she did not seem interested in asking why, she took life as it came, left decisions to him. It was the children who scarcely stopped asking questions, when, where, who, why, why, why, all the time they were putting their things into bags, why why why.

'When are we coming back?'

He did not know. He had made no plans, just been sure that they must leave and trusted to his feelings.

The traffic became heavy as they hit the industrial Midlands, there was a twenty-minute delay at roadworks, it poured with rain, slowing everything down. The children squabbled. Wini was silent.

There was a long queue at the entrance to the service station where Wang filled up the car, before parking as close to the mall as he could. Another car slotted in beside him, making it difficult for them to get out without walking through puddles, but no one felt like complaining, they just ran through the rain. The place was busy but it swallowed up dozens and still looked quiet, and while his family went to the toilets, he found a table in the centre, opposite a sushi, a Caffè Nero, a McDonald's, a Waitrose, a Chinese noodle bar. When he had first come south, there had been Granada all-day breakfasts and a W.H. Smith.

'Better?'

It was, with hot food, hot chocolate, comics and sweets.

'Why are we going?'

'Because Grandpa and Nana need us, I told you.'

'They've got lots of people all round, they don't need us as well.'

'That's not respectful – you should be wanting to see them.'

'I do.'

'Yes, they give us loads of cakes and those fried sweets.'

'Where are we going to sleep?'

'Come,' his father had said over the phone, 'we can decide everything when you're here. Just get in the car.'

He had told him a cut-down version of the story, not wanting to alarm his parents but needing to communicate the urgency of his need to come.

'Your brother can have the children, you can be with us, anything to make you comfortable. Of course we will look after you – as if we would do anything else.'

Yes. What he would do after the first few days he did not know but there was always work, with family, friends, even if it was not his own work, not at first, but his brother who lived next door to their parents was an engineer, the other brothers ran a wholesale warehouse. They had come a long way since the years of Chinese takeaways, fish and chip vans, small restaurants like the old Sun King and the Green Dragon, which had been sold while he was still at school. They were prosperous.

They had all left home to study and come straight back, to settle, raise their families, push ahead with their careers. He was the only one who had wanted to get away, see another sort of life, try a different part of the country, and they had been hurt and surprised, but they had not complained. 'You can always come home.'

But not like this.

They had pancakes with sugar and fat curls of cream from an aerosol. The place was full of movement, no one sitting for long, everyone on the way to somewhere else. A restless feeling came over him, and a strange sense of being no bigger than an ant among a million other ants. He looked at his wife and she looked back over her mug, and did not smile. He looked at his son and daughter, and they grinned and started to shove each other.

A picture of the pharmacy came to his mind, empty and dark, with the sign turned to Closed. He would have been seeing a woman with a bad bruise, a man with a cough wanting more of the linctus that he said was all he needed to do him good, though Wang had been trying to get him to see his doctor for months, he needed to see his doctor. He thought of the stock-room shelves, their calm arrangement of boxes, jars, bottles, like a satisfying pattern, and then packets that the men pushed in anywhere, disturbing the order.

He had never told his wife, his family, anyone at all, and even talking urgently to his father, he had skirted round the truth, what they did, how long it had been going on. The threats they had made at the start had been enough for him to let them do what they wanted, they had never had to repeat them.

A busload of pensioners had come in, lines of them tottering on legs cramped after a long drive, heading for the toilets, and after them, fifteen or twenty squaddies in khaki, with berets, boots clattering. The children stared at them.

'We should go, people will want this table.' He handed out five pound coins to each of them. 'Go and get a book or something. No sweets. Don't take forever.'

They scuttled across to Smith's.

'It's going to be fine,' Wang said, putting his hand over his wife's inert one. 'You like my family, your own aren't so far away.'

She shrugged.

'We'll be back.' Would they? He had no idea but she would want to and he needed to keep her spirits up, she was too easily cast into a depressed, passive mood in which she barely spoke, even to the children.

'It's safest for now.'

'You seem to know.'

'I do.'

'Not to know is hard, but then, I never do know.'

'Because I don't want you to be worried.'

'You think I'm not worried now? You think we can just run away in the middle of the night like refugees without me worrying at all? I like my home. I like where we live.'

'It's a break,' Wang said. 'Just a holiday and time with our families. Think of it like that.'

'But it isn't,' she said, as the children came racing back, hands full of comics with plastic toys taped to them. 'More rubbish.'

'Leave them. I said they could get what they wanted except sweets. Come on.'

The blue car was still hemming them in, but as they tried to edge the doors open, a woman came across the walkway, unlocked it and reversed just enough for them to get in. After that she did not move so he had to edge out slowly.

'Some people have no manners, no thought for anyone else. Look at this, and if I touch her wing mirror she'll be out screaming at me.'

'She's waiting for someone.'

'Makes no difference.'

He made for the exit road and joined the line of other cars, the blue one behind. In the back, the toys were being peeled off the comics. It was still raining, and as Wang reached the slip road, spray was arcing up from the fast-moving traffic, windscreen wipers could not cope with the deluge, some drivers had fog lights on. In such blinding conditions, everyone's focus was on the road ahead. Only on the road.

The blue car pulled out and came close alongside Wang, so that he had to steer left towards the narrow strip of verge. He swore and wound the window down, turned towards them.

They were experts. It was over in seconds, bullets fired into the car, front seat, rear seat, and even before it began to slip and lurch, with no one controlling it, they were onto the motorway, moving from slow to middle to fast lane, in and out of vehicles, through rain and spray, ignoring the blaring horns and squealing tyres, moving fast up the gears and out of sight, off at the next exit and gone.

The road from the service station was a chaos of stalled cars, opening doors, shouts, desperate phone calls while the Wangs' car was at standstill against the boundary hedge, the engine ticking, and inside, silence.

Fifty-Six

Her last call was a mile from the farmhouse and it was ten to one. For once, she had time for lunch.

The warmth and the rich smell of cooking came as she opened the front door.

'Sam?'

'Hi. This isn't for now, it's for dinner, but if you sit down I'll make you a salad when I've got this in. Should I start it in the top oven?'

'Till the liquid is bubbling, then down. What's brought this on?'

'I'm a fantastic son and so domesticated.'

'Hm. But thanks, whatever. I'll look forward to not cooking supper.'

'I've made a lot, plenty for the freezer, and I thought I'd take some to Rosie later, don't want her living off crisps and frozen pizza.'

Cat hesitated, but then said only, 'She's got too much sense.'

She got plates, salad and cheese out of the fridge, switched on the kettle, still carefully working out what to say, until her phone buzzed.

Mrs Ellen Boyden, 30 Grove Lane, Starly. Cough, sinus pain, after heavy cold.

'You're having lunch first, Mum.'

'I am, this one's all right for an hour. I take it you used all the stewing beef?'

'And what was in the freezer.'

'Heavens.'

'Carrots, mushrooms, red wine, stock –'

'Which red wine?'

Sam looked vague and shushed her out of his way.

'You sure Rosie will be at home? Wouldn't want you to have a wasted journey.'

'She's revising and she doesn't do libraries. She'll be there.'

'Maybe ring her first to check though?'

Sam closed the over door. 'Now, sit down and have lunch. '

'Just that . . .'

'What?'

He turned to look at her and she recognised her son's 'challenge me' expression.

'Just that I'll have to leave at two.'

'Right. Have we got any of those tinfoil containers?'

'No, take it in a lidded dish, in a box. Will she be OK about you taking her food? Might it not look a bit . . .'

'What?'

'Nothing.'

When they were eating, he said, 'I've applied for my old portering job back.'

'OK. Good idea to put fennel in this. I can never slice it thinly enough.'

'Sharpen the knife and do it slowly. You're all right with it then?'

'Sure. You haven't decided what else you might want to do, you enjoyed portering, it's a wage. Only thing is, the car . . .'

'Yes. Yes, right. I was going to mention that. If I'm living here it does mean I need wheels, and I'm selling the motorbike, one thing too many has gone wrong. Think I bought a pup.'

'Why don't you wait and see what happens?'

'What's that supposed to mean?'

'Don't jump down my throat. You mightn't get the job.'

He gave her a look.

'Yes, all right, stupid thing to say.'

'They're desperate for porters, always, and I've got experience. Done deal. You want coffee?'

'Please. Then I'm going to take Wookie across the field.'

'I'll come with you. Tell you what as well, there are some daffodils just showing through on the edge of the spinney.'

It was cold but the sun was out, the sky brittle blue. Wookie no longer raced up and down but he trotted ahead of them happily, his back legs looking stronger.

'You'd be all right about it, wouldn't you?'

'Sammy, I have absolutely no problem with you being a hospital porter. I'm not a career snob and I know it's a very valuable job. Hospitals couldn't function. Do it while you work things out.'

'Cool. But actually, I meant Rosie. If I went back to live in the flat.'

'You . . . could you do that?'

'Why not?'

Cat hedged her way round the question. 'Once she's qualified, she probably won't be there though.'

'Not that actual *flat*. You know.'

'With Rosie. Wherever?'

'Well, yes.'

'Sam, five minutes ago it was all off. You can't blame me for wondering if I've missed something.'

'Think I read too much into it.'

'Wookie! Don't you dare go under that fence. Remember what happened the last time?'

'He remembers all of it.'

'He should.'

'So?'

'It's up to you, Sam. Your life. Just go carefully, that's all I'm saying. Now, I've got to hurry up.'

'Did you hear about the fire?'

'Who didn't. Why?'

'There was a body found.'

'I didn't hear that part. Are you sure? Was it on the news?'

'Dunno. Probably. But when I biked over to Starly, everybody was talking about it.'

Inside the burnt-out shop the smell was choking, it caught the back of Serrailler's throat and within seconds he was tasting it.

The counter, shelves, displays were mounds of black melted substance, and the walls were burned out back to the brickwork. He looked up. Blackened boards, joists, cross-beams and, here and there, gaps into the room of the flat above. Water dripped onto his yellow hard hat, his shoulders, the ash and cinder piles that crunched underfoot.

'You did well to stop this spreading.'

'Near thing but that's always a priority. We more or less had to let this go, it was well alight by the time we got here.'

'Is that usual?'

'Depends.'

'Any idea yet what caused it?'

'I can't put it in black and white but this wasn't your usual electrical fault – difficult to tell until the investigators have combed through but it looks like an explosion, incendiary device of some sort. Firework possibly, petrol bomb even.'

Simon stepped slowly round the stinking room. At his feet, a glass bottle, blackened by smoke but intact, another nearby. The cash register, melted out of shape. The door to the office and stockroom was only burnt splinters hanging off burnt-off hinges. Inside, nothing was left at all, the shelves were buckled, piles of debris, cardboard boxes, melted plastic tubes gave no clue to what they had held.

He shook his head.

'But thank God no human remains.'

'No, place was empty. And I understand the upstairs flat had been untenanted for a while.'

'More or less,' Serrailler said. He looked around again. 'I'm not a fire expert, far from it, but this was deliberate. I'd put money on it.'

'Insurance job?'

'I doubt it. There's a much bigger backstory.'

He came out and stood taking deep breaths to clear his lungs and throat. Even the damp, muggy air was refreshing after the acrid smell inside the shop.

One engine and a fire service 4x4 were parked up and they would be gone once the building had been secured and sealed off, with flashing warning signs and cones outside. A few people stopped to look briefly as they went by but there were no sight-seers left, Starly had gone about its business of the day, the shops were mostly open again.

Simon did not feel much better for his heavy sleep and had wakened with a dry throat and stiff limbs, and even his run had not refreshed him.

He unlocked his car and threw his jacket into the boot. He smelled of rancid smoke and ash, clothes, skin, hair, he needed to shower and change again before he could go anywhere near other people. He drank a full bottle of water, still standing outside, and though it was not cold, it cleared his mouth and throat, and he was debating whether to get straight off or buy another bottle, which with luck would come straight out of the corner shop's fridge, when the message light flashed on his phone.

Fifty-Seven

Cat held the front door open as Sam took the box of food out and loaded it carefully into the car, the familiar ice chip of worry pricking. You carried every child for life, from the moment of birth, but the shards cut more deeply and painfully for Sam than the others. Hannah was her own woman, had been since childhood, and Felix lived in a quiet, purposeful world of his own, but Sam . . . sensitive, touchy, muddled Sam, kindest, most thoughtful of them all, marked by seeing his father seconds after he had died. He had taken that in and understood it, and of most people she knew, was least troubled by death, but it had helped to make him emotionally vulnerable.

He waved as he turned the car, heading off to take Rosie the lovingly prepared dinner, including napkins, candle, candle-holder, even matches, and his expression was open and cheerful. Cat went inside, to immerse herself in catching up on patient notes in the hope of putting it all out of her mind. Maybe it would be fine, Rosie would give him a welcome, they would talk and restore their friendship, if nothing more.

The country route was as usual until Sam reached the ford through Denningham, which had flooded across the road, and he had to take a detour, then another, as local radio was giving priority to reports of the river through Lafferton being danger-ously high. The journey to Rosie took him nearly twice as long as usual, but her light was on, he could make out the line of her head bent over the desk. She worked too hard, too long, too late, she had done ever since he had known her, but it meant she would do well, she was a highflyer intent on being at the top as soon as possible, when she had finally decided on the branch of medicine lucky enough to get her. His own indecision would have irritated her had she not, rather to her own surprise, suffered from it too.

He managed to ring the bell, holding on to the box and a chill bag. Since moving to London he wasn't there to insist that she take a work break, eat, go for a run. He ought to be back with her, seeing to all of that, whatever their actual relationship.

Quick footsteps.

'Oh.'

'Hi, Rosie. I know you're not eating properly, I have second sight, so I've brought your supper.'

Rosie looked at him, then at the box, the bag. Back to him.

'Can you let me in before I drop these? I've got absolutely everything, you don't even need to pour water, there's a bottle straight from our fridge, only it took such an age to get here, the roads are all flooded, so it probably won't be very cold now. The food needs putting in the oven anyway so –'

'What is all this?'

'Your supper. I said. Boeuf bourguignon, rice, beans and carrots, a –'

'I didn't ask you to be the Deliveroo man.'

'I know, but look, please either take the chill bag or let me in. It's heavy.'

'No.'

'I'm going to drop them, idiot.'

'You have to put them back in the car, Sam.'

'But it's your supper.'

'I've eaten.'

'Ha, I don't believe that one, unless it was a banana. Come on . . .'

'Sam . . . please. It's very kind and thoughtful, but honestly, I would prefer you to take it back now. I've got my head down and I have actually had a proper supper.'

He looked at her. Looked again.

'Rosie?' A male voice. 'Everything all right? Want me to come down?'

Sam did not know whether what ran through him was heat or chill, he only knew he felt something change inside him as the truth hit him, which it should have done from the moment she opened the door, as it should have done weeks ago when he had seen her in a clinch with . . . but somehow, it hadn't.

'I'm sorry but you can see . . .'

'OK, it's OK, I get it. I'm sorry, I should be the one, I'm the idiot here.'

He was backing away, still trying to keep hold of the box and the bag, trying not to drop his car keys, managing to grip them enough to open the door.

He drove back attentively, but a mile from home, he pulled into a gateway, switched off the engine and sat very still, letting himself cry for as long as he needed to, here on his own in the darkness. After this, he was never going to allow himself to cry about it again.

Fifty-Eight

Need to know what's happened.

No reply.

Ten minutes later. *Pick up.*

Another ten.

Have you got him yet?

He knew he couldn't just not answer or he'd be the next.

Not yet.

Why?

He's not around.

Fuck sake. Pubs. Cafes. Get on with it.

Done all that. No sign.

Then get to the bloody caravan.

Can't. Flooded.

What?

Field's under water.

Shit. But the clock's still ticking.

I'm not Jesus Christ.

What?

Can't walk on bloody water.

He wanted to call the text back, that sort of clever-dick reply got you into trouble.

He drove past the gate to the waste ground again, but the flood was seeping out from there now, trickling steadily over the road. He could see the caravan on the other side, near the warehouse, its wheels under water, but the rest was clear, and the flood was spreading away from not towards it.

Still, it was a question of getting over there, the water looked deep for over half the distance, you'd need more than rubber boots, you'd want a wetsuit. Meanwhile, they sat up in some lush house hundreds of miles north and gave him orders.

Gloves went back into town – nobody ever went by their real name, nobody even *knew* real names – and, by a miracle, a van pulled out of a parking space opposite the Black Cat Cafe as he turned down the street. He slipped deftly into it.

It hadn't rained for a night, but the small space was like a sauna and stank of damp gear, wet boots, mud. Steam blotted the windows. You breathed in air full of moisture, straight from other people's mouths and lungs. That'd be a cold then. Flu. Pneumonia.

He pushed his way into a space near a gang from the construction site, wet overalls, orange hard hats on the floor.

It was Nora on the counter, missing nothing, shouting out orders over the din, with little Benjy shoving through plates of sausages, bacon, eggs, burgers, chips, chips, chips.

Fats wasn't here though, he had a good look round, table by table, making sure the little weasel wasn't concealed by someone broader, taller.

His phone rang and he ignored it. There wasn't much signal in here and he wanted to eat in peace. Bacon. Two eggs. Mushrooms. Black pudding. Three rounds of toast. The extractor fan roared from the galley kitchen. He shook the plastic ketchup bottle and made worms of dark red round his plate, remembering doing the same thing as a kid, with the bottle glurping out too much in a huge pool, drowning his food, ruining it.

'That'll teach you, and you're eating all of it.'

He looked round as the door opened, and then again.

No.

He bent his head to his plateful. If Fats turned up, he wouldn't miss him.

*

261

'Serrailler.'

'Vince.'

'I'm on my way into a conference. I'll contact you later.'

Serrailler switched off. There was no conference and he had no appointments. He didn't feel like talking to Vince about a lowlife drug runner. Fats was a nobody, he didn't know anything, he couldn't lead them to those at the top of the food chain, so it was a waste of time to go looking for him.

He felt sick to death of the business, the way its tentacles reached out and curled round the innocent, and drew them in, enslaving them to men who got filthy rich on all the misery and fear. Liam Payne, dead in the now burnt-out flat, his devastated, shocked, grieving family, blaming themselves, other young men and women like him, dead from accident or suicide, in their teens and twenties. Girls working on the streets to feed their drug habits, kids with addicted parents. Kids like Vince's boy, innocently hooked in with presents by scum like Fats. It was sordid, degraded, filthy. Those who gained most paid nothing.

He sighed. That morning he'd rung his father, who had put the phone down on him. Cat had sent a message about Sam. That kind of a day. That kind of a year so far.

His laptop flickered. Ten minutes later, he was on his way to the Cypriot cafe.

'Hey? You out on calls?'

'In theory, but my next patient just cancelled.'

'What, they died?'

'Not funny – no, they've gone into BG with pneumonia.'

'Same difference. You anywhere near the station? I'm having a coffee and I've got something to show you.'

'No, I'm on the Bevham side. What sort of something?'

'Nope, you've got to see.'

'You have a puppy?'

'God, no thanks. Come on, try harder.'

'I can't, Si, my last call is near home, and then I'm off. Come to supper.'

'OK. Actually, that might be better because I'll know more by then.'

'Don't *do* this! More about what?'

'See you later.'

He laughed, and started on his espresso as his phone beeped.

'You nearby, guv?'

'What's happened?' You could always tell, by the tone of voice, or the expression if they were standing in front of you.

'Call just came in from West Midlands . . . It's the Wang family.'

Whatever lightness Serrailler had been feeling disappeared.

'What about them?'

'Killed in car crash coming out of service station on the motorway, WM confirmed it was the Wang family, parents and two kids, their car had rolled and caught fire. They didn't have a chance. Loads of people stopped, they got extinguishers from the filling area, but you can't get near that sort of blaze.'

'God almighty. They were running away, weren't they? Going to his family? That fire in his shop was arson, and Wang knew it wouldn't stop there, they'd be at his home and family next.'

'Right.'

'So he scarpered, he got out. It's what anyone would have done, he was going to somewhere safe, or safe-r. They could have got lost in the Chinese community, they could have stayed there. ' He banged his fist on the table. 'And he messed up. What was he thinking, what the hell made him hit the bank? He can't have been going any speed.'

'Thing is, guv . . .'

'What?'

'Witnesses said they saw the car behind get alongside them, asked him to open the window . . . shot all four of them?'

Serrailler was silent, taking it in. When he spoke again, Denzil could barely hear him.

'Christ. They'd been following. They guessed what he'd do and where he'd go.'

'Looks like it.'

Serrailler went to get another strong coffee, his head feeling as if it would explode.

'You've seen everything, but you haven't, everything has happened and then it happens again.'

'Sorry, guv.'

'We'll never find out exactly what he was doing for them but it would have been under extreme pressure. And for how long? Months?'

'My guess is longer. Bad drugs have been around forever, but as the county lines have spread and reeled in more and more users, there have been problems with supply. I don't know much about the chemistry of it, but they get round the problem for a time by mixing the stuff with something else, something they can obtain easily – or people like Wang can.'

'No evidence of course. The building has gone, so has Wang. Junkies like Payne are dead, they shut everyone else up, one way or another. God, these are evil men. I'm on my way.'

'Finish your coffee first, guv.'

Denzil spoke gently, as if, Simon thought, that he was looking after him. He felt warmed by it.

It was nearly four before he got away and he had to change the time of the meeting with the estate agent twice. He rarely left the station before six, but this was something he was anxious not to miss, something that had given him a thump of excitement when he had seen it.

The last hour with CID had been grim. These coppers were as tough as any but some things did not wash over you without leaving their mark, and as Serrailler looked round the room, he saw the different expressions on their faces – shock, revulsion. Anger.

'What are these people like? What kind of scum shoots a mum and dad and their two children point-blank, for Christ's sake?'

'Same scum who set fire to the shop.'

'Big difference.'

'They must have thought Wang was in there.'

'All of that,' Simon had said. 'I agree with every last word, and we're liaising with the West Midlands force, the motorway guys, Greater Manchester, everyone's together on this. They have to be found.'

A frisson round the table. They all knew the odds of getting the men at the top. Other, larger forces with far more drug-related crimes on their streets, had been working on it for years.

'Lucky strike,' DI Morgan said.

'Yes. Chance plays a part, always has, but dogged police work, routine searches, eyes and ears open, patrols on the motorways are usually what pay off in the end.'

'Come on, we all know it's the tiddlers who get caught that way – doing a ton, no brake lights, forgot to pay their tax, pull them over and guess what? The top men drive their Audis and their Range Rovers as if they had granny inside, they never forget their insurance, they have the cars serviced every month, keep them clean as a whistle. You won't find any little wraps and polybags of coke in their glove compartments. Never come under suspicion.'

'All right, but let's not assume every force is as idle and incompetent as this one.'

A good-humoured roar of protest.

'The scene of the shooting is cordoned off and they're crawling all over it, the exit road from the service station has been closed – they've done a temporary rerouting. They're throwing every-thing at it, including ballistics of course, which is something they're particularly good at. Don't assume your best policing never yields a result.'

'So what about us, guv?'

'Wang's pharmacy and the flat above – we won't get anything more, the building's pretty much obliterated, but fire service investigators are still there. Our main focus is the Wang house. I also need people delving into every aspect of his business – and his life. Every last detail. Bilaval?'

'Great, right up my street at the moment.'

'You still got that foot problem? Time you saw the doctor.'

'I'm seeing a podiatrist, thanks. Every week.' The DC looked pained.

The jobs were assigned and they dispersed. They would go at this one like Rottweilers, wanting results. Some things got to you.

A few of the country roads were still flooded, the river and several fords were right over, fields studded with pools, but there had been no more rain and the canal towpath was visible again.

Simon drove past the belt of woodland, then up and up from where he could see the cathedral tower and what was left of the old city wall, the Hill, and Lafferton contained in its elegant oval shape, on the far side of which the bypass cut across the countryside, fields gave way to housing estates and then, though he could not see so far, on to Bevham.

It was mild, the sky pearly grey. A black bird was singing. There were golden catkins, thick patches of aconites still bright under the trees. He stopped and got out. The slight breeze was blowing in the opposite direction, so that he could hear no traffic, only sheep bleating, and the birds.

He was four miles from Cat's farmhouse, six back into Lafferton. Harnham village was a mile away, hidden by the crown of trees.

A text came in. *On site now. Jonathan P.*

Two sharp bends in the narrow track that ran between trees led to a farm gate, and fifty yards beyond it, another bend, and the house. There was a very old oak to one side, a walnut to the other, and in front a great round-headed holly tree as big as he had ever seen. The house faced south-west, he could see the silvery late-afternoon light ahead, as if it were light from the sea. The estate agent's car was parked to one side.

'Chief Superintendent? Jonathan Purvis, Forbes and Chatto. You found it.'

'I thought I knew this bit of the country pretty well but I'd no idea there was a house down here.'

'Part of its charm.'

'We'll walk round to the front first. Don't be put off by the garden – the previous owners were great gardeners, I believe, but he died seven years ago, she lived on by herself until last summer, but the garden got beyond her. Would take some work to get it back but the bones of it are there. You a gardener?'

'Never had one but my mother was.'

'Green fingers are hereditary, they say.'

They turned the corner of the house and Serrailler whistled. Even on a grey day, the view was breathtaking, dropping away from the garden towards a spinney, then field after field, with sheep scattered about randomly, like confetti, a couple of horses, broad hedgerows, and the river.

There was no wind. It was all still, all quiet apart from the bleating of the sheep. The surrounding villages were to the north, behind the house, so that there was nothing but countryside in view.

A robin looked down and followed them as they moved.

A blackbird scuttled under bushes.

'The house was pretty much cleared out but the curtains and rugs were left . . . not much use, I don't imagine. I never think you get a proper idea of an interior when it's empty – have to use the old imagination a bit.'

But even empty, with bare floors, even with a smell of dry plaster and dust, and ancient faded curtains and rolled-up rugs, cleaned-out grates, spaces in the walls with the outline of picture frames, even then . . .

He walked through the garden-facing rooms, which led off a corridor but also in and out of one another, then across to the darker, back rooms, study, dining room, huge kitchen, pantry, boot room, then up the staircase with its wide banister, to the same arrangement, large bedrooms at the front, a couple of smaller ones, plus bathroom, at the back.

A short, narrower staircase led up to a bare attic. Simon bent his head and looked out over the countryside again. A buzzard was soaring on the air, looking for prey. In the distance, because the weather had cleared slightly, he could now see the train line that ran into Bevham, and the Hill, not much more than a bump in the ground from here.

They went back into the kitchen.

'Needs the lot ripping out really, though you might be able to restore the old range.'

'What's the heating?'

'Ha – coal – but you'd convert to oil easily. Rewiring would be essential, of course – not up to safety standards by seventy or eighty years I'd guess.' He tapped the walls. 'But the great thing is, this is a solid house, the walls are thick, the plasterwork is sound, there's no rot or damp, the roof was actually done just before the old man died. Obviously, you'd get a survey but this is a house built to last and it has and it will.'

'How old?'

'Not as old as you might expect – around 1800. There was an ancient farmhouse here going way back and probably some sort of dwelling before that. It's all in the deeds. There are some collapsing outbuildings – more were demolished fifty years or so ago, but what are left are way older than the house. You interested in all that sort of thing?'

They wandered back to the front door. Jonathan went to his car and got out a brochure. 'Hot off the press, they only came in as I was leaving.'

'How long has it been advertised?'

'It barely has but it'll go in the property pages of the *Gazette* next Friday and of course it's on our website. It's a very desirable property. It won't hang around.'

Serrailler knew the spiel. He also knew that the agent was probably right.

'I have to get back now for a viewing of an apartment in the Old Ribbon Factory. Those get snapped up. Can't get enough.' He reversed, stopped and wound down the window. 'Nice to meet you. You've got my details. And if you are interested in this, you need to jump on it.'

When he had gone, Simon paused, then went back, round the side of the house to the terrace, the garden. The fields. The sheep. The horses and the steely river. The cathedral tower, receding now into the gathering dusk. The close. His own flat at the top of the building he could not make out. But it was there, it was home.

He looked for a long time at the view, and then at the house, its windows darkening, chimneys half hidden.

When he had seen this first, as the pictures had come through onto his laptop screen, he had felt a stab of something – excitement, recognition? The feeling had intensified as he had driven here, down the track to see it before him, not a photograph, a real house.

Now, as darkness gathered, he no longer felt the same, his emotions about it and about himself were blurred again, uncertain.

He drove away too fast, sending a rabbit racing into the ditch for safety.

Fifty-Nine

'Shall I do those?'

Cat handed him the potato peeler. 'Drink while you work?'

'No, thanks. I'm not on duty but that hasn't been making much difference just lately.'

'Any more news?'

'On the Wangs? Fire investigation is pretty conclusive – crude incendiary device, on a timer . . . it was lucky it didn't go off while anyone was in the shop.'

'Depends what you call lucky.' Cat sat at the kitchen table, watching her brother carefully. There was something. In spite of his tough working week, there was a barely suppressed fizz waiting to surface.

'Story to tell?'

'Maybe.'

Something fell with a crash above their heads.

'Oh God. Sam. He's decorating his room, and the bathroom, after which I gather the plan is the corridor, the landing and the stairs. They do need doing but if it's going to take him weeks I'd rather have got in a professional.'

'I can give him a hand on Saturday, all other things being equal.'

'You might not be all that welcome.'

'Good a way as any other of mending a broken heart. When does he start back at the hospital?'

'He's got a bit of a wait. There's a job for him but they're doing some sort of restructuring, new shift patterns. If it ain't broke . . . but who listens?'

'Poor Sam.'

'He says he's done with women.'

'Oh, I've said that.'

'You? Really?'

Cat dodged the piece of potato peel heading her way as Kieron opened the front door.

They ate, cleared up, Kieron went into the den to watch the news. The sounds of decorating stopped but Sam did not come down, and when asked about supper, shouted that he'd get something himself later.

'Leave him be. I'll bring coffee in. Ask K if he wants one.'

'He won't. He says he's been having too much caffeine, so his mint tea is in the top cupboard.'

She knew the expression on Simon's face, even with her back turned.

Kieron came into the sitting room for half an hour, and they kept to their understanding that except in emergencies police talk was forbidden at home. Cat sent in a couple of patient reports from her iPad, Wookie spread out beside her, hoping to have his tummy scratched. Sam was silent upstairs.

Calm, Simon thought, calm and contented, quiet, peaceful. A family evening. Was this his family? Yes. No. Felix slipped in to report homework done and request time on his Xbox.

Family.

How the Wang family would have been – supper, homework, television, a bit of squabbling. Bed.

He banged his hand down on the table beside him, making the lamp flicker off and on again. Cat looked up.

Kieron said, 'Don't worry. We'll throw everything at it, so will the others. We'll have their heads on bloody plates, Simon.'

Cat glanced up as he went out. 'You going to get me a glass of wine, honey?'

'Anything for you Simon? Then I'm off for *Line of Duty*.'

The ban on police conversation at home did not extend to the Chief's favourite cop shows.

'Should I go and say hello to Sam?'

'I wouldn't. He's got to have his own trudge through the slough of despond. Aren't you going to watch exciting police action?'

'I get enough of that. It's all right for Kieron. What they don't show you is chief constables sitting in their offices all day, apart from being chauffeur-driven to the occasional meeting.'

'Bitter.'

'Sorry . . . don't you ever hate your job?'

'Not really. I get weary of admin, I get upset by things I can't make any better. I don't think I've ever hated medicine itself though. Come on, bro, think about it – that's exactly what you dislike, not the actual job.'

Kieron brought in their drinks and vanished into the den with his own.

'Right now, bloody drugs are my version of things I can't make any better. They're beating us, and sometimes I think they always will. But you've got to chip away.' He got up. 'Now, we're changing the subject.'

As he returned from fetching the house brochure from the car, he caught a glimpse of Felix, going slowly, softly up the stairs.

'Do you know this house?'

Cat looked carefully at the photograph. 'Harrows. Yes – or rather no, I don't know it, but I'd no idea there was a house down that lane until I was lost on the way to a new patient and I took the wrong turning. It looked very empty.

'It is empty but OK, not derelict or anything. It needs TLC but not reconstruction.'

She read through in silence.

'So . . . I didn't realise you'd started looking.'

'Neither did I . . . it was just a vague thought until this popped up.'

'You've been to see it?'

'Earlier but I want to go again. Will you come with me? I need your eye.'

'Have I got one?'

'You'd definitely have one for the garden. But you know me.'

'True – I think. The thing is, never mind what this house is like and whether you like it, or I like it, that doesn't matter at this stage, does it? It's whether you have sat down and thought carefully about what moving from your place would actually mean. Is it what you want, for the foreseeable future? 'You have to be dead sure – sure of leaving the close and your nice eyrie before you even think about where you might go. This looks quite big. Do you need all that space? It's pretty isolated.'

'Not really . . . a mile to the village.'

'Where there is what, exactly? No pub till the Plough at Foxley.'

Cat took off her shoes, and hitched her legs onto the sofa. Wookie grumbled in his sleep.

'The thing is, I suppose, you like your own space – maybe too much but you do – and that works fine in the close but look at this place – you'd rattle around. Echoing footsteps. Owls at night.'

'I'm never spooked.'

'No but you could easily be lonely. Of course, for all I know you could be planning to move in with someone – which would be quite another story.'

'Nice try, sis.'

On the landing above, Felix waited until things had gone quiet again, the sitting room door closed, sounds of the TV coming loudly from the den, before he crept his way along to the end and knocked softly on Sam's door.

No reply.

'Sam?'

'Go to bed.'

'Can I come in?'

'No.'

Felix stood for a moment unsure whether to try again or leave Sam alone and go to bed with his Alex Rider book, but then his brother's door opened slightly.

'What do you want?'

273

'Thought you might like something . . . a Coke or a cup of tea or . . . anything really.'

'Why?'

'Just thought.'

'You've been earwigging.'

'No!'

'Whatever . . . Thanks but I don't want anything. OK?'

'OK.'

'Night.'

'Sam . . .'

'Oh for goodness' sake, come in, or they'll all be up here. Uncle Si's downstairs, isn't he?'

'Yes.'

After a moment, Felix went in and shut Sam's door.

'I only wanted to see if you were OK.'

'Yeah, sorry. I didn't mean to bite your head off. You want some Maltesers?'

'Great, thanks.'

The small red bag flew across the room. Sam had been lying on his bed, iPad and earphones beside him.

'What's happening about Rosie?'

'Nothing.'

'Anything you say will not go any further than these four walls.'

'Ha, you're reading Young Bond again.'

'Alex Rider.'

'Love them. Anyway, Rosie and I are taking a break, that's all. She's got finals, I'm waiting to start my job.'

'I like Rosie.'

'Yeah.'

'I thought you two were really strong.'

Sam laughed. 'Ha . . . you're a good one to have around, you know that? OK, now take your Maltesers and hide them where no one will ever find them, I want to watch a film. Thanks.'

'What for?'

'Just thanks.' Sam threw a second small bag across. Felix gave him the thumbs up and slipped out.

So, he didn't believe the story, about his brother and Rosie just taking a break and his job and her exams, Sam was putting on a brave face, his mother had said as much to K, when he'd been coming past the open door, and that was not earwigging, he hadn't been able to help overhearing. Sometimes, you just couldn't.

Sixty

The floods had receded enough for the first earth-moving machinery to get on site, along with the stacked Portakabins. They had drained and laid down the heavy boards, the adjacent lot allocated for parking was filling up, but the first week would only see the men involved with ground preparations, so there were fewer cars and yellow hard hats than would eventually fetch up. There was not a great deal for them to do but watch, as the Caterpillars moved in through the gate and started to crawl across to the west side.

The place would be unrecognisable in a month's time, a new development of executive-style detached luxury homes would be under way and the show home ready by May, all flags flying, for prospective buyers. A sales office, with more flags, would go beside the entrance gate, on a temporary base which was already being marked out.

Ollie Drinkwater, civil engineer, and his assistant stood looking at the space, still a dark mess of mud, close up to the remains of a half-demolished bramble hedge.

'That should have gone.'

'Looks as if they made a start though.'

There was a gaping space through the undergrowth.

Ollie shook his head. 'Even they don't begin in the middle. Something's bulldozed through.'

They went over. It was drizzling and slippery where they walked. The hedge, ground, sky were a grey-brown wash. Only the Caterpillars, the hard hats and orange coveralls splashed brightness.

Arron scrambled down, steadying himself by holding the tough roots and lower branches.

'What the hell's that doing?'

Ollie joined him to look at the caravan which had slipped and rolled sideways, landing half in, half out of the ditch and verge on the side of the road beyond.

'Lucky it didn't stay upright and end up in the middle of the road.'

They went round to the other side and tried to see in. The door and steps leading to it were wedged, but by clambering Arron could lie on the caravan and look through the window.

'We need to make sure it's safe, nothing inside that could catch fire – they have paraffin heaters and Calor gas in these things, though that's when people are living in them. Shouldn't think anyone was, so we can call in the heavy lifters, get it upright and then find out who it belongs to. As if. It's been dumped.'

Arron turned, squatting on the toppled caravan. 'I think there's someone inside.'

'How can you see? The windows are all grimed up.'

'OK, you look.'

Ollie rolled his eyes. But there was something about Arron's expression that made him edge his way on hands and knees, until he could just see through the dirt.

A leg. A body half over on its side. One arm.

'Jesus.'

Ollie slid fast down the wet metal side, tearing at his overalls to reach his phone.

Half an hour later, ambulance, fire engine and two patrol cars were on site, passing vehicles which had slowed down were being moved on, and Serrailler, wearing borrowed overalls which was too short for him, hard hat and boots, was edging his way up the sloping caravan.

He always tried not to jump to conclusions before he had at least had a preliminary look at anything, even to guess whether it was a crime scene, and never to speculate about a body, even as to whether it was dead or alive. He had been caught out in the past, assuming the man found lying in a back alley was the same one they had been chasing in the area earlier, deciding that a woman had been murdered only for the pathologist to see a natural cause immediately. Why had the caravan over-turned, who was inside and why? Was it even a human being? Light played tricks and dummies had been planted before today.

Simon crouched and pressed his face against the caravan window. The figure was no trick of light but a dead man with his head bashed in, the thick stains on the linoleum were dried clotted blood. No dummy had been planted.

He slid back down to the ground.

Sixty-One

It went all the way back to the days when, as a rookie copper, Serrailler had seen his first mutilated corpse, that of a young man separated from his head, the latter having floated further downstream and caught up in reeds beside the riverbank. Inevitably, he had been shaken, but he had felt neither faint nor nauseous, and on returning to the station he had headed straight to the canteen where he had downed not only a pint of tea, but a plate of eggs, bacons and fried bread, and it had been the same ever after, was the same now, when he went straight to the basement canteen for breakfast.

'Is there something wrong with me?'

'Not exactly wrong,' Cat had said, 'but maybe idiosyncratic. Most junior doctors go off their food for a few hours after they've attended the aftermath of an RTA, or they faint their first time in the operating theatre, but we all react differently to trauma. Neurosurgeons are well known for going straight from probing into someone's brains to enjoying a Chinese takeaway.'

Simon did not have long to eat. He had been at the site for three hours, and the team on the ground had finished their part of the job, the caravan had been set upright and towed into the field, the buckled door had been crowbarred open – it looked as if the same had happened to the victim's head. The pathologist had pronounced death and set the rough time at between eleven the previous night and four in the morning. 'Difficult to be more exact till I get him on the table. Blunt instrument or possibly a heavy axe. I'll get back. Let's have him in as soon as you've finished.'

Forensics had been hanging about outside, suited and booted, but before letting them into the caravan, Serrailller had stood still, and let his eyes do the work in the cramped space, the floor of which was tipped sideways, giving him a peculiar sense of being at sea. The place had been lived in. There was a television, which had crashed to the floor, some mugs and plates, only one of which had survived intact, a small pile of clothes – jumper, jeans, two or three shirts. Socks and underwear were pushed into the corner of a shelf. The door of the food cupboard hung open, revealing tea bags, ketchup, spilled sugar, long-life milk and a random banana. A grubby bedcover and pillow were heaped on the bench seat.

'Guv?'

'Hold on.' He had taken a last look. He had no feelings whatsoever for the man, known variously as Fats, Ginger or the Weasel. If what had happened was any kind of escape, it was only one that had led down a short passageway to a swift and terrible end. He wore a washed-out grey T-shirt with some sort of slogan on the front. One trainer on, the other on the floor. Black socks. A navy-blue fleece jacket hung over the back of the door.

'OK, it's all yours.' The two of them had edged in, white suits and overshoes rustling.

'One thing – our guys will come in to take the place apart after you're done, but if you spot anything you think I should know about straight away, call me. I can't say what sort of thing, I don't think I know, but you'll know if you see it.'

Which was not strictly true, but he did not want to put a suggestion into their heads. Sometimes, you found what you expected to find, which was not always what you should be finding.

Work on the site had stopped, the machines were stranded and silent, the workmen's cars and motorbikes had left but morning traffic was on the go and still being waved past, a knot of women with buggies stood just beyond the crime scene tape, watching every movement in and out, an elderly man had parked his invalid vehicle as near to the entrance as he dared and was sitting smoking, the local television news van was being confronted by uniform.

As he'd left, Simon had lowered his window beside the media men.

'Nothing for you yet, sorry, I might have something for you around lunchtime. Or not.'

He had sped off, hunger gnawing.

Sixty-Two

'We've got everything and we've got nothing.'

All of the on-duty CID bar one was in the conference room, photos of the scene were up on the screen, and there was something in the air, a new sense that perhaps this was 'at last', though Serrailler had said nothing to bring it on. But it did happen, an inquiry could go on for months, dragging like boots through wet sand, meticulous data work getting them nowhere, and then there was something, often small, and it shed a ray of light which led to another, and the mood changed.

'They'd likely been on watch, waiting for him to get back, and when he did, burst their way in before he'd had time to get his hoodie off. Several blows with our friend the blunt instrument, any one of which would have killed him, and needless to say nothing found, they'll have taken it with them and thrown it in water a hundred miles away. No prints of course, no DNA so far but they've still got the fine-tooth comb running through on the van interior. Talking of vans, one was found parked up on the other side of the building site, behind a run of derelict sheds and that's on its way in, because the only thing found on the body was a set of keys, which fitted. Lucky strike, that. His living space has given us nothing but the van had his prints all over it and a couple of screwed-up bits of paper on the floor with some phone numbers scribbled on.' He pointed, and enlarged. 'Those will have to be trawled through.'

'Phone?'

'Nope but if it was on his person they'll have taken it, extracted the SIM card and sent the shell the way of the murder weapon.'

'Do we have an ID yet?'

'Sort of. He was known as Fats, and that was what he called himself when asked for a name, but also as Ginger and Weasel. In the side door of the van he'd stuffed dozens, literally dozens, of betting slips from the dog racing at Bevham stadium, he was obviously a regular, these weren't from a betting shop. Bilaval?'

The DC nodded. 'Surprisingly easy, this one. There was a meeting on Thursday night, and to anyone who's never been to a greyhound meeting, I'd recommend it, good cheeseburgers and hot dogs from the stands, lots of buzz, most exciting – I got quite carried away. But compared with a horse-race meeting, the place is small and there were only a few bookies and their slips ID them, so I found the name of the one on every single slip pretty quickly – Graham Reason, known as Bald Graham, though you wouldn't know it because he never takes his hat off. He was on to me in a nanosecond, wouldn't give me anything. He's in this somehow but for the time being I left it, got myself lost among the punters and found another bookie, asked him about regulars, ones likely to have a big stash of slips. He was a talker. Not many of those, he said, but there were a few guys who were there every meeting. One description fitted.'

'You didn't show him the pics?'

'No, guv, but I had them in my head pretty clearly. Height. Build. Clothes. And ginger. The name he used was Fats. Unfortunately, that's the only one he knew.'

'Fats,' Serrailler said, 'is the bloke who hooked up a young lad in Starly. His dad found out and came in here. I saw him. He's been useful.'

'Starly.'

'Yup, it's become home to more than the old flower power folk.'

'Flower power?'

Simon groaned. 'You're too young, Denzil. Google it.'

'So Fats is caravan man, and if he was grooming the kids to run the drugs, we've got the best lead we've ever had.'

'Don't get too excited. Yes, pretty sure of that, but he was a tiddler.'

'What about the phone numbers?'

'Chances are they won't be anything – contacts for the kids they're running, and some of them might be dead numbers, they change them all the time. Still, you're right, it's something. We need another break.'

'This anything to do with the Chinese pharmacist?'

'I was coming to that. This is what we have so far. The shop was torched, Wang and his family were murdered, there was absolutely nothing in their house as you know . . . clean as a whistle. We've got Greater Manchester on it, talking to the Chinese community up there, but my bet is they'll find nothing because they know nothing. Wang's people are shocked rigid . . . and the DCS is certain none of them had the faintest idea that Wang Lin was involved in anything – if indeed he was. The most likely scenario is that he and his pharmacy were being used and he was scared shitless. The whole thing stinks. The family might know nothing but there wasn't a word I said came as news to the Manchester boys.'

'The big bosses could be up there.'

'They could. Or in Leeds. Or Newcastle. Or even down in the Smoke. Meanwhile, let me remind you that we are here and we've got something. We have an ID of sorts, we know some of Fats's contacts and his haunts, we have the caravan he lived in and the van he drove. Denzil, you take the list of phone numbers. Donna, take your husband for a treat and a night out at the dogs. Enjoy a cheeseburger on expenses. Keep your ears open, get chatting to those who know their way about. Glam up as you would if you were a flash punter's wife and not a DS and use Bald Graham to place your bets.'

'Can I keep my winnings?'

'No, but you pay for the losses out of your own pocket.'

'Or the hubs'.'

'I expect the forensic reports on both vehicles later today and I'll be going through every detail right down to the invisible ones. There's got to be something.'

'What's the bottom line, guv?'

'Good question, and of course, it is who killed him.' He pointed at the body on the screen. 'To be honest, I don't much care who killed Fats but if anyone, down here or among our friends in the North, can lay hands on whoever murdered the Wang family I'd be very happy. If investigations lead nowhere else, so long as we get scum like that behind bars for life, my work here is done.'

'Aw, don't say that, guv, we'd miss you.'

'Right, toddle off and bring me something to make me proud of you.'

He went straight from the conference up to Kieron's room, but had to wait ten minutes. 'Come on in. I won't bother to ask if we've closed down all the county lines on our own patch and every surrounding one but give me some good news – any good news.'

'That bad?'

'Let me tell you now, if anyone asks you what a Chief Constable does, the answer is budgeting – resources, budgets, cuts, make-do. Seems I joined the police force to be an accountant.'

He shifted himself, stood up, moved the chair. Sat again.

'They still haven't got to the bottom of it.'

'Who? Greater Manchester force?'

'What are you talking about?'

'I thought you meant the Chinese family.'

'No, I meant my torn tendon.'

There was no polite answer Simon could give, so he just shook his head.

'You've got an ID for caravan man anyway. What next?'

Serrailler filled him in.

'The thing is –' There was a knock and Kieron's secretary put her head round the door.

'Can the DC have a word, Simon? He says he's got something.'

Denzil came in, face lit up like a hundred-watt bulb. 'Result!' he said, punching the air. 'We've got his phone!'

Ben Longley, aged fifteen, had lost his new, birthday-present smartphone when he was biking along a towpath thirty miles beyond Bevham and gone back, with his brother Zak, to find it or else. After forty minutes they spotted it, caught up in a thick clump of grass beside the canal, except that when they managed to disentangle and retrieve it, Ben saw that the phone was not his.

'Chuck it back.'

'No, it's all right.'

'It's dead, stewp, been in the water, like yours will be.'

But Ben had slipped it into his pocket and they'd gone on looking for his own half an hour longer, before giving up.

'It's a junk one anyway, bet you, some old pensioner's Nokia. You thinking of going home ever again?'

He had spent half the night faffing with the lost phone, then read that to dry it out he should put it into a bowl of rice and went to nick a bag of it from the kitchen cupboard.

In the early hours of the morning, the phone rang, waking him up, then rang again, so that in the end he had switched it off but still left it in the rice.

The police car had pulled up outside while they were having breakfast.

'What did I say we needed?'

'Stroke of luck, guv.'

'And you got it. Bloody hell, this is one of those that never happens until it does.'

As part of the routine, the IT support team had put a trace on Fats's mobile. When it had been reactivated, the signal had gone straight back to them.

Sixty-Three

Sam's phone rang.

He was pushing a semiconscious patient back from theatre to ITU, a nurse beside them attending to drips and tubes as they walked.

'Are you supposed to answer your phone on duty?'

'I'm not answering it.'

'Even have it switched on at all? Honestly, it's one rule for you porters . . .'

He was not sure how far she was joking.

'Hold the doors.'

They reached the patient's bed and Sam handed over. Back in the corridor, he called Hannah.

'Hi. Why didn't you answer?'

What's up?'

'Nothing in the wide world. Can you pick me up from the station at half five?'

'No, I'm on till seven.'

'Can't you knock off early?'

'No, I bloody can't, and I don't have a car. Sort yourself out, woman.'

'It's your charm that has got you so far.'

What was she coming home for so suddenly when she hadn't been back for weeks? Not since Christmas, now he thought about it, because she had gone straight from the end of her pantomime into the musical.

His beeper went and he headed back to the theatre suites.

The printout of numbers from the recovered phone reached
Serrailler as he was thinking of leaving. Voicemail and texts had
been corrupted and they were still working on them but the
stored list was intact and he glanced down it. Eleven mobile
numbers, fewer than he would have expected and probably only
the tip of the iceberg. Maybe Fats and the rest of the bottom
feeders in the drug supply chain had instructions to delete
anyone the moment they had dropped off the radar and become
uncontactable. He started to pack up, ready to take the number
sheet down to CID on his way out and get whoever to go through
them and report in if any were answered. But after he had done
so, he turned back.

'Just let me have that list again, Denzil . . . I need another look.'

'Recognise one, guv?'

'Not sure. Maybe.'

'If there's anything that looks like something I'll call you,
otherwise enjoy your evening.'

'Thanks. How's the newborn?'

'Noisy.' Denzil's baby son had arrived safe and well, and
clearly the fun had now started.

As he crossed to his car, Simon was pleased to be going back
to the peace and tranquillity of Cathedral Close.

And then his phone rang.

'Uncle Si?'

'Hannah! Hi, honey, how are you?'

'More to the point, *where* am I?

'Right.'

'Could you be an angel and pick me up from Bevham station?'

Since she had been at stage school and then working in the
theatre, inevitably his niece had changed, grown up and become
independent, but as Simon watched her come through the ticket
barriers, he realised that, essentially, she had not changed at all.
Her hair was blonde instead of its natural brown, because of her
recent pantomime role, but it was tied back in the old ponytail,
she was wearing jeans and a parka with a fur collar that he recognised from at least two winters back, and she carried her things

in a rucksack she had inherited from Sam, and her face was free of make-up. She might have been twelve again, not eighteen.

She flung her arms round him and gave him a tight hug, before taking the rucksack off and handing it to him.

'Sorry, I know you weren't planning on being my Uber, only Sam was on shift until later and Mum was out on calls. S'pose I should learn to drive soon.'

'Do you need a car in London?'

'Couldn't afford one even if I did.'

He put her bag into the boot. 'That's assuming you'll be staying in London of course. If not, you probably should start driving.'

'Oh I'll be staying in London all right.'

Hannah's face was like her face aged five, on Christmas morning.

'Tell,' Simon said.

'Oh . . . oh oh oh I really want to but . . .'

'No, your mother comes first.'

'I'll tell everyone at once, only I don't know when Sam will be at the farmhouse.'

'Sam is living at the farmhouse.'

'What?'

'Ah. Sorry, you didn't hear me say that.'

'Sam never says anything to me about anything – he's more likely to tell the dog than his sister. What's happened?'

'He'll tell you, Hanny, it's not for me, and anyway I honestly don't know much except that he and Rosie split up.'

'No bad thing, if you ask me.'

'Why do you say that? They seemed pretty happy.'

'Come on, Uncle Si, he's far too young. He doesn't seem to know his own mind about anything.'

'Whatever. So he'll be home later I imagine, plus your ma because she'll hand over at eight, and Kieron should be back. If . . . you count him, don't you?'

'What, as family? Of course I count him. Don't you? No, I guess it's harder, him being your boss and all.'

'Doesn't affect anything, we made a pact about that right at the start and it's worked.'

'And you'll be there.'

'Depends if I'm invited.'

'Don't be silly. Unless you've got some boring murder to go to.'

'I hope to God not, Han – too many of those just lately.'

'What's Lafferton coming to?'

'You may ask. Though it's more a question of what's Starly coming to.'

'Dopey Starly?'

'In more than one sense.'

'Oh, drugs schmugs.'

He glanced at her. 'I shouldn't ask,' he said, 'and I promised myself I would never wag my finger at any of you, but I've seen too much –'

'I smoked a joint a couple of times and it made me really really sick. Throwing-up sick, enough to put me right off, and apart from that I swear on whatever you like that I have never and will never go near any drugs. I've seen stuff as well.' There was no response. 'Did you hear me?'

'What? Sorry, Hannah, yes, I was just thinking about something. When we get to the farmhouse, I have to check out a phone number.'

'Light bulb moment?'

'Candle, anyway.'

They all arrived home in dribs and drabs, Simon and Hannah going up the drive moments before Felix's lift, because on Friday he stayed at school for homework, tea and late choir, and three sets of the parents shared pickups. He was halfway up the stairs with his bag and his oboe when he realised that the voice greeting him from the kitchen was not his mother's and tumbled back down again to be enveloped in an overwhelming sisterly hug, which Kieron's arrival interrupted.

He had been cautious with Cat's children since their marriage, never trying to claim either attention or precedence, just being there, taking things as they came, not crowding them. Inevitably, he knew Felix best because they were at home together and Kieron had taken him into early-morning choir practice from the beginning, because it was on his route into the station and he liked to start early. Hannah had been away much of the time, so that he knew her the least well but the hug she gave him was immediate and genuine.

Simon made a pot of tea, and even got his brother-in-law his own mint brew, and as he did it, as Hannah and Felix chatted behind him, he thought about the phone number, letting it run through his head on repeat.

He set the tea and mugs on the table, and went into the den. Wookie pattered after him, his limp making the sound of his feet out of sync on the tiles. He lay down at Simon's feet. Recalling the number and keying it into his phone took seconds. It matched.

In the kitchen, Hannah and Kieron were planning supper and Felix had gone upstairs. Simon gestured to the sitting room.

'Something?' Kieron said.

Simon filled him in.

'Well, you've a better head for numbers than me – you're probably right. What are you going to do?'

'I shall have to go to the house.'

'Difficult. I'm wondering exactly what would be achieved.'

'Some sort of answer,' Serrailler said. The words were all but lost in shrieks from the hall, as Cat and Sam arrived home to be greeted by Hannah, and Wookie ran round and round in crazed noisy circles.

Supper was in the oven, Kieron and Simon had taken drinks through, Cat had raced upstairs to shower and change. 'And don't you dare say as much as half a word without me.'

Later, what Simon kept on recalling was Hannah's face as she told them, the pride and excitement that made her glow as if in the theatre spotlight. He wished he could have captured it in a photograph, but it was too alive and changing every second like the surface of the sea, Hannah's every breath registered on her features. Yet it took only a moment to give them the news.

'OK, listen up.' Everyone went still. 'It's something this guy has always wanted to do, it's been on the back burner where I guess he keeps a lot of ideas, because other stuff always got in first. But *finally* . . . It will be different and all his own, and the librettist of course –'

'Spit it out, sister.'

'New musical of *A Midsummer Night's Dream*.'

'Wow!'

'And I went through five rounds of auditions and callbacks and then I auditioned twice for him . . .'

'And?'

'I'm going to play Hermia, in the West End, from September.'

It was Wookie who got there first, making the room erupt with shouts and laughter, Wookie who had been lying on the rug at Cat's feet, but who now leapt up, hurled himself onto the sofa and Hannah, and started to lick her joyfully, picking up the atmosphere on the instant and making her laugh and then cry, holding him tight and sending him into further ecstasies.

Simon watched, as proud and delighted as the others, as surprised and as impressed. But all the time, a shadow rested, just behind his shoulder. He glanced at Kieron, the only other person who might have picked up on it, but he was in the thick of a group hug, and when he moved away, Simon had to take his place and so that the shadow's presence was known only to him, pushed down and covered over, but there. Still there.

Sixty-Four

It was breaking light and he was the first up. Even Wookie only half opened one eye and immediately closed it again.

Saturday morning before seven, a pale morning, the air mild, the surrounding fields misty. He met only one car all the way.

But when he stood looking about him, a hundred birds were singing.

The house seemed set apart from him and its surroundings, settled within itself, needing no one. If he went inside, it would accept him, if not, fine. But he could not go inside.

Simon cupped his hands and looked in through the windows, and though he could see little, it was familiar, and he could picture it as it would be, with his elm table, the white sofa and chairs, wooden floor polished, his pictures, his books. His space.

Yet when he walked back to the car, he felt uncertain again, his mind still not made up, not because of what might be to come but of what he would lose. He sat for a long time letting everything have its voice. Too isolated? Too big? Too much work? Too much garden? Too expensive? Yes. No. Perhaps. In the day job, he was decisive and confident, in his private life, he was another man. He knew it, and knew he could not, would not, did not want even, to change.

The sun came out but purple-tinged clouds were bubbling up on the horizon and a wind ruffled the bushes. He drove away, leaving his thoughts about the house to settle themselves.

*

Two doors away, a man was polishing his car, a toddler riding a red plastic car slowly to and fro on the footpath beside him. The post van was turning out of the close as Serrailler turned in but otherwise, it was quiet. He parked fifty yards away and walked to the house, because there was less chance of his arrival being noted and, as he might have been recognised from his cluster of previous visits, accorded unwelcome attention. He had been in similar situations often enough to understand that however long ago a distressing event might be people remained raw, vulnerable, and so easily upset. Instinctively he wanted to protect her, save her the well-meaning but intrusive questions, if only for a time.

The man washing with the bucket and sponge ignored him. The toddler stared, then shuffled the red car closer to his parent.

She answered his knock in a few seconds, and several expressions flickered over face, enquiring, searching, recognising, recollecting, before her features crumpled in distress.

'Hello, Mrs Tonks. Superintendent Simon –'

'I know.' She stood back from the door to let him in, closed it behind her.

'I was just finishing my breakfast. The tea is still fresh if I can offer you some.'

'I would like a cup, thank you.'

He watched her. The immediate shock had cleared from her face but he saw that pained look in and around her eyes, and that they were sunken slightly, the little flesh there was, on her cheeks and jaw, had fallen. He remembered her as slight, thin, small-boned, but now she looked brittle as a bird, and old age lay in wait close by, though she was probably not far into her fifties. He felt anguish for her, and a flash of fury, too, as he had felt in this situation before, wishing that Olivia could see her mother as she was now and understand the lasting effects of she had done. It was an anger he could never admit to but of which he did not feel ashamed.

She poured tea and sat down, but said nothing, did not meet his eye, only looked down at the table mat, her attention far away.

'Thank you. I left home too early.' He drank, sat quietly, gave her all the time she needed. He was facing the window onto the garden, where a squirrel was leaping up the branches of an ugly fir tree with blue-grey needles. There was a rectangular lawn. A fence on all three sides. A shed. No shrubs, no other tree, no flower beds, no bird table or feeders.

'You've found out something,' Greta Tonks said.

Serrailler put down his cup and took out the folded piece of paper.

'Would you look at these carefully, please and tell me if you recognise any of them? Before I explain, may I be rude and ask if there's any more tea?'

'I'll make a fresh pot.' She glanced at him with a slight smile. 'Reminds me of all the pots I made at the beginning . . . all those visits and questions, all those people in white suits . . . I pretty much ran out of tea.'

'We should have brought some.'

'Pish, of course not.'

'Between ourselves, I'm delighted it's tea leaves.'

'I have never had a tea bag in this house, I hate the things, sopping round the draining board, and no matter if they're the most expensive brand, the tea just doesn't compare with freshly made from leaves. I don't drink much coffee, but if I do, it doesn't bother me what kind or where it's from – beans, a jar of instant – it's all the same. But tea . . .'

'I couldn't agree more, though we'll have to differ on the coffee.'

He was giving her time, giving her moments to take a breath and calm herself to prepare for what he was going to say. She had her back to him, looking out at the garden, but miles away, and he felt bitterly sorry for her, knowing what had happened to her over the past couple of years. She now had no one to shield her from whatever blows might fall in future. He wondered if she had friends and any sort of social life, groups she belonged to, people to visit away from Starly. She needed those things now and she would need them more as she grew older. How strange it was that he could be perfectly happy on his own, so that old age, retirement and loneliness never came to his mind together and yet this woman had loneliness in her DNA, as impossible to overcome as her grief. He was lucky, or so it seemed as he watched her pour the tea.

'Please tell me whatever it is, Mr Serrailler. Nothing can be worse than her dying and how it was, nothing I can possibly imagine, so you don't have to be cautious about what you have to say or how you say it.'

'Thank you. This is a list of mobile numbers and occasionally we are able to recover data from a discarded phone. This was probably aimed at the canal, but instead of hitting the water it got caught up in undergrowth. It was found by a boy who had lost his own phone in the area. He took it home, and because he's that sort of kid, started trying to revive it in case he could make use of the parts. In doing so he managed to trigger a signal. By a stroke of great good fortune, our technical team picked it up – they had been trying to trace this same mobile. The signal led them right to where the phone was, in the boy's house. They haven't recovered any voice messages yet and most of the data has been wiped, but there were some texts – and these stored numbers were saved. They're working through them but the phones we found in Olivia's bag resonated with me, so I checked.'

He drank his tea, letting her take everything in step by step.

'The phone belonged to a man who was part of a drug gang. His job was to recruit youngsters to carry drugs and deliver them to users. This is happening just about everywhere, and increasingly in country areas, small market towns, but we hadn't seen this sort of organisation in our force until just over a year ago and it had been growing while we were barely aware of it.'

'Olivia never ever would have taken drugs, I am sure of it. Cast-iron sure. She really disapproved of them, she despised people who took them – she often said so. It wasn't that we had to warn her, she was there first – she used to lecture us about it, if you like. She must have been on this man's phone list for some other reason.'

Her face was flushed and she was passionately certain of what she was saying. Simon recognised this brand of unshakeable conviction, usually encountered in parents but occasionally in partners, when confronted with information they could not bear to absorb, truth they could not bring themselves to acknowledge. Olivia Tonks had let it be known loud and clear and often that she was against drugs, and perhaps in a sense she had been. The part of her which had spoken out in that way was quite separate from another, deeply hidden part, and the two were never in the same place together, each would have been in denial about the other.

'I believe you,' he said, 'this isn't unusual. Olivia would have hated what she was doing, but for whatever reason, she continued to do it. Usually, this is all about enticement, intimidation, blackmail, and once she had started, she was caught and trapped, threatened in small ways and then much bigger ones. They all are – bribed and blackmailed, with money but more often with things, nice new designer trainers, a bit of jewellery, a smart bag –'

'No!' Greta Tonks knocked the chair over as she stood up. 'I would have known. Liv never got anything like that, and she only had pocket money from us. Her father might have slipped her a five-pound note sometimes after he left us, but that was out of guilt and she always told me. Always. This is not Liv, I can't tell you how sure I am, but whatever you say makes no difference to me, because it won't bring her back. '

'No. I can completely understand why you're saying this and –'

'I doubt it, Superintendent. You're not a hard man, but you're a policeman and you have no idea about any other aspect of this outside the job you have to do. It hasn't helped me – though it hasn't made things worse either, as if anything could – because it doesn't take me any closer to understanding and knowing why Olivia killed herself. Not an inch. Of all the unlikely explanations, this cock-and-bull story about drugs and drug dealers . . . I'm angry, I'm upset and hurt, you've made a fool of me, and – you have no idea how wrong you are. Now would you please leave?'

Sixty-Five

'Aw, no, Dad, please.' Brookie was biting his lip, determined not to cry and failing. 'Don't make me go.'

'You'll do as I say. Now get upstairs, wash your face and hands, brush you hair. Five minutes.'

'Please.'

Vince pointed again. Brooklyn ran.

It was just after nine and he had kept the boy from school in order to do what he hoped to God would make him see sense, understand what it was all about, and be frightened, yes, be told some facts. He was young enough for it to go home and stay home, but old enough, or so Vince thought, to face what he was sure was going to be a scary encounter and a lecture he would never forget. The other boys had left for the school bus without being told anything and he did not know how much Brookie had talked to them, how much he had hidden, though the business of the phone was out there.

He had asked himself enough times if it had been his fault, because he spent too little time with his sons, was working until all hours, couldn't be up to speed with their friends, what they did, where they went, if they were in any sort of trouble. He blamed himself but he blamed their louse of a mother more, and how could she never ring to ask how they were doing, let alone see them, send them birthday and Christmas stuff? They barely mentioned her now and Vince knew they were better off, but she was their mother and he couldn't make up for all of it, whatever she'd been like.

Brookie came slowly down the stairs. His face was still wet, his hair flattened. Vince wanted to hug him but he felt he had to keep things cool until they'd got the visit over with. He handed the boy his jacket, looked at his shoes and went to find a brush and a cloth. 'Look at you.'

Brookie did not look, nor meet Vince's eye. He brushed at the shoes hard, getting the worst of the mud off.

'Right.'

He did not speak all the way except to answer a question when he had to, and in the end his father gave up and they were silent. He had not called in ahead, and if it wasn't a good time, he'd ask what that was and just drive on to school.

As they went in through the doors of the police station, Brookie reached for his father's hand and gripped it for a second, a thing he had not done since he was five years old. The feel of it made Vince stop.

'Listen, it's just going to be a talk.'

Brookie gripped more tightly. 'Will I go in a cell?'

'Of course you won't, you daft bugger! What made you think that?'

'Because . . . we're in a police station.'

'Everything all right?'

Serrailler had seen them as he came down the stairs on his way out.

'Yes, Superintendent. I was hoping you'd got a minute. I've brought my lad in. Brooklyn.'

'What's happened to him?'

'Not happened exactly, but I think you could maybe have a word with him – only you look as if you're off out.'

'It'll keep ten minutes.' Serrailler looked at the boy. 'Let's go up to my office.' He would have seen anyone else in an interview room, for speed and convenience, but not someone looking so cowed and scared and much younger than his age.

He asked Vince to sit on the other side of his office and he would also have asked him not to say anything but Vince had already started.

'You know what this is all about, what he did, all about Fats, and I said to him that you'd make him see the harm that man could have done, because it'll have more effect coming from you, I can go on until I'm blue in the face but I doubt he listens – or any of them come to that. He has –'

'Right, Vince, I get it. Come over by the window, Brooklyn. You can sit down, it's OK.'

The boy looked quickly at his father, then did so, swivelling the chair to and fro, then all the way round. Simon let him do it a couple of times, then said, 'Now stop, it'll make you sick – and me.' He pulled his own chair away from the desk, closer to Brookie.

'This isn't a telling-off, and it's not a cross-examination, don't look so worried, but I do want to ask you one thing, if that's OK?'

He waited. Brookie realised he was actually being asked for a reply. He nodded.

'Thanks. It's this. When you first met the man who gave you a lift home because you'd missed the bus, did he ask you any questions?'

'What about?' The voice was almost a whisper.

'Anything.'

'No. Don't think so. '

'Did he talk about himself – where he lived, what he was doing at the school?'

'No. Oh, yeah, he said he'd taken his daughter's homework in or something. She was off ill.'

'Did he tell you her name?'

'Can't remember.'

'Did he tell you his own name?'

'Said it was Fats and I said nobody was called that but he said he was.'

'He gave you a lift another time, didn't he?'

Nod.

'Was it after the first time that he gave you a phone?'

'Next time. I think it was. It was in the rucksack.'

'Did he say why he'd given it to you?'

'No. It wasn't –'

'What?'

Brookie shrugged.

'It was just a present?'

'I suppose.'

'How much do you know about drugs? Dope and coke, those sorts of drugs.'

'A bit.'

'Tell me what.'

Now he did not glance at his father but looked straight at Serrailler, for the first time.

'People take them or they smoke them like cigarettes and sometimes, I think, they sort of have them like the injections you get at the doctor, needles in your arm. I know they make you feel weird but people like it.'

'Do you know that they can kill you?'

'Yeah, if you get the wrong ones. I know they cost a ton of money. It's not like getting the injections and stuff free from the doctor.'

'So where do people get them?'

'The chemist.'

'Really? Any chemist's shop?'

'No, just . . . some. Tommy said. He said you got them from the Chinky one in Starly, the one that got burned down.'

'How did Tommy know that?'

Brookie looked out of the window, then back. 'I dunno.'

'Did Fats ever talk to you about them?'

'No, but I know he had something to do with them.'

Vince did not speak, sensing that Serrailler had not yet done, but Simon saw he was shocked that another of his sons was somehow involved. He himself was unsurprised.

'All right, Brookie, now listen. You are not in trouble and you did nothing wrong. You made one mistake and that was not telling your dad. You should have done that the moment Fats brought you home the second time. The first time might have seemed OK, though you should never accept lifts from someone you don't know and I bet your father's told you that, yes? But you'd missed the bus and didn't know how else you were going to get home and this guy seemed OK, and so far as it went that day, it was OK. He drove you back to Starly and dropped you on the corner. But when Fats met you the second time out of school, and gave you a lift again, and the rucksack, you should have told your dad. You understand why, don't you?'

Nod.

'I'm not angry, Brooklyn, I'm just reinforcing what you already know. You need to understand that not everyone who seems nice and friendly and harmless really is. It's a tough thing to have to learn, but everyone does. Do you hear what I'm saying?'

'Yes.'

The boy was eleven, but sitting opposite Simon he looked small in the high-backed chair, and, with fine hair and soft skin, he might have been nine.

'Is it . . .'

Serrailler waited in silence, while Brooklyn swivelled again, looked back out of the window, thinking about what he needed to ask and at the same time shooting Vince a warning not to jump in.

'Someone said he got murdered.'

'Who did?'

'Fats.'

'Who told you that?'

'Tommy. He said he'd seen about it.'

'I can only tell you that Fats is dead. He was found dead in his caravan – did you ever go there?'

'No, he said he lived in a big house.'

'Right. But why or how he died I can't tell you at the moment. Did Tommy say he knew any more?'

'Here . . .' His father was standing.

'It's all right, Vince, we're asking just about everybody in Starly the same question.'

Which was not strictly true.

'Tommy didn't know anything.'

'You're sure about that?'

'Yes. I can bring him in as well, no problem.'

'Thanks but I don't think that's necessary.' Simon stood up. 'Now I have to go.

But I want to give you my card, Brookie, it has this station phone number on it, plus my own mobile number. Keep it somewhere safe and ring me if you need to.'

Brookie took the card, and they were out and down the stairs before Vince said that was that. 'Not going to say any more about it, only don't forget any of it, not now, not ever. Understood?'

'I'm late for school. You'll have to come in.'

'I'll come in.'

'Only, what are you going to say?'

'I'll think of something. And put that bloody card away.'

It was late afternoon before Simon got back to the station. He had been on the other side of Lafferton, following reports of a body being seen at the bottom of a quarry, and having to call out the full panoply of climbers, divers and support teams. It had been pouring with rain, visibility was bad, conditions underfoot treacherous, and two hours in, the body had been located and brought up.

'Poor old boy.'

'Slipped and slid down and that was that.'

'He seems pretty old . . . you know anything about dogs, guv?'

The black Labrador's mask was greying, his body battered and scarred by the fall.

'Anyone reported losing him?'

No one had.

'OK, stand down, sorry, everyone. Can you put him in the van and take him in to Lafferton Vets? He'll check if he's microchipped and do the necessary. Thanks, guys.'

Nobody minded. Better a dog than a child.

'Better a dog than a child,' Kieron said. Serrailler breathed a sigh. Operations like the one he had ordered cost money, and when the drowned body turned out to be that of a dog, the Chief might have been read him the usual lecture about resources, waste of.

'I'm on my way home to change,' he said now. 'Retiring dinner for Mike Bardsley. Downside of the job, never mind what you think – I hate these bloody dinners.'

'Rubber chicken.'

'Almost certainly. And interminable speeches.'

Simon's phone rang, but as it was the Greater Manchester Police number, he stayed in the room.

'We got them,' his counterpart in the North said, failing to suppress the jubilation in his voice. 'Routine motorway patrol set after a car going like the clappers and weaving in and out – pulled them over. Everything in the book on vehicle regs but it was what was tucked away . . .'

'Big fat plastic bags full of coke?'

'No, surprisingly, though we might find those when we strip it right down. Firearms – two, to be precise – and we're pretty sure one of them was used to kill your Wang family. Ballistics are onto it but even at this stage . . .'

'That's great work, Don. Well done, your guys. Are they talking?'

'Man and a woman, we're keeping them well apart but he's the talker. Terrified she'll spill so he did it first.'

'Often the way. Do you think they'll lead you anywhere?'

'Chances are they won't know much but we'll pump them until they go flat all the same. Miracles do happen.'

'Life.'

'Wouldn't that be justice? They'll be in the magistrates' tomorrow anyway. Will you pass the news on?'

'I'm with the Chief now, as it happens.'

'I'm not in favour of capital punishment, as you know,' Kieron said, 'but there are times . . .'

'A man and a woman shoot a family, including two kids, at point-blank – Christ, what kind of scum are they?'

'You know the kind, Simon. We just haven't had many like them on our doorstep before now.'

'I'm the first to admit that I didn't take this seriously enough. Certainly didn't take on board what it could lead to on my own patch. I suppose I've always kept the Met apart in my mind – things happen there that would never have happened in a smaller country force back in the day.'

'Definitely a wake-up call, Simon. It's here and it's not going away, it's going to become a far bigger problem unless we can smash it soon. If we're not on top of it, if we haven't seen this lot off by next Christmas, latest, we never will.'

At ten past six, Simon was at the butcher's counter in the supermarket, his mind on an earlier call from Adam Iliffe, giving him news he would eventually receive formally. Liam Payne had died of a self-administered, but accidental overdose, so Professor Shenfield's verdict had been correct and that was a relief but it would not make it any easier for his family, and Liam was another victim, probably guilty of nothing except weakness and naivety, of wanting to keep up with others, and maybe to relieve stress and soften the effects of disappointment. Whatever, such an end to a young life was all too common, always regrettable. He was still dwelling on it when the person in front glanced at him in turning away from the counter. Hesitated.

'Hello, Simon.'

Something happened, something startling, crystal clear – the bright whiteness of the store lights, the voice of a 'Staff announcement', the smell of cold above the meat display. The mundanity of it all, and the absolute extraordinariness. It happened and it was like a body blow, in its complete unexpectedness, and the effect it had on him, so that for a moment he couldn't speak.

'How are you?'

He looked into his empty basket, then hers, with meat, a few vegetables, a bottle of olive oil, a pack of washing powder, and every item locked into place in his memory.

'Simon?' She was laughing. 'You were miles away!'

'No,' he said. 'Actually, that's the last thing I was. I was right here. When I saw it was you, I couldn't have been anywhere else.'

'Excuse me, are you in the queue?'

'So sorry, no, we're not.' He took Rachel's arm and they moved sideways.

'Weren't you going to get something?'
'Yes, a steak. But I'm not now.'
She looked at him, and he saw it in her face, too
That face. The same as he had first seen among the silver and
the champagne glasses and chandeliers of the banqueting hall.
'Where would you like to go for dinner?' he said.

Sixty-Six

'I'm sorry,' Simon said.

'What on earth for? This is perfect.'

'Almost. I did try, but it's a new maître d', and however much I pleaded, table 6 was booked and he couldn't change it.'

Rachel raised her glass and the champagne caught the light, the surface broke into a thousand pieces. 'I don't mind where we sit. When were we last here?'

'Too long ago.'

'Perhaps too long was right. I mean . . .'

'I hope you know what you mean.'

She frowned slightly. 'I want to get my words straight.'

A couple came past them, going out. Two women went to the bar. Somewhere backstage, the crash of a tray being dropped, and instantly silenced. Simon had the sense of being out of time and in a different reality, and yet completely in this one, the rarest, most longed-for of senses.

'I just mean a long time was necessary. Anyway, it isn't that long.'

'It only feels that way?'

Rachel smiled but did not reply, and they were interrupted by the waiter, offering menus, which Simon waved away. 'We want a bit longer. Is that all right?'

'Of course.' He refilled their glasses. 'Take all the time you like.'

'Time,' Simon said.

Rachel looked at him. 'What's wrong?'

'Nothing. Work stuff. Not here and not now.'

'I read the papers, you know. I watch the news.'

'Even so. There are better things to talk about anyway.'

'Such as?'

'I think I'm buying a house.'

Was he?

'Thinking about it?'

'As you do. Or as *you* do.'

'Do I?'

'OK. I do. God, I'm ravenous.'

'Me too. An apple for lunch and now two glasses of champagne.'

Now they ordered, and then Simon took her hand. 'I wonder if I could –'

'No. If you're going to say what I think you're going to say, then no. Not yet. Time.'

'Sod time.'

'It's probably the most important thing of all. We have to get time right . . .'

'This time.'

'More than any other.'

'Your table is ready when you are.' As they walked into the dining room the waiter went ahead to the far end and the corner table slightly separated from its neighbours, beside the window. They looked out at the lights down the drive, the tiny lights, like glow-worms, in the bushes, and wound through the bay trees on either side of the entrance.

'You did it!' Rachel said. 'Table 6.'

'I just said if there happened to be a cancellation.'

The waiter held her chair. 'Was there?' she asked him.

He made a small movement of his head. 'We like to get things right.'

'I can't have any more to drink,' Serrailler said, 'so the rest of the champagne is yours and then whatever you would like with dinner.'

'No. At the moment I am perfectly balanced between not enough and too much.'

'Ah, but that won't last.'

Rachel looked at him.

This. Now. Time. Make this last.

She sat back in her chair, but went on looking.

'I think it will,' she said.

They were the last to leave the dining room, and there were just three people left in the bar by the time it closed at half past midnight. They drove back on empty roads, happy, in silence.

'Come and see the house tomorrow?'

'No, leave it a while.'

'Why? Why leave it a while?'

'Because. Time. Everything we said.'

'Don't you want to see it?'

'If you buy it, yes, of course I do, but I'm not going to influence you.'

'What if you hate it?'

'Whether I do or I don't isn't the point.'

He was silent. The edges of the evening began to curl up and shrivel.

'Don't look like that, Simon. Time, remember.' And she opened the car door.

He watched her safely into the house and drove away too fast, checked himself, went through Lafferton too slowly. If he had been Traffic he would have stopped himself, though he was very sober and very safe. But also, what? Angry? Disappointed? Deflated?

He turned into the close and looked ahead, up at the house, at his apartment. Home. Remembered when Rachel had moved into it with him and he had, not hated her being there, but been irritated with someone invading his space and changing it, making an impression on it that was new and out of his control. He had been surprised at how much he had minded and what a difference it had made to his feelings.

Upstairs, he switched on only a couple of lamps, poured himself a small whisky, and stood looking down the deserted avenue to the ancient gateway, and then across to the cathedral, its great stone bulk in darkness now, because all save a few low street lamps went off at midnight.

Time. How much? Fifteen years or so more in the job. Nothing would change there unless he moved to a larger force. No.

Fifteen years or so living here, which he loved, which was his. But it was not his, he owned nothing.

He sat down and looked round at his white room, the polished boards, the rugs, the pictures, books. His long table. What would he lose, irreplaceably? Only the situation and the experience of living at the top of a Georgian house. Everything else he could have again, and more, as well as so much outside space, and the country beyond, the quietness, plus the complete separation from work, which was a relief he had always found at his sister's farmhouse, though neither was more than half an hour into Lafferton.

He finished his whisky but he knew that he would not sleep even now, his mind was electric with thoughts, plans, worries, questions, hopes. Fears.

He had a warm shower to try and relax his mind as well as his limbs, found a book. He got into the cool cotton sheets, and lay back luxuriating, until the top that had been spinning in his head for hours at last began to turn more and more slowly.

He sat up. Idiot. He was an idiot.

No, this was not enough, this would not do for the rest of his life, or even the rest of the year. He had been ignoring the gentle insistent voice, turning his back, stubbornly pushing himself down deeper into the old pit, the old way of thinking, acting, living. Being.

Idiot.

He reached for his phone and it rang, but only once.

'Hello?'

'You're awake.'

'So are you. Do you have a day off tomorrow?'

'No. I have a long weekend though . . . Friday until Tuesday night.'

Rachel said nothing.

'If you don't want to or it's not the right time or not time enough, say so now.'

She said nothing.

'Oh God, Rachel . . . listen. I love you.'

'Yes. I know. I've always known.'

'I want to get up now and come over.'

'No. I'll let you know tomorrow. About the weekend. Goodnight, Simon.'

A second after he had put the phone down, he picked it up again.

'Simon . . .'

'I know. I'm sorry not sorry.'

She laughed and she did not mind, she had wanted him to call back, he was sure of that.

'Just something I want to ask you . . . you might know the answer. I should but I don't . . .'

'Google it?'

'Can't be bothered.'

'All right. What?'

'Do you happen to know how long it is after you've given them notice that you can be married?'

He wanted to kick himself because he should have stopped, he should not have said it or anything like it, anything within a million miles, and when she backed off and warned him again about Time . . .

'Sorry,' he said. 'Rachel, I'm so sorry, I blurted it out and you're furious now.'

'I'm not furious.'

'Well, annoyed.'

'Not even that. Oh God, Simon, dearest Simon . . . with you it's all either feast or famine.'

'Oh.'

'Think about it.'

'So which is it now?'

'I don't know about you but I've had a bit much of famine. I thought today marked the start of . . . maybe a feast. Didn't it?'

'Yes. Yes, yes, yes!'

This time, seconds after they had finished the call, it was Rachel who rang back.

'What you wanted to know and I said you had to google it.'

'Yes?'

There was a silence and he held his breath.

'I couldn't be bothered to google it either.'

'Oh.'

'But – I'm pretty sure it's twenty-eight days.'

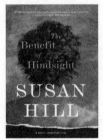

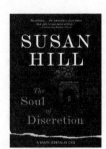